DAVID G BAILEY's latest work fea
realism, caustic humour and a mul
period from 2017 to 2025, encompassi
It explores relationships of baby boon
and subsequent generations, and what
world.

In David's previous contemporary novels, *Them Roper Girls* (2022) traces in their own voices the lives of four sisters from their 1950s childhood, while *Them Feltwell Boys* (2023) follows a Roper-girl husband's crude attempts at teenage love in counterpoint to his cynical womanising as an adult.

David debuted in 2021 with *Seventeen*, a football fantasy adventure novel aimed at and beyond young adults. From 2024 *The Sunny Side of the House* is the clear-eyed narrative of a 1960s boyhood in East Anglia, a first volume of autobiographical non-fiction in a projected series, *When Life Gives You Strawberries – Memories of a Fenland Boy*. The author currently lives in the Midlands.

To read more of and about David's work, including a quarterly newsletter and new content daily comprising extracts from diaries and other writing over more than fifty years, visit his website www.davidgbailey.com.

Also by David G Bailey

Young adult fantasy football adventure
Seventeen: or the Blood City Tommy O'Reilly Benefit Tour

Contemporary adult novels
Them Roper Girls
Them Feltwell Boys

Non-fiction
The Sunny Side of the House: When Life Gives You Strawberries – Memories of a Fenland Boy (I)

For reviews and to read opening chapters of each of these works, please visit the author's website www.davidgbailey.com.

THE TUESDAY-THURSDAY TONTINE

LAST MAN STANDING

DAVID G BAILEY

SilverWood

Published in 2025 by SilverWood Books

SilverWood Books Ltd
14 Small Street, Bristol, BS1 1DE, United Kingdom
www.silverwoodbooks.co.uk

Copyright © David G Bailey 2025

The right of David G Bailey to be identified as the author of this
work has been asserted in accordance with the Copyright,
Designs and Patents Act 1988 Sections 77 and 78.

All rights reserved. No part of this publication may be reproduced,
stored in a retrieval system, or transmitted in any form or by any means,
electronic, mechanical, photocopying, recording or otherwise,
without prior permission of the copyright holder.

This is a work of fiction. Names, characters, places and incidents either are products
of the author's imagination or are used fictitiously. Any resemblance to actual events
or locales or persons, living or dead, is entirely coincidental. Works of fiction may contain
themes, language and attitudes that some individuals may find offensive and/or outdated.
Readers likely to be affronted by accurate representation of real-world language, attitudes
and situations should not read on.

ISBN 978-1-80042-308-4 (paperback)
ISBN 978-1-80042-309-1 (hardback)
Also available as an ebook

British Library Cataloguing in Publication Data
A CIP catalogue record for this book is available from the British Library

Page design and typesetting by SilverWood Books

NO AI TRAINING

Without in any way limiting the author's exclusive rights under copyright, any use of
this publication to train generative artificial intelligence (AI) technologies to generate
text is expressly prohibited. The author reserves all rights to license uses of this work
for generative AI training and development of machine learning language models.

*To the Tuesday-Thursday Gang at Rugby Golf Club
— members past and present.*

Although I have not drawn these fictional characters and events from any individuals, I have drawn from you all great friendship and camaraderie over many years. If you do not find enough about golf in these pages, for me it has never been all about the golf.

Cheers, Dave.

Contents

PART ONE – THE TUESDAY-THURSDAY GANG 2017–2018
    Breaking 90   11
    The Flat   23
    The Tontine   27
    Out of Bounds   36

PART TWO – THE GATHERING STORM 2019
    Teeing Off   42
    Chips   50
    Golfer/Non-golfer   55
    The Shark   66
    Captain's Day   77
    Lotto   90
    Paris   97
    Birthday Etiquette   110
    The Minge of Fate   119

PART THREE – THEIR FINEST HOUR (NOT) 2020
    The Calm Before   126
    Bubbling Up   130
    Two's a Crowd   140
    You're Gorgeous   150
    Conversations with Friends   154
    Smokers' Corner   168
    Woman Down   173
    The Grand Mesalliance   178

Friday Night Dinner	185
Down Memory Lane	189
No Hat-trick Heroes	195

PART FOUR – TRIUMPH AND TRAGEDY 2020

Le Petit Pierrot	205
The Stag	212
The Road Home	226

PART FIVE – CLOSING THE RING 2021–2025

Valentine Bouffe	233
Maundy Thursday	241
Paris 2025	248
Roll of Honour	257

THE TUESDAY-THURSDAY TONTINE

PART ONE

THE TUESDAY-THURSDAY GANG 2017–2018

Breaking 90

'What's going on up there today, Reg?' Graham Cook asked the steward of Market Welham Golf Club, gesturing with his chin through the propped-open doors leading not only to the gentlemen's locker and bathrooms but up a half staircase to what was nowadays being marketed as the MWGC Pitcher Lounge for outside business meetings as well as members' events. The Tuesday-Thursday gang had fought a losing battle to keep it as a snooker room and still muttered that the table had not been fairly disposed of by the committee of the day.

'Birthday party in the name of Peter Goodwin, his mammy's I think.'

'Free grub for us later on then, no need to order our chips today?'

'It's little enough we make on them anyway. Herself is unhappy they didn't come to us for the catering, preferred to keep it simple and in the family they said. Wanted the tea urn muggins lugged up there, mind. No earner for us unless Pete slips me something for the extra bar work. Put a couple of hundred on his card and got his mates doing all the fetching and carrying for the old 'uns, so fair play to him on that.'

'Didn't say nothing about a round for the lads an' all, did he?'

'Not to me. Ask Harry here if you like.'

'What's he got to ask Harry?' a thickset, florid-faced fellow with a tray of empty glasses demanded as he approached the bar from the lounge, at a right angle to where the Tuesday-Thursday-gang member was being served.

'Graham here was wondering if there's a free drink for the TTers from the party.'

'Not my shout, Cookie boy,' his tone made it clear there would not be one if it were. 'You know we're not in your click.'

'Right, we got round a lot faster today without you in front of us. Cheers, Reg,' Graham said as the steward returned his swiped club card.

Harry Unsworth's face became redder as he placed his own order – four pints of London Pride, wines white and red, port and lemon, spritzer and a Coke. He would not give Cook the time of day, never mind the satisfaction of rising to the ancient issue. A more acceptable face of the TT gang appeared at his side from the toilets as he was carefully distributing the drinks onto his tray: a younger face, never quite clean-shaven, curly hair fighting a valiant rearguard action against an encroaching forehead, smiling at Harry as if it had already taken a good dose of alcoholic amiability.

'You buying for the whole party up there, Harry? Need a hand, another tray, that one looks tight-packed.'

Confident of his ability to manage the portage, Harry remembered another errand, with Reg now away serving other members. 'I'm good, ta, but if you don't mind we could use someone to take a group photo before we let them at the grub. Some will be off sharper than a Polaroid soon as they've had their fill.'

Happy to help, the TTer followed the older man's cautious steps to the party, where he was able to pay an additional service on finding the door to it closed. 'Reenie keeps 'em doing that, thinks she's Larry Grayson, says the draught does her rheumatics no good,' Harry thanked him incomprehensibly.

'Here you go, Pete, David Bailey not available so Jimmy Bradley will have to do.'

Peter Goodwin was the only one of the thirty or so people assembled wearing a necktie, under a light-blue sports jacket. A football-sized pot belly was incongruous against a slim build, sharp-features as immaculately shaven as his light-brown hair was shortly styled.

Jimmy took the phone Pete gratefully thrust at him – the armpits of the host's jacket were a darker shade of sweat – but was not confident enough to organise the guests for the shoot. A slim woman introducing herself with a firm handshake as Margaret took charge of that, getting everyone against the back-wall spread of food, above which floated a big silver-ballooned 90. Glasses of sparkling wine had been served while Harry was placing his lengthy order downstairs, so the white-clothed tables where the guests would sit to eat were pristine, save the tray he had not been given a chance to unload.

Anxious to do a good job, Jimmy thought he had everyone in shot, the cardiganed, white-permed old lady at the centre with arms folded and no hint of a smile, when she suddenly pointed at him. 'Wait, you can't take it without George.'

Returning from a cigarette break, George Pym stood in the doorway, which he would perhaps not have crossed except at Reenie's command. His hair still had as much black as white in it, swept back from his forehead and behind the ears but trailing down almost to his shoulders, marking him a young man of the 1970s as clearly as his porn-star moustache from that era. He reluctantly joined the party with a nod of greeting and pat on the shoulder for the photographer, to stand at the back beside Harry. He would not have needed the chair Jimmy was preparing to stand on to give himself a better angle.

The group photo was soon done, to a quick nod of satisfaction from Margaret who had broken away to check Jimmy's work. Her husband Peter was more effusive, telling him he was welcome to join the party.

'Thanks, mate, you're grand, I'm already in a round downstairs.'

'Put yourself a pint on our tab then, we might be down ourselves later when the crowd thins up here. I'll ask Margaret to do some snaps of smaller groups later.'

'Can our pal do us one of a group the missuses may not entirely approve of?' came in a soft Scottish burr. Andrew Wood, an upside-down head with closely cropped white beard and fringe around the ears and back below an unabashedly bald dome, was a few years older than his three friends. Peter liked the idea and there the mates posed for him: Andy with wine glass in hand, Pete between him and Harry with an arm around the shoulders of each, and George the tallest on the outside, raising a pint to the camera.

Pete's work was not quite done when Jimmy had escaped. After allowing everyone time to serve themselves a plate of food, Margaret – who had gone from nursing to a career in hospital administration – knew how to gain silence for him by a vicious crack rather than gentle tinkle on her wine glass. Although she had no close friends among the crowd gathered, she would have been glad to move to any table other than the one where mother-in-law Reenie held court, flanked by her sister Ruth and current best friend Pauline – a deal younger this one, a good thing as Reenie did tend to wear them out. Peter was hovering over them all like a nervous footman, on his feet already to make the speech to which Margaret now prompted him.

'Ladies and gentlemen, no that's far too formal, friends and family let's say,' he launched himself. 'I won't keep you long but I wanted to welcome you on behalf of my mother Irene – Reenie, before she might say a few words herself.'

'No fear.' Reenie's prompt refusal reassured her son she had in her hearing aids.

'I read recently that a child born today has a fifty-fifty chance of reaching a hundred. That's a big change from when Mum came into the world, before the Second World War. And though it's not true she fought directly against Hitler, it might have ended sooner if she had.' He heard a loyal chuckle from Harry or Andy to his left, but otherwise the crowd had its vacant, feeding face on. 'As Jane and Sally-Anne bring refills of champagne round – sparkling wine anyway, none of that French muck was Mum's command – I'd like to give the three generations of my mate Andy's womenfolk, including Little Miss Maddie, special thanks for the magnificent spread they've laid out for us.'

'Hear, hear,' Harry seconded, raising his pint to the two women as the younger one came to their table. Pretty enough, short spiky hair presumably dyed its blonde colour which matched neither of her parents. Fuller figured than Jane, or just had more of her boobs on display. She was also showing a lot more leg, but he appreciated too what he could see of her mother's. If he would ever be able to look at a woman below cronehood without assessing her sexually, he had not started yet.

'So, Mum, you've lived and seen a lot, some of it not so good, some we can't imagine nowadays. But you've come through it all. I honestly believe we'll be back to read out your telegram from Her Majesty in another ten years. In the meantime, let's celebrate your ninetieth among friends and family like I said, and here's to you: to Mum.'

'To Mum' from those hardly listening, though no one else had the right to call her that… 'to Reenie'… 'to Irene', the odd 'to Mrs Goodwin' came the ragged chorus. Peter asked again if she would like to say a few words herself, taking 'sit down and don't be so soft' as a no.

Reenie was normally more voluble, especially on the topic of her age, and how well she was doing for it. 'The twenty-eighth of September is the day I was born, 1927, so that's the day I want the do,' she had insisted when her only son floated a weekend event. 'If people can't make the effort to come on the day for my ninetieth, they're no big miss. It'll be my last party, make sure they know that, except for the one you'll all have when I'm gone.'

A widow for more than quarter of a century, Reenie's community was now mainly the people on her estate, not quite sheltered accommodation but with the stipulation that no one under fifty-five – also the age of eligibility for senior competitions at MWGC – could live there. She was making a point of speaking more to Pauline than her only surviving sister. Ruth, aged eighty-seven, had been brought by her daughter Marion. Peter wondered whether the weekday date had been so important to make it more difficult for Marion's children to attend, bring their own kids. Reenie had let him know often enough how disappointed she was that he had never been able to give her grandchildren. Not that she blamed him so much as she did Margaret, vexed at having no more to feed her curiosity about their childlessness than the words he made a formula years ago when 'none of your business' proved ineffectual – 'mutual agreement', which she liked just as little.

Harry had been quick to unburden himself between the photos and the long-overdue distribution of his tray of drinks, sitting with two of his mates.

'That snidey bastard Cook downstairs was only trying to cadge a pint for him and all his mates. Jimmy's all right, but most of 'em think they own the fucking course. I won't mention it to Pete, he's soft enough to let 'em have one.'

'Watch your language, Harry, there's kids up here remember. Hello darling, are you helping your mum and nan with the food?' Andrew addressed a ten-year-old ribboned-and-bowed girl.

'Yes, and Mummy said I can only have my Coke if I get her drink – a spitter I think she said it was – back to her first without spilling a drop.'

'Grandad'll watch over yours till you get back then, don't worry.'

'Tell you what, Maddie,' George offered, 'I'll take your mum's drink for you so you won't have to worry and you can carry your own. I need to go get my own food anyway, not like these two with wives to wait on them. Is that a deal?'

She looked up at him intently before accepting the proposition. 'Deal. She's the one with the short skirt on, the one Grandad said was up to her neck but it isn't really.'

'I know which one's your mum, thanks,' George replied quietly.

Harry watched Andrew – usually Andy to his mates, often Drew to his wife Jane – as Pym stooped off with the little girl. He knew there was some history between George and her mother Sally-Anne, for all their generational age difference, but had never been able to get to the bottom of it. It was true his best mate was the only one without a woman there to fetch him a plate of food – his current partner, Emma, guvnor of the White Horse in town, had said she might be along later when its lunch traffic lightened.

Andy picked up on the free drink for the TT gang, as if to soften the rebuke to Harry for swearing. 'They'll get no free drinks if it's Reenie's money Pete's using. Let's hope he can relax now. Lord knows why he got so worked up about his little speech, it's only his mum and he's among friends. Him a salesman as well.'

'Sales manager, Margaret wouldn't let you forget that. Or us anyway, she maybe didn't make such a big thing of it with you being the finance director.' It had been Andy's suggestion two years earlier that the four old friends should take up golf together at their local club when they all ended full-time employment, beneficiaries of a generous redundancy / early retirement package from a foreign car manufacturer, seeking to bow low as it left the UK in search of a cheaper workforce elsewhere. Already due to retire with a hefty bonus for his role in the divestment, Andy's company pension was big enough for him to have thought of deferring his state one, though he mentioned it only once to his mates before realising it might be regarded as showing off.

Harry's wife, Ellen, returned to their table with two fully laden plates. She knew he would not eat much, if anything, while he was drinking pints. He knew the heaped food would not go to waste. There was a base of sandwiches, a second layer of quiche, sausage rolls and pork pie chunks, then a generous covering of crisps and the cheesy Wotsits he thought might have been more aimed at the kids. A couple of cherry tomatoes added the only touch of colour; neither of them were big salad fans.

'Come and sit down, love, you've been on your feet since dawn.' Andy had prudently waited until his own wife, Jane, had put a more modest paper plate in front of him before speaking.

'Feels more like dawn yesterday. Tell the truth, I've enjoyed it though. I'm glad Peter mentioned Maddie, she's been a star. And Sally-Anne, I always knew she could have made a real go at catering college if she'd only stuck it out.'

'Sticking at things was never your daughter's strong point.' Andrew's tone was suddenly peevish. 'You'd think she's out looking for a new boyfriend rather than working. Nearly had poor Harry's eye out bending over to serve the fizz.'

Ellen came in right on cue, Harry thought. 'More like his eyes were popping out at her, don't bother to hide it with his own wife sitting right here beside him, more fool me. I tell you what though, Jane, this quiche is *really* good, did you make everything yourself?'

'With Sally-Anne, *our* daughter, Andrew, yes.' Jane turned her cool gaze away from Harry as he was on the point of justifying not rudely averting his eyes. With Ellen's never leaving her plate he wondered how she managed to keep so effective a track of him for anything she could wildly construe as 'perving'.

Andy too knew he had been telt. 'That's the way this lassie got to my heart, like they always say, through the stomach. By the time we wed, and I found out her mum had been doing most of that home cooking, she had other tricks to keep me interested.'

'So first I'm a liar, then I'm a tart. It was always your silver tongue that was the main attraction for me, Drew.'

'Sit yourself still a while longer, I was only joking.' But Jane had moved away to organise the ceremonial presentation of the birthday cake.

They had gone with just nine candles – 'one for every decade, Mum, the club said if we did it properly it would be too much of a fire hazard' – which Reenie enlisted Maddie to blow out on her behalf. She then entrusted the girl with taking round the thin slices she had confidently carved. She was fine with casual children, it was only those within her own family that irked Reenie, emphasising by their very existence an area in which she felt short-changed. Satisfied that Maddie had done a good job as she surveyed the crumbs – 'and them that hasn't had any will have to lick the plate' – Reenie foraged into her purse and stuck a 50p piece into her hand. 'There you are, sweetie, buy yourself an ice cream.'

Marion and Ruth were staying the night in Reenie's flat, having driven up from the other side of Peterborough. The two old ladies would be sharing her double bed, as everyone knew they had been more than used to doing with multiple other siblings as children. 'I wonder if they had rubber sheets back then as well,' Pete joked to his cousin, who would be berthed in the tiny spare bedroom. 'Ta for taking Mum home. You can leave 'em gassing with Pauline if you like and come back here, we haven't had much chance to catch up.'

'I'd like to, but Mum gets fretful away from home if I'm not with her. Yours is older but looks to have all her faculties about her.'

'Any sharper and she'd cut herself. I expect you've heard that saying a million times like I have. Luck of the draw, I suppose. Listen, thanks for coming. I'll bring her down to you next time, I promise.'

'Let's hope it's another birthday. We should be grateful, at their age you're more likely to be getting together for... you know. You take care, cuz, enjoy the rest of the party.'

There was in truth not much of it left to enjoy, what had hardly felt like a party to Peter. He had wanted to do right by his mother; the compliments came from everyone but herself. She had been gracious enough in thanking Jane for the catering and was allowed to get away with sniffing 'I thought she was just a waitress' when Andrew's wife tried to share the credit with their daughter. Pete had been a little exercised about Sally-Anne's involvement himself; her reputation extended far beyond the confines of the golf club, and not generally in a good way. Safely gone now, she had helped Ellen load a good proportion of the leftovers into Harry's car in exchange for a lift into town when he took his wife home. Harry returned to the clubhouse not alone but with George's partner, whose pub Margaret did not want Peter visiting, and another woman to whom the same would most likely apply.

'Had to escort these young ladies up the hill from the car park. Shame on you, George, for not having invited them before.'

'I wasn't sure it would be OK for Jackie to come along,' Emma greeted her man, 'and as usual you didn't have your phone on.'

Harry continued fussing over them. 'You missed the guest of honour, so whether we let you take your coats off is down to Pete and Margaret. I think you know Emma already, Pete, and this is her sister Jackie.'

'Her *younger* sister,' Jackie was at pains to point out, clearly not behind the party mood in drinks already downed that day.

Pete felt a fool the moment he stuck out his hand to shake in reassuring them they were very welcome, and more of one when Jackie giggled as she put the tips of her fingers into it before swiftly drawing them back. Margaret kept her own counsel.

Reg had invented an IT seminar in the Pitcher Lounge for the following day when pressed by the half-dozen remaining TTers, including Jimmy, to 'get some of that nosebag out here'. The birthday party took the hint when he said he would fetch anything they did not want to take home down to the bar, where they were free to carry on drinking. Jane decided she had had enough for the day, with Maddie also on her hands now. Whether she had expected to go home and put her feet up or not, she accepted with a good grace Margaret's self-invitation to join them for a cuppa before coming back to fetch Peter. 'I don't want to sit here watching him neck one beer after another now his precious mother's not around to see him,' she said, then turned to the man in question. 'I'll call you on my way back and if you're not outside ready you can make your own way home.'

'Fair enough. Thanks for all your help today.' Pete was careful to avoid any hint of sarcasm. 'And thanks a million again to you, Jane. Are you sure you won't take anything above the cost of the food for all the work you've put in?'

'Absolutely sure, thanks. I'll take some of it home though if you don't mind, save me making dinner for a couple of nights. I'll trust you to make your own way home when it suits you, Drew, no need to rush.'

The remaining group of the four mates – Harry, George, Andy and Pete – pulled a couple of small tables together, hemming in the late arrivals Emma and Jackie on the banquette seating against the wall. They were in what was designated as the Spikes Bar, the part of the single room with the shortest path to the counter, minimising muck and scraping on the carpeting from golf shoes. The TT gang were around the corner in the long narrow area looking out onto the first tee and the eighteenth green. Jimmy had said they should 'take a pew' when Peter gave his formal blessing to them digging into the remains of the feast, but Harry had already steered the women away from the other group of men. He was glad to see they had outlasted Graham Cook, so he would not get any of the free nosh.

When the friends had first joined MWGC, free of the constraints of full-time work it made more sense to play during the week than at weekends when there was more traffic generally apart from competitions and the like, which only Harry had much interest in entering.

With Mondays and Fridays clogged up by the seniors, and Wednesdays by the ladies, the long-established Tuesday-Thursday gang had already staked out the remaining weekdays. Its forty or so members were all male, mainly retired, aged from mid-fifties to mid-eighties, with a smattering of younger self-employed or shift workers. Depending mainly on the weather, anything from a hardy dozen to thirty might show up on any given T-day, drawn at random to play in three- or four-balls occupying the first tee from ten thirty onwards. The club pro, Cliff Lambert, had made the four friends aware of the TT gang, suggesting they might wish to join it or the seniors. They preferred playing in each other's company to being matched every time with new strangers, also to drink together – the TT convention was to stay after the round at the clubhouse (the 'nineteenth hole', indoors through the winter, outside in warmer months) with your playing partners rather than your particular friends. Added to which, except perhaps Andrew, they were not yet used to considering themselves as seniors, though they could not deny being pensioners.

Nothing stopped them turning up at any time before the TT gang went out, no booking system for members. The trouble was, in their early days they were not teeing off much before the first of the larger group. This had its own share of slow players, for reasons of neurosis or cussedness more than outright incompetence, but if they were playing in three-balls, and a good number of them, there could be a significant snarl-up behind a four.

Percy Parsons was the unelected but acknowledged leader of the TT gang, or at least its face to the club – he had served in his day as both MWGC's captain and president – and the wider world. He was finally prodded into having a word with the sluggards after a period of behind-the-scenes grumbling, or shouting in the case of Franny Rowland, held up at the back of the caravan into a rainstorm one day: 'Tell the fuckers to speed up or piss off and play with the split-arses.'

Andrew was disposed to be conciliatory, since he considered himself largely responsible for their slow pace. From out of nowhere – or nowhere he was going to get psychoanalysed to find out – he had suddenly developed an appalling case of the yips. He had found Cliff the pro sympathetic but unable to help, his friends loyal but equally baffled by his sudden inability to hole a putt from anywhere within five feet. Always a steady if unspectacular player, he now had everyone waiting almost as anxiously as himself when he addressed the ball on the green.

Harry took a more robust attitude. 'Course a four-ball's going to be slower than a three. This club's not only for you old farts to block out the best hours of the day for yourselves twice a week. If we let you all come through, we wouldn't finish ourselves till dark.' He had his say, what Percy reported as 'a rather dusty answer' to the gang as he urged them to patience.

Harry had dark suspicions of a put-up job, some collusion if not with Percy then between his own mates, when a couple of weeks later Pete suddenly found himself unable to tee off any later than nine in the morning. He did not trouble to invent a decent excuse, putting it down to a diktat of Margaret – though they all believed in her rule over him, what difference could an hour or so either way make to her? It wasn't as if he had kids or grandkids to collect from school, as the others had all neglected to do in their time.

While relations between the four mates and the wider gang had eased, to the point of friendship with the likes of Jimmy and other solid drinkers, there was no reason to join forces today, especially when they were in the company of women. Emma and George had been together long enough for him to treat the White Horse almost like his own gaff, which was in fact a tiny flat a hundred yards down the road from it. She had always been neutrally friendly to his mates, of which only Harry went in the Horse with any regularity. Emma was known to keep a baseball bat under the bar, with no hint that its use would be reserved to her male staff if there was any trouble. George would never confirm the rumour that she also kept a shotgun upstairs. His looming presence was something of a calming influence on her clientele, without him needing to carry anything but himself in a certain manner that earned respect whether they knew his name and reputation or not.

Jackie had not exercised her arms as much in pulling pints as her sister. A slighter figure altogether, she was a good deal more talkative, at least today when she had decided to treat herself to 'a night on the razz', she confided to Harry early doors from her corner seat.

'Don't tell me it's your birthday as well, like Pete's old dear? Only seventy years younger, twenty-one today is it?' he tried.

'It's not my birthday, but it might be yours if you play your cards right. I'm only joking, look at his face, Emmie, they come on to you like they think you was born yesterday, then they're surprised when you give 'em something back.'

But she wasn't joking, and he knew it. From the club they went on a crawl round town – 'see what the competition's up to,' Emma said, enjoying landlord's privilege of a free drink in every bar where the boss was on duty.

Then it was an Indian, then back to the Horse where Jem the superannuated hippie was locking the door behind him as he went home for the night. When Harry was allowed upstairs with Jackie, he had no interest in looking for the shotgun.

The Flat

Losing out on Reenie Goodwin's birthday gig could hardly have been the final straw for Reg and Glenda opting to leave MWGC that winter. They were popular enough as stewards during their five-year tenure, though it was the general opinion of the Tuesday-Thursday gang that he was the better half. Glenda acted like it was beneath her to pull a pint, rarely seen on those afternoons. She trusted Reg to handle their only kitchen requirement, a bowl of chips for each table.

Reg would always take a Guinness when offered one for himself and was rumoured to serve himself as needed to make up his daily gallon. The club committee did not make any great effort to retain the pair when they let it be known they had the offer of managing a pub over in Rugby. Neither of them was shy about moaning to members of the inadequacies of their current employment package.

'She should be grateful enough to get the free membership, out there on the course all hours when she should be ironing Reg's shirts or offering us bacon batches when we get here, like Mary used to.' Jack Roberts was a fierce partisan of the former regime.

'And if I supped as much as he does without paying for it, I wouldn't be complaining,' Billy Jackson answered as they waited at the bar while Reg was in the cellar changing a barrel. 'He's probably laying on the floor siphoning the first pint off into his own gob while our tongues are hanging out.'

'Apply for the job, why don't you, Billy? Beer on tap all day every day, your missus don't play golf so she could be the one grafting in here letting you get out on the course.'

'Fuck that for a game of soldiers, she might find out a round can sometimes take less than eight hours.'

Whether or not the departing couple had a case in moaning about their terms and conditions at the club, it proved impossible to confirm replacements before they served out their notice. Their biggest perk had been found accommodation, a flatlet above the ladies' changing room and pro shop, to which Reg was never known to have invited anyone. 'Why would he?' Billy asked more than once. 'He's the one to decide what time to close up down here, where he don't have to pay for the bevvies.'

'You'll be hearing it soon enough, so I'll let you know first myself. I'll be taking over the club flat,' Harry told his mates in the Rifleman's Arms, their regular Friday lunchtime haunt precisely because its lunch aspirations went no further than Pukka pies and pickled eggs.

'Are you serious? How'd you persuade Ellen into that? Bit of a drastic downsizing, isn't it?'

'You weren't listening, Andy. I said *I'*ll be taking over the flat, nothing to do with Ellen. She stays where she is. But don't you go off at half-cock, Pete, telling Margaret we're splitting up or anything like that, nor any of the TT gang, it's none of their business. It's only a temporary thing, most likely, till they find new stewards. It'll be extra income for the club, couldn't believe how little they wanted for it. It's not a palace or anything, but summer coming up, a bolthole above the clubhouse, no need to worry about drinking what I like afterwards, no jaw pie to soak it up neither. Anyway, there it is, can't stop people talking, let 'em say what they like. Only one bedroom but the settee will do as a spare bed if any of you don't fancy going home before dark one night.'

Peter was nettled at the accusation of having a loose tongue. 'Sure I won't cramp your style, Harry? Who is she, your latest shag-stick? Not one of the juniors here you could see from the upstairs window I hope, some schoolgirl still living at home, you can do time for that now.'

'He did some good numbers but I'm no mate of Gary Glitter.'

George said nothing. Barring a very recent development, he knew who the 'latest shag-stick' was. Harry had not been able (or wished) to keep from telling him about any matter in his life since he'd fancied Jane Fincham when they were both eight years old.

'Hold onto your cash, here comes Sally-Anne's latest, another one out for what he can get I shouldn't wonder.' Andrew had time to lean forward and confide this before a fellow in his twenties appeared at his elbow. Harry had noticed the flicker of not-pleased surprise on the kid's face when he spotted them from the bar, but he made something of a recovery by asking what they were drinking.

'No, you're all right, Dean, I'm in the chair. Go get yourself one then I'll introduce you properly to the lads.' Andy palmed him a note. 'What brings you in here?'

'Nothing much, between jobs, thought I'd have a cheeky lunchtime pie and a pint.'

'Take the pie out of that as well if you like then, can't speak for how good they might or might not be, we're strictly liquid lunchers.'

Returning to the table with a pint of Kronenbourg, Dean gave a cheers and a fistful of change to his girlfriend's father. 'Is this one of your famous sessions then, what is it you call them Sally-Anne says? After some old fogie pop star, forgotten his name again now. Lionel something?'

Peter was always the most outgoing of them when it came to getting on with strangers. 'If we still take Leo Sayer's name in vain it's like his singing used to be, just a bit of fun. We can't often claim to be up for an all-dayer now, like we used to.'

'Speak for yourself, mate.' Harry was on his mettle. He had a soft spot for the frizzy-haired dwarf because 'When I Need You' had been a sentimental favourite of his mum's in the few months before she followed the old man in death. 'George has beer on his cornflakes and doesn't stop till Emma serves him a tot before bedtime, all day every day.'

'Yeah well, George is a one-man band, we all know that.' George and Harry smiled at Pete's nod to one of Leo's hits, as Andy did not – the little man was never as big up north as he was down under – while Dean could barely contain his lack of interest.

'Anyone for another long tall glass?' George asked, keeping up the game. Dean was happy to have another pint put in the taps for him. Referring to the kid's paint-spattered white overall, George said to Harry later, when they were the only two left in the bar, 'I hope Andy gets some decorating out of him, cos he don't look as if he pulls his weight otherwise.'

'You're only jealous cos he's moonlighting in Sally-Anne's knickers. Thing I noticed was he didn't take in our names, just cheerio lads when he fucked off. And the way he treated Andy, you'd have thought he was the father-in-law waiting to be impressed, not the other way round.'

'I reckon Andy's already made up his mind about him, but what can you do? He says anything and Sally-Anne'll only be all the keener.'

'You should know, George.' Neither of them would hear a further opinion from Andy about Dean. The next time they saw the lad was at their friend's funeral.

The Tontine

Andrew Wood's death was the catalyst for Peter, Harry and George to join the TT gang, allowed to pay the £5 entry fee after some discussion within it to which they were not party.

When did you ever consult us, Percy, sounds like you've already agreed it.
Can't we still blackball 'em?
That Unsworth's a bolshie bastard.
I like the way they come running to us now Yippee Ay Andy's gone.
Why can't they stick in their own click, we'd get round quicker now?
I say welcome to 'em, none shy about getting one in.

Although Andrew had managed the yips to some degree using a long putter anchored under his chin, when that tactic was outlawed he manfully tried again, ending up with a stroke that had some of the characteristics of a push shot at pool. Realising it might be called into question by outsiders, he had limited himself to playing only with his three mates, while constantly assuring them that he would not mind in the least if they chose to go round without him. He was beyond worrying about any of that now.

It had cost them time to understand his other bequest to them, as explained by the solicitors helping Jane in the execution of Andrew's will. He had been given enough leisure to prepare one by pancreatic cancer, though no more than a few weeks after their last round as a four-ball. That was the only time any of them ever heard him complain or, Harry realised without remarking, swear. 'Christ, you'd think the fucking cancer would have the decency to kill the yips before it does for me.'

'The legacy is in a similar form to what is called a tontine, though you won't find that word in the will. Lawyers like me get nervous about it, though tontines are still perfectly legal and even popular in countries like France.' James McCreery, in a three-piece suit and a good twenty years younger than any of them, showed no sign of nerves.

'You can get away with anything in France,' Harry muttered.

'Sounds a bit like "la plume de ma tante". That's about as far as my French goes.'

'You're ahead of me with that, Pete,' George said. 'If it's anything dodgy it doesn't sound like Andy. He was a straight arrow you know, finance director and everything.'

'Of course, of course, nothing to do with French aunts, it was an Italian who first came up with it, Tonti, but that's by the by.' McCreery was flustered by George's growl. 'Perhaps I misspoke, it's tontines as investments or insurances that are frowned on, but a similar effect can be achieved in a carefully worded will, as Mr Wood's was.'

'And what effect is that?'

'Well, the simplest definition I could find of tontine was' – he held a piece of paper well away from him to read – 'a joint financial arrangement whereby the participants usually contribute equally to a prize that is awarded entirely to the participant who survives all the others.'

'Not simple enough,' George said.

'And I thought you said it wasn't a tontine anyway,' Harry weighed in.

'I'm sorry. Mr Wood left a lump sum which, with or without accumulated investment income, will go to the last one of you to remain alive. That's why these arrangements are also sometimes known as last-man-standing.'

'That's simpler,' Pete reassured the solicitor. 'We could do with Andy here to explain what the hell he was thinking.'

'I can share that Mr Wood felt your legacy would not represent a life-changing amount split three ways, but might for one person, especially if prudently invested over a period without any withdrawals being made. He also felt it was in the competitive spirit of what I understand was a long-term association that there should be, if you will, a winner.'

'So it's more like a bet, winner takes all?'

'You're right in a way, Mr Pym. That's why the authorities historically took an interest in such schemes. Because of the temptation a tontine gave for nefarious measures by the participants.'

'Come again?'

McCreery felt he was facing a tag team in George and Harry. He apologised again. 'In short, there were concerns that the concept of a tontine when translated to reality provided too much incentive for participants to wish the death of others, leaving them to benefit as sole survivors.'

'I'm glad that was in short. You mean we might try to bump each other off for the proceeds?'

'Exactly so, Mr Pym. That's probably a better way of putting it.'

'So Andy managed to tie the money up, for years touch wood. We can't split it between us now and walk away with a non-life-changing amount.' Peter Goodwin was looking for a positive spin. 'Always the money man. I suppose it may have been his way of keeping us together as a group, lads.'

'A bloody strange one if you ask me, Pete, more likely put us at each other's throats, literally.' Harry made the gesture of grabbing his friend by the neck.

'Before we get too worked up about it, how much did Andy leave for this one lucky chap?' George asked.

McCreery named a figure. He now seemed anxious to bring matters to a close. Perhaps, like them, he had somewhere else to be. 'Any income from the fund, interest say, is yours to dispose of as you like pending the final settlement, but the initial capital is governed by the terms I have just outlined. You may wish to seek the help of an independent financial adviser. While we cannot specifically recommend one above another, I can give you a few local names if you need them.'

'We'll ask if we do, I think there's someone at the club in that line. Nick Gregory,' Harry told his friends before returning to the lawyer. 'Far as I can see, we've just been given something with one hand, then told hang on, you've got to wait for all your mates to pop their clogs first. You might be drooling into your dinner but never mind, you take the pot. It reminds me of that Tommy Cooper gag, have you heard of him, Mr McCreery?'

'You bet,' the younger man said with sudden enthusiasm, pausing in gathering his papers together. 'Comedy legend, and no mean magician either. I do a few tricks myself but nowhere near his Magic Circle level.'

'Good man. For Pete and George then, you'd need to see Tommy do it really, there's an insurance man selling door to door and he's trying to persuade an elderly couple to buy life insurance. "So if you pay me sixpence a week for the next twenty years you'll have a death benefit of ten pounds, and if you live on the day of your ninetieth birthday I'll be right here to pay you that amount with a special bonus, a full twenty pounds." Then the old man says, "That doesn't sound like very much."' Harry opened his palm to the solicitor.

'"It's not much, but it's a start in life",' McCreery deadpanned.

They had purposely set their appointment for eleven of a Friday morning, so that they could discuss its outcome at their usual Rifleman's table. Drinking, more than golf, far more than work, had been the real common interest between the four men. Since their retirement they had made the most of the luxury of doing it by day, with only George still regularly also out at night.

They did not need to specify their order to Tom behind the bar, who served them two pints of Pedigree with a Wifebeater dash for Peter. He had got into the habit of the splash of lemonade so he could tell Margaret he had been on shandies, persisting with it past the return of his licence from the police eighteen months after they had found eight such shandies excuse enough to take it away from him.

'Right twat that McCreery,' was George's opening gambit as they took their corner seats.

'Good job he wasn't charging us by the word, but he was sound on old Tommy,' Harry qualified his agreement. 'Far as I can see, apart from watching what you fuckers might be slipping into me drinks there's nothing to do about it.'

'Andy probably meant well. He didn't have to leave us anything.'

'That's true too, Pete. Never look a gift horse and all that bullshit.'

'I like his definition of life-changing,' said Harry. 'All right, I couldn't run away from the missus to live in the Costa del Sol with it, but a couple of weeks in Benidorm would make a difference, I'll tell you. We could have used it to go to Vilamoura again, just the three of us.'

Pete did not remind Harry that he had already run away from his missus, if only as far as the golf-club flat. 'That's what it is, just the three of us now. You sure you don't want us to carry on like that, George? It was your idea to join the TT gang.'

'I know, and I still can't tell you why. It's not a matter of taking up Andy's offer to let us go, he can't give a toss either way now. And it's not because it would be unbearable to carry on ourselves without him, bring back memories, all that bollocks. Let's face it, he did get to be a trial at the end. He was ill and everything, poor old boy, but admit you thought it too.'

'Fuck me, George. I hope you speak as well of us when we're both gone. You've got to be the bookies' favourite to sweep the pot, living on your own, a landlady on tap and fresh fanny whenever you want it, no missus to drive you to an early grave.'

George was too used to Harry holding up the supposed idyll of his bachelor existence to protest. It was better than the endgames of his marriages, but that was not saying much. He had thought with his second wife he might not come out of it alive to continue drinking himself to death at his own pace. 'One of us ought to have a word with Jane, or maybe Ellen might do it, Harry, just to check she's all right about it all. Or Margaret,' he added for form's sake, though none of them would have considered Pete's wife a realistic option. Over the years she had been to various events where wives were allowed, without ever striking up much of a relationship with the other women present, whereas Jane and Ellen were friendly enough to see each other occasionally without their men.

'I said at the funeral I'd clear his locker out and take the stuff round to Jane,' Harry volunteered. 'I can do it then if you like. Are we agreed that if she is upset about him leaving us something we get McCreery on the case to reverse it, let her have the dosh free and clear? It's already giving me the creeps a bit.'

'Absolutely, yes.' Pete nodded several times.

'Sure.' George's single nod was just as emphatic. 'How good will all the beer in the world taste over the dead bodies of your best mates? Still, while you're there, might as well get her OK to finish up whatever credit he's got left on his bar card, hardly worth bothering the club to get a refund on that.'

If Andrew Wood did not view one third of the legacy to his friends as a life-changing amount, those won and lost on Tuesdays and Thursdays would not change half an hour. The basic stake was £1. If playing in pairs, better ball, the losers would pay for their opponents, so the most anyone could fork out was £2, plus 10p per birdie. Arthur Harrison reinforced the stereotype of the tight Yorkie by jibbing at this additional amount as if it were the poll tax, reiterating his disagreement to the principle every time it affected him though he would never say exactly what it was about the small-change outlay that tipped him over the edge.

Jack Roberts was not only self-styled 'number 2-IC' to Percy (his former boss in the world of work) but paymaster general, holding the money for those who had left before the cards were tallied as well as ensuring that the winners played off two strokes less their next time out. Handicaps used were set at seventy-five per cent of the official club ones.

The first time the reduced mates played with the gang there were eighteen present, six three-balls. In that case there was no competition amongst the playing groups, with the two best scores of the three aggregated. Playing with Mark Jones and Billy Jackson, George was a winner, sent up to collect their £3 each to cries of 'check his handicap' and 'put a mask on if you're here to rob us' along with half-hearted applause (not in any particular disapprobation of his win, it was the same for everyone, with various stalwarts never putting their hands together at all).

Only a few of the gang were in full-time employment. While its average income per person was higher than a random cross-section of Market Welham's older population, individually it ranged between the state pension, through company pensions to those who had cashed in on their own businesses – at least one of these a millionaire – with accumulated savings or investment portfolios in the background for various of the group. Most were homeowners, and Harry Unsworth had additionally the house his parents had left him, profitably rented out. If money was never discussed within the gang, holidays often were, a reasonable index of members' disposable income. Cruises featured prominently.

The tontine legacy, leaked indiscriminately by Peter during their early rounds with the Tuesday-Thursday gang, was a nine-day wonder. While Nick Gregory was talking to the three friends about how they should invest the fund to maximise their annual income from it, he was professional enough to keep the details confidential from the others. In the Rifleman's one Friday – oblivious of his honour in being invited to join them there – he accepted Harry, Pete and George's unanimous instruction to aggregate any investment income with the original amount, increasing the final payout to the sole survivor, and more reluctantly gave way to their insistence on keeping it in a simple bank or building society savings account. He also gave them a heads-up that the subject would be among Percy's parish notes the next week.

'What? People want to come in with us, how's that going to work? Why'd you have to open your big gob, Pete?'

'Didn't realise it was a state secret. I didn't say how much it was or anything like that.'

'You're right, Harry,' Nick mollified. 'It would be impossible to bring anyone else into your group. It's a matter of explaining the general concept to everyone, that's all.'

'I don't see why everyone else should know our business.' Harry looked darkly again at Pete. 'What say you, George?'

George shrugged. 'I don't think it's worth falling out over. I had enough of that with my brother when our old man died, I'm not going through it again.'

On the day Nick was to describe the latest ancient investment idea to the gang, there was not a noticeably bigger bunch of remainers than normal beyond the prize-giving – forty-two points earning the winners £3.50 each. Percy, Jack and Graham Cook stayed on, members of the gang's informal (but powerful) 'committee', as did Franny Rowland and Arthur Harrison. Cecil Ransom had no means of escape till his son or daughter-in-law came for him; although they said the pick-up was to allow him a couple of beers, he knew it was the opening shot in what he had every intention of making a tough battle to quit him of his driving privilege altogether. Billy Jackson, Brian Hammond, Mark Jones, Jimmy Bradley with his father-in-law Barry Knighton and one or two more made up the audience.

Although familiar with the concept of a tontine from his insurance career, Nick regretted the word had been mentioned when Hammo dragged in another Italian, forcing him to explain it was nothing like a Ponzi scheme. He tried to steer them to a more conventional saving plan if they were to go for anything.

'And how much would we be expected to invest?' Most of the TT gang were competitive as well as inclined to gamble, so reluctant to give up on the last-man-standing aspect of the arrangement imposed on George, Harry and Pete. There was a long discussion about setting up an internal handicapping system to adjust each man's contribution by age. Nick felt he was losing the room and was glad to see Percy raise his hand, the only one to have given him that courtesy before speaking. For all their good-humoured mickey-taking of PP, there was silence from the gang as he began.

'Thank you, Nick. I think we've thrashed out the main points. Art's right on handicapping. It makes no more sense to pit a fifty-year-old against a man of seventy in a matter of life expectancy than a pro against a hacker in golf. Still, it would be a major undertaking to satisfy everyone on a tariff, and I wouldn't want to waste Nick's time if there's not enough interest to warrant it. Why don't I sit down with him separately and come up with a minimum contribution? If we have any takers at that figure, depending on how many there are we can investigate further. Does that sound reasonable?'

It did. As Cecil's son shepherded him out, Graham spoke across the room to the younger man. 'You tell old Sess what to do on the way home, mate, don't let him go blowing your inheritance on a game of spoof between us old gits.'

Nick had not become the successful salesman he still was by leaving social engagements early. He was in the clubhouse with Harry, George, Jimmy and Billy, when Peter Goodwin reluctantly gave up his own seat to head home to Margaret. There had been no further talk of the tontine during that period. Harry returned to the topic as his friend left.

'Sorry lads, especially you, Nick, if it was all a waste of time today. I would never have brought the subject up, and George is a tomb, but you can't be with Pete five minutes without knowing all his business.'

'No problem for me, it kept Tight-Arse Art here till the fourth round so I got my pint back off him.'

'You didn't have much to say about it, Billy? Reckon you're too young to get a shot at it anyway, like me?' Jimmy was either an early leaver or a late stayer, nothing of moderation about him. In drinking mode he was careless enough to joke with the usually amiable but volatile Billy.

'Long as I've got enough for my beer and fags,' Billy replied equably enough, 'and a regular flutter, I'm square, not interested in saving for next week never mind next year or however many years it is. Same as life insurance. If 'er indoors has got any of that on me, good luck to her, she pays for it herself. I prefer something I can see and get half interested in, pick up my winnings as soon as the horse comes home. I weren't hardly listening, but it sounded to me more like betting than insurance. Is there any real difference between the two, Nick? Come on, you're not selling now, be honest.'

Nick had no inclination to take them back to his *Elements of Insurance* textbook. He knew already neither tontine nor saving plan would be formed by the TT gang. 'It's not a conventional type of insurance, I'll give you that. It's been compared to whatever we're supposed to call that Agatha Christie novel nowadays, *Ten Little* you-know and now there was one.'

'Ten green bottles. You want another Heineken, Billy? Harry, Jimmy?'

'Ar, one for the ditch, George.'

Declining a last drink himself, Nick continued. 'When I started out in insurance, my first boss told me it means you're worth more dead than alive. With a tontine or legacy like these guys', someone is around to spend the money, and if you distribute the investment income you don't have to outlive everyone else to get a return. But you *can* put it in betting terms, your slip may be the big winner.'

'There's that, but we've just buried one friend.' Harry could get sentimental in drink, a staging post for many in the classic track from jocose to comatose, with request stops on the way at lachrymose and bellicose. 'George was saying the other day, what fun you going to have on your tod, literally dancing on the graves of all your mates?'

Nick decided it wasn't worth quibbling over 'literally'. Insurance encouraged you to take the longer-term view. He had already declared to the group that it would be unethical for him to participate in any kind of tontine plan. He shared before leaving his personal, more practical reason not to do so. 'A tontine only makes any sense in times of war or plague.'

Out of Bounds

None of the friends' wives had ever expressed any interest in golf, though only Harry went so far as to say he had forbidden Ellen to play. She laughed in his face when he did say that, which – he would insist – was not the same as denying it. Margaret had been persuaded into the clubhouse a couple of times when fetching Peter home. He relayed her excuses – 'Why would I want to sit and listen to a load of racist bigots?' – when she took to sitting in the car park instead, driving off from it without him more than once, too. Some members failed to recognise themselves in such a description, curtailing their former elaborate gallantry towards Margaret ever after (she did not notice), while others took it as a badge of honour.

The TTers would always point to Chitrabahadur Paudel as their evidence of racial diversity; Chit, a retired Gurkha warrant officer and the only non-Caucasian in the club, had certainly chosen to be part of their gang rather than any other. They might have struggled to find any proof of diversity in sexual preferences; while various of them were widowers, divorced or bachelors, none were identified as gay. They had stood foursquare behind their mate Brackers as a permanent option when rumours of a same-sex couple applying for the stewards' post were leaked by one of the club committee members involved in the recruitment process.

'I hear the new bean-counter Brogan was all for the idea of giving it to Elton and the other one.' Graham Cook teed himself up. 'Said it would increase bar takings cos they'd be able to fit three poofs onto every stool. You know how, right?'

The fact there were no barstools in the clubhouse was irrelevant. They were in 'joke' territory. 'Go on,' Billy Jackson obliged him.

'Turn 'em upside down.'
Might need a good stock of stools now, they say one in ten people is gay.
That means we must have some in this group by the law of averages.
Who smelt it dealt it, Charlie. You trying to tell us something?
It's more like one in ten straight, if you listen to Radio 2 nowadays.
I don't see it matters what they do as long as they keep it to themselves.
Lezzers can show it off as much as they like for me, long as they're half tidy.

Andrew Wood's widow was amazed at the volume of stuff Harry brought round from his club locker one late-October afternoon. Apart from the fourteen clubs already in Andy's bag, the maximum allowable in a competitive round, Harry had crammed in surplus drivers, wedges, chippers and putters tried and largely benched over the years. There were shoes, gloves, hats against the sun and against the cold, waterproofs, sleeveless and sleeved jerkins and pullovers. There were pitch and ball markers and scores of golf balls, some still in their boxes but most rolling about on the floor and upper shelf of the locker as Harry gathered them all in a Sainsbury's plastic bag. The number of cigars was fewer, similarly floating loose or in packets, varying in size as well as brand. Harry suspected some of the Zippos were out of gas. Why otherwise would there be half a dozen – all red? He did not flick to test.

Half a dozen club head-covers were also in the locker, never used by Andrew which had made it hard for him to surprise his friends clanking up on them from behind, easy to put them off their swing. Harry had been thorough, pulling out his mate's old trolley, with hedgehog treads against severe winter conditions cobwebbed behind it in the shed where members kept them.

Standing either side of the huddled mass, Harry – with a hand on the biggest driver to steady the bag upright – offered to dispose of Andrew's golfing remains, while making it clear Jane should not expect much in the way of financial return for any of it.

'That's good of you, Harry, thanks a lot, but I think I'll hang on to it. You know I never shared that part of his life, but Dean said he might be interested in taking up the game and it won't hurt if he can use anything. I don't know how these things work but if there's any of the individual clubs or whatever you might fancy for yourself, or George or Pete come to that, Dean wouldn't know to miss it and I'm sure Drew would be happy for any of you to have one.'

'Definitely not George, you know he's about a foot taller than Andy. Our old mate had his clubs specially adjusted to his height – back in the year dot mind, that's why I said they won't fetch much. I'll take a packet of Hamlets if you like. I remember this old maroon pullover, holey relic we used to call it, not for me though ta.'

'Nor me. He must have rescued that from the bin, which is where it'll be heading next. I'll have to get rid of his clothes, there's so much to do even though he tried to sort out as much for us in advance as he could, as I'd let him. I couldn't bear the thought of him having to chuck out his own clothes. Like that bloody pullover, he could get so attached to them.'

'Tell me about it. If there's anything me or the boys can do to help, or Ellen of course and I'm sure Margaret too, you only have to say. We want to respect your privacy, but don't be a stranger. And about the legacy, the tontine as they call it…'

'The what? Oh, the money he left you. If that was his wish, I respect it. Sally-Anne had a word, but she had to learn some time to stop running to Daddy for everything.'

'Well, there's this… Dean?'

'Yes, her latest. I don't know if you talked to him much, the whole funeral was a blur for me. He's probably going to move in here now.'

'You're all right with that, are you?'

'Did it sound as if I'm not? I'm not as enthusiastic as Sally-Anne is, for all she says I should be glad that we'll still have a man in the house. He's good with Maddie, which is the main thing for me. I haven't properly got round to thinking about it, haven't been able to concentrate on much… I do have to consider the girls though, how the loss of their dad and grandad will affect them.'

'Course you do, but don't forget to think of yourself while you're doing all that, Jane. He was your husband above all. No need to rush into anything, I'd say. None of my business, I know.'

Harry had been unimpressed at the funeral by the kid Dean positioning himself among the head mourners. To comfort his girlfriend and her daughter, fair enough (though Sally-Anne remained dry-eyed and Maddie clung more to Jane); to act like he was the one responsible for the float behind the bar allowing free drinks to all the invitees, that was an abuse of their mate's posthumous generosity.

Nobody saw Jane again until New Year's Eve, when she came to the club's dinner-dance with Dean, Sally-Anne and a Maddie excited at the promise of being allowed to stay up till midnight. Peter and Margaret got there early to make sure of bagging a table, only to find the precaution hardly necessary as the place was half empty. It had been Ellen's idea to get together at what had been a fixture on the annual calendar for the four men and their wives or girlfriends, though not in recent years. The live band they remembered had been replaced by a disco run by one of the TT gang's newer members. Old enough to have an impressive collection of vinyl, he no longer had to lug boxes of 45s to his gigs, doing everything on a laptop.

The former sit-down dinners were now a buffet, MWGC's own catering facilities almost non-existent without a stewarding pair. Never imagining the problems they would have in replacing them, the club had neglected to contract professional caterers in good enough time for one of their busiest nights of the year. The Ladies' Section had done sterling work, but there was a heavy weighting of the buffet laid out in what club stalwarts still called the snooker room towards cakes and sponges.

While Peter could be persuaded to get on the floor with Margaret, who preferred that to the conversation and drinking at table, dancing had not been a thing for Harry or George since their teenage years. Among Andrew's curious collection of niche interests, one that would have worried his friends had he not been so safely married, was ballroom dancing. He took it beyond the ogling of the women on *Come Dancing* in the old days, so spectacularly revived with more acreage of female flesh in *Strictly*, to taking classes and involving Jane, a good mover herself.

George's partner was busy at the White Horse, where they ran an all-night party. The club event was not likely to extend much beyond 'Auld Lang Syne', so he would still have several hours to spend with Emma if he wished. Meanwhile he was happy moving around the room or standing at the bar talking to other members – there was a fair sprinkling of TTers, some muttering at the presence of Maddie and other children, which Jane had insisted Harry confirm was allowable before deciding to bring the usually quiet little girl along. Dean had not been seen in the clubhouse since Andrew's wake was held there, nor out on the course. 'Probably put Andy's bats straight on eBay,' George had suggested.

Sally-Anne was more animated than her boyfriend and had been since their arrival, more hyper than her daughter (who was not fuelled with

Prosecco) as they danced together to numbers Maddie was surely hearing for the first time. Dean resolutely refused to join them, gaining a point or two in Harry's estimation. He lost more than that, however, when he set to follow his girlfriend into town for 'something a bit sparkier', leaving Maddie with her grandmother when she proved stubbornly unwilling to be taken home to bed.

'You can't think of doing that, leaving her alone in the house,' Jane had said. 'Do you want to stay with me, or we can both go home together if you'd rather?'

'You promised we'd stay out till midnight, Mummy. Why can't I go with you?'

'Because little girls aren't allowed there, else we *would* take you, my darling. We'll do lunch with you tomorrow, won't we, Dean?'

'Sure, long as you're driving. Jane, I've got my mobby on vibrate so however loud it is wherever your daughter's going to drag me, don't worry about calling when you want to go home. I'll come back and take you and Maddie.'

'Thanks, Dean, that's kind of you.'

'No bother, mate, we can get them home when they want,' Harry offered on behalf of Ellen, driving them that night coincidentally also against the promise of a lunch out the next day. He was uneasy having his wife on the premises at all, though she had shown no interest in visiting his flat upstairs. He had not suggested they spend the night there, and she had never raised the possibility.

It was only when he saw George offer Jane a dance that Harry realised he might have done the same. Although her reluctance was obvious, and it was an upbeat number with Maddie bopping between the two adults, he was quick to task his mate when George appeared at his shoulder to help take the drinks back from bar to table – the club didn't run to proper trays for that nowadays. 'Now I see why you didn't bring your own bird tonight.'

'You what? Oh Jane. Leave off, Harry, she's strictly OB, you know that.'

'Why would it be? You're alone, she's alone, the night is yet young.'

'A mate's bird, you know that's always been a non-starter, otherwise imagine the number of times you and me would have fell out back in the day.'

'Too right, but is it out of bounds now?' Harry had been surprised at George's immediate insistence on the term. 'You know, Andy's gone, a new year coming up and all that. I've seen you do a lot worse than Jane.'

'She's a cutie, but she's got no interest in me. I keep trying to be polite, that's all. Time was, she wouldn't stay in the same room as me. That's not the point, though. It's principles, rules are rules. I can't believe you think I'd be trying to pull her.'

'I suppose it would be odd to go after her when you already fucked her daughter.'

'Take it easy, Harry. You might have Ellen driving you but no need to go mad on the bevvy. If you're worried Jackie might show up, or show you up, I got her key back for you. So don't get arsey with me. You don't know shit about me and Sally-Anne, so don't talk like you do.'

'All right, point taken. Fancy a chaser for these?' Harry looked sulkily down at his pint.

'Oh Christ, now I get it. You're only ragging me because you got a sudden itch for Jane yourself. Get a grip, man. I'm glad I didn't ask Ellen for a dance.'

'You can take my missus home as far as I'm concerned, Jane an' all, save me the trouble. Jackie knows why I had to have the key back, she was taking the piss with it, however good a laugh she is most of the time. If I'm jealous of anything it's you living the dream – shagging a landlady and still staying on the right side of the bar.'

PART TWO

THE GATHERING STORM 2019

Teeing Off

The golf clubs stayed untouched for months in the garage where Harry lugged them for Jane. He had given her his mobile in that period immediately following Andrew's death – there was no reason for her to have it before – yet was surprised to get a call from her in March 2019, just after the club's AGM where a three per cent increase in subs had been carried despite some dissent from the floor.

'I'm fine thanks, how are things with you? It's been a long winter, and it can't have been an easy one for you.'

'No, it hasn't. I'm getting ready for a proper spring clean. There's still a lot of Andrew's stuff around the place; turns out I was more sentimental about it myself than I thought.'

'That's not sentimental, it's…' He was surprised to find himself choking up, not knowing how to finish the sentence. 'We all still remember him, out on the course and in the Rifleman's especially.'

'I was reminded of you all golfing because I got a letter from the club. Ken Brogan, whoever he is, asking Andrew if he was going to renew his membership. He offered to discuss terms if there was, how did he put it, "any degree of financial constraint".'

'What a prat. Sorry Jane, he should obviously have known better, he's too busy watching the pennies to ever lift his head and see the members' faces. Otherwise, he would have known about Andy. That's unforgivable.'

'I wouldn't go that far, though it does still give me a pang every time I have to open a letter addressed to him. This one got me thinking. I told you I'm having a clear-out. Well, Dean never said anything more about golf, and I was practically as tall as Andrew' – Harry admired her delicacy…

she was taller – 'so I thought maybe I should give it a go before I throw the clubs out. You never know, I might even like the game and people never stop telling me I should get out more.'

If his Ellen had been one of those so urging her, she could hardly have had golf in mind. Had she not mentioned something about Jane growing concerned about becoming dependant on anti-depressants? That she had no trouble acquiring them after Andrew's death but some in leaving them alone? By Ellen's account she had fretted too, just like a woman, about putting on some timber over the winter.

'If you don't want to, that's perfectly all right, don't worry about it.'

'Sorry Jane, the line went funny there.' He tried to cover his inattentiveness. 'Want to what?'

'Take me out. On the course I mean, if that was what gobsmacked you, on the course, so I can get a feel for the game.'

Harry felt a prick of pride that she had come to him before either of his mates. Then he wondered if she had. 'Wouldn't you rather have a lesson or two with the club pro? Cliff Lambert's a nice chap and takes on people at all levels.'

'I'm sure he does but I feel too embarrassed at how bad I'd be. Obviously I'm a beginner, but I don't want to look a complete idiot. I'd rather start off with someone I know, someone I feel comfortable with.'

'Golf makes us all look idiots, Jane. There's no getting round that. George is a better player than me, you know. Or I could ask around the ladies…'

'All right, Harry, I get the message. I won't beg. I wouldn't ask George in case people got the wrong idea, him being single and a ladykiller and… I just didn't want to. You don't have to get nervous. I'll sort something out myself or go straight to the tip with the clubs, one or the other.'

'No, don't be silly. George isn't such a ladykiller nowadays, getting old like all of us are. All us blokes.' He was stung at the imputation that he might have been scared to engage with an attractive woman, on the golf course or anywhere else, the more so because he realised there might have been a touch of truth in it.

'Women age too, Harry. I shouldn't be prejudiced against my own sex but I didn't want to ask one at the club – even if I knew any – to show me the ropes. I thought that might drag me further than I wanted into a social group.'

'I see.' (He didn't.) 'You want what we used to call a deep meaningless relationship. I'm your man for that. We'll go to the practice area first, before we think about playing a round.'

'Playing around?'

'Yeah, "a round", two words, that's one of the first things you'll have to learn about golf, all the double meanings and jokes.'

'One of the first things you'll have to learn about me is that I can make a joke as well as take one. I knew what you meant, I was just teasing you.'

Harry could not remember the last time he had been teased.

'One last thing, Harry. What do I have to wear? Is there any special gear I need?'

This question brought home the magnitude of the task he had undertaken in introducing a woman to golf. Any man would have known not to rock up in T-shirt or jeans, and that would about do it. The TTers were generally conservative in this aspect of club life as all others within and outside its bubble. One or two, not necessarily among the gang's ancients, would sometimes sport plus-fours non-ironically, Henry Lawford with the particularly objectionable tartan socks.

A bitterly contested relaxation of the code had been endorsed at the recent AGM, championed by the club's new president Malcolm Shorten and his finance director Ken Brogan on the grounds that it might attract more green-fee-paying and bar-drinking visitors. Socks worn with shorts, as allowable from the first of May, would no longer have to be white or predominantly white – Percy had been sniffy about Mark Jones' United-logoed ones the previous summer – but Harry had no idea whether any such restriction applied to women.

Although he had noticed Jane was always presentable on the rare occasions he saw her socially, he had no fear she would come to the club dressed to kill. He advised her only to wear enough layers to keep warm without impeding the movement of her upper body, as they would be standing around in the practice area rather than walking the course in the early days. 'Well, a lot of them do wear skirts,' he guessed, wondering why, with the legs they had to show off, 'but trousers would be fine too if that's what you prefer. No need to think about proper golf shoes until we know for sure if you're going to give it a serious go. I assume you've got a pair of trainers knocking about somewhere. Don't bother bringing Andy's whole set either. The driver, five iron, pitching wedge and putter will be enough to start with.'

They had agreed to meet at the clubhouse that Tuesday afternoon at four thirty, giving them enough daylight and more importantly the TTers time to clear the premises after their own round. Harry was not exactly nervous, he just felt – as usual with women one-to-one – more comfortable with a few beers inside him. Tuesdays and Thursdays were when Ellen knew he was most likely to be staying over at his new flat – 'funk-hole' she called it, apparently not as suspicious as his friends of any sexual motivation in its acquisition.

He had not dreamed of spending almost their entire first session at the nineteenth hole. Keeping an eye open from its window he saw her pull up in the car park down the hill in Andy's maroon Volvo. Either she had sold the little Fiat he remembered her in, or she wanted the extra boot space for clubs and golf trolley. Ever the gallant, he went down to help her unload.

'Hello Harry, that's very kind of you. You did say I wouldn't need them all but I couldn't remember which to bring – I see some of them don't have numbers on them.'

'That would be the woods, not made of wood anymore but that's what we still call the big hitters. I don't know how much you're up on golf lingo, whether Andy used to bore you with it or you've read anything. Stop me if you think I'm telling you too much of the bleeding obvious.'

'Treat me as a complete virgin. Golf virgin,' she amended with a smile. 'Drew was good at keeping his life compartmentalised. The only thing I remember about his golf was the day he came home drunk as a skunk after getting his hole-in-one, and the shock I got when I saw the credit card bill the next month.'

'He was unlucky, middle of summer so plenty of our gang out there, then a society in the clubhouse when we came home. Some people duck out of buying the full round nowadays but not Andy – you could always depend on him for that, you know better than me. This is a good course for an ace, with six par threes when most only have four.' He saw he had lost her already. 'Par threes, where good players should get the ball into the hole with three shots, are the only ones where you have the slightest chance of holing out with your tee shot – unless you're a monster and can drive one of the shorter par fours. Let's not run before we can walk, though. It can be a long journey to a hole-in-one.'

She probably did not pick up on the hint of regret that it was one he had not yet himself completed. 'Oh God that makes me think of *Britain's Got Talent*, going on a journey like the contestants always say they are. I feel as jumpy as they must do. I'll probably be as terrible as a lot of them too.'

Harry had never thought of himself as a teacher, of golf or anything else. On the contrary, over the years he had spent far more money on golf lessons than his handicap reflected. Still far from happy with his game, he had curbed the worst excesses of showing his frustration by swearing and throwing his clubs around after a quiet word from one of the now departed club members in an early competition he played there.

'Why are you surprised when you make a bad shot? How often do you practise?' Will Something had asked him.

'I've had some lessons.'

'How often do you practise, think about your shots?'

'The more I think about them the worse they get.'

'You're not a good enough player to act so surprised when you fuck up, son. None of us out here are,' he added, to soften the blow Harry knew he had received.

Pulling the five iron from Andrew's bag – not a club he remembered his mate particularly favouring but conveniently in the middle of the range to get Jane started – he decanted half a dozen balls from the duffle bag full of old ones he'd brought from his own garage onto the pitching area, which along with a small putting green was all the club had by way of practice facilities. It was 150 yards to the canal so he had no fear of Jane reaching it.

'Just take a few swings, however feels most natural, then we'll see what we've got to work with.'

He did not stop her until the third swing, unable quite to believe what he was seeing. He struggled to find the right words.

'Hold on, love. You didn't tell me you was left-handed.'

She looked up at him anxiously – at least she had done a good job of keeping her head down on the shots she had taken. 'Does it matter? Is that why I'm not hitting it very far?'

'In a way. It never occurred to me. Andrew was right-handed.'

'Yes. What of it?'

They really were just sticks to her. He was sharply reminded of a brief teenage girlfriend who had proved her point about never having played pool by trying to break holding the cue crooked under one elbow and single-handedly stabbing at the white. 'So his clubs are right-handed. You'll never be able to hit them properly if you swing left-handed.'

'You told me to swing however it felt most comfortable.'

'Yeah, that's true, I did, but didn't it feel a bit… a bit clunky hitting the ball.'

'Course it did but I *am* only a beginner, I thought that was perhaps natural. I'm glad I've given you a good laugh anyway,' she said tartly, as Harry was no longer able to keep the grin off his face.

'No, we'll laugh about it together one day, it's partly my fault, just never occurred to me. Look at what I mean, you can see the two sides of the club are totally different, like a spoon.'

'It's not like a spoon, one side's flat. I can see that. You must think I'm a total idiot now.'

Desperately seeking to salvage something for her, he took out Andrew's putter. Luckily it was, like his own, one with a gap in the rear surface rising from the sole with the maker's logo in the middle, allowing it to serve to chip left-handed as well as scoop the ball up in disgust after failing to putt out. 'Here, try this one.'

She got it a creditable ten yards with her left-handed swing. 'That feels much better but you're messing around with me now. Even I know this one's a putter.'

'No, I swear I'm not messing, I just wanted to show you one club does swing both ways, so to speak. We'll have to get hold of some left-handed clubs for you. Funnily enough I used to carry a leftie five iron in my bag, in case I got backed up against a fence or tree or something.'

'Maybe I can use that one then to get started.'

'I don't carry that club anymore, not since I jarred my hand hitting it one time bad enough to break a finger. Couldn't wear my wedding ring for a month. Ellen was furious.'

'I bet. I'm not sure I want to spend a lot of money on a whole new set of clubs though, Harry. Not yet, anyway.'

'Sure, I get that. Cliff must have a set of left-handed rentals, might not mind us borrowing them except he's probably already knocked off for the day. If not there'll be plenty going cheap second hand. Amazing how many people take up golf then give it up – probably should have done that myself – so you're dead right not to put too much into it up front.'

'We can't do anything tonight then?'

'We can have a drink.'

*

It was already the same afternoon the next week he was going to see her when he remembered he hadn't done anything about the clubs. He had a word with Cliff, for whom he had been a good customer over the years – not just the lessons, the newest driver on the market, any number of different putters, three complete sets of irons, despite being perfectly conscious of the golf saying others might well apply to him – all the gear, no idea.

'That's a bit radical, Harry,' the pro said when he asked after left-handed clubs. 'I never thought you'd try switching to southpaw. Course you can try 'em out for free this afternoon as this is old stock, not much call for 'em. If you want to get serious, as ever I'll sort you out a fair price on a good set.'

'Not for me as it goes, I should have said, ladies' ones.'

'Got the missus taking up golf at last? Never thought I'd see her on the course, thought you always reckoned you'd barred her out. Decided to check up on you has she in that sha… sheltered accommodation for elderly golfers you've taken on?'

'Might let her clean it for me, that's as close as she'll get to the course, mate. It's for a sort of friend, friend of a friend… well, no secret about it.' He was suddenly exasperated with himself. 'Jane Wood.'

'Cos it's you, no problem, Harry. But if it's going to be a regular thing for a non-member I might eventually have to charge for the use of the clubs. And all modesty apart, you do know I offer special beginners' rates? Might get her out on the course and playing more quickly if she goes about it what I'd call the right way.'

'You would say that, wouldn't you? Don't think I didn't tell her the same myself, truth be told I wasn't all that keen on the idea. I tell you, talk about not knowing one end of the club from another…' He was about to embark on the tale of her left-handed swing with a right-hander's clubs, but decided to forego the easy laugh. If only for Andrew's memory, Jane deserved better than that.

He had been surprised at how much he enjoyed their time in the bar the previous week when he was able to neck four pints to her two bottles of cider. He could not remember the last time he and Ellen had gone out just for a drink; there always had to be a meal attached to it now. More recently she had broken their social contract by insisting on driving out while he drove home, rather than the other way around as had been their custom for over twenty years. Sometimes she wasn't even over the limit when they'd finished, so he could only put it down to sheer female malevolence.

Not that Harry had made the mistake of criticising his wife to Jane. He knew something about female solidarity too, without failing to notice women never had any trouble trampling over one of their so-called sisters if it was a matter of getting a man they wanted. How often did you hear of blokes getting into trouble for screwing their partners' actual sisters, blood sisters? You couldn't tell him that was all the men's fault, there had to be some come-on. As for so much else in life there was a handy golfing reference to it, the sister-in-law, a mishit shot that somehow flukes onto the green near the pin: you know you shouldn't be up there, but it feels good anyway.

With a proper set of left-handed clubs, albeit male ones, Jane's striking of the ball naturally improved exponentially. Naturally too, it was still awful. He did not pretend to her it would quickly get much better. 'Don't give up yet, it'll be a while before you can hit it consistently.'

'Who said I was giving up?'

'I can see you're getting frustrated from the steam coming out your ears. Get that son-in-law of yours to look on eBay, you should be able to pick something up dirt cheap, start with a half set if you like. Make sure they're ladies' clubs as well as left-handed, mind.'

'Afraid I might show my ignorance again, Harry? Dean's not my son-in-law, and I'm perfectly capable of using eBay myself.'

'I'm sure you are, turn the kettle off, love. There's a golf shot called that, the son-in-law.'

'What's that?'

'Not too bad, but you were hoping for better.'

'Oh. And by the way, I don't have to go for dirt cheap ones. Drew didn't leave me in the poorhouse.'

'And by the way he's not here to stop you pissing his money up the wall however you like.' It occurred to him that pissing up the wall was probably more a man thing. How could women do it, pissing down the drain maybe? He couldn't ask her since he hadn't voiced the irritable retort, but if she was going to throw a strop every time she failed to connect cleanly he would soon be passing her on to Cliff – let her pay his hourly rate if she had that much fucking dosh.

Chips

'Any news on replacements for Reg and Glenda? No offence, Carl, but by the time the chips come out on Tuesday there was only half a dozen of us left to eat 'em.'

Carl Bracknell, a widower pushing eighty, had been out of the pub game for years and was not looking for a full-time return. He played with the seniors on Wednesdays but had agreed to take on the other weekday lunch and afternoon shifts. He worked at his own pace.

'Still looking, I hear. Maybe it's dying out, the idea of having a husband-and-wife team working behind bars. No need to worry about your grub today, can't do it no more, under orders.'

Carl did not seem as put out at the imposition of such orders as Franny Rowland was. 'What the fuck, Brackers, here's an order for you: twenty players, so five bowls of chips to get started on soon as you fucking like.'

'Shout and swear as much as you like, Franny. I can't do nothing about it. I've had a letter from Mr Brogan with an official warning, after you all said it would be all right for me to carry on doing it. It's not my living, these few hours, but I've got used to it. I thought Percy had been told, did he not say anything?'

'Not to me, did he bollocks.'

The chips they had after each round were not a necessity for the TTers in the sense of serving anyone as lunch or tea, just a between-meals snack, nonetheless welcome especially on cold winter afternoons. They were a tradition, and as such to be defended to the death. Percy had a look at the letter from the finance director when he came in, to an instant doing-over from Franny. He addressed the matter in that day's parish notes.

'I hadn't realised they would threaten Carl with the sack for continuing to provide a good service to his old friends. I thought we were still discussing it with Ken Brogan on behalf of the club. Clearly, I was wrong.'

Been nothing but a disaster since they appointed that arsehole.
You'd think he'd be glad of anything that brought the club in a few extra shekels.
Twice a week without fail.
Bloody health and safety gone mad again, you can bet.
Paying him too, don't forget.
Can't we just send out an order to the Wood Street chippie?
Get Harry to cook us some up in his shag-pad.
Not allowed to bring your own grub onto the premises.
Even when they don't provide any.
And who'd fetch 'em? We need Brackers here to pull the pints.

'Ladies,' Percy called for order, 'you make some valid points. As far as I can see, it's not that *they* can't serve us chips. It's Carl that can't.'

'That's not fair. We had a few burnt offerings but he's got used to it now.'

'While he may have, Pete, the days of the gifted amateur are dying. It's about licensing of the individuals involved more than fear of Carl setting the kitchen alight. There are all sorts of rules and regulations about food hygiene.'

'The Wood Street chippie may not score too high on that either, not since them Turks took it over. Chips still good, though.' Graham Cook was already thinking that he might be calling there on his way home later that afternoon – Thursday was his wife's bingo night so he had to wait for his dinner till she brought them home their Chinese.

'Don't tell me Reg used to have a licence or whatever. He did 'em for us without anyone kicking up a stink.'

'Indeed. Ken can be a pain' – Percy paused until the rowdy rumble of agreement died down – 'but he *is* only trying to make things more professional around the place. That's what Malcolm Shorten, our esteemed president, tells me. Malkie used to be something in compliance in his last years at GEC, and he took it to heart more than many of the rest of us ever did.'

'And Brogan's just his lickarse fucking lapdog, we all know that.' Franny was still fuming.

*

'Room for a littlun still,' Brian Hammond said redundantly a few minutes later, turning his head from the otherwise unoccupied urinal trough in the locker room to see Harry Unsworth hovering behind him.

'I don't need a slash. Just come to have a word with you.' Harry leaned back against the sink, arms folded in front of him.

'Damn disgrace about the chips if you ask me.' Hammo fumbled at the wall with his zip, turning towards the sink with both hands still on it.

'Can't say I liked your idea of a solution,' Harry said. 'Or what you called the club flat. There's so much comes out of your slack gob you may have trouble keeping track, so I'll remind you. Shag-pad you said it was. Said I could do the chips in there.'

'Oh that, Harry, that was just banter, a joke.'

'That's the only reason I didn't call you out for a cunt in there. I still have to tell you I didn't find it funny. Who invented that name for the flat since I moved in?'

At that moment, Peter Goodwin appeared. 'All right, lads?'

Hammo wasn't sure. Harry suspected Pete had come in without needing to use the facilities any more than he did himself. 'I was just telling Hammo I didn't think it was very funny to refer to the club flat as a shag-pad.'

'Surprised you could make out who said it in the din going on at the time.' Pete continued more kindly to Hammo. 'I'm sure you didn't mean any harm did you, Brian? If you were serious, I'd have to get offended myself, being as I was the last visitor to spend a night at Harry's flat, after poker. You wouldn't be saying *I* was getting shagged there, would you?'

'No, nothing like that, course not. I didn't mean anything, honest.' While Pete was not as aggressive as Harry, he was not the white knight Hammo had momentarily hoped for. 'I was already saying, I meant no harm.'

'Good, no harm done then. Come on, mate, let's go have another pint while Harry washes up. We can share a packet of crisps long as there's no chips today.' He put an arm round Hammo's shoulder, his own body between him and Harry at the sink. The banterer was glad enough to leave the toilet without washing his hands, going straight home rather than returning to the bar.

*

'You shouldn't be surprised if people wonder what you're doing with the flat,' Pete returned to the topic at that week's Rifleman's session, updating George on how they had set Hammo right. 'I don't know how Ellen lets you get away with it. OK it's handy for the golf, but that wouldn't wash with Margaret for minute one. And we're still waiting for the poker-night invitations, least I still am whatever I said in the bog. Just between us, if you're not using it to get your end away what do you need it for?'

'Maybe I am using it to get my hole, or was anyway, but that don't give Hammo or any of that crowd licence to take the piss.'

George was not surprised that Pete apparently knew nothing of Jackie. Harry would have been scared of word leaking from him through one wife back to the other.

'Between us – and you're no Hammo, Pete, but I'll say it again, between us – things aren't good with me and Ellen just at the minute. I wasn't going to smack him, by the way. I just knew telling him would be the best way to get the message across to all the others'

'Don't say you've split up now. I thought you'd weathered the storm.'

'Nothing like that, George, no. Well, *something* like that I suppose. She told me to piss off once too often and I said no problem I would. It was lucky I had the flat in my back pocket, she was always bitching about that anyway so might as well rub it in. I was just throwing a scare into her, let her see how much she wanted what she kept saying she did. I fancied a bit of your lifestyle, being able to please myself about what I do, when and with who.'

'Nothing to envy in my lifestyle, mate. Remember when ole Kenny Lindsay told us it's no fun being single if you're past thirty, when we was still teenagers drinking in the Beehive? He seemed ancient to us but must have been only like the age he was talking about. It always stuck with me. Turns out we were nowhere near that position, married long before and more than once in my case. I'd say the same as ole Kenny every day of the week now, except changing over thirty to over sixty.'

'They do say sixty's the new thirty,' said Pete. 'For all you think she gives me a hard time, I wouldn't be without Marg. What about the kids, Harry? What do they say?'

'What do they care, more like? We were only sleeping together anyway when Jason or Janine come to visit us, just so they can have the second-best bedroom, not trying to con them. And I do mean sleeping, nothing else going on.'

'I hear you there, mate.' Pete and Margaret once had a sex life active enough for him to be secretly proud of it. He knew he could not match the historic number of partners of either of his friends, without letting that disturb him. If married sex was not the kind you could brag about or people envied you, so what as long as you loved and still fancied your wife? He could not envisage needing the blue pills he knew various of the gang used. Some had for years, Jimmy Bradley selling them cheap from an undisclosed source when they were not only expensive but prescription-only in the UK. If they stimulated libido, he was beginning to wonder if there was a female version. Since a prolonged menopause she had made sure he knew all about, Margaret had gone off sex. She let him know that, too.

'I thought Ellen was turning a blind eye to anything you had going on the side, as long as you didn't show her up, lose your head like you did that time with Sheila whatserface.' That one had been so notorious even Pete had not missed it. 'Taking her on holiday, when you could probably have her for a packet of plain crisps, that was a lot for any woman to stomach I expect. I hadn't twigged you had a new bird lately, or is it without one you've been pestering Ellen too much?'

'Hardly that. You won't believe it but she got jealous about fucking Jane.'

'You're fucking Jane?' Now George was alert.

'No, I mean just Jane, fucking seeing her for golf. I thought they're supposed to be friends. I could understand if it was Carly Devonshire or someone like that at the club, but...'

'Carly don't need lessons at golf, nor anything else. Could probably teach you pair a thing or two.' George's tone was wistful.

'I'm not after Carly, for Christ's sake. I wish I hadn't started telling you wankers about it. Try to be serious and that's all the support I get.'

'No, I'm sorry about Ellen, really mate.' Pete put a gentle hand on Harry's arm. 'If you have got a bird on the quiet though, just one thing... can I ask you just one thing?'

'What?'

'Will you get her to do us some chips from the shag-pad? At the end of the day that wasn't a bad idea of Hammo's.'

Golfer/Non-golfer

'Are we still on for Thursday?' Jane asked him on the phone without preamble.

'Why wouldn't we be?'

'Because I'm a bitch? I should have called you before now, you don't know how competitive I can be and I didn't want to look a fool in front of you. The next day there were blisters on the palms of my hands, right at the bottom of the fingers. Does everyone get them when they play golf?'

'I expect you were gripping the clubs too hard. I thought you were going to wrap them round a tree at one point, if not round my neck.'

'I knew I was bad but was I *that* bad?' Harry did not fill the silence with reassuring words. 'I don't know what got into me. I'll try to keep my temper if you'll bear with me.'

'Makes no odds to me, I'm used to being in the wrong with women. I will say one thing though, and it might be the most help I can give you at golf. You're going to hit a lot more bad shots than good for a long time, perhaps for ever. If you get pissed off every time you do, it will only make you hit more yet. I could tell you to scream and swear, let it all out, a lot of people do. It took me a long while to stop doing it myself.'

'And did it make you better?'

'Not so much that, I'm still crap. It made me enjoy the game more though, and it made others prepared to keep on playing with me. You don't see it when you're starting out, but if you're a Tommy – or Tammy – Tantrum, you put off your playing partners as well as yourself. George had to have a word with me about it.'

'Ah, wise old George, Grasshopper. Are you as much in love with him as Andrew used to be?'

'Not anymore, he broke my heart when he took up with Emma from the White Horse.'

'He didn't break Drew's even when he took up with our daughter. Anyway, thanks for the tip, I'll try to keep cool, and I'm into getting some clubs. What's the main difference between men's and women's.'

'Pink grips I suppose. No, I'm joking, only cos I don't actually know, just shorter and lighter maybe. I've never thought about it, any more than I've thought why they're never called women's clubs. All female golfers are ladies, apparently.'

'I'll try to remember that as well. Thanks for being a gentleman with me.'

Whether her child-minding commitment was real or not, she had not accepted his invitation for a drink after their second class. At the third she offered to buy him one, which he deflected by saying that only members' cards were accepted at the bar. She asked him about the golfer/non-golfer tournament posted there for the following Friday. 'Would I qualify to play in that?'

'No doubt. You're hitting the ball a lot better but you've still got a long way to go. Or did you mean as the golfer?'

'I'm not getting so far ahead of myself. It just occurred to me, I've never seen you hit a ball in anger. You couldn't be more patient as a teacher, no complaints there, but if you're free I thought it might make a change.'

'What, instead of having our session on Thursday?'

'As well as, if you like. I see they're doing chilli or a burger after, I'd like to treat you to one or the other of those meat-eaters' delights, a little thank you. I've already twigged you *can* spend cash at the bar, by the way. Carl told me.'

'You can, but you wouldn't get the members' discount.'

'Is that the real reason, Harry? Don't get me wrong, it's something I find very decent about men of your generation – ours I should say – always wanting to buy the drinks. It took me a long while to train Andrew out of it. Dean's a totally different matter. I can always give you the money under the table if you like. Baby steps.'

'You like taking the piss out of me, don't you?'

She laughed right in his face. 'I suppose I do. You've gone all red now, please don't get upset. I enjoy having a drink with you but I have my own self-respect. I'd invite you round to try some of my own chilli – I'll be interested to see how the club's shapes up to it – if I didn't have to be a lady now I'm a golfer. Or a non-golfer anyway. Go on, ask Ellen if I can steal you for it next week.'

'I don't need to ask her,' he grumbled.

The golfer/non-golfer was more a social thing than a proper competition, one Harry had never indulged in before. Always on a high-summer Friday night, the idea was that the golfer would get the ball onto the green, leaving his or her partner to do the putting. Who hasn't played a round of pitch and putt or crazy golf at some point? How hard can it be to hole out on a smooth surface without having to go through a clown's mouth or between the wings of a windmill? Nevertheless, there was a three-over-par cap on each hole to prevent too much dallying by any totally-non perfectionist. For the same reason it was limited to holes one, two, nine, ten, eleven and Heartbreaker eighteen, an abbreviated circuit back to the clubhouse.

George's partner, Emma, was suspicious of golf as a toffs' game, whether involving the official seniors' section at MWGC (The Over Fifty-Fives) or a subset of it whose TOFFS were Thick Old Fuckers From Sladen, one of the town's lower-rent estates. Other variants were too old for football, fucking or fighting. Besides, Friday was her busiest night of the week. George did not pretend he would pop in for a drink at the club, but Pete said he might persuade Margaret to make an exception to her rooted dislike for it and its members if she knew Jane would be there.

Cliff put in some overtime to organise the event, hoping to make it worth his while with the offer of a cut-price package of lessons for any of the non-ers he could interest. He would be starting people in half-dozens at most between six and seven, without formal tee times. Jane, unfussily punctual as ever, was happy enough to have a drink before they started out, Dean weaselling in for one as the price of dropping her off.

'I thought I might need a drink beforehand as well as after. I know it's only supposed to be a bit of fun but you wouldn't believe how nervous I've been about it all day.'

'She nearly gave up her place, Harry,' Dean said. 'Maddie was all for giving it a go if Sally-Anne would of let her come. Can't blame her for not letting our little girl hang about with a load of dirty old men. Only joking, chap.'

'Probably safer with us than hanging about with young ones, pal.' Harry would not dignify Dean with a 'mate', more vexed at being called 'chap' than any blanket imputation of paedophilia, and more vexed yet at Dean's 'our' for Maddie.

'You shouldn't joke about that sort of thing, Dean. It's not true either, Harry. She did want to play, that bit is, I said they could come after if it's all right with you, carry me home if I get too drunk with success. I didn't want 'em watching my competitive debut, enough pressure already.'

'Course it's all right with me, more the merrier.' Harry wished he could add 'except for you, dickhead' to Sally-Anne's 'chap', as he might fairly have been called if they were living in the 1950s.

They were sent out with a friendly face from the TT gang. 'Who's the golfer?' Harry asked Jimmy Bradley of the tubby teenage boy with him. He was not old enough to have grandchildren that age, and had never spoken of a son. The kid's palpable discomfort at being there ruled out a favourite nephew before Jimmy's answer did.

'If only, Harry. This is James, my girlfriend Barbara's lad. Her dad's our Baz Knighton, didn't fancy bringing his grandson. I said I'd give it a go, it was my Uncle Will first got me into golf here years ago, so felt like passing on the baton. I've had to give up on football with this one, accept it's not for him. However much I tell him you can play golf on your own, no need to talk to anybody or anything, he'd rather be in the bedroom on his tod than getting a whiff of fresh air. His mother practically had to kick him out tonight.'

When Jimmy confirmed Uncle Will had been a tall Irishman Harry remembered him as the one who had taken him to task about his own attitude in his early days at MWGC, a man from whom he had felt able to accept the instruction. Perhaps George's height reminded Jimmy of his uncle, since he seemed most devoted to him of the three friends he had christened the tontiners and liked to hang out with when in drinking mood. This was not always. Within the gang Jimmy had a reputation as a Jekyll and Hyde character, quiet to the point of anonymity most days when he would sit over lime and sodas to do the right thing of having a drink with his playing partners. Sometimes though, without any discernible pattern of regularity, he would be the life and soul of the party, flitting from group to group as they dwindled, to be among the last drinkers there, suddenly smoking as well with anyone who took a break outside the clubhouse to do so. He was always discreet about the customers for his Frankie pills. The boy James looked as if he was waiting for Mr Hyde to savage him, not raising his eyes to look at Harry as he submitted reluctantly to the old man's ritual of the handshake.

Appearances could be deceptive. With nothing to do until the men reached the green, Jane and James strolled together down the road less travelled by them, the middle of the fairways, soon enough chatting and giggling with each other. Despite being conscious of wanting to put on a good show for Jane, Harry somehow still managed to do so, breaking the cardinal rule of club golf (the harder you try, the worse you play). She did not let him down either, averaging two putts a hole helped by a couple where he managed to leave her tap-ins.

Jimmy's attitude to his playing partner was diametrically opposed. It was like he was on a bet not to talk to James, or after a while to anyone else. His golf was like his personality; tonight he was very much on the dark side, depriving the boy of any putt at all on nine after driving twice straight out of bounds onto the railway line to London. He popped into the bar as they passed the clubhouse for their back three, tossing a double Jameson's off without holding them up at the tenth. It changed his mood, if not his golf.

'Is your missus thinking of becoming a member then, Harry? She looks as if she's got the concentration already, very steady with the putter.'

'We're not together, Jimmy. Just old friends, only came out for a laugh.' He struggled to find something positive to say about James' work on the greens, for all there was no evidence of any step-parental pride to boost.

'James is a good lad really,' was the most Jimmy would allow. 'From Barb's marriage. She might drag her mum and Baz along later.'

'Good lad himself,' Harry was happy to say of Barry Knighton. He had soon learned how much like a village community the TT gang was, unexpected friendships and alliances everywhere so that it was best to keep your opinion of any individual to yourself unless it was one shared by everyone in the gang.

'New leader in the clubhouse,' Cliff remarked at its door on receiving their scorecards for checking as they went in after completing the six holes. Jimmy had neatly recorded on Harry's gross scores per hole plus the number of putts Jane had taken. Insisting on buying them both a drink, he was as quick to the bar as James at the trestle table with the big tureen of chilli and the stack of burgers on it. Harry hoped they were more fully defrosted than Margaret looked, where Pete handily had them all a corner table ready.

Harry somehow felt awkward with Jane now that Pete and his wife were around, despite the diluting presence of Jimmy and his stepson, the latter already tucking into a plate of chilli. At the eighteenth, Jane, relieved or elated, had hugged the boy first, then Jimmy. Moving in for his turn, with congratulations on her performance, Harry had been treated to a kiss, not an airy-fairy one somewhere up by your lughole either; right on the lips. In itself, that did not signify much between long-standing friends of their generation. They weren't French, where he had read that to kiss a woman on the lips in public was to confirm she was your mistress, but he struggled to remember her doing it in the past. He had no hope or wish for a kiss of any kind in greeting from Margaret, so he was not disappointed.

Having agreed they would wait until the queue for food headed by James began to subside, there was nothing else to do but drink. The lad had a pint of Coke, the men three of Pride, Margaret a martyr's Virgin Mary (a bloody shame) and Jane a healthy gin and tonic – Jimmy held no more than Harry with single measures of spirits.

When Dean arrived with Sally-Anne and Maddie, Harry watched with interest to see how he would avoid buying a round. They came over to the table first, and it was Sally-Anne who offered to get them in. Jimmy was as generous in drinking mode as he was parsimonious, a drink for a drink and not a tittle more, when on the wagon. 'Here you go, take my card to the bar, I'm in the chair. Your mum just handed us our arses out there by the way, outputted my boy – say hello, James, don't be shy – all day long.'

Harry gave up willingly for Maddie his meal voucher, part of the admission fee to the event to make it worth the cook's while to turn up. 'There's no need, Harry, we could have paid for it, but thanks anyway,' Sally-Anne said. 'Go up there with her to get the food, babe, will you? And me another double vodka Red Bull while you're at it.'

Again Dean was saved by the unwitting Jimmy. 'James can squire her. If Harry can throw his cloak down for the little lady, never let it be said that I can't be just as generous. Who needs lining for the stomach anyway? Go on, son, you couldn't make your mind up earlier, so have your two dinners. Get the burger this time, don't worry about anyone calling you half rice half chips.'

Dean laughed at that. James took the ticket before responding with some dignity, the heat limited to his face. 'The only one who might call me that would be a homophobe like you.'

Jimmy was the first to laugh this time. 'Where do they get the language from nowadays? Homophobe, you'll be saying I'm a heterosexual next, that's another insult, isn't it?'

'I remember at school people thought it was, because nobody knew what it meant,' Pete contributed, as James politely offered Maddie the lead so as not to show her his back before giving it to the table.

'What's funny about half rice half chips? I don't get it,' Jane asked Harry.

'Oh Mum, come on, you left that convent of yours a hundred years ago, not last week. Don't you fall for it, Harry, she's not that innocent.'

'What *does* half rice half chips mean?' Jane insisted, three hours later, in her own front room.

'You what?' Harry was paying rather more attention to the Malibu she told him was the only drink in the house. He wondered if he could make either that or the black coffee he had also not wanted more palatable by mixing them.

'You know, there was an atmosphere when that drunken friend of yours was getting on his son's case. I suppose he was hinting he was gay or something from the way Dean started to cackle. I'm glad you didn't.'

'I didn't think it was funny. If he is, it's no laughing matter, and if he isn't, it wasn't a very good joke.'

'So he *was* saying he was gay? But where do the rice and chips come in?'

'Jimmy's like that. He can go over the top when he's on the bevvy. All it means is someone who can't quite make their mind up, so not a full-on poofter I suppose. I'm sorry, there's so many names for 'em I don't know which one you prefer, they keep moving the goalposts. Don't give me that look, I didn't say it.'

'I feel guilty now for not speaking up myself. That poor boy, to be shamed like that by his own dad. He was great with Maddie, and with me walking round the course come to that, very polite.'

Harry did not bother to clarify that Jimmy was stepdad to James, not seeing any mileage in prolonging that conversation. He also resisted the temptation to say that getting on well in female company only proved Jimmy's point, worry or whatever it was. 'I wouldn't have minded if you did have to babysit Maddie, you know. I'm glad they could find a way round it, though.'

'I wouldn't have minded either if they'd given me some notice, and I would still have done it except in the end she was keener to go and spend the night at her friend Shevonne's house. It didn't hurt them to drop her off there on their way out on their Friday night razzle. If I'm honest, I don't feel at all guilty about having a night to myself for once.'

'Shouldn't, neither. Had to celebrate your win!'

'I was truly amazed at that. The best non-golfer in Market Welham I can start calling myself now. I couldn't have done it without the way you set me up, shame you didn't win out of the golfers.'

Harry had been surprised to come second, glad Jane did not go off on one like Ellen might have for his voucher being worth more than her winning one. He could have argued it was a golfer/non-golfer rather than male/female thing, that it was coincidence all the golfers had been men. She made light of the money, trying to give him the voucher. All right she wouldn't get her name on the honours board over the bar, but she had still won her first golf competition, something he was still waiting to do.

'I've seen you can play as well as teach now,' she continued. They were sitting a respectable distance apart on the three-seater settee he had gone for when they arrived and she disappeared to the kitchen, not so much hoping that she would plump down beside him as unwilling to risk choosing whichever of the two armchairs had been Andy's favourite. The men had never been ones to visit each other's houses, generally meeting wherever they were going out. The fact that Jane had made her third change of footwear in the evening, from golf shoes – bought for the occasion, she told him – to heels and now to fluffy slippers did not suggest a particularly amorous mood. Still, he was wondering when he should make the pass.

'Jimmy was very complimentary about your putting,' Harry passed on the praise. 'I bet he would have swopped you for James if he had the chance.'

'I was thinking when we were all sitting there, thinking we were the only happy couple. All right we're not a couple, but do you see what I mean? There was the drunk who wouldn't open his mouth to the boy except to say something nasty, then Peter and Margaret hardly speaking to each other at all.'

'Maybe they're contented. Don't you think they're happy?'

'I don't think she approved, somehow. I've never liked her as much as your Ellen, tell you the truth. You did invite her, didn't you, like I asked? It would have been good to see her, if only to thank her for giving me a borrow of you these last weeks.'

'You wouldn't need to give me back if it was up to her.' The bitterness in his voice surprised himself. He had not mentioned anything about the golf to his wife.

'I'm sure that's not true.' She tried a laugh, then turned serious. He had bent forward to have a go at his now merged drinks, and she put a hand on his unencumbered forearm. 'Look at me, Harry? Tell me I'm not coming between the two of you, cos that was kind of the impression I was getting from Margaret. Was Peter the same with you?'

A quick gulp at the tepid – foul – drink, the cup returned to the low coffee table, he half turned as requested. 'Pete's a mate, he wouldn't stick his nose in. Can we not talk about Ellen?' He managed to get his lips onto hers and kid himself she did not instantly withdraw, though he could not deny even in the moment she did so quickly enough.

Suddenly they were both apologising, he was getting up to run but she put a hand on his shoulder and took her drink off into the kitchen, as if she could not wait a second longer for more gin or more tonic in it. It was not a big glass but when she reappeared in the doorway she was holding it in front of her, in both hands like a priest offering communion. He could see it moving, any ice in it would have been clacking like a set of castanets.

'Jane, I'm sorry if I misread things.' He tried to adopt a brisk tone. 'You did start it.'

'You what? I *started* it? How's that?'

'Well, you know, the kiss, and putting your hand on my arm and… and being nice.'

'What kiss?'

He could see Jane was genuinely puzzled. 'Come on, when we finished golf, or was that nothing? We're not kids. I might have jumped the gun but there's no need to go running off like some little virgin, you can't have been surprised…'

'I think you'd better go, Harry. I don't like what I'm hearing and I don't want to say something I'll regret. I can't believe you thought you were coming back here to have sex with me.' She took a swig from her glass and put it down with some force beside his own on the low table.

'Well it wasn't for the Malibu,' he flicked a finger at the liqueur he would not now have to finish. 'OK bad joke, listen, maybe it's the Tyson defence but exactly what did you think you were doing with a man on your own at midnight?'

'I thought I was with a friend. You mean the boxer Mike Tyson? The convicted rapist Mike Tyson? Is that the way you were thinking, whether she wants it or not, once I'm in that door she's going to get it? Is it?'

'Now you're twisting things. She went up to his room and everything.'

'You're just the same as Andrew. He wouldn't hear Tyson was guilty either. Why did he bite that other fighter's ear off? Because he was an animal, that's why.'

'That was in the ring. Heat of the moment. He was billed as the baddest man on the planet, but an animal? Look, I wish I hadn't mentioned his name.' That was nothing less than the truth. 'Jane, you mustn't think I'd ever force you to do anything. *Anything*. Never mind an ear, don't bite my head off for what, one little kiss between friends?'

Jane was not quite ready to make nice again. 'A kiss I was begging for? Believe it or not, when I came back through that door I was going to say something different altogether, but you threw me off track. Never mind Mike Tyson, what was it Sybil said to Basil – at least if you're going to grope the guests have the decency to own up to it?'

Harry was more than happy to move from Madison Square Garden to Fawlty Towers. 'I think she said "have the decency to do it while you're in the same room as them" and if we're being picky, I thought I was the guest here. Look, I can see I've outstayed my welcome, I'll go now unless you've got anything more to say.'

'It is funnier the way you remember it. I was never much good with jokes. Are you going to be all right getting home?'

'Don't worry about me. I know my way around. I thought you did too,' he regretted adding as soon as the words were out of his mouth. She allowed him to take one of her hands between his. 'If it means anything, I honestly didn't come in here with any bad intentions. I'm more Basil Fawlty than Iron Mike, believe me.'

'All right, I hope I didn't overreact. I don't normally drink this much nowadays. I think we should both sleep on it then we can talk again. Is that all right with you?'

'Not really. I don't want to talk any more, and I'm guessing a shag's out of the question... Only joking, I keep forgetting you're a convent girl.'

'I'd forgotten Sally-Anne mentioned that tonight. You don't miss much. Why do men think all convent girls are sex-mad?'

'Must be something to it, probably St Trinian's, all them schoolgirls in stockings and suzzies.'

'That wasn't a convent, was it?'

He smiled. 'Boxing from the eighties yes, *Fawlty Towers* in the seventies OK, but I don't go back as far as the fifties or whenever it was them films were made. Christ, they were in black-and-white weren't they? Please don't come to the door, I might be tempted to pounce on you again for a goodnight kiss.'

'No trouble. As you say, you're the guest.'

He thought she meant seeing him to the door, but when they got there she turned his hunched shoulders round and gave him a kiss. 'We're past the days of black and white now.'

The Shark

'Since when do you drink wine?' Harry was accused rather than asked.

'Never too late to start. Or start again. Remember when we used to drink wine in bed together?'

Ellen did not answer, already digging two-fisted into her fish and chips, not waiting for him to put them on a plate for her. He had not been above the same tactic once, but had less appetite as he grew older. Time was he would have what he persisted in considering the drink-drive legal maximum of three pints (for all today's kids tried their own law of five-and-drive, with varying degrees of luck) in the Beehive before so much as entering the chippie. Now he generally stuck at two, and not from increased fear of plod. He was sober and would never have an accident to draw their attention. He knew Ellen would have enough wine for herself but had bought her brand anyway – Merlot, it was all the same to him – so he could offer her an extra glass. She was highly territorial about her own daily bottle, though as with the chips he was the one who did the weekly shop for it.

Cod and chips, haddock and chips, large curry large mushy peas. Their ageing, mainly black partly collie Judy had followed him into the kitchen, knowing she could expect nothing from her missus. He threw a chip into her bowl, then had to show the stupid mutt where it had gone. Once he had dripped the short end of both polystyrene cups onto his plate he would come back and pour the rest willy-nilly over the ravaged spread across his wife's thighs. She had found it amusing when he continued so long to bring her knife and fork, not realising he did it for himself rather than her. Now he tried not to look as she noisily sucked her fingers clean, down among the scraps.

'Go on then, but don't expect to get me going with a couple of extra glasses. It'll take more than that.'

'Tell me about it.'

'Go out and get it with your new girlfriend if you're desperate. Friday night not date night again this week? Or are you both too knackered after last night?'

'What are you on about now?'

'You don't ask *who* I'm on about then?' She backhanded her long straight hair away from her face as she raised her head at last from the white wrappings, nothing but grease left on them now. Had the start of her not taking care of her appearance for him been all those years back when he had innocently laughed at a perm? 'Sure you can afford her, on top of your flat? Or is this one kicking in something towards it, expect she's flush now.'

'I do have trouble keeping up with who I'm supposed to be knocking off, but since you've been going on about Jane all this week I assumed you meant her. Or have you moved on to someone else? You could have come last Friday if you wanted, then you wouldn't have had to trust whatever your new best friend Margaret said was going on.'

'Did you invite me last Friday? I don't think so.'

'Time was I wouldn't have to invite you,' he ducked. 'Friday night used to be our date night whatever happened, remember?'

'What's the matter with you tonight, off down memory lane? Are you getting Old-timer's on me already? You remember what suits you to remember, Harry. Don't think I'm that dumb you can throw me off the track. How many women would let their husband bunk off to a flat not two miles from home without thinking there's something behind it? You should think yourself lucky I'm so placid.'

He had no memories to come back with of her being anything but placid, it was true. Plump and placid, plumptious as Ken Dodd might have said, the body of a seaside-postcard siren until pushing forty. How he had enjoyed that body. He would still if she let him, even with an extra five or six stone on it.

'I'd say good luck to her if she keeps you off me, but I won't be made to look a fool. Whatever Margaret says I take with a pinch of salt, her and her perfect marriage, that's what no kids will do for you. Maybe. Didn't work for us, did it?'

She pulled a handkerchief from under her mush-and-curry-stained T-shirt – was she keeping the bloody thing in her bra? – to start dabbing at her eyes. He knew there was a genuine feeling there at the loss of their baby, though the memory was usually triggered nowadays by a slight overdose of red.

'We have kids, love, let's not go down that road tonight. I'd rather you kept on about my supposed girlfriends.' Ellen's younger girl Kerry still lived and worked locally, at the Melwood House care home, God bless her, while Miranda was down in London living the same life of leisure as her mother. He had brought them up in a way, that waster Tony Beamon had never contributed a penny of support when you could still get away with that. Only Kerry occasionally called him Dad, as his own kids Jason and Janine did not.

'Supposed? If I wanted the proof I daresay I could find it, though maybe not with Jane. She must be older than you are – not your style, I would have thought.'

'You were the exception there, my treasure.' He made sure to get his fair share of the Merlot, could feel his face flushing on it, like it always did on wine he only now recalled. Seven years between him and Ellen, his best ones already behind him when they met if you looked at it one way, already finished playing football – golf was all right but no real substitute – a marriage already dead in the water. He did not deny his fault in that, did not begrudge his kids their anger.

He did not know Jane's exact age, only that it fitted smoothly with his. He tried to lighten the tone by darkening his voice. 'You can ask me about my business, just this once. And I'll tell you that I have not had sex with that woman.'

'No need to stand over me like that unless you've come to put the chip bags in the bin. I'm not scared of you, you know, you're nothing compared to Tony.'

So now he was being compared unfavourably to her ex because he had never hit her. Admittedly he was no good at accents, but he was disappointed she had not caught the *Godfather* reference. He had not seen the film at the cinema on original release, but wasn't it a timeless classic? And had she never heard of Bill and Monica? One of the reasons he enjoyed being with Jane – one his wife might have laughed at – was that she more often picked up on his random allusions.

But it was not the main thing. A kiss with intent changes everything. His may have been bungled, and Jane had not gone beyond hers at the door the previous week, not a long or deep one but he knew it was in earnest. He had allowed himself to be gently turned outside, no breath left to talk further, standing suspiciously a moment before leaving yet hearing no mortice locks being thrown, bolts being drawn.

There had been no lesson yesterday. She did not call and he was determined not to. He had wondered what he was doing, sitting alone in his flatlet after the Thursday game and subsequent session. He had wondered what she was doing. He wondered again now. Could he say he had a green light from his wife to go ahead with whatever might develop between them?

'Come on, Jude, time for us to go walkies.' The dog beat him to the door. 'Let your mum go on dreaming about her fabulous first marriage.'

'Wasn't a marriage, maybe that's what stopped it ever getting boring.' He let her have the last word now, knowing she would eventually do so however long he kept her up. She was already laid out on the settee, which sagged at the centre in the shape of her left hip and arse.

He told himself it was not fear of discovery but respect for Ellen's feelings that made him make or take any calls from women, however innocent (they were not all innocent) outside her presence. She had only had to jeer at him once, when he declined to answer its ring, that he could speak to his floozie if he liked, see if she cared. Would he like her to leave the room, give them a bit of privacy? Now it was always on silent. Nobody needed him so urgently that he could not return a call when he saw it flagged.

Ellen herself had little need to tax him with unanswered calls. She rarely rang him, for all her phone was as often in her hand as a biscuit. He assumed she was all over Facebook, which he chose not to join. It had become her main social outlet, now that she rarely left the house. If he did not walk Judy, the poor little bitch would be getting as fat as her missus. He did not resent his walking duties, they gave him a chance to catch up on his calls and smoke a cigar. Ellen would not allow them in the house, annoyed that only she had remained a total non-smoker after they both gave up cigarettes ten years earlier. Concern for her heart – she had read some article about it. He could not help wondering if smoking would have been more dangerous for that organ – lungs fair enough – than the extra weight she had piled on.

Jane answered the phone as he was on the point of ending the call. 'Hello. Hello, Harry. I somehow didn't think you'd get back to me. Thought you were going to be a kiss-and-runner.'

'Kiss and run, haven't heard that phrase in years. I never was that, never a kiss-and-teller either.'

'Relieved to hear it, I wouldn't like to think of you bragging around the clubhouse about poor old widow woman Wood losing her heart to you and you had to let her down gently.'

'Have you been drinking, Jane? You're not talking anything I can make sense of.'

'I did have a drink before I called you earlier, yes. Dutch courage I suppose, then perhaps another to console myself when you didn't answer.'

'You know it's bad form to take calls at the golf. I have to put it on silent so often, I sometimes forget and leave it there. Anyway, I was glad to hear from you. I thought my services were no longer required or you'd taken up that special offer of classes Cliff was touting at the golfer/non-golfer.'

'It wasn't as good an offer as the free tuition I've been getting from you. Truth is I didn't know whether you would want to continue after I practically threw you out of my house.'

'You threw me out very gently, Jane. If my feet didn't touch the ground it was only because I was walking on air.'

'Wow, what a smooth talker. I never thought you had that in you.'

'Not bad, eh. If you come across it in some late-night flick don't tell me, so I can kid myself I made it up on the spur of the moment. I was worried I might have overstepped the mark and you wouldn't want to see me again.'

'I do want to talk to you about that, but there's something else as well. I think I've definitely caught the golf bug, so if you're still ready and willing I can be there next Thursday, late afternoon as usual. Then – I don't want to sound forward or anything – I'd like to invite you out for a bite to eat.'

'You don't have to do that, Jane. Not that I don't appreciate the thought, but I might not see the mark at all if you get a bottle of wine down me.'

'That's why I said invite you *out*,' she laughed, sounding relaxed for the first time. 'And it's funny you mention wine, because there's a bottle chucked in at The Bell with its Thursday-night meal deal. So don't worry about me breaking the bank for you.'

'If you put it like that, how can I resist?'

They continued talking golf at The Bell after their session on the practice patch at MWGC. It felt great to have a woman listen to him with something like respect. 'Soon be time to take you out on the course, I think. That's the only way you're going to progress, now you can get the ball away.'

He was drinking a Pedi, thinking that if he knew the guvnor he would tell him it really shouldn't be chilled like that. They had come straight from the clubhouse bar, only polite to have one there after using the club facilities. He was glad there had been no fuss and nonsense about going home to get dressed up or anything. It made it less like a date.

'I don't know about playing properly yet. I'd be worried about holding up people behind us.'

'Got to start sometime. Anyway, we can always pick up the ball and move on, you mustn't be afraid or ashamed to do that.'

'I'm thinking about the other members because I might be getting to know them better. That's one thing I wanted to talk to you about tonight.'

'You're thinking about joining the club? That's great but they do have a flexible membership you might want to try first, glorified pay-and-play but you can upgrade it to full if you get into the game.'

'I may not have to pay to play. I've been talking about doing some work on the catering side and they might throw in a membership. The money's not that good to be honest, they'd need to, but then I'm not doing it for the money.'

'You could do it, could you? You mentioned this famous chilli I still hope to try one of these days, but you could run a full kitchen?'

'I like to think so.' She prodded at her steak. 'Don't get me wrong. I'm not talking cordon bleu any more than The Bell is, but I have got some experience and it would help get me out of the house. I don't know why, but I hanker after that more now than I did.'

'I can give you a job as a dog-walker if you like. Cordon bleu would be about as welcome at our club as that Scottish arsehole Ramsay, good old bacon sarnies would be a start. It's a disgrace we can't offer anything to members or visitors. I told them I'd give up the flat in a heartbeat if they found a couple to take it on who could do a proper job stewarding again, you know, food and drink.'

'Why not invite me to move in with you?'

Surely her timing had been deliberate. Rather than choke on his beer he took a longer swig than he had been planning. She was watching him without giving anything away, only smiling when he lowered the glass, before he could speak himself.

'I thought you were going to down the whole pint. I didn't mean to terrify you. Just when you think you've got yourself a cosy little bachelor-pad set-up some woman comes muscling in on it, cramping your style. I was joking, don't fret, but there is a serious bit to it. You can bet if I start being around the course and the clubhouse a lot more, and we keep our lessons going, people are going to start talking about me and you. If they're not already.'

'They probably are. I've had a few comments from the TT gang. Like a bunch of old women some of them are – speaking of which, I'm guessing the ladies' section aren't above a bit of gossip. Do you know any of them?'

'And how does that make you feel? Them talking?'

'Nothing like as bad as being asked how I feel. Can't we talk about the steak instead? Not a bad cut but how you can eat it cremated like that I don't know.'

'I don't like the sight of blood is all. Too squeamish maybe. I suppose I keep asking you these questions because I honestly don't know much about you. You can take the strong, silent thing too far.'

'Strong and silent, that's more George's line. Not that I had Andy pegged as chatty either. Pete's the one who can gas. I shouldn't wonder him and Margaret do nothing but talk about their feelings when they're out for a meal together.'

'What about you and Ellen?'

'We never go out for a meal together. Look, I'm not going to give you any wife-doesn't-understand-me bullshit. Maybe she understands me too well. I've not been the greatest husband.'

'You don't have to tell me that. It wasn't that my husband judged you, don't think it. Your little gang of four meant the world to him, I was almost jealous of it. He liked Pete just as much as he did you and George. I think although Drew was the oldest of you, he and Pete always felt they were like the junior partners, that was how he put it anyway. George, we had a serious issue but Drew and him worked through it. I heard everything you were all up to sooner or later, and some of the tales about you weren't pretty.'

He resisted the temptation to ask which ones. If it mattered, she would not be here now. He would ask her at some other time about the 'serious issue' with George.

'You don't owe me any explanations or justifications, Harry. I don't need them.' (He had not been planning to offer any.) 'And I don't feel I owe anything to Ellen either. There was never the same friendship between any of your wives, or women, as you four. I sometimes used to think I wouldn't be able to count on Drew if it came to a choice between me and his mates. I think Margaret hasn't accepted that element of doubt, so she gets worked up at times trying to pretend it isn't there.'

'She keeps Pete on a tight leash, right enough.' They all thought they were the different one, that history meant nothing. The only man a woman can change is a baby, he liked that cracker philosophy. He was happier to talk about Pete than himself. 'I've never heard him say a bad word about her though. I don't mean to put him down, I'm closer to him than nearly anyone else, except me and George, we go right back to primary school.'

'All right, so what does the strong, silent George say about me and you?'

'Why don't you ask him? I'm sure I can fix you up if you like.'

'Fix me up? Where did that come from? Did you ever leave primary school?'

'You were the one who asked about my feelings. You might regret it. I might talk all night like Elvis, not the big E, the little Costello. Do you mind if I get another Jameson's? I'd be more than happy for you to join me but don't feel obliged. When I say me and George are tight that doesn't mean we don't have a niggle at times. When you're at school, when you've always lived within drinking distance of each other, there's a lot of bodies. I wouldn't say he's ever deliberately set out to take a bird, a woman, away from me, but over the years a few have turned out to prefer him. I wouldn't like it if that was you.'

There were a few beats of silence. Harry knew he was being outwaited. He gave in with a good grace. 'Getting back to your original question, for what it's worth he disapproves. Says there should never be anything with a mate's wife, that it's OB.'

'OB?'

'Yeah, out of bounds is a golfing term, two stroke penalty if you hit the ball outside the course's marked limits, so beyond the pale, verboten, way out of order, however you want to put it. He caught me on the raw with that, probably because deep down I know he's right.'

'Harry, until these last few weeks I knew George if anything better than I do you. You said it yourself, in some ways it would have been more natural to ask him to help with my golf. I chose you.'

'Yeah, but that's golf. I thought somehow we weren't talking golf anymore.'

'Maybe we're not. I still chose you. I'm not a daft teenager, don't think I've fallen passionately in love with you or anything like that. Though I do feel younger around you, however silly that may sound. Most of all I don't feel like a widow. I want to respect you and your marriage, that's why I'm asking if you would mind me getting involved around the club. I was joking about moving into the flat, but I wouldn't mind moving a tiny bit more into your life.'

'There's a first. I thought it was always the man who had to say how much he respected the woman and all that jazz. You already have moved into my life, and I *have* been feeling like a daft teenager. Let me pay you the same compliment and be straight. I know Andrew's gone. I'm not religious, don't believe he's somehow looking down on us all, but I do respect his memory. If it had been Margaret in your situation I would have helped out with the golf – after exploring all the other options, including paying Cliff myself for a course of lessons for her. If your husband, God rest you Andy, didn't tell you, or you didn't work it out for yourself, you should understand that I don't normally do friendships with women.'

'Do you chase after them and pull their pigtails?'

He nodded to acknowledge the hit, before steaming on.

'You know sharks? They have to keep moving forwards else they die. That's me with women. I keep going forward until I'm knocked back or she comes along with me. I don't know if I can be any different with you. Go ahead, start working at the club, that's your choice, hundred per cent. We can make like friends for the gallery, but you know I want more.'

As he broke eye contact with her to drain his whiskey, she came in quietly. 'There's a reason *Jaws* was such a monster film, Harry. It frightened people. Sharks are scary.'

'There was no happy ending for *that* shark. You should already know from the other night that if you tell me no, you don't have anything to fear. Unless you do, I'm going to keep coming forward at you. You won't even have to punch me on the snout to stop me, the offer of a glass of Malibu will do the trick. If there comes a day when you say "I hope we can *still* be friends" that will be different, because it will mean something's happened. Friendship's fine for a mate's wife, but you can't squeeze me back in that box now. Its spring's bust. I don't need any more mates. Besides, maybe we didn't get off quite on the right foot at yours, but it was a foot forward, that I do know.'

She was silent another moment, but her gaze never dropped. 'I'm not sure I got all that, Harry, but I see now how to get you talking about feelings. A few tots of Jameson's will do it. There's a lot going on in that head of yours after all. I wonder if you don't need a friend or two as well as your mates. One day you must explain the difference for you between the two words. I'll put my cards on the table too. I'm not prepared to be just a sexual mate. Nor a friend with benefits, a fuck buddy.'

They were not talking loudly but Jane caught his uneasy glance at the next table, where a young woman was wrangling a toddler while her husband opposite chomped on his steak. 'Spare me that disapproving look. Don't deny it, did you think I wouldn't have heard the term or is it just because I used the word "fuck".' She used it a bit more loudly this time, as if enjoying Harry's evident discomfort. 'Women do, you know, including some of your lady members I bet.'

'I know they do, it just surprised me coming from you.'

'Well, I'm sorry if I disappointed you. Don't go putting me on any kind of pedestal, Harry, that won't work at all. Cheer up, let's live to fight another day. I'll tell Claire on the House Committee I'll be happy to give it a go for a few months, like you said you did with the flat. If anything better comes along, we can both step aside. Your shark analogy was one of the things I didn't get, but let's take our first step forward by me settling up here without you making a big fuss about it. You can pay for a minicab home for me, if you want to be a gentleman.'

'I can easily run you home myself, why not?'

'One step at a time, Harry. I think we both got a bit confused when we tried to move too fast. I may be the best non-golfer with the trophy to prove it but I'm still a novice. It's the same with whatever there is between you and me – and I'm not denying there is something. Surely even sharks don't go full tilt all the time. Give me a chance to swot up on them and find out if I can live in your crazy ocean.'

Captain's Day

Although the TT gang boasted three former captains and two presidents, their race was mainly run for the club's major offices, particularly the captaincy which tended to be for a man younger than most of them by two decades or more.

If the captaincy were decided by popular vote rather than behind closed doors (ratification at the AGM, where Percy could have turned up each year with thirty TT votes in his pocket for any candidate, was the merest formality), then Brendan Foyle might not have made it. He had the advantage of being the serving vice, as which you had to shit in the president's shoes to fail to graduate to the captaincy, but there was still talk of a concerted move to buck the standard procedure in the first months of 2019.

The country's political turmoil over Brexit from 2016 onwards was hardly echoed at the club, in a pro-leave constituency and with a stronger majority of its members voting that way than in the wider community. It was enough that clumsy, sexless Theresa May affirmed Brexit means Brexit for her to retain the TT gang's qualified approval beyond her humiliating failure to draw a pass from the pussy-grabber-in-chief. None of them had any thought that the Brexit deal she was peddling was a good one, but parliament's failure to pass it was what began to turn the tide against her.

Holding hands, my arse. Trump knew he could do better than her.
Birmingham's like Pakistan now or Nigeria, no offence, Chit.
Johnson's got something about him, he'll sort things out.
He's no Churchill but you know he'll be sound on immigration.
Another shagger, you would support him.

Best we've got, especially when you look at that dipshit Corbyn.
And look at his taste in women.
I was thinking more of his taste for Venezuela, but good point.

Brendan had not been strident in his views, but they were well-known from one evening when subbing for the captain he had drunk more than usual from fear of the debut speech he would have to make. Many felt he should not be expressing any view at all as an Irishman – any more than the various Scots at the club had been given the right to vote a few years earlier on the separation of their own country when they chose not to live in it.

The gang lacked its own Irishman since the death of Will Gallichan, but had a sizeable minority of Scots, whether Corby overspill or reflecting only a higher percentage of that nation playing golf. Their referendum in 2014 was a matter of little interest or discussion, perhaps because nobody believed the separation would happen. The same was largely true of the 2016 referendum that did for Call-me-Dave Cameron, not least among those who had stoutly voted to leave.

Immigration was the prime topic of resentment in the Tuesday-Thursday gang, of which very few had jobs to lose to foreign workers. Many of theirs had disappeared with the country's motor industry, but not so early as to leave them financially strapped. There was an element of grumbling resentment that you could no longer claim to be English, on official forms or elsewhere.

It was easy to identify people by the colour of their skin, the language they spoke or the accent with which they spoke it – English, not British – but the real civil war began only with the cries for a second referendum, or people's vote as its proponents soon took to calling it. Surely uneasy at the thought of being cast as nothing more than sore losers, they sought to brand the first as a mismanaged political affair while the second would truly express the mood of the nation.

Although there were already dark mutterings of what would happen if 'they' tried to overturn the one and only legitimate referendum, it was not yet time to take to the streets against the wishy-washy, liberal posh London feminist elite or within MWGC against Brendan Foyle. With typical English tolerance or disdain for the beliefs of others, and above all the desire to avoid a fuss, his appointment as captain went through at the March 2019 AGM with no dissenting voices.

Three months into Brendan's tenure, Theresa May resigned 'the honour of my life' with greater dignity than she had ever occupied it. She was already a dead duck at her second meeting with Trump, who used it to give Boris his open blessing as the man to succeed her. Surely here were the makings of a new Atlantic Alliance, and Europe could go fuck itself.

No one ever said the new captain was unsound on the bevvy front. Apart from a lottery ticket to each starter at his Captain's Day, always at MWGC the first Saturday in July, there were tots of whiskey at the turn and pitchers of black velvet served at his expense on a side-table in the clubhouse.

Peter had taken over Andrew's role as administrator and got the three mates signed up together at a plum tee-time, well before noon but not so early that they couldn't have a Spoons breakfast and pint together before heading to the club.

'Thought you might have wanted to break with our tradition today, Harry, support Jane with her breakfast batches.' Pete set carefully on their table the full array of condiments and sauces.

'She's not bothered, but I can recommend her chilli afterwards, or her curry for that matter.'

'I hope she won't be offended if I pass.' George had already been nearing the end of a pint when the other two arrived at the Frank Whittle. 'What's the point of a full English if it doesn't keep you going through the rest of the day?'

'No wonder you stay so skinny, mate.' The Captain's was not only a major day in the club calendar, but had been one of the four friends' high and holies. They had always contrived that Andrew played with two of them, the other joining a different three-ball behind some fictitious pledge or request he must have seen through but was grateful enough not to challenge. This was the first time they would spend the whole day, golfing and drinking alike, as tontiners. Before their Jameson's at the turn, they had toasted Andy with a Lagavulin on arrival, from the bottle they insisted the House Committee continued to stock as his favourite single malt.

None of them greatly distinguished themselves that day, posting Stableford scores between twenty-two and thirty-four (one point for a bogey hole, two for a par and ever upwards for the rare birdies, vanishingly rare eagles and academic albatrosses). Harry was low man and George took all three legs of their Nassau bet. When they reached the clubhouse, it was already full, people choosing it for a degree of coolness greater than on the outside where they would have gone anyway to allow George his smokes in company. On the course he would toss a smouldering tab behind the tee box as they drove off from every other hole, and whenever he had a drink in his hand he wanted a cigarette in the other. Pete had not smoked for years, pussy-whipped out of it by Margaret the others insisted, while Harry was half rice half chips. He would smoke cigars with George – or anyone else for that matter – at the club, paying over the odds in buying them singly rather than admitting his own addiction by stocking up with supermarket packets.

The club still did not have a daily food offering for members, but Jane had received plaudits for reviving the meals it was customary for the home club to offer both teams in official matches, as well as a couple of social events for the ladies' section. She had confessed to Harry a greater degree of nervousness at those than for the men, feeling they were looking to catch her out in some way.

Their relationship had not progressed as he had hoped it might. Had he imagined greater keenness from her than existed? He could understand her being reluctant to invite him back to her home after he tried to jump her on his first visit. He had no great wish to go there if he was likely to find Sally-Anne and Dean still up, him now apparently living there full time. Jane had not complained about this, so maybe he was projecting his own dislike of the kid in thinking her not best pleased by the arrangement.

He took Jane out to dinner in return for her treating him, careful not to take too many supplementary drinks on board that might loosen his tongue unduly. She seemed more edgy when she was not the one in control, choosing to his suspicious eye lower-priced items on the menu.

'Have a fillet steak, not sirloin. I'm good for the few quid extra you know?'

'Don't be silly, of course you are. I happen to like sirloin better.'

Cars were another embuggerance in their courtship. She preferred taking her own rather than letting him pick her up, much less drop her off afterwards. It would have been too ridiculous to tail her home on the pretext of wanting to see that she arrived safely; Market Welham was rougher than it had been, but hardly a warzone yet.

He was ambivalent about inviting her to his flat, and not just because it might not meet female housekeeping standards. He had frankly not cared what Jackie thought about it; its use for her to him was bluntly what his mates had said it was. He wondered if he was being over-nice with Jane because of Andrew. He told himself he didn't give shit one what George said, but his mate had injected a niggling little inhibition with his BS talk about OB.

He was not entirely comfortable himself in the flat, never mind inviting anyone else. Jackie had been a distraction, the drink too that always accompanied their snatched meetings, from the desperation of being an ageing man living on your tod. George coped with it fine, but he had been alone for years. Perhaps it was not so much loneliness as the lack of service. Harry had always had a woman to do for him, his mother until he married at twenty, then Diane followed soon enough by Ellen. It had been all very well to storm out of their house and say he wasn't coming back, but for what? To watch a smaller telly, sleep in a smaller bed (he could usually spread himself in their double king, since Ellen preferred to sleep on the sofa in front of the outsized downstairs screen and closer to the kitchen) yet still have to walk Judy.

It was not a threat but a matter of historic fact that his wife would not walk the dog. (Could you still call them bitches now that word was absurdly rendered b-tch in tabloids? How would the current local press record the adventures and obituaries of all those Bl-ckies from his youth?) No longer needing the excuse to get out of the house to make his phone calls, he resented the task falling to him, while enjoying its performance. He would not see the old girl miss out or suffer any harm, would have brought her to his flat if the terms of his rental agreement with MWGC had allowed it. Judy was company. It was an undeniable wrench on taking her in again to close the door with himself on the outside and return to the deserted golf club.

A couple of girls from the junior section had been conscripted on Captain's Day to help out Jane, not so much with the cooking but in bringing the food from the kitchen to the punters. Surely the club hadn't supplied the rather smart black skirts and white shirts they wore? There was nothing so uniform about the dress of Jane's own daughter, Sally-Anne, pierced belly button on display in the six inches that separated the top of her jeans from the knot of her blouse.

'Got a fag for us, George?'

Wordlessly he handed her the packet. She fished out two, sticking one behind her ear. 'For ron. Got a light, Harry? You all talking about me, gone quiet all of a sudden?'

'No, not at all,' Pete hastened to reassure her. 'Helping your mum out then?'

'Trying, as far as she'll trust me. I might be applying for a job behind the bar, that would be more in my line.'

'How is Jane doing? Let her know there's a drink in behind the bar for her, will you? Hope she can find a few minutes to come out and have it in peace with us.'

'What's it worth? Is there one in for me as well, Harry?'

'We're looking to toast your dad with her, you're welcome to join us.'

'My round now anyway. What are you on, Sally-Anne?'

'Double vodka Red Bull please, Uncle Pete. I'd rather toast Andrew in that than his disgusting old whisky if that's what you're planning. I can still smell it on his stinking breath.' Having silenced the men, she resumed more brightly. 'Will I still be able to call you all uncle when I start working here?'

'Come off it, Sally-Anne, you haven't called any of us uncle for years except to take the piss.'

'It got to seem not quite appropriate, George, especially with you. It's nice to be part of a family though, isn't it? So nice, Harry wants to be in two at once.'

'How many of them double vodkas have you had so far?'

'Maybe I should call you Dutch Uncle Harry, sooner that than Dad anyway.'

'Give it a rest, girl, nobody's trying to take your dad's place. No need to be a cunt to Harry.'

'Always the sweet talker, George, can't believe I fell for it once. Thanks for the smoke, and for the drink, Pete' – as he returned from the bar she almost knocked the tray from his hands in snatching her glass and can off it.

'Did I really hear you use the c-word to her, George? Bit much, that. I don't like to hear it used against a woman.'

'Why not, you dippy cunt?' George answered Pete with more force than his comment warranted. 'They want equality, don't they? See, we can use it to each other friendly as you like, why can't they take it that way?'

'Because you didn't mean it that way. You're getting to be a mean drinker lately, what's up with you?' Peter was a people-pleaser, yet no pushover.

'You don't know the half of it, mate. I hope Margaret doesn't check your bar bills else she'll soon start seeing a lot of double vodka Red Bulls on it.'

Whenever two of their group got at it there would usually be another to pull them back, physically on the odd occasion. It was Harry's turn. 'If you're not going to spill whatever happened between you and her that's fine, George. But I agree with Pete, you should never use that word to a woman. She's not been too bad with me, all things considered. The poor bitch probably *has* to cadge her drinks from what I've seen of that workshy little fucker with his feet under their table.'

'Whose are those feet, under the table, where my old feet should be? You might be grateful for him one day, mate. Look, I'm sorry if I offended your delicate ears, both of youse. I mean it. Don't let that sweet girl get our backs up, especially not with each other.'

Their only hope of a tickle on the prize front was a few quid for George's two on the eleventh hole. Almost before they realised it, they were close enough to the announcement time not to bother leaving until it was all done. If they scored a bottle of something from the raffle, Harry said they would do it upstairs at his place, whether wine or spirits, with no votes to the contrary.

Sally-Anne was long gone when her mother at last appeared from the kitchen. Harry, keeping a bleary eye out for her, put himself in the way before she could escape to the ladies' changing rooms. 'Jane, come on, you look knackered, take the weight off and have a drink with us.'

'I'd love a drink, Harry, a huge gin and tonic, but I think I'd prefer it on the edge of a bath with me soaking in it.'

'Carry on Cleo, want any company in that?'

'No, honestly, I feel like my clothes must stink of chilli and curry sauce.'

'No worse than we stink coming off the course on a day like this. Come on, it'll help you unwind, you'll appreciate that bath all the more.'

'We'll see, Harry, but without being rude can you let me get by to the toilets first, or else the bathroom might get flooded.'

'You what? Oh, gotcha, yeah sure.' He fetched Jane a G and T from the bar – a triple, since a quadruple might have been construed as spiking, for all it was she who had said huge. He set the big bowl glass down on their table, his poor male equivalent of the sexy negligee come-on. He was rewarded with a hand resting lightly on his shoulder when she reappeared, briefly though and possibly to stop him rising to wheedle her into the extra seat he had drawn up.

'Thank you, Harry. Ta very much' – she took a token sip. 'I tell you what, let me pop home and freshen up. If I can get a second wind I'll come back. If they call the numbers first, will you do me a favour? I don't suppose for one minute I'll win anything but take my raffle tickets. That lovely Brendan bought up the last few strips left in the book to share around all of us working today. You know I prefer white to red, dark chocolates to milk if that's what it comes to.'

Did she actually ruffle his hair, as much as that quarter of an inch on the back of his neck would ruffle? 'Maybe see you later then, no promises. Have fun, bye Pete, bye George.'

'No promises' was not much, but it was all Harry had. He pulled out his own two strips of five tickets to put with the one Jane had left. He had taken to protecting his minor reputation for luckiness in raffles by buying twice the number most people went with.

Jane had not returned when Brendan started the speechifying. Not absent from public view for any appreciable amount of time during the whole day, he must have brought a change of clothes with him as he was in the club-badged jacket and tie. He was swaying slightly but spoke clearly enough.

'Thanks to everyone for making this such a special day for me. My charities will be very grateful for our efforts too. Joe behind the bar, I fear your work is not yet done my friend, but Jane our great new find as catering manageress can relax now... is she here to take a well-deserved round of applause? Is that her seat you're keeping warm for her, Harry, good man?'

He gestured at the pot- and prize-laden table behind him without looking round. 'I'd like to thank the board of MWGC for getting behind my day – our day, though I challenge anyone to say they've had as much fun as myself. If I may be serious for a moment, it may be our last such day as part of' – was he overcome by strong emotion or drink? – 'as part of the Rutland County league, sure I'm only kidding with you, no politics today.' Was there a tinge of relief in the laughter, or disappointment that he had not stuck his head above the parapet on Europe? 'Let's all raise a glass together, if not to a bollix of a leader on either side of the pond then to our own president Malcolm Shorten, who's kindly agreed to do the honours of the awards. And his lovely assistant, Ken Brogan, will be ensuring the tickets produced match the ones drawn out, keeping everyone honest. Maybe you were needed more out on the course today, judging by some of the scores, Kenneth.'

'That arsewipe cost us our chips,' Pete moaned, too loudly. If the earlier spat with George had stirred his fighting spirit, he might be needing the settee upstairs tonight, Harry thought, without relishing the prospect of making that call to Margaret.

The raffle prizes were interspersed with the golf ones. Harry's honour was satisfied early, but not before he had forgotten Jane's stated preference for wine colour. In the end he went for rosé, which he believed all women (and only women) liked.

George had not bought any tickets. He was outside smoking with Jimmy Bradley and Mark Jones. Leaving the bottle beside Pete on the table, Harry went out to join them, lighting a cigar on the threshold after parking his pint on an outside table beside those of his friends, who were facing into the clubhouse. It was still a lovely warm evening, surely too early for Jane to have given up on it. He imagined her in a big bubbly bath when her number rang out, then through to her voicemail. 'Good news, Jane, see if you can get back here, missing you.' He realised he had been premature in considering himself the only sober one of his mates left.

'Can't wait to give the missus the good news then?' said Mark innocently. Apart from being considerably younger than most of the gang he could not usually stay for more than a courtesy drink on Tuesdays or Thursdays before heading round the country for his maintenance shifts on the railways. 'I was going to offer you a fiver for the wine, mine's birthday's tomorrow and she'll know if I get out of the scratcher early to fetch her a bottle the only day I can get a lay-in.'

'See me before you leave, we might be able to do business on that. You should be flush anyway, weren't you right up there on the leader board?'

'I was. Never thought forty would win it and lost out on back nine to Lee Simons anyway, before our captain's new buddy blew us both out of the water with forty-four. First time out here they're saying an' all.'

'If that don't stink there's never been fish come out of Grimsby, Uncle Will used to say,' Jimmy chipped in. 'Still, I'd get indoors, you should have a few quid coming to you for third.'

'Think you might get lucky for the price of a bottle of wine then, mate?' George asked when Jimmy had followed Mark inside, leaving him and Harry alone on the terrace.

'Fuck off, George. Still twisted and bitter about all the vodkas you poured down her daughter's throat?'

'Hope it was her ticket, so you're not out of pocket.'

Harry did not dignify the jeer with a reply, pinching a pause into his cigar as he went back inside.

He was in time to join the applause as Mark took away from the table his envelope of winnings, cash on Captain's Day by tradition rather than vouchers for the pro shop. Lee Simons had not returned to pick up his second prize, maybe unaware he was in contention since he had been one of the earliest out.

Brendan had taken the microphone again. 'Before we confirm the winner – since you can see who it is, whether on the leader board behind me or your own phones – I want to say a couple more words. Patrick Trent will be a new name to many of you. This should hardly need saying, but I will. His handicap transferred in from Cold Ashby so it's not a case of a sandbagger catching us unawares, come here to take our money. I didn't have the pleasure of getting out on the course today, too busy trying to ensure things went smoothly for everyone else, but I've spoken to Jack' – he nodded to the TT gang's committee man eking out his third half of bitter – 'who marked his card and told me he played out of his skin. So by all means when he steps up to accept his prize, shout "bandit" as much as you like, that won't bother Patrick I'm sure, but let's keep it good-humoured and recognise a fair-and-square winner. I also ask you to remember there's still the top raffle prize to come, which I will ask him to introduce.'

'Fair and square, fat and round more like, I thought Bob Hoskins died years ago,' Pete gave his tablemates the benefit of his opinion. It was as well Harry's earlier drunken vision of a Jane so delighted with her rosé that she would fall into his arms upstairs had receded, because it looked more and more likely he would have another guest that evening.

'Thank you, Brendan,' Patrick said, getting to his feet, 'and all the other members of this fine golf club for giving me such a warm welcome.

At least until today! No reason why most of you would know that 2019 is shaping to be a record year for the business I'm in, which is travel. Something like one and a half billion international trips. And 2020 will be the United Nations Year of Tourism, so it felt like a good time for me to open a couple more of my own little shops in the Midlands.' He preferred to address the restless movement from the captain at his side than Pete's blatant yawn, using both hands to cover his gaping mouth. 'OK Brendan, this isn't an advertisement for Trent Tours, and I'm no threat to Thomas Cook just yet, but if you want friendly personal service right in the town centre precinct I hope you'll pop in and give us a go. One lucky fellow is going to benefit from our arrival right now, since I'm giving away as the main raffle prize an overnight break for two in Paris, chance to score some brownie points with the missus or, if you're lucky, score with the girlfriend.'

Patrick looked disappointed at the underwhelming response to his prize and what he'd thought a neat little gag; obviously a tough crowd, a smattering of applause sparked by Ken Brogan never catching. 'In fact, I'm going to boost the prize to mark my win today, by throwing in two return Eurostar tickets as well.'

'First class?'

Patrick ignored Pete's loud query. 'If the winning ticket has done an Elvis and left the building, there'll be no redraw. The prize will be kept on hold until it is produced.' He passed the microphone back to Brendan.

'Thank you, Patrick, more than generous. My fellow committee members have agreed that if any of us should win it, and we all did contribute to the raffle, we will put the prize back into the hat, so don't despair immediately if you haven't got number... number...'

'What is this, the fucking X-Factor? It's only a mini city break, you can get 'em for fifty nicker out of the *Mirror*.' Pete was on a roll.

'Will someone tell that gobshi... I'm sorry, Ken,' the captain heeded the restraining hand on his arm, 'but enough's enough: two, four, three, number two hundred and forty-three.'

'Bingo,' Pete hollered. 'Or should I say... er, beengo.'

Brendan looked more likely to swallow the ticket he held than submit it to Brogan's matching audit to give the star prize to the man who had just dissed it. Then he realised the drunken old fool was pointing not at his own five tickets but the three strips to his right, where he had spotted the winning number ahead of his mate. Harry stepped up to collect his second prize of the day.

Except this one was not his, any more than the bottle of wine had been. Someone was luckier than him after all; Jane's single strip had two winners. He knew it would be unwise to claim it in her name. Brendan would only be likely to make a fuss about it after bigging her up earlier, while the others would be all over him sure to be the one going with her and whatnot. If he knew anything about women, she would not have glanced at the numbers on her strip. And who would remember the winning one by the end of this evening, let alone tomorrow?

As Malcolm Shorten – always more comfortable in front of a spreadsheet than a boisterous crowd, but doing his duty – handed him the envelope, Harry took the less-than-enamoured look from Brendan to be a reproach for Pete's comments throughout the speeches, as if he had been egging him on. The travel agent made sure to get his fizz in the photo standing between them as well, some mate of his snapping it not from a phone but a proper camera; a wonder little Bob hadn't brought a giant cheque with his firm's name plastered all over it. Harry smiled for the snap without showing his teeth. Deciding he was unlikely to need what was now very much a second prize, he found Mark again to do a deal on the bottle of rosé. 'Hope you get lucky with it tomorrow.'

Pete's mind, foggy around the edges though it was, remained enough his own to insist on finding his way home unescorted, allowable as he was not in his car. George had not come back into the clubhouse to hear the closing stages of the award ceremony, so Harry was suddenly left with the prospect of either watching Joe swab the tables and close the bar or going alone to his flat. He knew he should not drive, but Jane's house was a manageable walk. Might clear his head, he reasoned. He found himself knocking on her door before he thought to consider it might be late to do so, already gone half ten.

'Who is it, Dean?'

'Give us a chance to open the fucking door and I'll tell you,' that gentleman replied to his girlfriend. He did not offer a greeting to Harry, much less a way past him into the house.

'Is Jane in?'

'I should hope so at this time of night. Did you think she might be out running around with another of your old buddies?'

Before Harry could reply, Sally-Anne was speaking at him over Dean's shoulder. 'Hello Harry, yeah she flaked out, your lot worked her like a dog today.'

'You look fresh enough yourself.'

'The old dear's getting on a bit, I suppose.'

If Jane's daughter did not pick up Harry's hint that she might have helped her out a little more, Dean was onto it. 'I told this one not to spend all day and night there grafting, we've got our own lives. We're having a date night as a matter of fact, takeaway, movie, you remember the sort of thing. Or are you back into clubbing now, is that why you're knocking Jane up at this hour?'

'He'd better not be thinking about knocking Mum up.' Sally-Anne dug her boyfriend in the ribs. It looked as if their date night had included joints or drinks, though Harry realised he should not be casting stones in the latter regard.

'All right, I'll leave you to it then,' he addressed the girl, hoping to suggest by his tone that a date night with Dean must be a disagreeable chore. 'Tell your mum tomorrow I called, will you, she wasn't answering her phone.'

'That was the clue then, chap.'

That was the cue to smack you, chap, Harry thought before realising he must not respond to it. 'She said she might come back,' he said lamely instead, noticing a flicker of what might have passed for sympathy in Sally-Anne's eyes and realising he was making a sap of himself. 'I'll be seeing you, anyway.'

'You're not driving, are you? I'd get Dean to take you but he's already had a whole bottle of wine, ain't you, babe?'

'You and me both, babe. We was just about to go for the hat trick,' he added pointedly to Harry.

Fuck you then. 'Don't worry about me, I can still find my own way home without a minder.'

And so he did, to all lights out at the club. He put his phone to charge in the kitchenette so he wouldn't be tempted to use it again before closing his eyes. An invitation to Paris was something to be given in person rather than by text. His last thought before sleep was that Jackie would jump at the chance to go there, and might be easier fun than Jane.

Lotto

Patrick Trent got his picture in the paper, but not as the central character between the winner and presenter of the prize he sponsored. He had brought the *Advertiser* photographer to the event thinking to provide the copy himself, but his story was blown out of the water before the weekly rag went to press.

Trent could be seen if you looked closely behind Mark Jones, smiling shyly with his thin envelope (luckily the pressman had been sighting up for the star prize). 'IN THE HOLE! – Local Golfer Aces Lottery Millions' was the frontpage headline.

He should've stayed anonymous, nothing but begging letters from now on for the rest of his life.
I already sent mine.
Good luck to him, I say.
Can you believe that bullshit about he'll carry on working.
They all say that. I give it a week tops before he tells 'em he's getting off the trains.
He always was a lucky beggar.
He could buy the fucking railways, how much was it he won?
Somebody said eight figures, maybe nine.
What's that in English money?
A few to a shitload of millions.
Don't you remember his luck with that bird?
'What bird?'

Graham Cook had the floor now, the others only realising the joke was generic rather than a dig at Mark when he started being unfaithful to his wife in it. 'You remember, said he come across this woman one night down by the tracks, did her every which way, front, back, between the tits. His workmate Eddie's tongue was hanging out. He said, "What about a blow job?" Mark said, "No, I never did find her head."'

Confident he would not find a decent bitter in France, Harry ordered two of their tiny lagers on the Eurostar, remembering as he paid the excessive price Mark dickering over a fiver for a bottle of wine bigger than both of them together. He would probably be lapping up the sangria now, breaking into his winnings with a treat for the whole family in Benidorm. If Harry had only known to ask for the lottery ticket instead of a bluey, he could have been there himself. The whole family, that would have been more of a challenge.

Judging by the hassle the small treat of a dirty French weekend – midweek, no doubt a lower tariff for Trent Tours – had caused, he thought poor old Mark's troubles had only just begun, then told himself not to be so soft. Tens if not hundreds of millions in the pocket and still young enough to enjoy spending them. How long would he stay with the wife he had been so anxious not to disappoint?

If Harry was going to stay on in the poky flat it might be worth joining the winter league, something to do on Sunday mornings. For the moment, he kept up his old habit of taking Judy for a long walk, though not as long in distance as Ellen might have guessed from the time he was out of the house. The Imp had gone downhill since the days he used to play its quiz machine – the snooker one hosted by the Hairy Arsehole – in the hope of winning a fiver while beering up an appetite for Sunday dinner, but it was still in a convenient enough loop back from the paper shop with the *Mail* and Sunday *Sun*, *News of the World* replacement these last few years. He'd not thought anything special of the *Screws* last edition till he found he couldn't get one anywhere in town that day, something to leave your grandkids. Sometimes he caught himself wanting to tell Jane little stories like that, fragments of his memories meaningless in themselves, but surely not as boring as Ellen's ostentatious mouth-fanning would suggest.

Once he had his pint, papers and dog laid out in front of him, he returned the call from Jane. She had phoned when he already had Judy on her lead anxious to be off from home, if never as anxious nowadays to get into the pub as when a former landlady would serve her by hand choice cuts of meat, not just a battered old bowl of tap water. Seeing Jane's name come up (as Jack, for plausible visual deniability), from habit he did not answer immediately, though Ellen had naturally not come to the door to see them off. Not for the first time, he wondered if she was developing a touch of agoraphobia, rather than simply preferring others to do for her.

'Sorry, I was driving.' It was a pointless lie, he had walked through town, but he knew women generally expected you to offer some excuse for not being at their instant beck and call. 'How are you feeling this morning?'

'Much better, thanks. I'd forgotten what hard work catering can be, either that or I'm getting old. Anyway, I'm the one who should be apologising for not getting back to you last night. At least by phone, I couldn't face putting my glad rags on and coming out again. I hope that monster gin you fetched me didn't go to waste.'

Harry had forgotten that. 'I expect Pete scarfed it. No matter anyway.'

'I hear you were pretty... merry... by the end of the evening?'

'That's not exactly the word I'd use.' He could not recall ever being merry in drink, but he appreciated her not repeating the harsher word he guessed Dean or Sally-Anne might have applied to his state. 'They said you'd already gone to bed.'

'So I had, but I would have invited you in if they'd let me know. I mean not to bed, a coffee or whatever. Is that what you were after?'

'Whatever, yes, that would have been lovely. Coffee not so much.'

'Come on, where are your manners, a dinner first.'

'I thought we'd already done that one. How about starting again with lunch? There really was something I wanted to tell you, good news I hope.'

'What's that?'

'I'd rather do it face-to-face, that's why I was banging on your door at what wasn't as late as that Dean probably told you. Are you free today?'

'Not exactly. I said I'd treat them and Maddie to a carvery, spend my earnings from yesterday such as they were. To be honest I couldn't face doing a roast myself. Why don't you come and join us, tell the whole family?'

'Do you know where the Imperial is?'

'Imperial what? We're going to The Bell. Don't you fancy it, then?'

'It's not that, only I'm in town at the minute. If you didn't mind popping over maybe we could have a swift half before you go off to get your Yorkshires.'

'All right, I get it Harry, you're at home. I remember now you've got a wife who's probably cooking your dinner as we speak. Why didn't you just say?'

'You may remember Ellen, but you don't know her too well if you think she'd be cooking for me at this point in time. I'm up the Imperial, the Imp if you need to ask anyone, halfway down Railway Lane opposite the garage. You can probably park in the street if you get here in the next half hour.'

'Bit cloak and dagger, isn't it? All right, I'll come and if you disappoint me you've got to take up my invitation to lunch. Deal?'

'OK.' He had no fear of disappointing her. He did not have the voucher about him, and anyway it was not an official thing, just a kind of credit note on Trent Tours headed paper so you would have to go into the shop to sort things out. He hoped little Bob hadn't got too pissed to remember throwing in the train tickets that didn't appear on the typed IOU.

'And it was definitely my ticket that won? You always say you're a demon for winning stuff like that, but I never am. You're not just being nice by giving me your own ticket because you're on the outs with Ellen, are you?'

'Christ no, but if I had won it I'd have invited you sooner than her. Don't put on that face, it may sound nasty of me but you said yourself you don't owe her any favours.'

'So *you* would have invited *me*,' she said slowly. 'Does that mean you expect to be my plus one if I go? Wouldn't that be kind of a big statement to Ellen?'

'Only if you made it one.'

'Right, you wouldn't have any intention of telling her yourself. Better keep stringing the two of us along in case I don't work out and you need to go back to her, back to your home comforts. Or is it the three of us, what about your other flatmate?'

'What are you on about now? Has somebody said something about me?'

'Has anybody *not* said anything about you? You've got the advantage of knowing everything about me and I know nothing about you, nothing you've told me yourself anyway.'

'Yet you were seriously thinking of going to bed with me and old Andy not gone a year yet.'

That was a hit, a low blow he instantly regretted but hadn't she been goading him? She sat there looking at him, struggling to maintain a glare while blinking back tears. 'You've not disappointed me, I'll give you that. Somewhere deep down I knew what a shit you were. Consider yourself excused lunch.'

He liked it that she travelled light, no handbag or other belongings to fiddle and fart-arse about with, but now she was gone before he could find a way to make her stay. He was the one encumbered, with mutt and smut, reduced to shouting at her back that he would leave the prize behind the clubhouse bar and she could pick it up from Brackers whenever she liked. The Imp barman had not looked up from his phone so there was no need to joke with him about women – can't live with 'em, can't get away with killing the fuckers.

And yet… three weeks later, here he was, on the train to Paris, 'Gotta See Jane' on constant rewind in his head.

He owed it all to Dean (not R Dean), from what he could make out of a terrifically confused switchback narrative. Jane had been in 'a bit of a state' when she met up with the rest of her family at The Bell, still coming to terms with having the tickets, never mind deciding how to use them. Dean was quick to speculate that Harry had been round the night before to stake an early claim on one, for reasons of naked self-interest rather than chivalry. Paris was for *young* lovers anyway, ones of about his and Sally-Anne's age, an already established pair. She could give them a break and have some quality time with her granddaughter.

'Why couldn't Nan take *me* to Paris? That would give you two some private time at home for your *date nights*.' Maddie could not know she was making those sound as unwholesome as Harry had tried to the evening before,

'You can take me to Paris whenever you like… long as I've got a ring on this finger.' Sally-Anne waggled her third left in her boyfriend's face, followed by the equally unadorned middle right straight up at him when he took too long to reply. 'An engagement one would have done, but you've missed the boat now. Not so long ago you was taking me and Maddie to Euro Disney, now you're trying to cadge raffle prizes off Mum. Can't you see she's upset? Harry can be a dick, but if she wants to go with him we've got no business trying to stop her.'

Jane was the only one to address Maddie's plea. 'Don't listen to them bickering, love. Harry isn't so bad and we shouldn't call anyone names like that. If your mum's all right with it, I'd be pleased to take you along with me. You've been doing well in French at school, so you can be my interpreter.'

'Are you sure, Mum? She's good at it and everything, but would you be able to manage to get around just the two of you?'

'Do you think Harry would be any more help?'

Jane had that curious way of drawing him in then pushing him away, without quite letting him go, like some elaborate dance of which only she knew the moves and he was constantly on the spin, off balance. She called and thanked him again for picking up her winning ticket, again insisted on his reassurance that it was hers rather than his (he gave its number but as expected that meant nothing to her), then said she could not let her granddaughter down once she'd asked, though otherwise the idea of taking her would not have crossed her mind.

Maddie showed similarly commendable loyalty to her nan when Dean sought to revive his fortunes, or just vent his spite, by promising tickets to her latest girlband crush in Birmingham, a one-night stand that happened to fall on the same one she would be in Paris. It was Sally-Anne who had to approach her mother.

'He's got two tickets for The Sundaes, like gold dust they are, says he'll drive us up to Brum and everything, maybe stay in a hotel there the night. I couldn't force him to sit through the concert, otherwise I might have been able to take her place with you to Paris. She says she won't let you down but I can tell she'd rather go and see them. It's nothing personal, you know this lot are the biggest thing since Little Mix.'

'So what could I do? I had to let her go.' Jane had sought out Harry that Sunday in the Imp, his first alert Judy's wagging tail when the newcomer to the bar walked over towards their table.

'What's the group like, is it The Saturdays moved on or something?'

'No it's like the ice creams, a mix of all tastes and colours I suppose is the idea but if you ask me it all sounds the same.'

'There speaks a true grandma. But it can't be the Imp's retro jukebox that brought you down here. Why didn't you ring if you were looking for me? You might not have caught me.'

'A game I was playing with myself, I suppose. You're a creature of habit, and we didn't part on the best of terms last time, so I thought I'd come back today. If you were here, we'd talk like we are doing, if not well I probably wouldn't have made it to the bar.'

'Used to be a few unaccompanied ladies in here for the lonely rail traveller, but not normally of a Sunday dinner, you're right. I'm glad you found me, anyway.'

Since he declined to ask the question she had been hoping for, Jane eventually continued. 'So, I'm not going to give Dean the satisfaction of scuppering my trip altogether. I came here to offer the tickets to you. You can take whoever you like, no strings attached.'

'Half-price parachutes for sale. Can I take you then?'

'You know what, despite everything I was hoping you'd say that. On one condition.'

'Go on.'

'You don't assume this means automatic sex. OK we'll have the same room, I'm not being silly or naïve about this, but when I booked it for me and Maddie it came with two double beds, so we won't have to be on top of each other.'

'Unless we want to, right.'

'I'll give you that one. Unless we want to.'

Paris

Harry was convinced Jane *would* want to – if not in Paris, at what amounted to her invitation, then when? But less than forty-eight hours before their scheduled departure there was another phone call. Dean had made an almighty fuck-up, something that would normally have pleased Harry a lot. There was either no concert or no tickets, Jane herself had only heard half the story from her enraged daughter while Maddie sobbed in her bedroom. Yes of course, of course he understood that she would have to take the little girl with her and he was once again off the bus if not thrown under it.

And yet again… here he was, on the train, a couple of hours ahead of the females on their prime-time schedule for a leisurely lunchtime arrival. It would certainly outrank her surprising him at the Imp in terms of romance, and Pete had been right in that it wasn't costing him a fortune. The little girl might be an inconvenience, but possibly also an icebreaker, not to mention a convincing alibi back home.

It had not occurred to him that his effort to secure a room in the Montmartre hotel as close as possible to them would be frustrated by the receptionist's unwillingness to tell him which one was slated for Mrs Wood and her companion. There was only one available as it turned out, and that not immediately, so he booked it and left his canvas sports bag behind the counter to visit a café bar across the street. While he would have preferred to sit at the bar, the lack of seating there excusable only by the narrowness of the establishment put him at a table in the street. It was all he could do not to buy a packet of Gauloises to crumple in front of him beside the dumpy glass of lager as he waited for the girls to arrive.

When they did, an access of nerves or shyness would have prevented him from greeting them if Jane had not been so clearly struggling with the suitcase, for all it was on wheels scuffing along the uneven pavement behind her. Maddie was chattering excitedly up at her gran, thumbs hooked into a rucksack that looked way too heavy for her skinny frame.

'Je vous aidez, madame?' He saw no smarmy Frenchie offering but thought he would impersonate one to add to the surprise when she turned with delighted relief to fall into his arms. Part of him was glad that she ignored the insinuating foreign tongue behind her, showing a proper reserve and at the same time complimenting him on his schoolboy accent's greasy authenticity. Maddie was less cautious or more curious. When she said, 'Harry,' Jane did spin round in a hurry, at the very door of the hotel.

'What the… Harry, what on earth are you doing here?'

Mindful of escape routes and children's attentive ears, he saved the romantic guff about following her to the ends of the earth for later. 'You know I have business in Paris sometimes. You wouldn't believe it, I was sitting in that café across the road when I saw you dragging your bags down the street. I can hardly believe it myself.'

'I believe the café bit, because here comes the waiter after you with a bill to pay.'

'Cheeky bug… so and so. I haven't finished my beer yet. Look, let me get your gear into reception, thought they'd have a doorman here offering to help, then maybe I can invite you to lunch. OK, monsieur' – he turned to the waiter now at his elbow – 'je… fineesh… bière.'

'Mais naturellement. I thought you were joining your wife and daughter. Très charmantes. Ladies, can I offer you a drink?'

Jane was clearly flustered by the little knot they now formed on the pavement, joined at last by a bellhop from the hotel. Harry could not judge whether his own arrival had been a pleasant surprise to her or otherwise. His usefulness at check-in would have been limited, so he recrossed the road telling them not to hurry, to get settled in their room, he would be waiting for them whenever they came out again.

There was still half an hour or more to midday. Having already drunk a red wine to follow his lagers, Harry was torn between continuing on that route or going for the better impression a soft drink might produce on the ladies. Except wouldn't that make him look a pussy to the waiter, likely to be sniffily superior enough anyway despite his immaculate courtesy so far. He compromised with a coffee and cognac, tipping the latter into the former and asking the man to make away with the spirit glass.

Jane and Maddie soon reappeared. It did him good to see them looking out for each other against the treacherous French traffic as they held hands to cross the street – cars parked bumper to bumper all along both kerbs – to join him. The waiter was instantly out to take their order, time on his hands in that lull between breakfast and lunch.

His fictitious business in Paris came in handy when they told him they were planning to go to some kind of kiddies' science museum. Maddie must be a swot, or at best an apple-polisher following up on some teacher's recommendation. When he had been thinking to travel alone with Jane he had not got much further in things to do than eating and drinking, supposing she would take care of any sightseeing. He would have been on board for the obvious Eiffel Tower and Louvre without caring much either way, while Quasimodo's cathedral would have been a no-brainer, handily within walking distance, if it hadn't burned down a few months earlier. He had dusted down a suite of jokes about the hapless hunchback for his girlfriend's delectation, of which only one might be suitable for Maddie's ears.

As the crumpled body lies on the cobbled street, an officious gendarme asks if anyone can identify it. 'Not sure, but the face definitely rings a bell.'

He did not begrudge the girl her unlikely alternative treat of a museum afternoon, but saw no reason he should have to suffer through it with them. He would soon be put right on that.

Insofar as he had thought of himself and Jane in Paris together, the scenarios all headed in one direction – to bed: a long and boozy lunch, seven or eight courses by all means as long as none of them were more exotic than Steak Frites, then afternoon delight under a lazy ceiling fan, curtains billowing gently at the unoverlooked window; a late-night show at the Moulin Rouge, or anywhere the girls still did the cancan, not even knickerless like he'd heard it used to be, frilly bloomers if you like but stockings as a minimum, something risqué (as the French said, but not too anatomical) to put her in the mood for love; dinner in a piano-bar restaurant, some ugly little twat like Charles Aznavour crooning 'She' in the background not loud enough to interfere with conversation, Harry and Jane holding hands across the table, no need to hide the brandy in its big balloon glass beside the coffee in the debris of delicious French dessert confections, closing the joint and leaving only as the waiters began apologetically to stack the chairs on all the other tables; strolling in the moonlight beside the Seine, the Tower in the background, her hands linked through his arm, head snuggling into his shoulder, both with the same eager anticipation of their return to the hotel bedroom where a bottle of champagne and two glasses awaited them in an ice-bucket.

The reality of the next twelve hours matched none of his daydreams. A bigger treat for Maddie than any French restaurant was a McDonald's hard by the Pigalle underground station. Harry would have found the layout and décor very similar to the Market Welham Micky D's if he had ever been in that one. Although Maddie giggled and Jane was on the point of telling him off, he had the last laugh when his nose and vision proved correct and they did after all serve him a beer to go with his burger. While he could have used another against the saltiness of the chips, he politely refrained from going back to the counter for it.

'You really can't make it to the science museum with us, then?' asked Jane, who had less reason to be convinced of his 'business' in Paris than Maddie might.

Something in her tone made Harry think again about his post-lunch plans. Having long given up any hope of afternoon delight, he sensed a stab at midnight magic might also be prejudiced if he were to duck out of the earlier part of the day's schedule. Maddie was slurping at her milkshake, so he did not need to make a big pretence of cancelling a high-level meeting, did it just for fun.

'Hmmm. It could make a big difference to the future of Unsworth Enterprises. Still, I guess I can fit an educational museum trip into my busy schedule. I'm the boss, so why not? Only thing is, don't expect me to be much help navigating you around Paris. Or in explaining the exhibits to Maddie.'

'It's more likely she'll be doing the navigating and the explaining. I would be glad of your company, though. I suspect it won't harm your business prospects too much, and you never know it might do your personal ones a world of good.'

'If you put it like that…'

The museum Maddie wanted to visit was part of an immense complex, the Cité des Sciences et de l'Industrie. As on the Métro, she took the lead in finding the right entrances, then exhibitions that appealed to her. A lot of it was interactive, a kind of cut-price funfair in Harry's view. In the section devoted to water, the pistols might have tempted him to interact, except apparently you were not allowed to fire them at anyone else. Archimedes' screw might have been fun for the old boy himself but did not stir his interest, or amuse Jane when he tried to sell it to her as a chance to look at classical porn together.

Maddie enjoyed filming herself at the TV studio, persuading Jane to join her in one or two of the scenes but still a little shy of Harry, which was fine by him. He was secretly hoping there would be some big screen film show, no matter how educational, where he might catch a few Zs. It only lacked Maddie lecturing them on the various exhibits for the whole thing to be a straight inversion of Harry's previous experience of museums, limited as both child and adult to the parents doing the cajoling and encouraging while the kids dragged and sulked their way behind them.

He would probably not be talking much about his brief cross-channel adventure back home, certainly not to his wife who had been told he was on an overnight golf trip to Wales with George. While unusual, this had some historical basis in fact he could rely on if questioned, which he did not expect to be. Audience for the holiday snaps or no, he still felt that if you were going to Paris you ought to see the Eiffel Tower.

Jane and Maddie had tickets for an early evening ascent; not having booked in advance it was quite likely he would not be able to join them. He would take pot luck on that and if necessary sit at the bottom. He could still say he'd seen it, just as he had the London Eye with his own family, over a beer exorbitantly priced to be sure but still cheaper than the ride and less likely to disappoint.

In the end, none of them got up. Emerging from yet another successful tube transit organised by Maddie, they found the approach to the tower blocked off by police, a bomb scare they managed to deduce from the multi-lingual chatter around them. Le Plod was in the process of evacuating all those on the site already, so it seemed prudent to duck straight back underground and make an earlier than scheduled return to Montmartre rather than risk getting caught up in an enormous crush.

It was still warm enough, nowhere near dark yet, when they came out of Pigalle to walk the couple of hundred yards to their hotel. Harry was relieved that Jane put her foot down about revisiting their lunch venue for dinner. 'Your mum would kill me if I let you have fast food twice in a day.'

He had no pretensions to being a gourmet himself, had given up all hope of the cosy piano bar never mind the Moulin Rouge; nevertheless, he still expected to eat something substantial to end the day.

Whatever his feelings about Sally-Anne as a person and a parent – she ranked in both respects far higher than Dean in his estimation – he gave her a substantial credit for Maddie. If she was disappointed at not being able to go up the famous tower, she did not make a big thing of it. She refused outright her gran's offer to try to rearrange it for the following morning, knowing that would mean Jane sacrificing her own trip to the Louvre.

'It's a shame old Trentie wasn't generous enough to offer a two-night stay,' Harry returned to an earlier grievance as they sat in the same café from which he had risen to meet them a few hours earlier. Their hotel was acceptable and they would probably eat there, but it had a somewhat fusty atmosphere. The lobby bar and dining area had not looked particularly inviting earlier.

'Mustn't look a gift horse in the mouth. You said he would have sold us an extra day or however much longer we'd wanted, he is running a business.'

'Yeah.' While he had told Jane it was a matter of principle not to feed the fat man's face further by supplementing their tickets when they had been heading to Paris à deux, his real motive was somewhat different. If things did not work out on the first night, he did not want to be stuck longer than necessary as a failure with Jane in Paris. If the planets were to be spectacularly aligned in his favour, he would surely gain more kudos in proposing a spontaneous extension to their stay than from having booked it in advance, showing undue confidence in his prospects. If they were lovers, he would be more than happy to go to extra time with her. If she regretfully had to decline a crazily romantic proposal to stay longer in the city of love, it would surely do him no harm. Ellen was not to know whether he was sleeping under les étoiles de Paris, the stars of Welsh sheep-shagging country or the cloud cover over Market Welham Golf Club.

'Do you mind staying here with Maddie while I go and have a shower, Harry, maybe get changed for dinner? I won't be long. The room's hardly big enough to swing a cat in, so with two women getting ready I'd rather do it in stages. I'll take her to get herself dolled up after that and you can have some time to yourself before we meet up again.'

Once it had been conceded that Maddie could get her dessert in early, a brownie with ice cream as a pre-dinner snack, she was happy enough to stay with Harry. 'You play cards at all?' he asked when she was coming to the end of her pudding. The Waddingtons pack in his pocket was not a prop to add verisimilitude to the trip to Wales; though he and George might very well have played crib on such a trip together, he was not that much of a method actor. He carried them everywhere.

The United Legends deck was the only Christmas gift from his only son, Jason, a few years earlier. There was no conversational mileage with Maddie in the players from the fifties through the noughties appearing in it. She thought it might be Top Trumps at first. He offered to play normal trumps, knockout whist, but she preferred rummy. Proving a capable player, she grasped at once the possibilities in using Fred the Red jokers as wild, though she had until then only played the vanilla version of the game with no card worth more than its face value.

'Good job you arrived before she cleaned me out altogether, you never told me she was a proper card sharp.' He surprised himself by feeling only the mildest relief at being stood down as responsible adult. He could not complain either that Jane had abused her liberty pass by staying away too long. If she did not know it was his favourite colour, the day's first genuine coincidence was in a red sweater she had changed into, accentuating her full breasts. Whatever the supporting infrastructure to keep them at their respectable height, they pleased him now as much as they had occasionally distracted him during her golf lessons.

Maddie's energy was not inexhaustible after all. He accompanied the two of them to the hotel, where he was soon done with his own ablutions. There was little temptation to linger in the boxy single room which had been his only option, not adjacent but on the same floor only a couple of doors along from theirs. He was sitting at the bar with half an eye on Dijon v Marseille when Jane walked in alone.

'No Maddie? What can I get you?'

'Can you do me a G and T please? Heavy on the ice and tonic, it may have to last me a while. Maddie's fine, totally tuckered out is all. She had a bath and then wanted to get straight into her jimjams and onto her phone. I do ration it when I'm with her, but she's been such a good girl today and she is abroad for the first time.'

'Don't you need to watch the cost of that?'

'Harry, I must get you onto WhatsApp. You can tell you haven't had young kids around for a while, Mr Texter. As long as she's going through the hotel Wi-Fi it's all free, and I trusted her when she told me she is – not sure I could have hooked it up myself even if I am a few steps ahead of you. I don't want her to go to sleep this early or without a proper supper so I came down to fix her up some room service if I can. Thought it would be easier to point at the menu than try to make them understand over the phone.'

'You going to eat with her then?' Harry was ashamed to hear the slight whine in his voice.

'No, that's not my plan. I have to say I could understand her, it's been a long, long day. I do want to spend some time alone with you, honest. I haven't had the chance to thank you properly for turning up out of the blue. That was a lovely gesture.' She leaned in to give him a kiss on the lips, her mouth fresh with minty toothpaste, disengaging only when the barman showed signs of having waited long enough and wanting to return his attention to the football.

She kept a hand on his forearm as she relayed Maddie's instructions for her day's second order of burger with French fries. Harry, unable to see how this was any different (except in price) from the McDonalds she had refused to allow her, said nothing. 'If you don't mind waiting before the two of us can have dinner together, I'll see her through hers and settled down for the night. She's a responsible girl and anyway I think she'll go out like a light, so if you're happy to eat here I think we can do that. Together,' she repeated, as if he might be slow on the uptake.

'Sure, of course, no problem.' He now overdid his extreme lack of whininess. 'You take all the time you like, I'm fine here in front of the football.'

In fact it was a dull game, 0–0. Equating *Ligue 1* as Sky billed the top tier of French football (was there anything worth mentioning below it?) with the second or third division in England, he was pleased to see his prejudice confirmed.

He had no objection to drinking alone, without the occasional exchange of pleasantries he might have ventured with a barman who spoke his own language. The post-match analysis of no goals and precious few highlights was impenetrable to him.

When Jane returned, he was pleased to see she had kept the red sweater, while changing into a smart black skirt just above the knee, flesh-coloured tights and high heels. He wondered briefly if he might have made more of an effort himself, but it would have had to be at the packing stage. The white shirt he wore was the only collared one he had with him; at least his black trousers were an upgrade on the jeans he had worn during the day.

The dinner was a success. Harry stopped drinking beer to accompany Jane in a bottle of wine, her choice the house white. It was not too bad, as much as he hoped for on the rare occasions when he would touch wine. If not now, when?

He was generous and sincere in his praise of Maddie, who did not disturb them though in case of need she could have contacted her gran through the bedside phone to reception or on WhatsApp from her own. Jane apologised for leaving her mobile on the table in front of her – 'I hate it when anyone else does that, and all Sally-Anne's generation do' – but there was no more traffic on it than on his own. Grandmother and child had already spoken cost-free to Sally-Anne, who professed to be jealous of her daughter's cross-channel excursion.

'How does Maddie get on with Dean?' Harry asked.

'They get on well, I hate to disappoint you. He's not all bad. More of a kid than Maddie herself, yet still better than some of Sally-Anne's exes. She was hopping mad about him letting Maddie down over that girl band though. Between you and me, I think he may be on his way out, not only because of that.'

'And would that upset you?'

'Better the devil you know, don't they say? No, Harry, if I'm honest it wouldn't upset me. You probably know yourself it's no good expressing an opinion one way or another about your kid's boyfriend, partner or whatever. It will only drive them in the opposite direction.'

'I hear you.'

When it became clear he was not going to elaborate, she nudged him. 'You never say much about your children. You never say much about anything personal. Let me in, Harry, tell me a bit about them. I promise I won't ask any follow-up questions about you and Ellen.'

'It depends which ones you're talking about. We've been friends so long you knew Diane as well as Ellen. You could only remember Jason and Janine when they were kids, it wasn't easy for them when me and Diane split up and I took most of the blame in their eyes. Not saying I didn't deserve it. I always thought there'd be time to make up when they were grown and could form their own opinions. That time still hasn't come with Janine. She didn't get on with Ellen either when we did have her and her family over once, so that never helps.'

'What about your boy, Jason? He never said it outright, but Andrew would have loved to have a son.'

'Be careful what you wish for. No, I shouldn't say that, he's not a bad lad. Some of the things I hear about Derek, George's oldest boy, I've not got too much to complain about with Jason. We'll always have a pint if we meet in town, long as I shout it anyway, that's about it. Kerry is a proper sweetheart, works in a care home.' His tone softened as he moved on to talk of his stepdaughter. 'I couldn't imagine doing that but there's no nonsense about her, not some wishy-washy angel, knows I'm no saint either but still seems to care for me a bit. Ellen's older one, Miranda, is more like her mum, hasn't got any time for me, don't see a lot of her.'

This time she called him out on the whine. 'Don't ask me to get the violin out for you and Ellen. You must have had plenty of time for each other once – weren't you both married when you hooked up? You'll be telling me next the two of you live separate lives, practically divorced. Don't take me for a fool, Harry, even if I am one to be sitting here with you in the first place.'

'You're no fool, I've always known that. I thought we weren't getting on to Ellen. I don't know exactly what's bugging you. Let me say this much. Me and her don't sleep together nowadays, haven't for a while, years rather than months. I'm not bullshitting you on the absence of sex, and I won't bullshit you by saying it's my choice. I still would if I got the chance. It's her decision.'

'"Still would if I got the chance." Modern man, or is it just man. Proper cowboy you then, Harry, always with a hard-on in his pocket ready in case of need.'

Surprised at her sudden direct language – though what had cowboys got to do with anything? – for a second he thought she was somehow as aware as he was of the blue pill in his trouser pocket, awaiting the call to duty. He had not cared to ask how far in advance of likely need he should pop it, nor research it online for fear his computer would ever after be deluging him with footage of Pelé past his prime or other ads for horn pills.

It was not a party hotel. By ten they were the only diners still in the main room. Harry panicked slightly when Jane said she was about ready for bed, without specifying it as her own bed. He pretended to want a coffee and she let herself be persuaded to take a tisane – some sort of fancy French tea. She would not join him in a cognac. On his way to the toilets to pop his tablet there were only a couple of men still in the bar, gays he assumed or at any rate not English because they were drinking coffee and speaking to each other in moderate tones, without either the exaggerated volume and movements or conspiratorial leaning-in and loud whispering of drunkenness.

He wondered briefly whether he could trust the tap water to help him swallow the pill, before reasoning there would be enough stimulant and depressive liquids in his system to neutralise any ill effects from slack French sanitary standards. He arrived back at their table as the waiter was making rather a show of setting out the two hot drinks and a big balloon glass for what he had to admit was a generous brandy, placing the tab for signing or settling annoyingly in the middle of the table rather than at Harry's elbow.

Not fancying a debate in the close corridors of the hotel, he leaned across the table to clink the unwieldy glass against Jane's china. 'I can't very well ask you to my room for a nightcap, so I suppose I'd better come clean and admit my intentions are altogether dirtier. I'd love to invite you to my bed.'

'You haven't got any chairs then?'

'Chairs?'

'To sit and chat. Oh Lord, you didn't think I meant something acrobatic, did you? I was only joking, or trying to, should have known better. I think I'm tiddly, and nervous too, if you really want the truth.'

'I can't handle the truth.' His imitation of the vein-popping Jack Nicholson in *A Few Good Men* lacked volume as well as any dramatic talent so on reflection he might as well not have bothered, particularly as Jane didn't give that flicker of recognition at a shared reference he so enjoyed. 'I'm nervous myself. How about it, darling?'

'Well… we are in Paris, admittedly more autumn than springtime. Rude not to be rude. You will let me go and check on Maddie first though, won't you, and you do understand I can't stay the night.'

'Whatever you say. You won't have to throw me out tonight, and you'll be free to leave whenever you want. I think there might *be* a chair if you want to sit and chat.'

She was unwilling to accept his key at first until he told her he would not need it again until morning. It was one of the old-fashioned affairs of a simple Yale on a bloody great hunk of wood to encourage you to leave it in reception rather than make off with it around the larcenous streets of Paris or to your own home where the return postage would be too much hassle to contemplate. 'Go on, you can hide it in your handbag if you're afraid Maddie will see it and wonder what you're doing with it.'

'OK. Don't come right up to my door. I don't want to wake her.' Again, she took the initiative in kissing him. He put everything he had into making it one that would not discourage her from using the key. Her touch or the tablet was already stirring him towards more vigorous action.

Expecting her back at any moment, he brushed his teeth and wondered if there was anything he could do to make the room look more inviting. He had not mentioned to Jane that the bed was only a single one. If the pill was good for a morning shot as well as the evening performance, he might be missing out on that by her returning to her own room to sleep, unless it enhanced that performance so significantly that she could not resist sneaking back for an encore in the small hours before her granddaughter awoke.

Having stowed his discarded arrival clothes back into his sports bag, and that into the wardrobe, he was at a loose end. It felt presumptuous to get undressed, lacking say an embossed bathrobe (the hotel was not of the category to supply these) over silk pyjamas, or in fact any pyjamas at all. He took off his shoes and socks before settling onto the bed outside the covers. Rather than sit looking at the door he lay down for a moment, saw too late the remote over by the TV not on the bedside table, couldn't be arsed to fetch it. Should he check out his prick for stiffenability or was it likely to come off in his hand (Jimmy had said he'd be good to go all night, without specifying whether this was in a single or multiple encounters). Always the most comforting way to fall asleep, hand on the control lever, and so he did.

Harry prided himself on being a light sleeper – a minor and not so very useful accomplishment in his generally unthreatened life – but Jane reached his bed and tapped him on the shoulder more than once before he opened his eyes and almost headbutted her as he started upright.

'Easy, it's only me. I was going to leave you to your beauty sleep if you hadn't stirred that time.'

'What? Yeah, how long has it been? I didn't give up on you, must have just closed my eyes a minute.'

'And opened your fly?'

He had struggled upright by now, feet on the floor with his head at the level of her still red-sweatered boobs. Looking down he saw what she meant but decided to brazen it out. 'Don't worry, little lady, if it can't get up it can't get out.' He couldn't remember the film that came from, the words from John Goodman (was it?) clearly meant nothing to her. 'Sorry, where's my manners? Sit down, there is a chair, I wasn't lying, but I'm hoping you'll be more comfortable beside me.' He took her hands and sure enough she sat on the bed, pillowside of him.

She started to babble something about Maddie having been awake, had to wait till she went off again, but he stopped her mouth with a kiss and for a while everything was fine. The red sweater was great but soon discarded, a black bra, she had changed from the tight skirt into the looser one from earlier in the day which made it easier to slide his hand up her now bare leg as he reclined her towards the pillow.

'Wait a minute, can we get under the covers? You will be careful, won't you?'

'Yeah sure, let me just go to the toilet. You get settled in.' He would have agreed to anything at that point.

He didn't quite have to stand on his head to take a piss as the old joke went, but he did have to sit down and apply some downward manual pressure. He had not needed pills to have a satisfactory sex life with Jackie. Good enough for him anyway – he had not liked to ask her. She was uninhibited and resourceful, as he did not expect Jane to be. Not the first time, and something in him hoped she never would be.

The room was small enough for him to keep his gut sucked in for the short return trip to the bed in only his underpants. He had been confident and considerate enough to buy new boxers, from M & S too, the first time he had ever shopped for his own underwear.

Birthday Etiquette

She's had more cock in her than I've had hot dinners.
I wouldn't let Harry hear you say that.
Who says, anyway? She's always polite but she never goes over the top.
Harry can't have dibs on mother and daughter both.
I'm just saying, and if not him there's George.
That proves my point, so many running after her.
Pete never fails to get her one in, proper drink with mixer she rooks him every time.
Say what you like about Glenda, she'd only take ten bob when you offered her one.
Yeah, but nobody wanted to give her one.
Can't see her hanging around here long, no fresh young meat for her.
Not in our gang, never keen to hang about when we're in.
I'd sooner look at her than Brackers anyway, front or rear view.
You always were an arse man.
As well as an arse.

From the autumn of 2019 both Jane and Sally-Anne were on the MWGC payroll, the mother laying on lunches and catering occasional evening functions while the daughter took a few bar shifts during the week. They could only be present together during Maddie's schooltime.

While Sally-Anne never turned up at full wattage for the benefit of the golf club members – it was reportedly a different matter at The Windmill, especially on karaoke nights, from where her reputation had spread as far as the TT gang – she was still bright and hot enough to stir memories of their lustier days. Peter Goodwin had clearly taken a shine to her, though he was always generous in tipping bar staff. The fact that Dean was apparently out of the picture surely meant Sally-Anne had many offers of male company far younger than the run of TT members.

George was curt when Harry started to tell him about his excursion to Paris, after checking that his alibi had stood up without any corroboratory calls from Ellen to his mate.

'No, she wasn't in touch. What makes you think she'd give a shit where you are? It's not like you live with her anymore.'

'Christ, take the head off that pint quick, you miserable bastard. Who pissed on your chips? And I might as well still live there, who else takes Judy out every day? Not her, that's for sure.'

'Same old story, since you asked about my chips. Derek's in trouble with his latest piece, wants to come up and stay with me. Reckon he thinks he can get back to being a teenager once he's back in Welham. Two kids there, one of hers and one between 'em.'

'Yeah, well in Paris it wasn't…'

'Spare me the details, mate, for once in your life. I'm not jealous, before you start. I'm not taking Ellen's side, I just don't want to know. I've already had my say, you go ahead but keep quiet about it and I promise I'll say nowt when it all goes tits up.'

'All right, keep your hair on.' Harry did not pursue the topic, though it would not have involved boasting. It was no use trying to explain to George that he got all the stuff about a mate's wife, that it was not about spotting a chance and going for it with Jane. It would have been nice for his best mate to sympathise with him, be someone on his side, that was all.

The hotel breakfast on the day of their return had been awkward, would have been more awkward yet but for the excited chatter of a well-rested Maddie over her chocolate croissant. Harry had a headache on top of his usual queasy stomach after a night drinking. The fried eggs he was served were so slippery snotty it looked as if they had hardly touched the inside of the pan.

Jane tried to be friendly, pouring tea for him – how hard was it to get a drop of milk to go with it? – but he was well-mounted on his high horse. They were as studiously formal around each other as if they had slept together the night before.

He thought of ducking the trip to the Louvre; the last thing he wanted was to be in a crowd of tourists gawping at art he seriously doubted would impress or interest him. Nothing against the French this time, no doubt it was all top-class stuff, but would it be more fun than a cold beer in the café across the road for which he had developed a forlorn affection? Maybe bring the trip full circle with a cognac-infused coffee. He could offer to manage all the luggage for the girls and meet them at the Gare du Nord.

He was shamed into going by Maddie's enthusiasm to give her nan a proper treat as part of their trip, no mention of the missed Eiffel Tower. He hung behind the two females as they followed a mysterious route around the museum, including the *Venus de Milo* which he knew was not just a piece of busted old junk but all the more famous for not having any arms. Not much in the way of tits either, plenty of those on display but none to stir him as much as Jane's had the night before. He tried not to think of them, though as if to keep them in the front of his mind she was again in her scarlet sweater.

A thickening of crowds and slowing of pace alerted him they must be close to the main object of their visit, the *Mona Lisa*. As they entered the room in which it was exhibited, Jane turned to look at him with something like exasperation in her face and attitude.

'Are you going to sulk all day? Look, this means a lot to me. You may not be into art – you've made that very clear – but can you look at this one painting with me?' She had both hands on his left arm. 'Don't leave me standing in front of it all alone, like Princess Di at the Taj Mahal. You've come all this way, let's make a memory we can share, else I'm going to fall out with you.'

He choked back the quip that he was the one enjoying Paris about as much as Princess Di, knowing people – not just women either – got hysterical about her. He had bemoaned the continued good health of John Paul at the time ruining his trifecta bet, looking good after her and Mother Teresa, only to friends he knew would sympathise. He did not want to spew out too much bile in front of Maddie either, ruin her little holiday. If Jane was trying to make him feel bad, it was working; he allowed her to take him by the arm as they shuffled towards the portrait, by no means the biggest in the room but the one given the most space to itself and the one where everyone lingered longest.

He forced a smile for the picture Maddie snapped on her nana's phone of the two of them with the *Mona Lisa* in the background – he hadn't realised she went by a different name in France, that already sounded foreign enough to him. Maddie's and Jane's smiles together were unforced, the girl making a ta-da gesture over her shoulder at the famous painting. He didn't like to say, but it would not be a very big part of the photo if he wanted to get the two real people in, forced to stand away from it by protective barriers. It was behind glass too, probably bulletproof glass at that.

'All right, we can head for the doors now I've seen her. Thank you both for letting me do it.'

'Did it live up to expectations?'

'Smaller than I expected.' She was looking up at him with a teasing smile. 'NOT like anything else on this trip, oh for God's sake lighten up, Harry,' as he disengaged her hands in a huff.

'No chance of getting close enough to touch it, was there. That might have made it bigger.'

'I don't care. To be in front of it was the main thing.' She tried to land a kiss on him, aiming for the lips but he was not to be mollified so easily. She only caught him on the cheek.

'Tell me Jane, I'm honestly curious, does it really count?'

'What do you mean?'

'The protection. I suppose there's always going to be nutters around, fair enough, but can we say we properly saw the damn thing? If you're looking at it through a shield, behind glass, how different is that from watching it on telly? And if it's on telly they can zoom in on the bird's features as close as you like. Not that I can see anything that special about her myself,' he took a final swipe.

'They say her eyes follow you all over the room,' Maddie interjected. 'Isn't that kind of spooky?'

'It is a bit.' He tried to be jolly. 'You'll learn that trick yourself as soon as you get married, Maddie, if it doesn't come to you automatically.'

'You might not marry one who needs so much looking out for, Maddie. Harry's only joking anyway. I don't care what you say, course I knew what the painting looked like, I think nearabouts everyone does, but this may be the only chance I ever get to share a moment in front of it with you two, and that means a lot more to me.' Rebuffed by Harry, she gave her granddaughter a hug, who accepted it with pleasure. Perversely, he now wanted to be included in it, too late.

He was almost pleased that another couple was already occupying the opposite side of the table pre-booked on Eurostar for Jane and Maddie. Rejecting Jane's offer to move and look for free seats for the three of them, he found himself one beside a beanied Rastafarian apparently unconscious, head against the window.

Harry envied the man his sleep. Now that he was on his own his thoughts kept dragging him back to the end of the previous evening, whether he kept his eyes open or closed (he opted eventually for the former, so as not to miss the drinks trolley).

It was painful to recall, impossible to recapture that sense of self-confidence as he approached the bed in which she lay with covers drawn primly up to her chin. He did not fail to notice her skirt folded neatly over the sweater on the otherwise redundant chair.

He saw again the black bra and a glimpse of knickers the same colour as he pulled the bedclothes back to get inside with her. If she looked at him below the belly button, she must have known he was ready to take their relationship to the next stage.

She insisted he switch out the light, not a problem. She responded at first to his advances, did not baulk at his penis butting against the side of her thigh, brushed against it with her hand as she helped him remove her pants. Only when he moved to get on top of her did she stiffen and ward him off. 'Harry, you promised you'd be careful.'

'I will, darling. I can tell you want it, I'll take it as slow as you like, gentle as you like. I just got to get inside you, I've waited so long for this moment you wouldn't believe.'

'That's not what I mean.' She had now turned onto her side and backed against the wall, still with one hand planted firmly on his chest. 'Where's the thingy?'

'The what?'

'You know very well what, the Durex, condom, whatever you might call it. How much clearer can I make it?'

If the blood had not all rushed to his head in rage and embarrassment, it had left his penis in a hurry at these words. He tried to keep calm; he had passed this way before, if not recently. He had known how to persuade women to do without the rubbers by gentle persuasion or emotional blackmail, without ever resorting (as he cared to remember it) to physical force.

'Darling, listen, I don't mean to be tactless or anything, a lady and her age, but you can't tell me you're worried about falling pregnant. In any case I've had the snip.'

'Don't be daft, that's nothing to do with it. I'm nervous about STDs. I—'

'STDs? What the fuck's that when it's at home?'

'Don't swear at me, Harry, please. Don't spoil tonight. I saw the doctor, you're not the only one been looking forward to this. He said it may be different for me with another man, you know one I'm not used to. Semen or just contact could cause a problem, like an allergy or an inflammation.'

'Are you kidding me? What's STDs then?'

'Oh God, sexually transmitted diseases, don't tell me…'

'You what? You think I've got the clap? Or is it syphilis you're worried about? Aids, why not? If you think I'd come to you poxed up you might think I'm a druggie or queer as well? Christ, what are you doing in the same city with me, never mind in bed?'

'I'm not saying that, Harry, don't twist my words. There's other things like HPV. You've had that woman round your flat, might still be seeing her for all I know, or other ones. You do have a history, you can't deny that.'

'Oh no, I can't deny that, I've never denied anything to you, always been straight. Fucking hell, why don't you ask if I'm sleeping with whores? All these initials, do you think I'm an HGV driver picking 'em up for company in the cab of a night, or visiting brothels or what? You'll be wanting to know about the ones I chopped up and buried next. For fuck's sake.'

'I thought you understood me. It might help with lubrication as well. We can still do it as long as we use a condom, and later on we may not need to.'

'You didn't feel like you needed no more lubrication. Do you think I carry rubbers around with me all the while in case a scrubber comes tapping at the car window when I'm at a traffic light? I obviously bought the wrong pack of three for this trip, thought clean pants would be enough. Couldn't you have brought some dunkies yourself if you were that keen on using the bastard things?'

'I didn't know I'd be seeing you here, did I?'

He hardly heard the whisper, she had a hand over her face. It gave him pause, and he did his best through the crying that followed until he could get rid of her.

So no, on balance he did not have anything to boast about to George. He was surprised how hard her suspicions had hit him. He wanted to call her a prick-teaser or worse while knowing that was unfair. Hadn't she hinted she would have got the nodders if she had known he would be in Paris? He had no answer to her having been surprised by that. On the other hand, couldn't she have popped into a chemist at some point during their endless afternoon at the science museum, or tipped him the wink to do so?

He did not care about the money he had spent on the trip, and as the weeks went by he remembered some parts of it with affection; even standing awkwardly in front of the world's most famous smile (yet not one that made you think she was necessarily up for it; enigmatic was the word all right). He tried to persuade himself the trip had taken their relationship forward. Jane had definitely responded to him at various points, right up to the sticking point in the bed. He regretted before she was out the door having pushed aside the shy movement of her hand towards his groin when she had suggested there were still things they could do to prevent the evening becoming a complete disaster. It would have been a happier ending than the brutal tug he finally imposed on his pecker in the hope it would help him get some sleep.

It had all been too much like his adolescent fumblings the minute she brought up that primitive form of birth control. It would never have occurred to him to think of dunkies as a protection against disease rather than pregnancy, not between people of opposite sexes when neither was a sex worker. He now remembered some campaign about the benefits of using them when Aids was at its height, without ever having regarded that as something affecting him. There was always a big part of him wanting to go bareback or go home. Maybe that was the cowboy Jane had mentioned.

Those teenage trials had included the loss of wood more than once as soon as Durex came into play. The girls expected the boy to do all the work of getting it on, usually not in idyllic circumstances, as it might be a warm summer's meadow beside the remnants of a picnic – freezing nights up against a wall came to mind more readily. Ellen had trained him out of what she called his bullshit, insisting on their use over a period of months before she trusted him to begin planning a baby together. He did not know whether the miscarriage of their daughter had broken her, their marriage or both. Rather than trying again she soon began to talk of him having a vasectomy, at a point when he felt he could deny her nothing.

He found himself spending fewer nights at his flatlet. As the daylight hours contracted, the Tuesday-Thursday gang brought its starting times forward so that they could all be in the warmth of the clubhouse before the light started to fade, and home by dark or not much later. It was not worth the club keeping the bar open beyond say six o'clock, which made for a long evening alone.

Pathetic as he knew it was, he tried to get back into Ellen's bed for more than just sleeping. He got short shrift, though he thought her comment – 'Between girlfriends again, are we? Keep looking, but not here, mate.' – was uncalled for.

In saner moments he could admit his attitude towards Jane was also somewhat pathetic. Since seeing her and Maddie safely home on return from Paris, he had not phoned or been alone with her. He thought she owed him an apology, sticking on that long after it became clear none would be forthcoming. Could she think he was only upset because he had missed out on sex? What about his feelings, accused of whoremongering and spreading VD (he would have grasped that abbreviation more quickly than the one she had thrown at him)? While he did not quite go to the lengths of blanking her, she made a far better fist of cordial friendship than he did. The appearance of that was enough for the Tuesday-Thursday gang to think there was still something more serious going on between them. Apart from George, they had no reason to know or care about the trip to Paris, with everything else that happened on Captain's Day overshadowed by Mark's multi-million lottery win. Although still with his wife, within six weeks he had left the railways and was playing more golf in Spain than at Market Welham.

Harry had assumed the romantic phase of his relationship with Jackie had run its course (if 'romantic' was quite the word for something so resolutely unsentimental on both sides). He was surprised when she called to ask what he had planned for her birthday, yet bucked too. It did not clash with golf, so he suggested a lunchtime drink. She agreed the daytime aspect but preferred a village pub with pretensions to offering a full restaurant experience and prices to match. After sharing a bottle of wine, she made no objection to taking their coffee back at his flat.

There was no coffee, and she made no objection to that. The sex was as good as ever, but apparently not enough of a birthday treat for her. On the previous two they had been involved, she had rejected the idea of a present as potentially difficult to explain to her proper boyfriend, who could be madly jealous or crazily supine according to her day's mood. She had found a way to suggest that cash would be welcome, and he had been happy to slip her some notes. She explained this time that she had a 'girls' night out' to prepare for and was short of readies. She had never put her hand in her pocket all the times they had been out together, which he had never begrudged her until now. He said he had no cash on him, strictly true though he always kept a monkey in the inside pocket of a greatcoat hanging up in the flat as well as in a bedside-table drawer at home. She bluntly reminded him there was a cashpoint he could use by the Co-op, where it would suit her fine if he dropped her off, ta very much.

Ta very much indeed. The boost to his ego was substantially dimmed by the mercenary sequel. He wondered how little he could get away with, without her calling him a cheapskate. Could he contrive a plausibly accidental jamming of her ankle in his car door, which she expected to be opened for her as if she was a lady? Precisely at that moment in the club car park, Sally-Anne emerged shamelessly (red panties) short-skirted from another vehicle, making a point of calling out a cheery, 'Hello, Harry.'

The Minge of Fate

Sally-Anne's friendly greeting when he was being robbed by Jackie was pure theatre. Her attitude towards Harry in the clubhouse was all business, totally lacking in warmth. The car she had come in, which roared straight off, was not Jane's so she was presumably not its driver. Nevertheless, he did not doubt she would soon be hearing about the female company he was keeping. What the fuck! Jane did not own him, and if that girl thought she would be getting free drinks from him as well as Pete from now on to keep her trap shut she was sadly mistaken.

In fact, neither woman's attitude towards him changed noticeably over the next week or two. As expected, he did not hear from Jackie to thank him for whatever she had spent her birthday money on. Probably to pimp herself up for the next sucker, or one round of fancy cocktails for her and her 'girlfriends' around town that night, he thought sourly.

He knew better than to expect any contact from Jackie on his own birthday, 22 November falling on a Friday this year. He was treating himself to an extra round of golf, with George and Pete. They had always marked each other's dates as a four-ball while Andrew was still alive; though they were not looking for an extra player, Jimmy Bradley talked himself in with them on the back of a heavy session the day before.

MWGC was mainly a members' club, relatively few outside visitors and fewer yet on a cold day past Scorpio. The four men had nobody holding them up in front or pushing them hard from behind, teeing off around ten and back in the clubhouse by half one. Only the five extra shots granted by usage and custom to the birthday boy allowed Harry and Pete to beat George and Jimmy two up.

'You kept it going to the last putt,' Pete said to Jimmy after they'd shaken hands at the eighteenth flag. 'I thought George was going to salvage your fivers when he crushed it up the hill off the tee.'

'I should pay his as well as mine. He was the one kept us in it. I was shite all the way round. Are you getting the cards then, Harry, same pairings, let's see if we can earn it back by luck if not skill?' Jimmy had been excited when the older men reminisced on the course about formerly having a drinkers' triathlon on birthdays: cribbage and dominoes following the golf. 'I used to play here with Uncle Will. He taught me everything when I was still a kid.'

It took Harry only a couple of minutes to fetch his own cards, prized set of dominoes and pegboard from upstairs, but Jimmy was already halfway through his pint. It was going to be one of those days, then.

They had got in before the heavy rain started. By four o'clock there was nobody left outside on the course, and they were just switching from cribbage – George and Jimmy, whose uncle had clearly taught him well, took the honours there – to dominoes, arguing about whether to play Out or Fives and Threes.

'Talking of out, are you getting out of here any time soon?' Sally-Anne called over from the bar, where she had little to do beyond attending to them in the last hour or more. The men's volume had risen enough for their conversation to be more than clear to her, insofar as she was listening rather than playing with her phone.

'Why, you looking to bunk off early? I'll report you to Shortie, you're here to serve the members until six o'clock minimum, house rules.'

It was not the club president but head barman who organised his staff, calling on Carl Bracknell nowadays only rarely. Sally-Anne referred to her direct boss in her prompt rebuttal.

'If you must know, Jimmy with your big boy pants on, I'm doing you all a favour being here at all. Joe should have been on at three, asked if I'd take his shift. He said I could shut up early if there was nobody in, which there isn't apart from you lot since Mr Hall and his wife left. Poor dear probably couldn't stand the racket you're all kicking up.'

'Surely you'll do a favour for all your friends here,' Jimmy persisted, ignoring her insult to his drinking persona. 'Not me, you and I have already had that conversation, but Harry, come on, the birthday boy, your mum'll want you to look after him all right. Then there's Pete, isn't it time you bought Sal-Anne another drink, keep her sweet?'

'Don't know why you can't all go up to Harry's flat over a few cans,' she retorted peevishly, nevertheless taking the pint glasses to refill from Pete, who had sprinted to the bar. She looked at him with something like pity when he suggested she could pull up a chair and watch them play since there were no other customers.

Perhaps as a further sign of favour to Sally-Anne, it was Pete who broke the party up as soon as he and Harry had won at dominoes in straight legs. They laughed out of court Jimmy's desperate suggestion to extend the game to best of five. All but Harry agreed to share a cab to carry on around town. He reluctantly declined: 'Kerry's organising a takeaway for me tonight when she finishes work. I wouldn't want to disappoint her.'

'What time's that? Come and have one while you're waiting.'

'I mean disappoint her by being shitfaced more than not being on time. I'm going to try to get my head down for an hour or two in the flat. Her shifts are erratic and she may want me to pick up the nosebag.' (She had his credit card details down to the secret three digits on the back, something with which he would never have entrusted her mother.)

They were all standing outside despite the cold and wet, waiting for the taxi to be sure, but more to be able to smoke the cigars which were another tradition of the now tontiners in which Jimmy was all too happy to join. The days of smoking fine Cohibas had died with their aficionado, Andrew. Pete had forgotten about his charge until he felt the packet of five Henri Wintermans as he pulled on his parka. The one left over was for Sally-Anne, he insisted. He went back inside to offer her it, with as little success as he had in inviting her to cheerlead at his joker round of dominoes.

'Won't one of you tell him he's wasting his time there?' Jimmy asked with the frankness of consecutive long drinking sessions as they watched through the window Pete leaning confidentially, elbows on the bar, towards Sally-Anne.

'His money more like, and he can spare that. She's probably the only woman he's spoken to in twenty years beyond his missus and his mum. I'd have to leave it up to George to tell him that.'

'Easy, Harry, don't keep setting me up as the expert on Andy's family. It might not be all that pleasant for the girl, either.'

'I wouldn't worry about her, George, she's had more…' Jimmy saw something in the older man's look that choked off the rest of his sentence. 'She can look after herself,' he amended lamely, with a nod towards Pete, foiled again, disengaging himself to rejoin them.

The lights in the body of the clubhouse were off when Harry returned from waving them away in their minicab, suggesting the bar was now closed. He realised he needed to go to the toilet with some urgency and preferred to do so in his own flat. Sally-Anne could look after herself right enough. He gave a sharp knock on the window, saw her raise her head for his wave half of goodnight and half a gesture that he was making tracks.

It was a closer run thing than he might have wished. Sitting on the toilet afterwards he wished he had given himself a courtesy flush, though the stink was not enough to prevent him almost nodding off, shoulders hunched and elbows on knees.

He was debating whether to shower before or after hitting his bed for half an hour when he heard a knocking then the ring of his doorbell, both unusual enough sounds.

It was Sally-Anne. He stood there stupidly facing her at the foot of his stairs.

'I've got something for you, Harry. Are you going to keep me out here getting drenched? If you've got one of your women in here just say, and I'll be on my way.'

'No, all right, come on up, I'll lead the way, hardly enough room to turn round in here, you know it's all upstairs, my flat.'

'All about the upstairs with you, right?'

And he had thought he was doing the decent thing, heading up first so she could not accuse him of wanting to ogle her arse. What the hell was he doing anyway? What could she have that she could not have handed to him on the doorstep?

He was slightly shamed when they reached his sitting room and she wordlessly pulled from her capacious shoulder-bag his compendium of games.

'Oh, thanks, can't believe I left them behind, could have waited till tomorrow, but thanks anyway. That bag you've got reminds me of my old school satchel.' He was casting at random for a neutral topic.

'You're not far wrong there.' She pulled open the flap to reveal in heavy block capitals on its inside ANDREW J WOOD.

'Your dad's.' He knew he was stating the obvious but wasn't sure he could get any more words out. Whether sensing his sudden sentimental turn or not – he feared for a second he might start blubbing – she returned to his thanks.

'Don't mention it. You're right, I could have left it behind the bar with a note for you. Probably would have, but there was something else, and I wanted to ask you a favour.'

'I don't know if I can run you home, love, if that's what you mean. I was planning on getting a cab myself later. You should have left Joe to clear up all the shit in the bar in the morning after the shift you put in for him. I'm sure Pete would have been delighted to give you a lift.'

'A bit too delighted, don't you think?' She was looking around the room with undisguised curiosity, which would soon have been satisfied by the single armchair and a settee facing the telly with a low coffee table beside it, bearing a pint glass and tea mug stuck on an old magazine. If she took in that both drink containers were United-branded and could deduce from the title *Golf Monthly* that their coaster was about that sport, she was certainly not curious enough to wonder how exactly it would meet the promise of helping its reader make more birdies.

'You mustn't mind him, he's harmless.'

'Not a heartbreaker like you, then.'

'That's not...' He realised she was point-scoring rather than looking for a debate, so let her have that one.

'Look, Harry, I know it's a cheek, but can I borrow your shower? I'd planned to go home and get ready to go out tonight but it'll be easier for me to do it from here now. If you don't mind,' she added politely, when he hesitated.

'Don't they have showers in the women's changing rooms then, they do in the men's?'

'Do you ever use them?'

'Well no, but some people do. Besides, I've got one right here now.'

'Exactly, that's what I thought too. The girls' showers don't come equipped with bath towels. If it's a problem don't worry, I didn't expect you to make such a big deal of it.'

The thought that had first struck him when she mentioned the shower was the stink that would strike her from the toilet when she entered the bathroom. He stalled again. 'I've got a towel sure, but what about a change of clothes?'

'Nothing you can lend me from one of your girlfriends? No, I'll go out as I am, put my dirty knickers in the bag, won't be needing any for a Friday night at The Windmill.'

'Too much information. Yeah sure, wait a minute let me just go check there is a clean towel.'

He knew already there was no such thing as air freshener. He vaguely sprayed around some Lynx deodorant not exhausted since his last birthday, then returned to the living room. Deciding to match her coarseness rather than fanny about as if he never took a shit, like a woman, in handing her the towel he said, 'I'd recommend giving it a few minutes, but there you go, knock yourself out, should be plenty of hot water.' Yes, at the cost of his own fucking shower, but he wasn't drunk enough to risk a joke about sharing one. He couldn't tell with this girl if she'd start screaming blue murder or drag him in with her fully clothed.

A text told him Jimmy and George were in the Rifleman's. He thought he might join them after all, as Sally-Anne looked to have stolen his warm-down time. On the other hand, she might want to come along if he mentioned it, which would lead to more gossip about him and the Wood women. George could be trusted but a drunken Jimmy was a blabbermouth, and lately he was often drunk. Maybe he had troubles of his own.

He couldn't decide where to put himself in his own house, a ridiculous position to be put in by a chit of a girl. He could imagine a sarcastic comment if she found him in his bedroom, similarly if he was sprawled out on the settee. He rarely sat rather than lay in either room, but when she did emerge – in such short order he thought she must be wanting something else before she could get started – she found him sitting at the end of the settee nearest to the TV screen.

She had the towel held tight around her, covering from an inch or two above the nipples to three or four below the join of her legs. That was soon on display to him, Windmill ready, when she perched on the edge of the armchair facing him.

'Not exactly a wide range of beauty products, Harry, but I'm not high maintenance. You getting an eyeful?'

Of course he was. There was not a single hair to hide her sex from him, and it had been pure reflex to check out the view he had surely not been granted by accident. He could feel himself reddening as he tried desperately to rally. 'If you weren't winking at me, I might not have noticed anything.'

'You want any more?' She stood and leisurely stretched out her arms, parting the towel completely.

'God help me, Sally-Anne.'

PART THREE

THEIR FINEST HOUR (NOT) 2020

The Calm Before

'Was that all right then?'

He was surprised she would need reassurance. 'That was wonderful. I didn't realise how much I wanted it, but I guess you could tell that from the start?' He knew he was himself asking for reassurance now.

'I did wonder if you really fancied me. A woman always wonders, you know.'

'So you say, but I think a woman always knows. I've never been good at keeping that sort of thing hidden.'

'From what I hear you've been free enough at letting women know exactly what you feel about them.'

Where was this suddenly going? He wanted to give in to his drowsiness rather than get into another fencing match. 'As long as you know now, that's all that matters to me.'

'You are serious, then?'

'Serious as a heart attack.'

'Oh Lord, don't say that. For a second or two there I thought you might be having one, that noise you were making before you…'

'Before I came? Before I came inside you. I couldn't help myself, I couldn't, the noise I mean. The heart, I think it was your letter melted that.'

She rose up from the crook of his arm to give him a kiss, and there were no more words for a while. Those of Jane's daughter two months earlier came back to him as if it were half an hour ago.

'Well done, Harry. You passed the test.' She was suddenly all business again.

'God help me, Sally-Anne,' he had answered her stunning invitation as soon as he could find his voice. 'I'm going to regret this in the morning, if not within the next thirty seconds, but will you get dressed? Please? As far as you're going to get dressed for The Windmill, anyway.'

'You sure? You no likee?'

'I'm an old man, so I prefer a few straws around the nest, but you're spectacular, honestly you are. I don't know whether you're taking the mickey anyway, just trying to get a rise out of me – you managed that no trouble, by the way – but even if you *were* serious, things have gone too far between me and your mum for me ever to consider anything like that.'

'With me, or with anyone?'

'Trust me, gal, if I can resist you, I can resist anyone.'

That pleased her. She pulled the towel to again and returned to the bathroom. It wasn't yet thirty seconds and here they came, regrets. He would obviously have to wait for the feeling of being virtuous and moral to kick in, maybe after he had a wank once she'd gone.

'Here you go, Harry. Mum asked me to give you this.' She had reappeared quickly to hand him a folded envelope, closed but not sealed. 'I just wanted to check out for myself whether you deserved her birthday greetings. And I think she may be offering you more, a second chance.'

'And if…'

'If you'd blown it? You don't seriously think you had a chance with me, do you? You'd have had to be like a fourteen-year-old about it, not sixty-four or whatever you are, blowing your stack practically before you got it in, cos my cab's already waiting downstairs. Want a lift into town?'

He felt she was playing with him, but the measure of her skill was that he could never be certain. 'Er no, thanks, you might find me NSIT, especially if you're commando.'

'Commando? Oh, that was part of the test. I do have a spare pair in my bag. Never know if I might have to make a present of one during the evening. What's NSIT anyway?'

'Not safe in… never mind. It's something nice girls used to worry about a hundred years ago. Your mum might have heard of it, but I shouldn't expect you to.'

'She's not that old, plenty lively enough for you. Mind how you treat her. I can put a whole different spin on today if I need to, trust me on that.'

'Oh, I trust you on that.'

He relived every word of the dialogue before he nodded off in Jane's double bed. He had read the single sheet of paper enclosed with her anodyne birthday card so often he had that too by heart:

Dear Harry,

Do you remember Millie Jackson? Fabulous soul singer and a rapper before there were rappers. I've still got her *Caught Up* from the seventies. She proved concept albums weren't just for the self-indulgent white kids whose songs all sounded the same and went on long after the ideas and words ran out. Pink Floyd and Yes and Genesis not a single hit single between them, not that I can remember anyway.

I'm rambling again. Get to the point, Jane, that's what Andrew would always say with that touch of irritation would always make me clam right up. But this isn't about Andrew. You've made me realise the rest of my life needn't be played as his widow.

I want you to know you're only the second man I've ever slept with. I was frightened, Harry. I can see now I wasn't so much worried about the wretched STDs or whatever other excuse came into my head. I was just plain scared of letting anyone get that close to me again. I've read enough agony columns over the years to know about performance anxiety. Believe me, it doesn't only affect men. I think we need to forgive each other that night in Paris, and without getting all woo-woo forgive ourselves as well if we can move on.

I'm caught up, and much as I love my work at MWGC I can't stand to continue there if you're going to keep up that frosty show of indifference. I do believe it is only a show, covering some real feeling for me, but if not then just leave this letter unanswered. I hope I can trust you to destroy it, if only from a sense of self-preservation with Ellen who you need have no fear of reading my birthday card. I know that's a dig, I can't help myself and there I go again talking in sixties Motown titles. So I'll close by admitting what it took me a while to admit to myself. If loving you is wrong, I don't want to be right.

(Ready to be) Your,

Jane

The feeling of being virtuous and moral had taken a kicking the same night Sally-Anne took her taxi, when he made it home in time for his takeaway treat with Ellen and Kerry. He had brought two bottles of wine to the table, more as a courtesy than in the expectation of getting through them. It had already been a heavy day for him. Kerry drank very little anyway, a token birthday toast as she ate her bowl of soup while he and his wife gorged on sweet and sour mixed pork, chicken and prawn. The pork option of those had been the only Chinese food either of them thought of eating for many years. If Kerry's selection that night had been designed to provoke nostalgia, it succeeded. He had stupidly driven his car across town, feeling invincible after reading the letter from Jane, but was not prepared to compound the felony by taking the car back to his flat. Kerry had no need to threaten to take its keys to bed with her.

'Good birthday, then?' Ellen asked in a friendly tone. 'Come home for your present?'

They had tried every sexual position and variation of love-making their imaginations and physiques allowed from their earliest days together, when they were both on their mettle. What had begun in a moment of forgetfulness one year, by Ellen not Harry, had led to a tradition of no birthday gift other than a last-thing sex treat. The key aspect, taken as the birthdayer's due that night, was permission to be a pasha, free of any sense of obligation to respond to the other's ministrations. It was a luxury. He told himself it *was* his birthday, she was still his wife, it could hardly be cheating on Jane, there was presidential precedent that a gobble didn't count as sex, in any case it was just harmless banter and she was setting him up to slap him down. 'That would be nice,' he found himself saying, in the same way you don't know if you're going to ask for a virtuous Coke or a cheeky pint until you answer the barmaid's waiting face.

'Come on then, you daft bugger.' She took his hand and led him upstairs.

The next day he went into Trent Tours and booked a luxury break for two over Valentine's Day 2020. Call him unimaginative, but despite the salesgirl's best efforts to sell him something more exotic, he went for the classic Springtime in Paris option. No last-minute deal, he caned his credit card with full payment up front to convince himself as well as his travelling companion it was a long-term commitment.

Bubbling Up

They don't know what they're doing.
What government ever did?
Elbow bumps, don't know their arse from their elbow more like.
If you're scared to mix you just stay at home, problem solved.
How are we supposed to get away from the old woman now?
It's a conspiracy.
They know golf can't do any harm, but won't let it be cos they're taking all the sports off the young 'uns.
Punishing us for being old white men, that's it.
Don't forget Chit, we're proper ghetto here.
If they close the clubhouse, what's the point of coming anyway?
Der… a few of us do put the golf ahead of the bevvy.
Bring a hip flask round with you, mate, like Billy already does.
No more sharing tots out of the cap, mind.

The clubhouse chorus was already at reduced volume on Tuesday, 17 March 2020, a week before government diktat pissing in the wind against the COVID-19 pandemic shut down MWGC completely and indefinitely. Some members of the TT gang were already self-isolating, either on their own initiative or indoors' instructions. Others on the same basis were hunting for toilet rolls. Among those who showed up to play, the first four-ball made it clear they would be social distancing between themselves and not entering the clubhouse once their round was done. While no longer the criminal offence against club etiquette it had once been, this was still not viewed as quite the ticket.

Peter Goodwin and George Pym were drawn together against Arthur Harrison and Jack Roberts. 'They say smoking's a good protection against the Corona,' Pete said, as Jack and George lit up on the first tee. 'Maybe I should take it up again, whatever Margaret says. Be loud and proud about it.'

'Nothing to be proud about literally setting fire to good money,' the tyke Arthur said.

'I have to make the most of it here, don't smoke at home out of respect for the missus,' Jack replied. 'She's got asthma.'

'Watch out, Klopp's scouse cunts'll be trying to sign her up,' George warned.

'No football, no golf, the pubs shutting an' all, there'll be more men topping theirsen than die of COVID.' Arthur was always one to look on the bright side.

In the natural pauses between shots on the way round, Pete confided to George that he was already coming under female pressure himself on two fronts. 'Margaret's flat-out refused to have Mum come live with us till this thing blows over. Reenie probably wouldn't anyway, to be fair. She's still doing OK physically but she's not supposed to go out because of her age, classified as vulnerable you know. Looks like I'll be shopping for them both, and that's more of a nightmare than usual now. No public transport to get across here so I can have a beer after playing or visiting Mum. I thought my days of living in the car were over when I retired.'

'I don't miss having one, I tell you. Walk everywhere I need to go. Corner shop and White Horse, that can be my bubble if that's what they're talking about. I'm within reach of Reenie, mate. If you want me to do some shopping or just look in on her, let me know.'

'That's the trouble, George. I don't think we're even supposed to look in on them, and she spends enough time on her own as it is. I haven't said much about it to anyone, but her mind's starting to go already. Nowadays when I catch her talking to herself she's not making sense anymore. If she's left to brood and stew by herself twenty-four seven it won't be good for her. Imagine all those OAPs shut up in their own flats, can't so much as have a cuppa together.'

'I can't tell you how to manage your mum, Pete. It will be hard on the oldies – hark at me, we're no kids ourselves – but if I was you I wouldn't worry too much about whatever bullshit rules the government brings in.

How are they going to enforce them, for one thing? You never see a copper on the beat at the best of times. If we go into lockdown, I bet they won't be changing that habit to trap someone helping out his ma.'

Resuming their conversation walking up the sixth fairway, Pete asked, 'What about you, George? Will you be moving in with Emma at last, or is it too late to make an honest woman of her?'

'She's the most honest woman I know.' Pete nodded in quick acknowledgement of the hard tone and look from his friend, who continued more amiably. 'I wouldn't mind being on me tod again tell you the truth. I'd gotten used to it. My boy Derek's often either shut up on his machine – I mean a fucking *Play*Station he calls it, and him nearer forty than thirty – or out on the piss, but it's not the same as having the place to yourself. Like I said about you, I can't see anybody kicking up too much of a fuss if I shift between the Horse and home just like I do now. If I catch this flu, I'll take my chances.'

'It's more serious than flu, mate. You can get vaccinated against flu.'

'You can if you're a fussy old woman. What is it they say about a cold? You'll get over it in a week if you take something for it, and seven days if you don't. Same with flu, same with the Corona shit. I can look after myself.'

'Has Harry told you what he's planning? He puts my problems into perspective, trying to keep two serious women on the go, plus your Emma's sister if that's still going on, three different places to lay his head. He's the one with some choices to make.'

'Yeah. I wish he'd make 'em and shut the fuck up about it. And since you don't bang on about her, I'll give you some free advice about Sally-Anne. She's damaged goods. Leave her alone.'

Rightly considering George was closing the conversation with that, Pete satisfied his own talkative nature for the rest of the round with the taciturn Yorkie and the always affable Jack.

Despite some reservations from Jane about travelling overseas, with different countries naturally assumed to be more infected with the Corona bug and less efficient at keeping their populations safe – not to mention lower standards of personal hygiene where the French were concerned – Harry was able to persuade her to return to Paris with him to celebrate Valentine's Day. It was everything he had imagined for them from the previous trip apart from the cancan dancers. She fancied instead *Chicago* the musical at the Mogadon theatre (as he chose to misread it), which did nothing for him.

He had wasted no time after his birthday in sharing his advance plans with her, which relaxed them both in the present. They became lovers before Christmas, after a good bottle of wine at his flat, in the most natural way (apart from the blue pill, which he persuaded himself he took as a modern stud cream, to prolong her pleasure rather than as a precaution against him failing to turn up with the right tool). She was more reluctant to let him stay overnight at her house, and indeed he felt a similar reserve, not so much from the presence of Sally-Anne as her daughter, Maddie.

Although they could not be together over Christmas, Harry took a calculated risk for New Year's Eve. It was true that MWGC was not holding its own event, from lack of support the previous year rather than the impending pandemic of which no one was aware then – it was months before Harry would realise the number in COVID-19 stood for its year of origin. It was not true that there would be a big party at the White Horse, which he correctly predicted would hold no appeal for his wife. He and Jane did meet there early doors to give his fiction a gloss of fact, but saw in 2020 at his flat in the deserted golf club with champagne in bed.

He became increasingly reckless, not troubling to cook up an excuse for the couple of days he would be away on their spring break, as he followed the travel agent in selling it to Jane, though the February weather in France turned out to be just as cheerless as in Market Welham. He felt guilt only at the delight with which Judy greeted his return – deprived of her walk for those days unless Kerry had made time to take her – not at Ellen's surly enquiry if he had run out of clean socks.

While he acted in part to provoke a confrontation, and told himself he would use it to make an all-seasons break with his wife, it was still a shock when Jane showed her own sharkiness in asking more and more pointedly how and when they would move forwards. He hoped the French honeymoon had gained him breathing space, without quite knowing why he needed it. He was sure that he wanted to spend whatever might remain of his life with Jane. For all that, he did not want to be the man who ran away with another woman and abandoned his wife. Not again.

'Well, you're going to have to make your mind up, Harry, or else we won't be seeing each other at all for God knows how long. Is that what you want?'

'You know it's not. Won't we be able to keep on meeting at my flat?'

'Are you taking this virus seriously at all? Because I am. I won't risk exposing Maddie to it for anything.'

'Let's stay together at the flat then, form a new bubble of our own. Might do wonders for our golf game, nobody else on the course and nobody to see us out there.'

'That's not possible. Sally-Anne needs my help with Maddie. I can't say I'm devastated that Dean upped sticks over Christmas, but it was a big upheaval for her – and him being around the house meant we could leave her with a semi-responsible adult if Sally-Anne and I both had to be out for any reason.'

'So what, are you inviting me to audition as a babysitter?'

'You didn't like Dean, you made that very clear. I thought you might be more comfortable staying with him gone. And before you get any ridiculous macho ideas, it's nothing to do with anyone in our three generations of women feeling the need to have a man about the house to protect and provide for us. We can manage that ourselves, ta very much.'

'OK darling, keep your hair on.' He looked uneasily around the crowded Costa, her choice of venue rather than the Imp or Rifleman's he would always have preferred. She was not shouting, but the irritation in her voice was evident. 'Do you want to get married then?'

'Do you have to say it like that? Would it be such a crazy idea? But no, or not yet. I realise these things take time, and I'm not hung up on having a new wedding ring on my finger any time soon. It does show commitment though. I suppose that's all I'm looking for. You're still living like a single man, two women on the go and your own little pad where you can get up to Christ knows what in your own time.'

'So you'd want me to give up the flat?'

'Would you think of living for nothing with us? Or cut Ellen off without a shilling, as they used to say. Like so much else, you never talk about money, and I'm not saying you're not generous with it, but can you afford to keep three households? And that's not the real question. The real question is, why would you want to?'

'A pint is what I want more than anything, tell you the truth. I hear you, Jane. Whatever you might think about my womanising as you call it, I'd never thought about leaving Ellen until you. Now I can't think of anything else. And I'm not sure she needs me around the house either, let alone loves me anymore. There's Kerry, and Judy she's got.'

'And you're more bothered about leaving the bloody dog than having to choose between your women? Let me spell it out for you, since you don't seem to have watched the news or read a paper over the last few weeks. Family groups will be in almost total isolation when this lockdown happens. I will respect the law, not only because it is the law but because I believe it makes sense. If you stay with Ellen, or for whatever twisted reason decide to set up a bubble of one above the pro shop, I shan't be seeing anything of you for as long as this thing continues. Without being melodramatic, that may mean forever. People are dying from coronavirus, Harry. The offer's there to come live with me, cos I can't move. I won't beg. You decide.'

'I decided on my last birthday. By my next one, if I'm still above ground' – he tried a smile, but her face remained stern – 'I'll buy you a ring. If you can still stand me by then. Can we go for a proper drink now? I feel like I've got coffee coming out of my ears.'

In the end he was spared further discussion. Days before the lockdown was confirmed, Kerry came home from work in tears and physical distress. She spoke to him and Ellen at the tea table from the kitchen doorway, a handkerchief clasped to her face.

'Listen, guys, we had a briefing today at work and Melwood say this thing is going to get really bad. They're not prepared to wait for the government, so they already stopped a week ago anything but essential visits. That cuts out nearly all of them unless the person is at death's door. You can't imagine how that's upset residents, not to mention their families. Some of them build their whole lives around coming in to see them every day. More than one don't eat anything except what they have with their loved ones and us. If some in the home are playing up – I don't mean that, the poor things are only lost and confused – it tends to affect the others. All makes more work for us, we're already understaffed and now I'm going to have to let them down, I feel shitty. Sav made me come home.'

'Good on her, she's a keeper. You don't need to feel bad about it, love, when have you ever had a day off sick?'

'Not shitty about letting them down, Mum. Too shitty to function at all, rotten cough, ache all over, can't concentrate on anything but feeling sorry for myself.'

'Maybe it's just one of them twenty-four-hour bugs, Kerry. Or are you thinking it might be the dreaded Corona?'

'It's no laughing matter, Harry, believe me. The trouble is we're not equipped to tell whether the patients have it or not, never mind ourselves. I plan to stay in my room here until it passes, can't be responsible for passing it on to people at the home. And I suggest you give me a wide berth if I come downstairs to get anything.'

'The house isn't that big we can give anyone a wide berth, love. And besides, I'm your mum. I'll look after you, his lordship here can bugger off to his funk-hole if he's scared.'

'Who says I'm scared? Your daughter's just accused me of the exact opposite,' Harry protested. 'We *should* listen to her though. She's in a better position to know about this whole business than we are. And with all due respect, Ellen, I can't see you rushing up and down the stairs playing Florence Nightingale. It's often too much trouble for you to get yourself to bed of a night, times I've had to throw a blanket over you on the settee and found you still here in the morning. You go get your head down right now, Kerry. The wonders of modern technology, we won't have to give you a broom to bang on the floor or anything. I'll stick around and you ring me if you're too weak to holler for anything you want. You look as if you might have trouble with the stairs yourself at this present moment. Do you want me to help you up?'

Kerry dabbed again at her nose. 'I'll be OK, ta. But it would be nice if you'd stay over. Above all, start taking COVID-19 seriously – you especially, Harry. And one other thing, guys. Try to be kind to each other.'

'Is that one of the symptoms? Start talking like a yankee marriage guidance counsellor? No, I hear you, Kerry, I'll do my best to keep an eye on your mum for any signs until you can pick up the reins again.'

'Hey, I am here you know.' It was Ellen's turn to protest. 'I'm not some old nag you need to keep trotting along to market or whatever.'

Before Harry could dispute whether Ellen was a nag or not, Kerry directed her next comment at him. 'One thing they did stress is the importance of personal hygiene. You should be washing your hands every time you come in and out of the house, not only when you go to the toilet. And a proper wash, long enough for you to sing happy birthday as you do it.'

'"When you go to the toilet", that would be a great start for this one.' Ellen laughed. 'He never washes his hands unless he goes for a sit-down, and don't you deny it, Harry.'

'I wouldn't dream of it.' She had him bang to rights. He stopped himself asking if he was supposed to murder the whole Stevie Wonder birthday-jingle single or could pound through the squashed tomatoes and stew like a kid impatient for party cake. While he doubted it would make any difference, he decided to humour his stepdaughter if not his wife. 'I'll try to do better. The first thing is to get Kerry well again, so come on, baby. Off you go to bed. Do you want me to bring you up a cup of chocolate or something?'

'Thanks for offering, Harry, but no. Nothing hits the spot for me lately as far as taste goes.'

'If COVID does that to you, bring it on. Maybe if I lose a few pounds, this fellow will start looking at me again like he used to.'

Harry was shocked to find himself tearing up at the passing poignancy of this remark. He had persuaded himself to think Ellen had lost interest in him as much as he had in her.

He would remember Ellen's remark frequently over the next three weeks. Although Kerry was properly sick for a few days, by then she had already moved far enough towards recovery to be in significantly better shape than her mother. Who knew whether she had infected her with whatever she had, or whether the two things were unrelated. Harry himself only needed to seek his bed at night in sheer exhaustion after days of shuttling between one sick woman and the other.

Kerry was thankfully at home when things suddenly got much worse with Ellen. None of them had wished to burden the NHS with their problems, relying mainly on the all-purpose over-the-counter paracetamol to fight whatever lurgy had gripped mother and daughter. A generation younger, and by running around all day at work plus serious gym sessions on her days off much fitter than Ellen, Kerry returned to active duty as soon as she felt able. Nobody at the nursing home troubled to check whether she was or ever had been infected with COVID, only too glad to have another pair of hands back in service.

It was Kerry who stroked Ellen's hair after calling for an ambulance while her mother fought for breath. Harry hovered and havered, desperately sad for his wife but not daring quite to approach her; not from fear of infection, but that she would call him out on not caring enough. She was not a gracious patient in terms of thanks for his attentions and poor efforts at cooking. He had tried to hide his resentment at being the household skivvy but knew he had not always succeeded. Kerry had taken him to task when he used that word.

'"Skivvying" may be how you see it, Harry. What I think you mean is looking after a sick person like women always do their husbands in sickness *and* health, when the lazy bastards are perfectly capable themselves.'

Kerry was not as militant as her girlfriend Sav, head chef at Melwood House, who Harry always felt viewed him as a lower lifeform. He did not know her name's derivation, whether surname (Savage?) or first (Savannah felt somehow unlikely). Still, he knew when he had to take his chosen daughter seriously and when he could tease her. Now was a time to listen.

While he devoutly hoped he would never end up in any sort of care home, if he did he wanted someone like Kerry there to look out for him, ideally the girl herself. He had assumed she would be the one to go to the hospital with Ellen after the scandalous hour's wait for an ambulance to arrive, two masked paramedics coming into the house.

'I'm sorry, sir, we can't take anyone else with the patient,' the younger, female green uniform told him briskly.

'But what if she…?' He would not complete the sentence yet could not cut off the thought. 'She'll be all right, won't she?'

'The sooner we get her into the ambulance, the sooner we'll be able to help her. You did right to call us,' was all the man said.

'It's OK, Dad, we can't do any more for now, she's with the professionals. Can you go and make us a cup of tea while I take Mum to the ambulance doors?'

'She's a carer herself, surely professionals are allowed to stay with them, I'd be no use, I get that but…' They were already manoeuvring Ellen to the street in the wheelchair they had brought. 'Let me at least say…' Goodbye sounded horrible. 'You take care, darling,' sounded pathetic as he croaked it to his wife's back.

He had the tea ready when Kerry returned. She took it from him but made no start on it.

'What did they say? Did they tell you anything?'

'They've got oxygen in the ambulance, quicker to get her out there than bring it in here.'

'So she'll be all right, then?'

'Let's hope she's strong enough to fight it. I can't lie to you, I'm worried.' She put a hand to her eyes.

Now he felt ashamed. He should not be the one bleating and seeking reassurance. Without speaking further, he moved over to give Kerry a hug, and to hell with social distancing.

Two's a Crowd

George Pym's son, Derek, had chosen the wrong time to pack up installing residential shower units around the country from a base in Birmingham. Perhaps he had not been given a choice, George thought, remembering various other jobs which ended in differences with his employers, who never seemed worthy of the lad's respect. He would hear the full story in due course, no doubt. Derek was prone to overshare when in drink.

Although the work would have dried up in lockdown, he would be sitting on his arse with eighty per cent of full wage under the government's furlough scheme, ridiculously generous to George's thinking. Derek was on unemployment benefit now; there was little job-seeking to be done in a ghost country.

Little entertainment either. George had tried to support his son's short-lived interest in golf as a teenager, until the kid started throwing his clubs around after making a bad shot. In the clubhouse afterwards, having stayed silent on the course (as he would not have done if they had been playing with others), George told him quietly that would be their last round. The boy knew his father too well to argue or appeal, and did not show much interest in continuing with anyone more accepting of his volatility.

Golf courses had shut down along with the rest of the country in March, as had the football leagues they might have followed together. Once deliveries of beer stopped at the White Horse they could not get a pint of bitter from the taps, though in the early days the two of them worked manfully to run down Emma's stocks. They played cards, tending to quarrel over poker and lose patience at cribbage, Derek in trying to tot up his hands and George in waiting for him to do so.

Father laughed at son bemoaning the lack of anything but terrestrial television in his new digs, telling him to consider it as one more way in which he was regressing to his childhood. The satellite sports channels, the only ones of interest to George and now in the absence of football only minimally so, were all on tap for him at the Horse, where he was still spending some evenings. On others, in sheer boredom he asked his son to show him what all the fuss was about on his latest video games. They had not played one together since *Mortal Kombat*, which he also remembered taking the boy to see at the cinema, already long separated from his mum.

Resident Evil was apparently a big thing nowadays, but did not lend itself to mano a mano competition. George could hardly believe that many games – Derek mentioned *Fortnite* – nowadays counted on the players being in different rooms, on different PlayStations, Xboxes or whatever to maximise revenue for the purveyors. *Clash of Heroes* sounded promising, as they sat side by side in the flat's second bedroom.

How the years passed, though but. When had George lost his eyesight, the speed in his trigger finger, his ability to absorb the ground rules of a game kids picked up intuitively? It was not Derek's fault, chuffed that his dad had made the effort to enter his world rather than always expecting him to be in that distant man's one he inhabited. He put up with George's irritation at the thought he might be going easy on him, and did not say he would never play with him again when his father gave up after half an hour, throwing his controller to the floor in vexation.

Only then did Derek allow that *Mortal Kombat* still existed; he had a version of it. George was persuaded to go ahead by the prospect of becoming once more Kano, whom he had always referred to as Kip Kano without his son ever asking why.

If the *Kombat* Kip had beaten the odds in terms of gaming longevity, why should he be bound by the human ageing process? He had more hair than George remembered, though no doubt in the long-ago he had been shave-headed rather than bald. He had new opponents nowadays too, any one of the DC comic range including Superman and Batman. Derek chose to prance around in front of George's warrior as the Joker. For all his tricks, Kip still had his old-school punching and kicking force, and came out on top two rounds to one. George remembered there were theatrical coups de grâce on the permission *Finish Him*, but not how to execute them. He would need to mug up on that. Derek also mentioned a football game that had not been around in his childhood, and they agreed to have a go at *FIFA* another night. There appeared to be plenty of time ahead of them.

The two men's weekly groceries were not quite the old student-flat joke of seven crates of beer, five boxes of wine, two bottles of whisky, and what idiot wasted money on the loaf of bread, mainly because neither of them drank wine. One thing in which son had followed father faithfully was in a steady to outrageous daily consumption of alcohol, and now there was nobody, no commitments to set much in the way of limits to it. What else was there to do?

There was Reenie's shop.

Peter, the only one of the tontiners who knew how to set up a WhatsApp group, did so in his mother Reenie's name. The government rules and regulations about what travel was and was not permissible, as interpreted by his wife Margaret, were enough to deter him from driving to visit her every day. The two women had never had a comfortable relationship and now the daughter-in-law was suffering advanced paranoia at the thought of her husband spending time with any other human being. Unwilling to risk leaving the house herself, she had to let him do so to bring in their own provisions through click and collect at the local Sainsbury's, but not to include within the order anything for Reenie. Peter was shocked when Margaret told him he could make his choice and go live with his mother in Market Welham if he wished, she would find a way to manage alone, vulnerable though she was and supposed to be shielding.

'What do you mean? Why are you vulnerable?'

'If you don't know I'm not going to tell you.'

'Come on, Marg, I know you're stressed but I didn't think you had any breathing problems. That's the main reason for people of our age having to shield, isn't it? It's not something more serious you haven't told me about, is it? My God you haven't got some kind of cancer you've been hiding from me, have you?'

'No, it's not cancer. I don't have breathing problems and I don't have a spleen either.'

'You what? Since when? I swear to you that's the first I've heard of it.'

'Maybe I didn't want you to think you were getting damaged goods. I can imagine what a field day Reenie would have had if she'd known, turning you against me. I was never good enough for you anyway, in her eyes.'

She let him come and perch awkwardly on the side of her armchair, helplessly patting her back until she got her sudden sobbing under control. He had never known she rode as a child, much less that she had taken a fall which caused internal damage serious enough to require a splenectomy. He had no idea what the spleen did but supposed it to be more important than say tonsils or the appendix. If she had lasted without one more than forty years then the lack was self-evidently survivable, but it turned out to reduce the body's defences against infection. He had thought nothing of the fact that Margaret always insisted on an annual flu vaccination, long before everyone was getting one. COVID-19 was a different ballgame and there was no vaccination for it. She had spoken to her GP, was as she said on the NHS list of the vulnerable.

Peter shared none of this with his friends, nor Reenie with whom he spoke daily on the phone and sneaked to visit once or twice a week. She had never gotten to the stage of texting on her mobile phone, could rarely be trusted to have it on, but her landline was available unless she had knocked it slightly out of true in the cradle when dusting or cleaning it. That had happened more than once. On the other hand, the compulsion to keep her flat spotless might give purpose to days now emptied of the social interaction she had always enjoyed. The bus trips to town – in which she took particular delight because they were free on her pensioners' pass – for shopping and the library, the shared coffee mornings with friends in the small estate where she lived, all that had gone. He feared for her, yet always tried to view his first loyalty as to the wife to whom he also owed so much.

The purpose of the Reenie WhatsApp group was unashamedly to take up the offers of Harry and George to help her out. Because he had a car, Harry had been the first port of call, quite prepared to add her shop to his own and drive to her flat to deliver it. He would knock on the window on arrival, never yet able to take her by surprise in doing so. She was not a professional curtain-twitcher, just liked to know what was going on in her neighbourhood.

Passing through the communal hallway in a dozen steps, Harry would leave Reenie's carrier bags, carefully calibrated to match her lifting capacity, at the door of number fifteen. He would retreat outside the now wide-open window and when she reappeared with a cup of coffee – she was most insistent on this part of the ritual, however inclement the weather – take it from the sill where she left it. When she had finished checking her order was complete, while leaving the careful cupboarding of the groceries till later, she would return with a plate of biscuits she expected him to sample if not finish. She would hand him the bags (her own reusable ones, no way was she paying supermarkets for them) through the window. The first time he thought the Galaxy chocolate bar was a mistake, then learned to accept it graciously. 'Give it to your Ellen if you don't want it yourself, it's the least I can do. I won't be beholden to anyone, friend or not. Now you're sure Peter has sorted the money side out with you?'

As soon as Ellen became ill, Harry let his friends know he had better stop going anywhere near the old lady. George immediately offered to take on the shopping detail. He found the orders pitiful, hardly enough to keep a sparrow let alone an adult: a single small loaf a weekly centrepiece rather than afterthought, a single litre of milk. Who knew they still made those little glass jars of fish paste he remembered as a childhood sandwich-filler? They could be found in Sainsbury's, though the staff struggled to tell him in which aisle.

Harry put a message on the Reenie WhatsApp group when Ellen was taken to hospital. He did not trust himself to talk to his mates, even over the phone, without breaking down. She was gone by midday and Kerry left for her afternoon shift at Melwood House. Finding he could not sit down, he took a delighted Judy and supply of poo bags in the car to the golf club. If he could not play, he could surely walk the course, as long as he kept his obedient bitch well away from the greens.

He knew it was too soon to expect to hear anything from the Pilgrim Hospital. Kerry had said she would get in touch with them from work to make sure they knew someone was looking out for Ellen. He supposed Melwood might have some sort of hotline to medical services of all kinds. Their daughter would have more patience than him in getting through to the right area. More understanding of what was going on, too. He tried to persuade himself he was not being lazy or cowardly in letting Kerry, barely recovered herself from what might well have been COVID-19, take some of the strain off him.

He told himself also his intention was not to unload any of that stress onto Jane when he called her from the third hole – he walked the course as if he were playing it, from habit rather than any need to do so with no clubs and only Judy for company. Jane had instantly accepted that he could not move in with her when he had reported Kerry's initial illness.

'You do understand then, really? You're not just saying that?'

'I don't know if I understand or not. Part of me wishes you'd made up your mind, chosen me, to be blunt about it, long before now. I do see there's no alternative at this point, and I'll try not to think of that as letting you off the hook. The important thing is to get that girl of yours well, look out for Ellen and try not to catch the blessed thing yourself.'

Although it initially took him an age to compose the briefest of messages on his phone, putting his glasses on then punching out the letters one by one as he found them, his keyboard skills were improved by increasingly regular exchanges with Jane. She was more fluent and prolific, but he realised he owed her the effort of trying to keep up. She never phoned him, explaining that it still broke her up, if he did not answer, to think it was because she was only his 'bit on the side'.

She did not always pick up his calls, but he was glad to get through to her today. He found himself unable to say anything more than that they had taken Ellen to hospital.

'Oh Harry, that's terrible. It's the safest place for her though. Is it true what I've been hearing, no visitors allowed?'

'They wouldn't let Kerry go with her, and she's one of them.'

'And are you all right? Physically I mean, you must be suffering mentally.'

'You'd think I would have caught it from one or the other of them, wouldn't you? We've been trying best we can to keep ourselves to ourselves in the house, and you know I wasn't sleeping with Ellen long before this anyway.' Birthday presents did not count.

'I wish you were sleeping with me. Does that sound too brazen? I hated that it was so hole-and-corner, but I do miss us being together in that way.'

'I'm right here at MWGC, come over any time you fancy some TLC. I miss you too, darling. I wouldn't run away if you did come.' He paused briefly; nothing from the other end. 'All right, I understand it's best if you don't. I hope you're looking after yourself too, keeping that Sally-Anne from running around all over town like she used to. From everything I hear you shouldn't have too much to worry about with Maddie. Don't they say kids are immune?'

'I don't know what they say any more, Harry. I still worry about her, and there's her education too. This whole home-schooling thing. It was lovely being together for a start, like a half-term holiday, but though they're my two dearest people in the world – not to disappoint you, love, you're edging your way into the top ten – it feels strange, three women in the house together.'

'Don't tell me you're missing having that arsehole Dean there?'

'Not that, never that. I wonder sometimes if Sally-Anne is. Her social life is zero now, like everyone else's. Which reminds me, I asked Pete to put me and her on the Reenie WhatsApp group. I'll be happy to help out and I think it might do Sally-Anne good, give her a chance to get out of the house and have a bit of conversation.'

'Listen to Reenie sounding off, you mean. I think it's because she can't hear what *you* say she keeps on talking all the while herself. Not that I can hear *her* properly, through the window with the telly on loud enough to reach London Road. Pete must feel like he's caught between the SS and the Taliban, with Marg and Mum controlling his every move. I think George has already stepped in with Reenie as it goes, looks like her social life will be taking an upturn. Another friendly face can't hurt. I plan to put updates about Ellen on the WhatsApp so it will be good if you are on it. We can keep it out of our own conversations then. I don't want you to pity me.'

'And I don't want you to feel you have to play the macho man all the while, Harry. You don't, not with me. Look at Boris Johnson, thinking he could bluster his way through the whole thing, say he's got a cough but can still run the country then ending up in intensive care. If you start feeling ill yourself, don't try to tough it out. And for Ellen, I can't believe she's less fit than that barrel of lard, and he pulled through all right.'

'Will they watch her round the clock like they did BoJo, that's the thing?'

Harry had no direct way of knowing what treatment his wife was receiving, having conceded next-of-kin status to Kerry for the duration. Kerry berated herself for not having thought to put Ellen's phone among her personal effects, so that they might have been able to stay in touch with video as well as voice calls over WhatsApp. She gave Harry an update based on her conversations with the Pilgrim at teatime every day, whether she was at work or home, where he was doing his best to coincide with her and prepare some rough and ready meals.

The updates did not test his texting skills unduly. Ellen was under observation on the first day, with tubes up her nose to boost her supply of oxygen. On the second day, COVID-19 having been confirmed, she was moved into a different ward, still on oxygen. On the third day she was breathing through an oxygen mask rather than the nasal piping.

On the fourth evening he had fetched fish and chips against Kerry's arrival. She let him get them out of the oven and said she was fine to eat them from the wrapping, at the kitchen table with him. He had cut open the batter to pour additional vinegar on the whiteness of the fish and was adding his tub of curry sauce when she told him Ellen had been taken into ICU.

'Intensive care? Christ no, when was this?'

'Only just. She's needing more help than they can give her on the ward.'

'How do you mean? What fucking help are they giving her?'

'Dad, there's no need to swear. That won't help Mum or anybody else.'

'Well there's no tablets that do any good far as I can tell. If it's just oxygen she needs surely to fu… surely they haven't got a shortage of that to give her what she needs.'

'I'm a carer, not a nurse. If she's in ICU we know she's getting one-to-one attention, they're not going to miss anything.'

'Boris got one-to-one, maybe two-, three-, five-to-one, but is it the same for Joe Public? I don't know what questions to ask, Kerry. Did they say what her chances are? With all the shit news was there anything to keep us hoping?'

'Even with the prime minister it was touch and go. The truth is nobody can tell how different individuals will fight along with the medics to beat the virus. They'll let us know if and when there's any change. That's all they can say.'

'And if the worst happens, what will they do? Throw her in a plague pit? Get rid of the body without us being able to say goodbye.'

'Harry' – he noted the stern shift from *Dad* – 'I'm looking at this stuff all day long at work, people coming into MH looking more dead than alive, because the hospitals are overflowing. It keeps me busy, and you may have more time to dwell on things, but I can't be around you if you're going to be so negative. Everyone's doing their best, that's what we have to believe. If you can't stay positive, I won't let you drag me down with you. There'll be time enough to think about the worst without calling it in advance.'

'Ellen in ICU but staying positive, cheers' was Harry's message on the Reenie group that night.

'Still fighting in ICU' he wrote the next evening, though he had no idea whether Ellen was conscious, let alone battling. After apologising to Kerry and sharing a hug with her before they binned most of their dinners the previous day, he had drunk his way steadily through eight of the two dozen large Kronenbourg cans in the fridge (no one to keep him from stocking it as he chose now). The only reason he did not finish the rest was that he moved on to Jameson's. He did not call Jane.

Harry was no longer bothered about lockdown rules once Ellen went into ICU, yet except for wanting to be present for Kerry he did not care for human company either. Waking from his K and J binge, which had somehow not helped him either to sleep well or feel better, he was probably technically still over the drink-driving limit when he took Judy to the golf course again. What did it matter, there were hardly any other cars on the road to worry about? He took a single club out with him, beating the hell out of a five iron all the way up to the greens without bothering to putt out. He briefly wondered if Judy would chase and attempt to retrieve the ball for him, but she showed as little interest in his golf as he felt.

Not knowing anyone who had been seriously ill from COVID, Harry's main reference point remained Boris Johnson, who like Christ in the tomb had passed three nights in intensive care before rising again. Harry had no deeper faith in religion than in BoJo yet still felt it keenly when Ellen entered her fourth night in ICU. He did not dare raise the topic with Kerry, but feared people might only be given so long on the machinery before they were disconnected to give someone else a go.

He was dozing uneasily, fully clothed on his bed after another random, solitary round of golf followed by more home boozing, when the vibration and sound of the phone on his chest woke him. Seeing Kerry's name on the screen, well before the time she would normally call, he almost chickened out of answering. Could he process a voicemail better than having to respond to a dear daughter? He had to answer.

'Dad, Dad, listen, it's good news. She's not coming home yet, nowhere near the all-clear, but Mum's out of intensive care. Dad? Are you there? Can you hear me?'

'Yes, yes. That's fabulous, sweetheart, thank you thank you I don't know what to say.'

'Don't say a thing. Just make sure you've washed up the saucepans from last night before I get home. It's Thursday.'

The reference was lost on Harry, but he did as he was told. At eight o'clock that evening he found himself at their front gate with Kerry banging pots as spiritedly as anyone in the street – not everyone was out by any means – in appreciation of the NHS and its workers. Although he could not see the sense, it felt good. He then got so drunk George could hardly understand him when he returned his mate's congratulatory call in response to the original WhatsApp: 'Ellen on the mend. God bless the NHS.'

You're Gorgeous

'Hello, handsome.'

'Well hi there, gorgeous, what you been up to?'

'I was talking to George. Who are you?' Sally-Anne and Jane had rounded the corner to Reenie's flat to find the two men standing outside her window.

'Don't you fancy me no more?' Derek was not at all daunted. 'It was a different story when we were kids. I remember I wouldn't give you a kiss, but I defo would now if it weren't for this COVID lark.'

'It's not all bad then.'

Each of the parents had to wait for the opportunity to tell their child not to get involved with the other one until the awkward foursome had been resolved. Reenie would not have minded them all standing at her window, in truth she still invited all and sundry into the flat, but George and Derek were already finishing their coffee and cigarettes having delivered her shop. 'Hey, can I give you a call sometime, Sally-Anne? You'll be safe from falling in love with me all over again with this social distancing?'

'I'm safe enough, lover boy, believe me. Suppose I can't stop you writing to me direct with my number on Reenie's WhatsApp group. I warn you though, I have higher standards than when I was a kid. Ask your dad.'

George was already halfway up the road.

Harry was not quick enough onto the new tee-time booking system to get a round in on Wednesday, 13 May, the first day allowed by the government. Playing together was limited to two people, or three if from the same family bubble, which ruled out a tontiner three-ball. He had an idea, which Jane was able to implement online rather than over the phone with Cliff Lambert, the pro still not allowed to earn from soft drinks and confectionery, let alone sales of golfing equipment or clothing, by reopening his shop.

Expected to play more quickly, George and Pete would go out ahead of Harry and Jane on the Friday afternoon, a longer fifteen-minute gap between start-times part of the new regulations. In the absence of any need to book at all, this had previously been left to members' discretion and judgement. Percy Parsons, having served in all the club's major offices over the years, now had the new title of Preventive Director of COVID, shortened to PDC then lengthened by Graham Cook to Pox Doctor's Clerk. Percy said most members thought he was doing a sterling job keeping them up to date with government decrees and guidelines as incorporated into the club's own rules and regulations. It was doubtful if many matched his commitment by troubling to read as carefully as he wrote his regular email dispatches.

A new prohibition was of taking alcohol onto the course, just as it became a more pressing need with the bar passed at the turn as well as reached at the eighteenth hole now closed. There was to be no congregating in the patio area either. Nothing daunted, Harry stocked his flat's fridge with a case of Kronenbourg to match the one at his house. Pete did not join George, given a key, in putting two lagers in his bag at the start of their round then a couple more for the back nine, any more than Jane did to accompany Harry in similar consumption. The host almost regretted the gallantry that had obliged him to play with her rather than his best mate.

They had only a small window to sup together outside Harry's flat – Jane vetoed an indoors reunion – since you could never be sure who might be on the PDC's books to grass up other members for non-compliance and prejudice what was of late snootily referred to as their golfing privilege. Still, it felt good to Harry, and he had enjoyed the chance to spend time playing the course with his girlfriend, who made it clear playing around was not yet on the cards.

Others were seizing their own window of opportunity, he found out later that day in an almost incoherent call from Jane, breaking her habit of not initiating phone contact.

'Can you believe it, there he was cool as you please sitting in my living room, shirt off like some yobbo sweating against the back of my sofa, her with her head practically in his lap. They didn't bother to deny they'd been in bed, that cheeky mare saying I'd had my afternoon delight so not to grudge hers.'

'Hold on, Jane, what you on about? Who was on your settee? I assume you're talking about Sally-Anne but who now, not Dean…?'

'Not Dean no, he could actually have made part of our bubble but now the whole thing's been burst. This had better not be something you cooked up with your precious mate George, lure the she-dragon out of her lair so the kids could trash it. And Madison there too, she spends enough time shut up in her room without being forced there to escape that sort of thing.'

'Slow down, Jane. I cooked up nothing except what I thought was a nice afternoon out golfing, and you can't be talking about George cos he only left my flat ten minutes ago – and before you start, we sat on opposite sides of the table. Give me a clue, love.'

'I thought she hated him, was genuinely disgusted like I was when he sent her obscene stuff, dick pics they call 'em for Christ's sake. I told her to make damn sure she didn't keep any of that on her phone, you never know if Maddie might pick it up, and she swore she'd block him or whatever it is they do. Some block. Like father, like son. He needn't think he's coming in and out of my house whenever he pleases. I told him that straight.'

Harry was at last getting a blurred picture of what had happened. While he could not imagine at any stage of his life having the confidence or pride in his tackle's allurement to send photos of it as a courting card, he knew it was a thing nowadays. He felt best not to mention a sudden certainty that Sally-Anne would be well up to indulging in the female equivalent – gash flashes? Snatch snaps? 'So you mean Derek, George's boy, he's been round your house?'

'God, Harry, how many cans have you had? Are you totally gone? Isn't that what I've been telling you for the last ten minutes? Of course it's Derek, who else? I should have known he'd be all over my daughter given half a chance.'

'Is he still there?'

'He might as well be now. Don't you get any of it? He's compromised our bubble. It's like he's brought tramping into our house whoever else he might have been mixing with these last few weeks. God knows how many skunks and drunks if he's been living in that dossers' pub with George and his woman.'

'No, the Horse is closed.' He did not add 'except to regulars'.

'If he was even a nice boy, but he's so cocksure of himself. How long do you think he'll want to stay with Sally-Anne when he realises she comes as a package with Maddie? My poor little girl will only end up getting hurt again.'

'Cocksure' seemed a peculiarly apt description of Derek, though he did not feel it the right moment to congratulate Jane on her choice of words. He could hear she was upset, but eventually established that she did not want or expect him to do anything about it, was just calling to have a good rant and get it out of her system. He could hardly be expected to ask the lad, with whom he was not sure he'd ever had an adult conversation, whether his intentions towards Jane's daughter were honourable or not. Then he realised he could. For good or bad, if he was to make something of a life with Jane, her daughter and granddaughter undoubtedly formed part of that package, another whole set of responsibilities he was reluctant to shoulder.

Conversations with Friends

They don't know what they're doing.
One minute you can't go nowhere, next they're fucking paying *you to go out to eat.*
Yeah, not subbing the drinks though are they.
That Richie Whatever chancellor of the exchequer, he won't care about that.
He's a Muslim can't have a pint hisself so don't care about us.
Be making pubs and caffs open all night next just cos they can't eat during the day.
No change there for the Horse then.
They're not vampires, it's only in Ramadan they don't eat during the day.
Leicester's still in lockdown anyway, that's where a lot of 'em live.
Ten or twelve living in the same room, that's why it's spread more there.

Reenie came out of what the still popular, COVID-survivor Prime Minister Johnson called a 'long national hibernation' (three months, but then a week is a long time in politics) without having caught the virus but undoubtedly in a worse state than she entered it. As soon as the buses were running again, she got out her pass and pushcart to go shopping in town. Peter was supposed to have come for her, but if he could not be bothered she would manage on her own. She was not helpless.

It was the first time she had been more than a hundred yards from her own flat since the whole lockdown business started. The walk to the bus stop on the side road serving her little estate of Carlton Close had never taxed her before, but now she noticed its slight uphill slope. She leaned more heavily on her shopping trolley. Empty as yet of shopping to serve as ballast, it slipped away from her. She would have fallen more heavily onto her face if her shoulder had not first struck a lamp post. That hurt. She dared not move. She looked down at the pavement. Her shoulder hurt. She would miss her bus.

It was six thirty in the morning. Reenie lay for half an hour before Sausage came to lick her face. 'Reenie, Reenie are you all right? Whatever's happened?' She thought it was him talking but told herself not to be so daft. Sausage could do a lot of things, but not quite that. He was not *only* a dog, she loved him so much, but he *was* a dog. And anyway, Sausage always called her Mum, not Reenie.

Pete had sanctioned the unofficial bubble formed by his mother and Pauline as something to help keep her sane. The younger woman was strong enough to walk her well-trained yellow lab, Bella – sometimes pre-lockdown accompanied by Reenie whose flat they would both still visit. Pete had been secretly relieved when the fat, unruly King Charles Cavalier given the commoner's name of Sausage had died in 2016. The little bugger had once pulled his then stronger mum to the ground, with an excited, unexpected switch of direction in hopeless pursuit of a glimpsed cat.

Since Pauline had to let Bella out anyway first thing, and some of the neighbours were looking for any excuse to have all dogs banned from the estate, she would put her on the lead and give them both a bit of exercise. That had been an important coping mechanism for her during the lockdown, as well as another walk later in the day on which she hoped Reenie might soon rejoin them. Pauline kept her mobile phone about her and had Peter's number on it, without Reenie's knowledge. Ridiculously jealous of the most common courtesies exchanged between him and her friends, she would have found it highly suspicious for them to be in contact other than through her.

Peter beat the ambulance to them to find his mum propped up against two heavy cushions a nosy neighbour had come out and supplied. Reenie was fiercely embarrassed. 'Where the bloody hell have you been? I shouldn't have fallen if I hadn't had to make my own way to town. Look at all the trouble you've put these poor people to.'

'It was tomorrow…' he started to say before realising that would not be helpful. He reassured Pauline and the other elderly lady that they had been right not to try to move her, then proceeded to do so himself. She winced and gave an involuntary cry of pain as he touched her right hand, before clumsily wrapping his arms round her waist to hoick her upright. He wondered whether to lay her flat across the back seat, but then he could not seatbelt her so she might end up in the footwell from her own fidgeting or his driving. While it was not particularly warm, still early in the day, he was sweating heavily by the time he at last got her riding shotgun beside him. 'That's right, Mum, we won't bother the ambulance people, I'm sure Pauline or Mrs… er, Connie, thank you… won't mind letting them know we'll be making our own way to the Pilgrim, but you do have to go.'

'All right, George, you know best. You will look after me, won't you?'

He felt a pang that she had grown more accustomed to his mate George helping her out than his own presence, before she added, 'You always have, my Georgie Porgie.' That endearment had been reserved for his father.

The consecutive two-balls Harry had thought such a good idea were never repeated, only in part because such restrictions were no longer imposed as the country moved out of lockdown. Although George had confirmed he had as little idea as anyone else what his son was cooking up with Sally-Anne, Jane still blamed him for it to some degree. While Derek was superficially contrite that he had compromised the Wood family bubble, she saw it as another sign of his opportunism that he so promptly moved himself and a few belongings into Sally-Anne's bedroom.

George himself was not pleased at the situation, seething over the phone to Harry. 'The kid wasn't exactly much company for me, but I did think we were starting to get along. I wish I'd never took him to Reenie's that day, it wasn't as if he was really interested in helping the old dear out.'

'Maybe not, but that's the only half good thing Jane can find to say about the pair of them. They did carry on seeing her, until she had to go to hospital.'

'She was keeping them together then, cos he buggered off back to Brum soon after that far as I recall. Can't see me getting any sickbed visits from him, let alone poor Reenie. Is he still in touch with that girl at all?'

'Not that I know of, and she does have a name, George. Sally-Anne's cut up that he ran out on her, according to her mum.'

'She'll soon be able to get back to work, take her mind off it.' George's tone was hardly sympathetic. 'This pig out to help out or whatever they call it, Emma thinks it could help put her back on her feet businesswise. But *don't* suggest Sally-Anne comes round to the Horse looking for shifts, that girl will be the death of me.'

'Before she does kill you, I hope you'll tell me what happened between you and her.'

'I was in the wrong, if that's what you want to hear. One of the ways I accepted that was by agreeing, not with Jane but Andy, never to tell my side of it, never to pretend there was any justification. If I have to break that pledge it might be to Pete before you, I can see him making a bigger mistake around Sally-Anne. Don't think I don't know her name, all too well.'

'He snuck round there and helped himself while her mum and dad were out playing golf,' Reenie confided to the waiter at the Green Man as Sally-Anne followed up the old lady's order of a jacket potato – 'just butter and cheese, no other muck' – with one for burger and chips. Reenie was pointing at her son, Pete – who by now knew better than to deny the accusation and merely stated his own preference, cottage pie and peas with an order of chips on the side.

'Cottage pie *and* chips. Must be wonderful to have a pot belly like you and not give a shit about it.' This time it was Sally-Anne having a go at him, with that tone of amused detachment one of the more friendly she used on him. He could imagine what others would say – what George did say the last time they spoke: 'She treats you like shit, man.' Well, so did his wife and mother, and they offered him scarcely a moment of respite as Sally-Anne had been known to do.

He was besotted, he could admit it to himself and recognise that part of being so was that he could do nothing about it. He was always courteous and attentive to bar staff, unlike Harry for instance occasionally tipping male ones the conventional 'one for yourself'. It had been a reflex to do so for Sally-Anne, whom he considered almost family through the various tontiners' friendships.

He did not dream of a sexual relationship at first. His tipping was innocent of any such motivation, which he knew was sometimes behind Harry's. George never did it, was more likely to be offered one on the house himself.

Reenie was not at all censorious of Sally-Anne's status as a single mother, as Margaret emphatically was. At times he suspected she was envious of any mother. As the years passed without them making a baby he had offered to have tests to see if the problem lay with him, and if necessary consider adoption. Her reaction had been violent enough to discourage further discussion of the topic.

'Then you'll want me to have tests I suppose as well. Look, if it doesn't happen it doesn't happen. I don't need someone to blame. And I don't want to bring up someone else's brat, clear up someone else's mess. If you want kids more than you want me you've got a decision to make, my lad.'

And so the years had passed, happily for the most part he would have thought. With his usual optimism, he had told himself initially the menopause might be good for them both, allowing them to give up finally all hope of conceiving. He now wondered if giving up that hope went for her with giving up sex, almost giving up on their marriage. Always scrupulous to avoid taking sides in the undeclared war between Margaret and Reenie, he felt his neutrality under threat as his wife became less sympathetic and his mother more frail. Did need trump love? As he indulged himself in such speculations, he knew the real pull away from Margaret was coming from a much younger woman than Reenie.

He could obviously never be a father to Madison, but he hoped he could be a benevolent uncle. He found the girl charming, by Sally-Anne's account valiantly struggling to mediate between her mother and grandmother when Derek's arrival put them at odds with each other. While the three of them lunched at the Green Man today, Maddie had opted to go with Jane and Harry to the Dun Cow. Nobody had suggested a joint party.

Margaret was not prepared to eat out anywhere, suspecting along with a sizeable proportion of the country that the idea was a populist move by the ever keenly people-pleasing prime minister rather than one justified by a sudden disappearance or diminution of the virus and its menace. Pete could respect her opinion, without being prepared to deny his mum the opportunity to socialise again beyond the confines of Carlton Close.

This was Reenie's first outing in her new lifestyle since leaving hospital. He had expected a routine check-up there and prompt discharge, without realising that nothing happened promptly in hospitals anymore. It was evident on her admission that she was confused or disorientated, yet he was shocked to be told she could be suffering from dementia or Alzheimer's disease (he was not clear on what the difference might be, though the latter sounded more serious, capital letter foreign name and all). She certainly had a urinary tract infection or UTI, which might be causing some of the problem. He was equally clueless how the waterworks could be linked to the brain. The broken shoulder was about the only thing he could readily understand, that and the fact that Reenie would be needing a good deal more support than she had ever allowed anyone to give her up to that point in her life.

He would not demean Sally-Anne's contribution to that support by saying it might be due to boredom in the young woman with lockdown routine, since she continued it beyond the end of that, beyond the departure of Derek, right into the August scheme which would save him money on today's lunch. The Green Man's tariff, and the ineligibility of alcoholic drinks for the discount scheme (Sally-Anne's vodka with Red Bull she no longer needed to tell him was a double plus his own pint and a half of Doom Bar would have been worth a few bob), meant he was in no danger of cashing in the maximum £10 per person.

'And when are you two going to give me and Georgie Porgie a grandbabby?' Reenie turned her embarrassing focus on them full beam, the question more archly worded but the same she had put in many forms over the years to Peter and Margaret, long after she must have realised it was not funny but hurtful to them. She took it for granted that he and Sally-Anne were now a sexually active couple, referring to his wife only to say that Sally-Anne was an upgrade on 'that beanpole you had before'. While she got on well with Maddie, her mind was clear enough that the little girl was no grandchild of hers. 'This one can definitely give you a bab, we know that, if you're up to it yourself, Pete. Pity you lost interest in me years ago.' This level of being taken for his father was another thing Peter was yet to come to terms with.

He was only too aware – she had made sure of it – that Sally-Anne did not view him as husband material. The one and only time they had so far made love – if the coupling, frantic on his part, indulgent on hers could be called that – had been a much bigger deal for him than Sally-Anne, who seemed in no hurry to find opportunities to repeat it. Derek was already away on his toes, she had come round to make sure Reenie's flat was in a good enough state for her discharge from hospital – it had not occurred to him that any look at it would be needed. Changing the bedsheets, he felt she was deliberately provoking him, brushing past him with her tightly denimed backside. His throat was dry when he said, 'That Derek must need his head testing.'

She turned to him and cupped his face in her hands. 'I'm the one who needs my head testing. Do you want to take this further, Pete?'

He half expected her to shake or nod his head, deciding his fate, so hopelessly out of his depth did he feel. She only repeated: 'Do you?'

He nodded and she steered him out of his mother's bedroom, into the spare single one where no one had slept since she moved in. They christened it.

The logistics of taking things any further were deterrent enough to an unpractised adulterer. He could not pitch up at the house Sally-Anne shared with Jane. He did not dare suggest a country drive in his car – what was he going to do, pretend to run out of petrol? He felt himself enough of a laughing stock already, though his befuddled mum was the only one to suspect – to insist on – a sexual relationship between him and the woman (he was training himself to think of her as that rather than 'girl') how many years younger than him he chose not to calculate. Margaret was always in his own home, where in any case he still had enough respect for her not to wish to bring Sally-Anne. The girl – woman – was no help, referring flippantly to their consummation as a 'mercy fuck' to him, or a 'revenge fuck' against Derek.

Reenie needed professional care. She got it on an emergency basis they were told would be free of charge for six weeks before a means test was made to determine the extent to which she would have to contribute to the cost. 'Can't you look after me, Georgie? I'll take the spare room and you and your fancy piece can have the main one, being as you never want to share it with me now anyway. We can get a divorce if you like, I'll give you that.'

Taking the dementia as more than a short-term effect of the UTI, which had been sorted in hospital, Pete put in train health and financial powers of attorney for his mum, prepared to present them to her as divorce papers, a new will, whatever it took to get her signature on them.

Harry's lunch with Jane and Maddie at the Dun Cow was embarrassing in a different way to the one Pete had endured. The girl was as chatty as ever, on holiday from a school she had not visited in several months. He did not doubt her proud grandmother's claim that she had been conscientious in carrying out the remote classes the teachers had cobbled together. Derek and Dean were equally off limits for conversation between the adults when she was present. Today it was a figure from Harry's own romantic history that threatened to set Jane off on another rant.

'Hello Harry, you must be happy with Boris's latest brainwave. I remember you always liked eating out.' Their server smiled at Jane at that point, before resuming. 'And now you're getting paid for it as well, coming to a better class of restaurant than I remember, wanting to max out the discount? I hope you won't forget to work out my tip on the full amount though, times are still hard for some of us.'

'Would you mind taking our order please? Jackie, isn't it?' Jane returned an equally aggressive smile. 'I'm sure Harry will look after you, he's always very generous to us.'

Maddie was engrossed, turning expectantly to their waitress for the next volley. Tempted though he was to run for the gents, Harry did not dare leave the two women together. 'How is this business going for Emma? I thought you might be helping your sister out in the Horse instead of moonlighting here?'

'I would if she paid family. They're going gangbusters I hear, she's got your mate pulling pints instead of supping them for free while she runs around like a blue-arsed fly. Sorry, honeybunch.' She put a hand on Maddie's shoulder, far too familiar for Jane's liking, he could tell. 'Didn't mean to swear. That son of George's soon skedaddled when there was a chance he could of been some use, no fear of him helping out.'

Harry had no idea whether Jackie was aware of the situation between George's boy and Jane's girl, but would not have bet against it. He could not get out of the Cow quickly enough, and knew he had not got away with it just because Jane remained tight-lipped that day. She remarked at their next 'lunch out to help out', just the two of them this time in a venue safely out of town: 'No twenty per cent tip for this one then, Harry. Or was that more for services rendered from that old brass of yours. They'd better be past services, that's all I'll say.'

The last day of the subsidised-meal scheme coincided with the Monday bank holiday at the end of August. Not that he was cheap, but Harry somehow thought it typical of Sally-Anne to suggest a lunch the very day after that. She wanted neither her mother nor daughter to be with them, which made him nervous. She was indifferent to where they met, so he opted for the White Horse, where he could be confident of not meeting Jane. Although his mate might be a dubious witness in her eyes, he thought he would be able to call on George as such if necessary, or to bounce the girl out if that proved the better option. You never knew with Sally-Anne.

She was not noted for her punctuality either. They had agreed half twelve, but Harry was there at noon. That and the choice of venue were part of an uneasy feeling that he had not been as loyal a mate to George as he might have since the Derek debacle. They had not played much golf or drunk together recently, George confirming what his sort-of sister-in-law had said in that he was extra busy in the Horse. Sure enough, he was behind the counter when Harry walked in, pulling him a pint without comment or charge. He took one himself too. He looked thin and pale.

'You should get out more, mate, if it's only to the fucking smoking area, get the sun on you.'

'Hello to you too, Harry. Cheers.'

'The boss not in?'

'She's in, in bed. Sick.'

'What? You should have said. What's up?'

'I'm saying now. COVID, you might guess. Going from table to table for the last month, mask or no mask you can't eat with a mask on and you've still got to breathe. There was people we've never seen in here before, the all-day breakfast special never been so popular, but it took its toll on her. The bastard virus hasn't suddenly gone away, she would have been exhausted and it must have caught hold of her.'

'What about you, haven't you caught it off her? Shouldn't you be isolating as well?'

'I don't give a shit. I'm not taking their poxy tests. I'll look after myself.'

'They want to get their finger out on this vaccine for it, probably be all over before it's ready. Is she bad? Scrub that, stupid question, I don't think I've ever walked in here without seeing Emma on one side of the bar or the other. Have you got in some extra help? I saw Jackie the other week, expect she's been laid off at the Cow now the cheap meals are done.'

'That's when we could have used her. Trouble is she owes Emma a shitload of money and wouldn't let her take a penny of it back out of her wages. That was the least the bitch could have done in my opinion – which I didn't give her sister, they fell out all on their own. I won't go begging her to come in now. I shouldn't wonder trade'll fall off a cliff again, before that cunt Johnson shuts us down altogether – that'll be next. You hardly needed to call to book a table. I nearly told you to fuck off when that was what you asked for.'

'I meant it as a joke but I don't suppose you're in much of a mood for them. I can see you're stressed.'

'Don't tell me you've got another bit of fanny on the side now? I can't see Lady Jane wanting to slum it in here. Anyone I know?'

'Nothing like that. I'm doing my best to hang on in there, but it's not easy.' Fearing his guest's name would hardly cheer George's mood, Harry plunged in and told him anyway. He was surprised at the reaction.

'Poor cow. I feel bad for her, the way that lad of mine treated her...'

'I think she was always going to be a handful for anyone. I wouldn't necessarily be too hard on him.'

George laughed, without any trace of amusement. 'Here's me going on about Emma and Jackie and I'm just as bad with Derek. The more you try and help 'em out the more they piss on you, family. You look after your own, course you do, but he's left me on the bones of my arse. No bother, what he had now he won't get when I go.'

'You're going nowhere, mate. You're bulletproof and plague-proof.' Only as he said it did Harry realise how much he wanted it to be true, had always believed it so until these recent times when everything started falling apart. 'Look, if it's money...'

'Don't even go there. I'm the guvnor of this dump now, I can chuck you out for talking shit.' His tone softened. 'I shouldn't have mentioned it, mate. Plenty have it worse. I hope you've still got an eye on Pete with Reenie. I haven't been able to keep up there as much as I'd like, just in case I have got the Corona. Looks like your date's here. You can pick your own table, come up to the bar yourself if you want any nosebag.'

'Fair enough. Give us another pint and...?'

'Morning, men, what are you two cooking up between you? Don't suppose you've got any Red Bull, George?'

'Morning. No, this int a kid's pub.' For all the sympathy he had just expressed for Sally-Anne, there was little of friendliness in his voice.

'You don't have to tell me. It's a long while since I was a kid. Vodka and Coke then please, Harry.' George was already at the optic.

*

When Harry updated Sally-Anne on the reason for the landlady's absence her only comment was, 'Yeah, lot of it about. That's probably why they call it a pandemic.'

'Easy for you to be blasé about it, I hope it never catches anyone dear to you.'

'Emma should be all right. She's nothing like as old as you and George. My mum's tough as old boots. And Maddie, kids don't catch it, God showing he's not a total bastard, must be. Not that Boris isn't doing his best to fuck up their education, all the same.'

'God forbid anything happen to Maddie, but I think there's some cases all through the population.'

'Are there? Let me ask you a question, Harry. How worried were you about Aids? Didn't they talk about that as an epidemic, not so quick to put the "pan" on that one. Come on, that was more your era, wasn't it?'

He saw the trap just in time. It was true that he had considered gay men and drug-takers the only ones with much to worry about for far longer into the eighties than he should have, laughing at the sick jokes ('Is toast good for the patients?' 'Don't know, but it's the only thing we can fit under the door.') until they dried up. He should have guessed that Sally-Anne would be all over the alphabet soup of minorities to be not only respected but almost worshipped – he kept that second bit to himself. Kerry was the same, like all the young people nowadays. He would not say they were wrong, only that their cast-iron assurance of being right vexed him at times.

'Well, were you worried? Or did you just keep right on chasing women?'

Sally-Anne was obviously not going to be satisfied with silence, and he could not share his thoughts. 'I didn't realise I was walking into a grilling here.' He said it with a smile, almost added 'sweetheart' or 'darling'. He would have to Kerry, but thought his girlfriend's daughter might bridle at such an endearment. 'I don't know where you get these ideas. Whatever I was in the past, you know better than anyone I can keep away from high-risk areas nowadays.'

'I'm more worried about you *being* a high-risk area than avoiding them, Harry. I'm thinking of Mum.'

'This is all upside down. Are you asking me if my intentions towards her are honourable, like your dad might have had to with your boyfriends?'

'I never had a boyfriend with honourable intentions.' She quickly recovered herself from what sounded a moment of rare, raw honesty. 'Credit where it's due, you put up a more decent show that time in your flat than I ever thought you would.'

Again he avoided the snare, this time of asking if her brazen offer had been genuine. He only wished he could put the scene out of his mind, or at least gain more control over when it would make its appearance. 'Trust me, honour damn near lost out. I don't think what you and George's boy did was right. I'm not talking morals, I'm in no position to do that, but I wish it had worked out better for you. I honestly thought he'd be a better lad than your last one, that Dean.'

'My fiancé Dean? Didn't Mum tell you?'

'What? You…'

'Your face! I bet you're a crap poker player. He'd have to crawl back on his hands and knees, that one. It's not him, or deadly Derek I came here to talk to you about. Look, it's bad enough COVID being everywhere again without risking salmonella or plain old food-poisoning from the Horse's kitchen, especially if George has been left in charge of it. Set me up with another voco – and make sure it's a brand I've heard of this time, not that house one made from Polish potato-peel – and I'll let you off the nosebag as he called it.'

Wondering how much else of his conversation with George the girl had overheard, and if there was anything in it that might have been grist to the mill she was putting him through, Harry went to the bar. She was instantly tapping away on her phone, set on the table in front of her to make it clear her focus on their own conversation was not total, but did not make him wait too long to resume it.

'It is a bit of man-trouble I think you might be able to help me out with, Harry.' She was looking down at her drink, swirling the ice cubes as far as George's rationed two could be swirled, rather than directly at him.

'I'll be happy to tread on his fingers if Dean really is crawling back to you. And kick his arse while he's down there, if you like.'

'So sweet of you. I wonder if you'd do the same to Derek. He likes to think he's as hard as his old man.'

'That'll be the day,' Harry responded instantly. Then he wondered if that day had already come, if the acting landlord's gloom was in part due to a feeling that the baton had been snatched from him by the next generation. Snatched and run with, like his money from what he'd said.

'It is somebody in your generation I'm thinking of.'

'Jeez, Sally-Anne, what is it with you and old codgers. I don't count myself but G—' He just stopped George's name coming out of his mouth. 'Jesus Christ, you had them all eating out of your hand at the golf club, especially poor old Pete.'

Now she *was* looking him full in the eye.

'Holy shit, it's Pete you mean, isn't it? Don't tell me he's gone and done something crazy. Don't tell me he tried to attack you or something.'

'Were you tempted to do that, Harry? No, he's a gentleman through and through. If he wasn't so… well, innocent is the only word I can think of, I wouldn't be worried for him.'

'So *you're* worried for *him*. Tell me if I'm being thick, I haven't got a scooby what you're on about.'

'It's hard to explain. You know him better than I do, and I don't want to sound big-headed, but I think he's got a crush on me.'

'A crush? Fuck me, he's not fifteen years old! Say what you mean, girl. You think he wants to sleep with you?'

'I know he does.'

'And have you given him any encouragement? I used to notice him resting his belly on the bar plenty when you were at the club, and I don't blame you for taking a drink if he was fool enough to offer it, but I thought that was just barmaid love.'

'You can explain to me what "barmaid love" is another time if you think it's something worth me knowing. It's clear enough if he wants to sleep with me – I can handle that. I'm more worried in case he's building himself up to something a lot more drastic. Can you tell me if he's happily married?'

A few months earlier Harry would have answered 'yes' with more confidence than about anyone else he knew. Now he realised he wasn't sure. Was his friend being torn apart by two nags pulling in different directions, his ma and his wife, like that Red Indian torture – maybe Jane would remember the film it had been in, the hero bound hand and foot to separate horses sent galloping off in opposite directions by a smack on the arse? And shouldn't Jane be the one having this conversation with her daughter? It was not proving a pleasant lunch. As with George, he was being forced to wonder whether he had been there for his mate Pete.

He had masked his indecision by taking a long pull of beer. By God, he needed another one. 'He's been married a long time, Sally-Anne, and so have I. You can never tell what's going on in someone else's relationship, however close you might be to that person. Are you saying you think he's prepared to chuck up everything he's got with Margaret for you, without being big-headed?'

He had not troubled to avoid a touch of sarcasm, which Sally-Anne ignored. 'I do think so. To be honest, more than I do with you and Mum. COVID should have made everyone think about whose bubble they want to be in, but you still can't make up your mind. I hope you're not just stringing her along, Harry.'

'I'm not here to talk about my love life. You're the one who was asking for help. I'm sorry, I didn't mean to shout.' He hadn't quite, but loud enough for one of the pub's other denizens to look up from his racing pages anticipating something other than horses going off. 'You want me to warn Pete off, is that it? Tell him you're no good? Tell him you're a prick-teaser and nothing more?'

She did not ignore that. He knew at once he had gone too far. 'I shouldn't have said that, I'd never have said it to him. Let's have one more drink and I promise to talk to Pete, whatever you want me to say. You'll have to help me get it clear what that is.'

Further conversations with George and Pete were much on Harry's mind after that lunchtime session, where he and Sally-Anne both had the sense to make their next drink indeed the only one more. It was his mates who had other priorities. Soon Emma and Reenie would both be in hospital. Only one of them would come out.

Smokers' Corner

Reenie's fractured shoulder gave her surprisingly little pain. Even in hospital it had been impossible to get her to keep the sling on. She would accept attendant nurses' reasons for doing so obediently enough, then quickly be plucking it off, probably more in abstraction than defiance. The mental and emotional side was the real issue for her, or rather for those around her. Pete had been reading up on the subject and saw the truth that family and friends live with the dementia, not so much the person affected for whom it is the new normal.

He found almost a release in the bureaucratic side of things, harking back to his years of office work. The procedure for the health and financial powers of attorney was straightforward, and Reenie amenable to sign them. She had already been reliant on him for all kinds of paperwork, including banking. He had no need, as an only child, to have a solicitor rather than any upstanding citizen countersign the powers, but it comforted him to do so. James McCreery had only recently helped them in a free-will month, one for Reenie and mirror ones for himself and Margaret. His mother had been distressingly adamant that he should be the sole beneficiary of everything but her (negligible) collection of jewellery. That, she left to her niece, Pete's cousin Marion. He should have known better than try to apologise to Margaret for her exclusion.

'You don't think I'm surprised, do you? I've long since given up expecting any sign of kindness or affection from your mother.'

He could understand Margaret hardening her heart, yet not quite forgive her for leaving care of Reenie in all its aspects to him. He was grateful that the professionals on their twice daily, half-hour visits, took a lot of the strain, given his authorisation to dole out her pills, of which she had lost all track. They would help her in the shower, a task he hoped would never fall to him. Reenie was still capable of using the toilet herself, barring occasional accidents. Only Margaret insisted there was always the smell of urine about her favoured armchair.

The carers would fill in a log after each visit, where he would interleaf his own notes to indicate if he had called and given her lunch. He still took her out on occasion. She seemed to find Sainsbury's soothing, whereas for him its aisles soon became claustrophobic. He would make these trips outside the carers' calling windows, the variety they brought to her constricted world too precious to lose. They would try to see her have a good breakfast and prepare something in the evening if necessary. He gave them full permission to use the stock of ready meals he kept in the freezer and could manage in the microwave that Reenie had always been too frightened to use. Her friend Pauline proved as faithful as Bella/Sausage in keeping up their visits, which he did not at all mind agreeing with his mother were more frequent, welcome and cheering than his own.

It was mainly young women who called, letting themselves in from a lockbox in the hallway outside the flat (the three-digit code the day and month of his birth chosen when Reenie could still remember them). There was a kerfuffle when she once found a large black man in her living room, the agency calling to assure Pete that he was a trusted member of their staff and had left the premises quietly, unable to complete his duties, immediately her distress became evident. Pete accompanied him on his next visit, when Reenie was apologetic for not having grasped who he was. He became thereafter something of a favourite, though she would look to find him odd jobs about the house and try to make him coffee rather than the other way round.

Reenie's hearing aids were a constant chore. Some carers were more conscientious than others in putting them in for her of a morning, and she could be recalcitrant about letting them do so. It mattered less because she had lost all interest in her television, as well as the capacity to read which had been a big part of her solitary life.

If he had to restock on batteries and stick them in the hearing aids less frequently now, Pete did not feel he could be so relaxed about the council's lifeline he had organised during the lockdown, before Reenie's hospitalisation. She soon found herself unable to activate it, without the strength in her fingers (or was it focus in her mind?) to trigger the call. They were helpful in replacing it with one far more sensitive, so sensitive indeed that she would bell them fifty times a day, dutifully keeping it round her neck but fingering it in moments of boredom, distraction or – who knows? – wanting to have a word with the nice people whose disembodied voices always greeted her by name and asked if she was all right.

The alarm went off at night too, if she moved in bed. Before dispatching help the service would phone Pete. Since they could not promise to reach his mother in less than forty-five minutes, which he could always beat, he would drive to find her sleeping peacefully, then call the service to stand down.

He was investigating alarms that could be worn as a bracelet, or promised to respond automatically to 'loss of altitude and speed', when Reenie had her second serious fall, indoors this time. Her existing lifeline proved as useless as a strand of spaghetti thrown to a person drowning, not least because it was beyond her reach. Pete had not always been called out at night. Sometimes she heard the patient, calm voice of the 24-hour service from the living room of her small flat and would feel obliged to get up to reassure them. So she took to hanging it on the bedpost when she retired of an evening. Pete could now blame himself for having seen it there on one or two mornings and said nothing, for the sake of a quiet(er) life.

The carer came in the chosen window between eight fifteen and nine. Reenie would usually be up and waiting for them, having done some housework in the better earlier days so they would not 'find the place a tip'. She did the same initially with the actual cleaner who now came in once a week, a former carer herself and the only person to report to Pete proud words from his mother about him.

It was not clear whether Reenie was asleep or unconscious when the carer found her this morning. Her nightclothes were dry, so she had possibly made it to the toilet then somehow fallen on her way out of the bathroom, going by the light from her bedroom so that she was wedged uncomfortably – to say the least, best case – between the wall and the half-open bathroom door.

'Hello, boy, what you doing here? Fancy woman kick you out of bed again?' was her greeting to Pete, showing awareness of the morning hour. It was the hospital again when the paramedics arrived, another UTI, a bang on the head that gave them cause for concern and the need to check for any other injuries of which she was unable to advise them.

He normally avoided looking at the group always right outside the big revolving doors into the Pilgrim Hospital, for fear they would think he was judging their smoking habit, especially the patients in nightgowns and inappropriate footwear for outdoors, under perhaps a puffer jacket and hooked up to a drip or portable oxygen.

'What's up, Pete?' His friend did not speak loudly but he knew the voice well enough to divert instantly from the entrance.

'George. You going in or coming out?' He would have thought him a possible patient, so gaunt and tired did he look, except the current generation of the Levi jacket he had worn winter and summer for over fifty years was not hospital gear.

'Hard to know if I'm coming or going at the minute. Don't tell me Reenie's in trouble again?'

'Afraid so. She keeps fighting the furniture and coming off worse. We're hoping there's nothing broken this time. Sooner we can get her out of here the better. I reckon every day in hospital sets her back a week or more, maybe gives her a temporary reboot but at the expense of her hard drive.' Suddenly realising his private thoughts, apart from being too fanciful, might not be the most tactful to voice to someone at the threshold of a hospital, he tried to strike a more cheerful note. 'But Reenie's a tough old bird, you know that as well as anyone. She's come through worse. Who you here for? I did hear Emma wasn't too cracky?'

'Got it in one. We'd have had to drag her kicking and screaming out of the Horse if she'd still had the puff to scream and the energy to kick. It's the Corona with her, pig out to wipe out they should have called that shitstorm. I just said goodbye to her... I mean I'll be back tomorrow, not goodbye goodbye... but they've told me it's intensive care if she don't buck up quick. I think they mean when some poor sod croaks in it, cos if you ask me she needs that right now, probably has for a couple of days.'

'Better late than never.' Pete's optimistic tone sounded fake even to himself. 'Emma's a fighter like Reenie, I'm sure she'll pull through.'

'I wish I was. If she does, I might put a ring on her finger, too much hassle having Jackie as next of kin, even if she did come through and tell 'em I had to be let in – I was ready to kick off if not, I'll tell you, protect our fucking NHS or not. "Immediate family and very close loved ones." Never thought I'd have to see it in a hospital's poxy visiting rules to realise that's what she is.'

George realised he had gone beyond the usual bantering, upbeat tone between him and his mates, but these were unusual times. He did not shrug off Pete's hand on his denimed shoulder.

'There's a lot of people having to change their way of thinking lately. Never thought I'd hear you talking about marriage again. Things are getting serious between Harry and Jane too. I wonder if he'll be going in the opposite direction with Ellen.'

'Only you and Marg rock solid then?' He was not smiling.

'It's not easy for anyone. Her and Reenie never got on, and I'm stuck in the middle.'

'I've told you before, don't think another woman will make things better. Sometimes they only complicate matters more. Especially the one you know I'm on about.'

'I've got to get in and togged up to see Reenie now.' He could not have been clearer that he did not want to talk about Sally-Anne. 'Do give Emma all my best. I tell you what, we all need to get back to the Rifleman's. Me, you and Harry, the three muppeteers.' (He had coined that term for them, uncomfortable with what he thought was braggadocio when Harry once christened them as musketeers.) 'It's a different world since COVID turned everything upside down.'

'Muppets more like. The world keeps coming at you, only sometimes it's harder to roll with than others. Hark at me bullshitting, that's too long away from the Rifle with you boys doing it, you're right. Give Reenie a hug from me if you're allowed. I won't visit her in case I've picked the Corona up spending so much time around it lately. Can't wait for the day we can bin these fucking masks.'

Woman Down

The Horse was more crowded than at the peak of the discounted dinners plan. The three tontiners had been through the mourning formalities – 'so sorry for your loss', 'lovely service' – at the crem. All that remained was to eat, drink and be miserable. They expected to be done before the usual evening session, though none of the pub's regulars or afternoon men had been turned away. The mates did not have a table to themselves; Harry was accompanied by Jane, chatting with Margaret.

'I didn't want to come, tell you the truth,' said Peter's wife. 'I wouldn't have just for her, but I think he's been sailing too close to the wind with drink-driving again lately. I hoped he'd learned his lesson before he kills someone in his car. It's something practical I can do to chauffeur him today.'

'Snap.' Jane jerked a discreet thumb at Harry beside her. 'They pay lip service to it, but I think deep down they don't believe the drink-driving law applies to them. They had so many years getting away with it. I wish Harry's wife was as conscientious as you so I could have a couple myself, but I'm not sure Ellen gets out of the house at all nowadays.'

'Can she get through the door? That's too catty, but she must have been pushing twenty stone when I last saw her – and that was before lockdown.'

Margaret had always been proud of her slim figure, taking various initiatives to maintain it, nowadays including regular visits to a gym. Although they had once been close, 'fighting the flab' together for a brief spell, the guilt Jane felt towards Ellen whose husband she was sitting beside would not let her pursue this line of conversation. It was debatable whether she would have felt similar sympathy for Margaret had she any idea of what was going on between Pete and Jane's own daughter Sally-Anne. Harry had wondered whether to mention something on that subject to her, but in the end remained close-mouthed.

Far from clear himself where he stood with Sally-Anne, despite the sombre circumstances and Margaret's presence Pete was finding it difficult to keep his eyes away from the barmaid, his… his what? Girlfriend was too ridiculous, lover too presumptuous, mistress too sleazy, and as a good Catholic boy he would not descend to the other words he had heard Harry use of his affairs. How about his amour, *amour fou* he had looked up from *The Sopranos* (which had its own freight of Catholic guilt)? How he wished he could call her just his Sally-Anne.

Sally-Anne was the last person Derek Pym had expected to see when he walked into the wake for his dad's missus. Although he had already downed a couple of pints, he did not want to go over to the old man's table empty-handed, from embarrassment rather than any fear of his mates flanking George. Like everything, he would have to style it out.

'Hey babe, how's it going? San Mig please, whatever George is drinking and one for yourself.'

Sally-Anne had her own style. She served the pint of lager, told him the first drink was free and that George had more in than he could drink in a week. 'As for myself, I'm working, which is the only reason you're getting the time of day. Don't offer me a drink again unless you want your own served in your face. Fuck off and talk to your dad, there's a good little chap.'

'You OK, babe?' Jackie was supervising the food mainly but had the instinct of the landlady she aspired to be for potential trouble. Speaking to Sally-Anne, she was looking at Derek, who chose to turn away from the bar, flushed as he approached the only reserved table in the place.

George made no acknowledgement of his son's arrival from his seat against the back wall. Derek had known Harry and Pete all his life and greeted both by name, with a slight nod to which only Pete responded in kind. Habits of politeness died hard in him, less pleased than anyone else in the room to see pitch up the boy – he would not call him a man – who had left Sally-Anne. At the same time, he was uneasily aware that he might owe his own opportunity with her to that same boy.

Derek walked round the table past Jane. Harry made no move to shift his chair to allow him to move in for a hug with George, if that had been his intention. He spoke to his father over the other man's head, not quite daring to offer a hand to shake.

'I'm sorry for your loss, Dad. Emma was always good to me, and I know how much she meant…'

George raised the palm of his left hand to quiet him. 'All you need to know is the kitty is fifty quid down if you want to have a drink with us. And leave yourself enough for a hotel in town if you're thinking of staying the night.'

'You know I haven't got… aw bollocks, all I wanted was to come and pay my respects. I wanted to be here for you as well, but it looks like you've got your precious mates hanging around like always.'

'Precious is right, they are and so is Emma. We'll talk another day, you and me, when I'm ready to be a dad again.'

'I think it's probably best if you leave, Derek. You've showed your face, fair enough, paid your respects.' Harry was now standing between father and son.

'You acting as minder for my dad now, Harry? Thought it was the other way round back in the day. Bit late to start playing the heavy now, too late to do it with me, anyway. If you've got your own nose in this business with the Wood family women, why don't you concentrate on keeping that clean?'

'Derek, I don't care what you think of the Wood family women, we can live with it.' Jane had scraped her chair back and was speaking to the younger man almost over his shoulder. 'Harry, if you think I'm plating up your food for you, you've got another think coming. Get yourself over to that buffet table with me. Please. Now.'

Without either of them wishing to appear to be stepping backwards one inch, Harry somehow squeezed past Derek.

'Thank God somebody remembered this isn't a wedding.' Margaret spoke loudly enough for all to hear, all of them with experience of those events ending in fistfights or worse.

It was the first thing to make George smile that day. 'Sit down and finish your free pint, Del. Thanks for making the effort.' He indicated the seat beside him just vacated by Harry.

George had lied about the amount per head to be pumped into the kitty, but not its existence. It was so typical of Pete to offer to manage it that his mates thought nothing of it giving him more time to exchange small talk with Sally-Anne or simply be in her presence. He took the hint of Jane and Harry moving off to suggest now might be a good time for him and Margaret to visit Reenie. She stood up and surprised him by taking his arm, then more by what she had to say on the way to the door.

'A sniff of the barmaid's apron and you're still all over the place, aren't you, Pete? Maybe I once found it endearing, or amusing, but there comes a time to act your age. Don't think being responsible with your mum gives you a pass in other areas of your life. I won't be made a fool of.'

'Wow, where did all that come from? Have you been sneaking an extra drink or two yourself, got a hip flask in your pocket? Sit down here a minute.'

She waited until he had also taken a seat, almost knee to knee with her. 'Some of us can talk about serious things without being pissed, Peter. I expect we'll have to listen to you and your mates get to it later on, with whatever you say forgotten tomorrow and nothing changing. I tell you what, stay here and get an early start at it. I'll take this visit to Reenie.'

'You? I thought you couldn't bear…'

'She's not so bad when you're not there, believe it or not. When you are, if you disappear for a few minutes to fetch coffee or whatever, she can get quite confidential with me.'

This worried Pete. 'You do know she's demented, literally demented. She doesn't mean anything of it, *it* doesn't mean anything, most of what she says.'

'I do though, I mean everything I say. Look, I'm sure she's OK, you stand down. Your mate probably needs you more today, and you do need a break. I get that.'

'But will you come back for me? How will I get home?'

'I'm sure you'll manage, and I'd rather you weren't tempted to do it with the car keys still on you. To be honest I'd rather go straight home from the hospital, but I'll swing back for you if you like.'

'No, that's all right, ta though. I can't see George's boy sticking around, so he may be grateful for the company later on. And Harry's got Jane to think of.'

'Plus a wife at home, just like you. There's always a taxi, or this marvellous new invention called Uber. I'm sure your little friend behind the bar knows how to work that.'

'Sally-Anne, Jane's daughter, you know her name, love.'

'Course I do, I've heard it in your dreams.'

'You what? Never. Are you going crazy like Mum?'

'Maybe, but that was just a little experiment, a sanity check if you like. Only thing I hear from you at night is snoring, but the look on your face just now told me more than I want to know. I suggest you follow Harry's example and get some food down you if you're going to keep on drinking at your current rate. It may be a long night.'

The Grand Mesalliance

The three friends' Rifleman reunions dragged themselves on, more sadly, like a crippled dog.

'What's the latest on Reenie, mate?' Harry asked Pete.

'Still waiting on accommodation for her. She's moved out of the Pilgrim, into St Mary's. They still have a few beds there, kind of halfway house. I won't let them discharge her back into Carlton Close. She can't look after herself anymore. I'm hoping we can wangle her into Melwood House. That's the best one I've seen and it's not too far from the Close.'

'Right. Our Kerry works there.' On the rare occasions he had picked his stepdaughter up from work, Harry had almost superstitiously preferred to stay in the car park waiting for her rather than cross the threshold. 'I thought it was more a hospice than sheltered accommodation or whatever? Are you still hoping to get her back home one day?'

'Hope's the last thing you lose.' Pete took another drink. 'I wish I never had to find out the difference between hospices, care and nursing homes. People die at Melwood. They soft-pedal the end-of-life care when you talk to them. Some go in voluntarily, so they've got everything from sheltered snug to last-chance saloon. It's a nice coincidence that it's close by, makes it easier for her old friends and neighbours to visit.'

'I'll get back to visiting her myself now I'm a free man. Same again?' George asked. As he went to the bar without waiting for a reply, the other two fell briefly silent. It was almost a fortnight since Emma's funeral, and he was looking worse than ever. His son had not stayed long at the wake, and the three men had ended up closing the bar before George went upstairs at the Horse. There was no invitation from Jackie for Harry this time.

'I'll put a word in with Kerry to look out for Reenie if you do get her into Melwood. How are you doing yourself, coping? I hear Sally-Anne's been a help? She's not such a bad kid.'

'I think I'm going mad if you really want to know the truth, Harry. I love her, that's the trouble. I can't stand the thought of losing her altogether.'

'That's only natural, mate, she's your mum. I remember…'

'I'm not talking about Reenie.'

'I didn't think you were,' Harry admitted. Watching George bring the three pints back with practised ease, he did not know which of his mates' misery to address. 'When are you two dossers getting back to the Tuesday-Thursday gang anyway? Cecil Ransom has decided to keep on self-isolating, but he's eighty-six for Christ's sake.' He almost added 'What's your excuse?' but realised he didn't want to hear them. He was getting tanked up more than usual on a Friday afternoon because he'd been summoned by Kerry to a family summit that evening, including not only Ellen but, something of a rarity, Sav. He and his wife could probably get away with sharing a bottle of wine but he always felt anything more than a single drink drew her disapproval. Did the two girls have an announcement of some kind to make? Couldn't be a pregnancy, he assumed, but you never knew nowadays. A wedding? What sort of role (if any) would he be expected to take in that?

Pete was the first to excuse his absence from MWGC. 'I don't like having my phone switched off in case the hospital calls, and I don't like playing with it left on. Can't concentrate on anything much, tell you the truth. Thank the Lord for small blessings I don't still have to go to work.'

'I find that helps, myself.' Never a chatterbox, George's contributions to general conversation had become rarer than ever. If they did not all huddle up against the autumn cold to join him in the smoking area he would be out there as much as indoors with them. 'If you can call it work, drinking a pint for every one I pull. People must stop pitying me soon, standing me drinks, wish I could stop myself. I could always get married, there is that option.'

'Oh yeah? Who's the lucky lady?' Pete was glad to think George had not entirely lost his sense of humour.

'I've had a proposal. Don't get jealous, Harry, it's young Jackie, least she thinks she's young cos my Em had a few years on her. Sister hardly cold and she's suggesting we could do worse. She says it's purely a business proposal, but I bet it's my body she's after.'

'You're having a laugh, right?' Harry could not say exactly what made him uneasy about his best mate's tone. He squashed a brief feeling of smugness that for once he had got the girl first.

'No, straight up. It is a leap year, like she said. I did think she was joking at first. Got her arse into gear quick, while I was still in mourning... in bits really...' He blinked fiercely and swiped a hand across his face. 'I would have got round to contacting the brewery sooner or later, somebody had to.'

'Perhaps she was only trying to help.' Pete, who hardly knew the woman, was as ever prepared to believe the best of her.

'Help herself, I'd say. If she knew how little return we got from running this place, and how hard Em had to work for it, she wouldn't be so keen to become a guvnor.'

'Well, she's got bar experience so she ought to know the trade, but I still don't see where you come in.' Harry tried to keep the tone light. 'Stud and stallion of the town, we can all see that, even if you do look like shit on toast just at present, but – now don't take this the wrong way – to marry you? She wants to *marry* you?'

'If she don't *want* to exactly, she don't want me hanging around the bar like a fart in a spacesuit either. The brewery have said they'll consider her for the tenancy, sympathy on the loss of her sister etc etc, understand Jackie was already playing a major part in running the business – pure bullshit that, we all know – but they prefer married couples.'

'Can they still say that? What about the couple of poofs who run the Red Hart?'

'They might be married, Harry. Anything goes nowadays. And I'm surprised your own women haven't dinned that sort of language out of you yet.'

'I hear you, Pete. Jane's sound. Kerry's a sweetheart and don't say much. Sav wouldn't stand for it and I wouldn't want to get on the wrong side of her. Never mind about gay, the one who's out back in the kitchen at the Hart looks a right miserable sod.'

'You still go there then?' George asked.

'If the price is right and the pint kept proper, I'm not prejudiced. But hold up, how did Emma hang on to the tenancy? You hadn't gone and got hitched to her on the quiet, had you? I don't remember any fucking stag do.'

'Not that, no. Brewery probably wouldn't have woken up if Jackie hadn't stuck her oar in, long as they keep taking their prime cut. Maybe Em's old man's name was still on the books, though he's been gone for years. You know I'm no good with paperwork. She took care of all that as well as running the whole pub, bless her. Jackie's not saying it would be a proper marriage, no sex or anything she reckoned. I said that sounded like marriage all right, so she wasn't exactly selling it to me. I don't know how you two find it, but sex isn't the main thing anymore, it's… shit, I'm going to start bawling if I'm not careful… the companionship I suppose, the company. And the odd cuddle. Anyway, I'll let you know what I decide, you can toss up for it, loser gets to be best man. Don't expect any bridesmaids to shag though, for all I hear you're both up and at it still.'

Pete would find whatever pretence he could to get Sally-Anne round Reenie's house, sometimes offering Pauline's Bella a longer walk than his owner could comfortably manage. Another positive feature of Melwood House was that it was determinedly dog friendly. He had stopped trying to involve Margaret in the choice of his mum's likely last home after he mentioned that to her.

'Why wouldn't it be? They'll have the inmates pissing and shitting everywhere, so dogs can't make things much worse.'

At first Pauline had been delighted to see them both whenever they called, but lately he had sensed a cooling in her attitude towards Sally-Anne in particular. Maybe it was disapproval of what she thought went on behind the closed doors of Reenie's flat; not frequently enough for Pete, but there were still moments of mercy for him to enjoy and treasure.

He tried to persuade her to a cuppa when she came out of the shower ready to be off – George was right, a cuddle would be nice sometimes, however much he prized the sex. As well as working again at the golf club now it was back in full swing, Sally-Anne was putting in some shifts at the Horse. He asked her whether his friend's unlikely tale of the would-be landlady's proposal had any substance.

'Why not?' She shrugged, sitting down in one of the flat's two armchairs to put on her make-up, a face mirror perched on Reenie's heavy old electric fire. 'It's only a bit of paper. He's not the catch you all think, it's like you and Harry worship him. If he had something about him in his day, maybe it rubbed off on his boy. Derek did make a fool of me, but I can't see

George doing that to Jackie. She's got her head screwed on. And he looks like a sad old man drinking himself to death.'

'He's always been able to take the booze better than any of us. Don't forget he's grieving over Emma as well. They might not have been married, but he was with her for longer than I remember him with most others.'

'And how do I stack up for you against "most others", Pete? What would you say if I was to propose to you?'

She had spoken lightly, but he took her question seriously. She could not read his face. He put his mug of tea on the mantelpiece, beside the framed photo of his mum and dad, and clumsily got on his knees in front of her chair, his hands on its arms as if to hem her in. That was how she felt, anyway. 'Hang on,' she yelped, 'what are you playing at?'

'Don't worry, I'm not about to propose, that would be on one knee. And I'm not going to beg either. I just want you to hear me out, not go flying out the door the minute I try to talk seriously to you.'

'All right, but you're making me claustrophobic. Get up for God's sake while you still can, wouldn't want you stiffening up in the wrong place.' She smiled at him and put a gentle hand on his cheek. He pushed himself backwards, resumed his own chair but pulled it closer to hers before speaking again. He put his hands on his own knees now instead of hers.

'For a start, there weren't any "most others" for me. I had one serious relationship before Margaret, who I met when she was a nurse and I was… she helped me recover after an accident. And I've always been faithful to Margaret. It was never a hardship either, not from religious conviction about the sanctity of marriage or anything like that. Even so, that Catholic upbringing can come back to bite you on the bum when you least expect it. I didn't think anything could ever develop between you and me. What you might have thought was barmaid banter or flirtation caught me by surprise, and soon it caught me good and proper. If you're one per cent serious in what you've just said, don't think I haven't gone much further in wondering if we could make a life together. Margaret's not a Catholic but we did get married in a Catholic church. I have thought of leaving her… and yes, you were behind those thoughts. But whether I could get married again, well, I guess I hadn't got that far.'

'Pete, Pete.' Only as she repeated his name did he realise how rarely she used it. 'You've gone way *too* far. I didn't want to get into any sort of religious discussion. I've been out of Sunday school a long time. I suppose

I was only daydreaming, joking with you bringing up George and Jackie. It's only natural a girl's thoughts turn in that direction when she's pregnant, and there aren't too many other candidates about.'

'What? What did you say? You're pregnant? So I might be…'

'Are you all right, Pete?' It was her turn to rise from her seat and kneel in front of him, taking his face between her hands. 'You've gone white as a sheet. Don't worry I won't be keeping the bab, and in any case it's got nothing to do with you. You couldn't be more in the clear as a jaffa.'

'A what?' He had trouble getting out the two syllables.

'Come on, don't tell me you're the only person in the country never to have watched *Fools and Horses*. A jaffa, seedless, can't have kids, firing blanks.'

'Who told you that?'

'I don't know. Haven't you and Margaret been married for ever? Maybe Mum or Dad mentioned something once when I was a kid. Anyway, that's what I always assumed. And you might have told me if it wasn't true.' Her tone became suddenly accusatory.

'Yes, I should have, would have. I assumed you were taking care of that side, and to be honest it was the last thing on my mind that first time. You're right Margaret and I never had kids, and we agreed that if it didn't happen it was neither of our faults, just – don't laugh, I don't know what she thought but I would say God's will. We agreed we'd never take the tests, neither of us, to avoid getting into the blame game. I suggested adoption but Margaret wouldn't have that either.' He was speaking more dispassionately now, eyes on a point somewhere above Sally-Anne's head. 'I thought I was being noble – I have these crazy notions sometimes – that I should let her go and have children if I was the problem. She kept her part of the bargain, never once reproached me. Perhaps she didn't mind if we never had any as much as I did. I see that now. Anyway, long story short, I took the tests behind her back, told myself it was for her benefit and found out there was no reason I couldn't become a father. And I never told her.'

Sally-Anne put a soft hand on his shoulder as she stood up. 'Thank you for telling me, Pete. And you didn't ever think that set you free to try and fulfil your own dream elsewhere? Noble might be one word. But it makes no difference.' She withdrew her hand when he tried to clasp it. 'Don't forget Derek. I can't say whose child it is – and don't start about

DNA tests and all that, I can read you like a book. I don't care who the father is, I'm not going to keep the baby. I can't.'

'But there's no sin worse than abortion.' The words were out before he knew they were coming, and she was at the door before he had any opportunity to speak further.

'It's a sinful world, Pete, about time you realised that,' she spat before shutting the living room door on him. He heard the outer one slam. He could not move. His eyes were on the photo of his parents, but they were too blurry to see.

Friday Night Dinner

Harry's Friday night dinner was a three-whip line with Kerry's girlfriend Sav slated to join her and Ellen. There was no sign of the Melwood House chef when he opened the door, not noticeably (he hoped) the worse for his Rifleman's afternoon; nor any Judy, he missed first, to hurl herself at his legs in frenzied greeting. When Kerry appeared from the kitchen she explained Sav was out walking her. 'She's doing us pasta tonight, Dad. We thought it would make a change from takeaway.'

'Long as she doesn't mind. Bit of a busman's holiday cooking for us after being at it all day.' He was not much of a pasta fan, but could always eat it, unlike some of the more exotic efforts the two women had tried on Ellen and him.

He brought them up to date on his mates' different trials, particularly mentioning Pete's efforts to get his mother into Melwood. Kerry was non-committal.

'We're usually full, but nothing is usual now. Higher turnover than I've ever seen and that's not a good thing like it might be in business. Mum was unlucky to catch it, but once she did she was luckier than plenty of others.'

'You're still not fully over it though, are you, Ellen?' His wife had hardly opened her mouth so far. She was sitting up on the settee rather than in her usual sprawl along it, though that might have owed more to the presence of Sav – he suspected Ellen found her intimidating; he had to force himself not to – than how she was feeling.

Kerry had brought him a big can of Kronenbourg and pint glass (knowing he preferred to pour for himself), to join them with their red wines. There was no sign of a drink for the other woman, but he knew she was teetotal so had nothing to be in a hurry about.

Judy was glad enough to see him when she was released from her lead in the doorway, followed by the bulky figure of Sav in jeans and what looked like a man's rugby shirt. He could not blame their dog for haring after her when she went into the kitchen. It was dinnertime for Judy too.

'OK, everything coming along nicely, prawn linguine, Harry. Hope that's all right for you?' Her brisk tone suggested she would not be heartstruck if it were not.

'You're spoiling me, ladies. Why do I get the feeling of a condemned man's last meal?' He had never seen the slightest display of public affection between Kerry and Sav, who had now preferred to take a hard chair by the kitchen door rather than the armchair left over for her, with him on the other and mother and daughter side by side on the settee. He saw them exchange a look, before Ellen inched herself forward in the seat – a tectonic shift, he thought uncharitably – ran a hand briefly across her face and began talking.

'Harry, I'll speak first because I don't want to do it at all. If I don't start and hide behind the girls I might never. You're right that I still don't feel well at all, but I do feel I have a life ahead of me again. I didn't think I was coming out of the Pilgrim, you know.'

'I do know, love,' he sympathetically mirrored her action by moving himself forward in his seat – they did cling a bit, he found. He meant to pay her tribute for bravery, but it was clearly not his turn to speak yet.

'I want to thank you for your support over that time. I really felt it.' Ellen's curiously dismissive hand gesture lessened the impact of her kind words.

He shook his head vigorously, a dismissive gesture of his own. The two younger women held their silence, though he doubted that would last.

'I realised there I wasn't ready to die, and when I came out I knew I couldn't go on living like I had been. Intensive care will take off a few pounds and following our dear prime minister I want to do my best to keep that good work going. Take better care of myself.'

'I'll take your word for it more than I would a politician's, any day.' He wished he had thought to reinforce her resolve in that direction, remarked on the weight loss of which she was apparently so proud.

'Especially *that* politician,' Sav chipped in with what sounded like the venom of a Remainer. Apart from both loving Kerry, he wondered if he would ever find any common ground with her.

Ellen glanced at her daughter, who took her hand. Blood would always side with blood in the end. 'I can't go on living with you, Harry, if you can say we still do. If you want me to go into more detail on the reasons why, I will.'

'Please yourself. Or just tell me where you're planning to move, and when.'

He saw his wife redden. Sav stiffened in her seat before snatching up Judy (sitting peaceably at her feet), as if to distract herself from any more violent move. Kerry was suddenly their spokeswoman, in the calm and reasonable tones she must be well used to deploying at work.

'I hope you won't get defensive and unreasonable about this, Dad. It doesn't change the way I feel about you when I say I think Mum is doing the right thing, and that she has the right to stay in the home she's made for you – for us – over the years.'

'One he treats like a flophouse, only appearing when he wants something.' He had recognised Ellen's flushed face as a sign of rising temper rather than embarrassment, not for nothing had they been together twenty years. She turned back from Kerry to face him. 'You already took the decision to move, to find whatever you're after elsewhere. I'll say it again, I can go into more details if you want and if I give them to a lawyer there's enough to take you for every penny you've got. I'm going nowhere.'

Although his own temper was rising, Harry strove to sound as calm as Kerry. 'Everything favours the woman in divorce cases nowadays – if we're talking about that, don't be afraid to say the word, I'm not Tammy Wynette's little man you have to spell it out for me. Even so, last I looked it was my money bought us this house. All right you made it a home, and I don't begrudge you equal shares, but no more than that.'

He had given not so much as a courtesy glance in Sav's direction, but she put a bemused Judy back on the floor to speak. 'Harry, I didn't want to get involved in this family discussion, but now I'm here – at Ellen and Kerry's invitation – I can't stay silent.'

'You *are* family, Sav, you've got every right to speak.' The conviction in her voice and the look Kerry gave her partner made him see it was true, confirmed by the nod and smile Sav returned her.

'Kerry and me have been doing some thinking as well. We want to take things to the next level between us.'

'What's that then? Getting married? Having kids? I mean if so, good luck to you, to each their own, but is it strictly relevant here?'

'Sav and Kerry will be living here with me, Harry. Deal with it.'

'Thank you, Ellen, can I just finish what I need to say?' (Harry noted the flash of impatience from Sav with a muted glee that any such coming together would not be frictionless.) 'I don't want you to think I'm coming here as a freeloader, Harry. It's true Kel and me don't have the money to put down for a house of our own, but we're both going to pull our weight, help Ellen financially as well as to live her best life.'

'Just as a matter of interest, does that best life exclude all men or is it only me?' Judy had come over to Harry – at last – but stroking her as she knocked at his knee was not yet soothing him.

'Dad, don't embarrass yourself. This is about you and Mum, as individuals, but I won't put up with your golf-club petty prejudices and outdated thinking. I might for myself, have done if it comes to that, but I won't take it for others I love. Which still includes you, let me say. Why mention lawyers, Mum, can't we talk sensibly between ourselves?'

Sensing a chink in the women's united front, Harry focused on the one he felt most sympathetic to him. 'No problem. I hear you, Kerry, but I feel kind of outnumbered, you know three to one. That's all it is.'

Ellen had heard enough. She could not quickly lever her bulk out of the settee, but she had her fists balled into its cushions as she screamed at him. 'If that's all it is, go tag your fucking girlfriend to join in then, see if I care.'

Sav suddenly found their dinner needed her attention in the kitchen. Kerry got her arms as far round her mother as she could. After an initial attempt to shrug her off, Ellen subsided into her and started to cry.

'Where are you going, Dad?'

It was the tears Kerry was blinking back that changed his mind when he was already on his feet to get out of the lesbian madhouse. 'Into the kitchen to fetch myself another can. Maybe see if Sav needs a hand. I'll bring the bottle back for you two.'

Steam was rising from the pasta as the chef strained it at the sink. 'Will you set the table please, Harry?' She spoke over her shoulder. 'And pass me four bowls out of the cupboard for the salad if you don't mind.'

He realised he was hungry. He did as she asked.

Down Memory Lane

Despite their promises to do so at Reenie's ninetieth birthday party three years earlier, and the genuine affection between them, Peter Goodwin and his cousin Marion had not kept in touch more than by Christmas cards and the occasional phone call since then. When his mother was hospitalised, he had thought first to write rather than call with the news. He had revived an old habit of keeping a diary, one he had given up in the face of derision from his then new wife. 'Do you honestly think anyone's going to be interested in what you have for dinner every day?'

He had lost the diaries somewhere down the years, so could not remember if Margaret's judgement of their banality was justified. The aim of his new exercise book (it was too late in the year to buy a cut-price diary from the last one, too early for the Christmas gift season) was to compartmentalise Reenie's suffering, gain a distance from it. Menus did still feature, her favourites among the Marks & Spencer microwaves to which he had treated her from her own funds – not wishing to give any leverage to Margaret on additional expenditure from their joint account she monitored far more closely than ever his diaries. He was now cheerlessly finishing off the cottage and shepherd's pies, the chicken casserole meals for one from her freezer before or after visiting his mum in Melwood House. The visits were harder than the bangers and mash to keep within the pages of his daily exercise book.

In the end he decided it was too chilly to write rather than talk to family about Reenie's state. Although he understood Aunt Ruth, who would turn ninety herself in October, still had all her mental faculties, he thought it better to let her daughter mediate the message. He reviewed his notes to be sure of having the right data to give Marion. Or was it to prove he was a dutiful son, on the ball? Such personal reflections were more and more finding their way into his jottings, as were others of equal or guiltily greater concern to him.

'Hello, Marion. Thanks for getting back to me. As I said in my voicemail, it's not the worst news about Reenie, but it's not that great either. Before I fill you in, please tell me Aunt Ruth is OK. I've been kind of assuming no news is good news.'

'There isn't much in the way of good news when they get to that age, Pete, but you're right, she's bearing up, still as active as this damned pandemic lets any of us be. Don't tell me Reenie's come down with COVID?'

'No, she's been spared that, so far. I was going to say luckily, but sometimes I wonder if it is such a mercy. She's taken a couple of falls since the summer, and whether or not it's related she's been diagnosed with dementia. Hopefully you won't be too familiar yet with all the stages of caring and carers, we kept her in her own flat for a while with people going in to see to her but now I've had to put her into a home.'

'I'm so sorry, Pete. When was this?'

He could be precise. 'She was discharged from the local hospital last Friday, 11 September. They like to get them out before the weekend if possible, but I'd made sure it was straight into Melwood House. She needs constant supervision now.'

'Is she bedbound?'

'No. She *was* mainly in bed for the first two or three days, from muscle wastage after being in the hospital, where you know they can't be walking them up and down as much as they need, sometimes not as far as the toilet, poor devils. It was for the best at that stage, she would have been disorientated. Now she gets up most days, going into the common room, getting to know the other patients, residents, inmates, whatever the right word is. They call the section for the ones with dementia "Memory Lane".'

'And is she up to receiving visitors? I'm sure Mum will want to see her if possible. I'm not just saying this, but I was going to get in touch with you anyway about a do we're planning for her ninetieth in October – nothing as big as the lovely one you gave Reenie – we were hoping you might be able to come back to the Fens for it.'

'Maybe we can yet. She lives in the past more and more, when she's making any sense at all. I thought she'd be devastated not to be back in

Carlton Close, but she loves to tell me that I've swindled her out of her home and this is the best of a bad job until we can find another place for her. There's a bench in the hallway by the back doors at Melwood. She's taken to sitting there as soon as she gets dressed, afraid to miss the bus, she tells them. Maybe it's one to East Anglia she's waiting for.'

'Pete, are you still there?'

He took a deep breath. 'Yeah, line's not great. Anyway, they have wheelchairs they let you borrow if you want to take your family out, gives the staff a break I suppose. I've done it a couple of times, just to lunch at Sainsbury's and a quick tootle round the aisles, but let's see how it goes. And as she's getting settled, you might be able to come up and see her here.'

'Now you say that, it must be her own birthday in a couple of weeks. Do you think she'd insist on us coming on the exact day like I remember she did for her ninetieth?'

'She still tries to insist on a lot of things, Mar, but I think we can make her birthday whenever it would suit you.'

'And how are you and Margaret coping with it all? It must be tough on you both.'

'What can you do? We have to look after her as best we can but try to keep on living our own lives as well. You probably know the score, especially having your own kids. How are Karl and Lesley?'

'Mixed, I'd have to say. He's on the point of divorce, and she is about to make me a grandma again.'

'A new baby in the family. Listen, Marion, I've got a call coming in from the home so I'm going to have to leave you now. Love to Aunt Ruth, and let's make sure we do get together, whether out your way or ours. Let's make it happen.'

'OK Pete, you take care. Love to all, especially Aunt Reenie, give her a big hug from me.'

They had never been much of a hugging family, but they could talk about it. He sometimes wondered if he was laying on a show for the Melwood staff (Harry's stepdaughter Kerry had said she would keep a special eye on his mum, and he was making a point of getting to know the others' names without having to read them off their chests) when he tried to hold Reenie's hand and on leaving put his arms briefly around her. He hoped they did not realise he was also checking that she did not shrink from physical contact. Without having seen anything to make him suspicious, he was morbidly concerned at the horror stories you heard of patients in such facilities being physically abused. He did fear his mum might not endear herself to staff for different reasons, with comments they could not fail to hear on anything from their weight ('you know the one, the big fat lump') to the colour of their skin or their accent. Those were linked, in that if she saw a darker complexion she would find it harder to hear the person, however precise and fluent their English.

Although protocols about masks and social distancing were still enforced, he was able to visit his mother daily, something to which he waited in vain for Margaret to object. A violent row would lead to him storming out and beginning a new life. He recognised it as a fantasy – violent rows had never been his style – while indulging himself with an admixture of what he thought of as hard-nosed business decisions. Checking for post on Reenie's doormat – junk circulars mainly, the pizza flyers would never have had a hope with her – he thought about renting or selling her flat. Melwood House would not keep Reenie for free once the six-week grace period ran out, when fees would start accruing at an alarming level.

He was more cautious about indulging himself in fantasies of a life with Sally-Anne. To be starting afresh with a beautiful young wife – why not go the whole hog, offer the ring? – and a baby in a pushchair, their baby as he had convinced himself it was or would be, that was pushing his luck too far.

It was no stretch to play the besotted, bewildered old fool struggling to cope. He left Sally-Anne a lengthy voice message on WhatsApp, thanking her first for continuing to visit Reenie in her new surroundings ('Your fancy piece was here,' his mother had alerted him, impatiently giving the name when he had mildly asked which one). He then put it to her as a business proposition, an extra shift in her gig economy, to help him transport his mum outside the home, initially for a lunch and then possibly a longer trip to visit his aunt and cousin. He was acknowledging a genuine need, squeamish about having either to sit his mother on a toilet or clean her up, one of which would surely become necessary if they were out in the world together more than ten minutes away from her new home.

Aunt Ruth proved reluctant to come the two hours from the other side of Ely to visit her only remaining sister. He had to agree with the merciless judgement his cousin apologetically retailed that Reenie had had more than enough time before 'falling bad' to come to them after her ninetieth, when they had made the effort. Marion suspected the bluster was hiding a fear of what she would find, a possible foreshadowing of what Ruth herself might face; he could understand. They were more than welcome to come to Ruth's own birthday celebrations before the clocks went back, obviously a tight affair with COVID still not subdued but it would be marked. He said they would see, had to take everything day by day, but thanks for the invitation.

He wondered whether there was a fear too behind his wife's reluctance to visit Reenie, or whether it was more a licensed continuation of her attitude while his mother had still been in relatively good health, in her own home. He had to respect Margaret's need to continue self-isolating. Her splenectomy pulled out of the hat did not make him feel any better about the failure to share the results of his fertility tests, though both could have argued they had only been trying to spare their partner grief or concern.

Another birthdate than his mother's and aunt's was much on his mind. One reason for his barrage of messages to Sally-Anne was that he still had hopes of saving their baby. He could not help thinking of it as such, vague though she had been about its most likely conception date. He did not believe abortion was murder, was trying hard not to view it as a sin; still, he could not repress a horror of it as the worst possible outcome for child (self-evidently) and mother. And what about the father? Should he not have a voice? During his many years with no expectation of becoming one, he now considered he had minimised their skin in the game. He had no one to turn to on these matters except Sally-Anne, whose primacy in the decision he accepted, hoping only she had not yet acted on the one she had insisted was already made.

COVID had accelerated an existing trend where many pubs did not open at all on Mondays (except for the brief period of eat out to fuck up), some not at all during the day except at weekends. Reenie's ninety-third birthday fell on Monday, 28 September 2020 and Sally-Anne, without a shift that day, had agreed to meet him at Melwood House to take her to lunch at the Featherbed Lane British Legion. This had been a weekly date for mother and son in her better days, one that met her demanding criteria of simple fresh-cooked food and reasonable prices. Reenie had usually insisted on paying before he took her debit card into his own wallet with full control of her finances. One of many distressing aspects of her changed circumstances was that she was constantly begging him for money, to get a bus if not a taxi, she said, just a couple of pounds. He gave her some coins one day, to be warned off doing so again by Dasha on the Melwood staff. It was not only that they might be a temptation to others; they had found them in Reenie's underpants, no doubt the only safe stash she could think of until she could seize her opportunity to escape. She had her own paranoia about her fellow patients, accusing one of them loudly of being a thief when she turned up at lunch one day wearing Reenie's slippers.

Before agreeing to join them for the birthday lunch, Sally-Anne had laid down a law on no talk of babies or sex, though the latter had somehow retreated since she mentioned the former. Was he nothing more than a classic case of Elvis-syndrome, only able to see women as mother or lover? He did not go to the outer reaches of picturing Sally-Anne as either Madonna or whore, was clear this would be no virgin birth. He could not determine whether there might still be the prospect of any birth. Was she looking fuller in the face? There was no give-away stomach swell, but would that come later in a pregnancy? How late was abortion feasible? Was there still hope? Did a putative father have any legal rights? Was it Billy Crystal's voiceover he heard, promising him at the end of *Soap* the answer to all these questions and more in the next episode once he got the girl in front of him again? She had reacted badly to it before, almost violently, so he would not claim he loved her. Surely she could not object to him saying he wanted to take care of her. Her and the baby, and Reenie made three. One more question, Billy. Would he be up to the job?

No Hat-trick Heroes

'Do you want the chance of a hat-trick, Harry?'

'Long time since I've pissed, puked and shit myself, and hope I've got a few more years before they put me in nappies again. You planning a bender then, George?'

'If you like. Two out of three ain't bad, but I've always felt a bit guilty you didn't get to stand best man for me with Melanie as well, good cause or not. It won't be a church do or anything this time, just registry office but I'd be glad to have you with me as witness.'

Harry remembered watching Melanie's Down's syndrome brother hand over the rings, without the slightest envy of the poor kid. He felt the same about George now. 'So you've caved in to Jackie after all?'

'Who else? I don't want to be barred from the Horse. I probably love that more than her, but she's already kind of family. She did show me she cared for Em at the end. I'm assuming you've moved on yourself, if you were ever stuck on her. You don't have to come though, I can pull in people off the street, half eleven Friday, see you and Pete at the Rifleman's from half twelve as usual. No need to make too big a deal of it. One thing though – what you've already said is said, but don't go badmouthing my future wife to me or others. You in or not?'

'Course I'm in, mate. But won't you need two witnesses?'

'I'd say bring Jane along, but she's no friend to Jackie. I thought it was only fair to let her have one pick, turns out she hasn't got many more mates than I have. She's chatty with Sally-Anne since they've been working together, so it might be her.'

'Christ, mate, and does she know about your history with that girl? Not that I know much myself. Are you ever going to open up about it?'

'See how many drinks you stand me at the stag party. You've been yapping like a terrier at a cornered rat so long I might tell you, just to shut you the fuck up.'

'Stag party? Now you're talking. Where we going? Prague, Dublin, down the Smoke?'

'No fear. It's after the wedding. We're doing it all arse-about-face. I suppose neither of us wants to admit there might be any real feeling behind us getting hitched, no writing in for a shout-out on *Sunday Love Songs*. She's having a hen party stroke pub crawl after the registry with Sally-Anne and maybe a few others. We should be safe in the Rifleman's, so I thought we might make a Leo of it there, invite a couple of people from the TT gang, but if it turns out just me, you and Pete that would be fine too.'

'Sounds more like a wake. Pete could do with a break from his own life, if you ask me. He's taken the thing with Reenie hard. OK it is shit, but he's worse than I'd ever have expected from that.'

'All the more reason to drown our sorrows together. I'm depressed myself, and I'm getting married next fucking week.'

Pete had detoured on their way to the Legion to avoid passing the turn-off to Carlton Close, where he had thought it too risky to take Reenie back to visit her old friends. He never knew whether the precaution was necessary or not, and perhaps that varied from day to day.

Arriving late as usual, if not *as* late as usual, Sally-Anne joined them at the club when he had already put Reenie's customary lemon and lime in front of her and made a dent in his pint of London Pride. He had seen the girl dolled up to the nines but he preferred her as she was today, without make-up and looking the younger for it, dressed simply enough in jeans and baggy T-shirt.

'You look lovely,' he said honestly. 'Are you feeling well?'

'I'm fine. To put you out of your sneaky misery snooping I'll tell you right off I haven't had the D and C yet, that minor surgical procedure. I've got until near enough Christmas but I'll do it before then, can't be out of shape for the party season.'

He wanted to tell Sally-Anne to call the abortion what it was, angry that she was almost teasing him about it. He tried to credit her instead with sparing Reenie inconvenient information. His mother may no longer have been capable of following full conversations, even wearing charged hearing aids in the correct ears as Pete had ensured she was today, but she did like to seize the odd word to riff happily or – more often – spitefully on it.

'Not much of a birthday party this, is it, gal? Not like the one I had when I was a hundred. Do you remember that? He took me to the golf club then, we're obviously not good enough for that nowadays. When you get too old, people forget about you. That or he's ashamed of me, I shouldn't wonder. Or been told by his mother he shouldn't spend his cash on the likes of us.'

His wife, a couple of years older than Pete, had not found it as amusing as he did the first time Reenie referred to her as his mother. It had soon palled on him too, in truth. If reminded that she herself was his mother, Reenie would usually admit it, but with ever less conviction, increasingly as if only humouring him while hugging the truth to herself. 'She means Margaret,' he answered Sally-Anne's enquiring look with a brief smile, before responding to Reenie as he could not yet quite stop himself doing, in tones of reason. 'Remember I told you, Mum, the golf club don't do food except for big parties, so we'll save that for your ninety-fifth, then have an almighty bash when we can show off your telegram from the queen.'

Sally-Anne took the old lady by the hand to draw her still bright blue eyes. 'That one was a great party. I think it was the first time me and you had a proper chat together. With only us three here today, we can do that better than in a big group.'

'Two's company, three's a crowd.' Reenie tapped a finger against the side of her nose then pouted her lips to it. 'So you lovebirds would rather be alone, you haven't been married to him thirty years. I told him he can have the divorce papers easy as wink, I won't stand in his way. All I ask is he gets me out of that place. There's buses every day but they never stop for me however much I wave. I want to go home again. I'm not from round here, you know. He can go then, long as he leaves me with a roof of my own over my head.'

Sally-Anne was taken aback by the intensity of Reenie's plea. Pete tried to help her out. 'We'll talk about that later, Mum, but let's get you fed first. Do you want the soup then a jacket with cheese? The usual?'

'Depends on the soup. Find out what it is, first.'

'I'll go and ask, Reenie.' Sally-Anne was out of her chair and gently letting the other woman's hand go. She gave Pete a look in which he thought he saw pity or sympathy, at odds with the sharpness of her next words. 'Have you started a tab, or have I got to buy my own drink? I need a big vodka Red Bull. Take that look off your face, Pete, it doesn't matter. I could be drinking gin by the bottle in a bathtub. Maybe I ought to try that, old-school remedies. Lighten up, man, for Christ's sake, don't try to drag me down with you. Let's make it a good birthday for your mum, as far as we can.'

The lunch went OK. Reenie ate most of the bread roll that came with her soup (a minestrone acceptable when he sold it to her as vegetable), but only a couple of spoonfuls of the liquid under her own volition. She allowed him to feed her one or two more, before batting his hand away the better to complain to Sally-Anne about her current housemates. 'They're all nuts,' she repeated more than once, after it drew a smile from the girl the first time. She ate some of her jacket potato but roundly refused a dessert, casting Pete once more as his father. 'You'll only say I get fat, and you don't want me anymore as it is.'

While family and friends were free to visit patients at Melwood whenever they liked, joining them (sometimes helping them) to eat if they wished, the afternoons were generally a quiet time. Apart from the three squares of breakfast, lunch and tea, the most active periods were the morning bustle of medication rounds and any group activities – Pete had seen Reenie resolutely refuse to bat a balloon one volunteer was lobbing to a half-circle of residents – then the sundowning spurt of anxiety some suffered. As night fell, they would become more acutely aware that they were not where they wanted to be, not in a happy place. At times the fever would spread to others not normally affected, a raggle-taggle platoon following the boldest up and down the corridors as best they could, to closed doors at each end. The staff would sometimes infiltrate them, mainly to ensure nobody found a tool with which to attack the doors or injured their own feeble fists against them.

The biscuits and pastries in the visiting area where hot and cold drinks were also available were a favourite with Reenie and indeed Pete. Desserts of crumbles, pies and roly-polies with custard took him back to his childhood, when Reenie would make them for him and Dad. The chef would also produce a splendid birthday cake for all patients. Whether the celebrant was in a state to recognise let alone eat it, there were always plenty of takers.

Kerry had agreed to bring out Reenie's cake in the afternoon lull, so that Pete could be there with his mother. Sally-Anne needed some slight persuasion to join them, with Reenie's sudden enthusiasm for the treat proving more effective than his urging. He had asked Pauline, Reenie's bosom pal in the Carlton Close community, to let her other friends know there would be tea and a slice if they should want to stop by. She and another lady whose name he was glad to remember as Connie arrived in the Melwood car park at almost the same time as them. Reenie's main interest and excitement was at seeing Pauline's Lab Bella, who minded as little as the humans that she was now being addressed as Sausage.

Pride in her advanced years had not yet deserted Reenie. One of the oldest in the home, she frequently pretended an interest in other patients' ages, so she could top them. She was only temporarily disconcerted when one potential competitor answered with the Swiftian saw, 'As old as my tongue and a bit older than my teeth.' Persisting, to draw an exasperated, sarcastic 'thirty' from Mary, Reenie chose to take that as year of birth rather than age, triumphing with, 'Well, I was born in 1927 so that makes me older than you.'

When Kerry appeared with the Victoria sponge (another of Peter's boyhood favourites), candles and all, along with a smiling happy birthday chorus from the other staff on shift, it was to half a dozen people around Reenie on a settee with Sally-Anne at her side, Bella/Sausage nuzzling her knees and Pete at her shoulder. She could still be trusted with the big cake knife – her arguments with Mary had never quite escalated to physical violence, though threats of it were not lacking – but it gave Peter a pang to see her puzzled by it, remembering the casual competence of her ninetieth. He awkwardly guided her hand as Pauline eased her dog aside, to be invited back by Reenie as soon as she had her slice, feeding the Lab a sizeable chunk and about to take the next bite from it herself until Sally-Anne stayed her hand.

'It's my cake, it's my birthday, you get off me. Georgie, tell your fancy piece to leave me alone and get her own cake. They think they can have their cake and eat it nowadays, but you tell her.'

'It's OK, Mum, we'll leave the rest of that piece for Sausage now.' He avoided looking at Pauline, who might not have appreciated her already portly dog being fed so much or realised he only meant it as a distraction, not a serious offer.

'I'm ninety-nine now and it's my birthday. And you said Ruth would be here. Where is she? I didn't expect you, thought you'd be off gallivanting, but you said she'd be here.'

'No, Mum, I said I'd been talking to your sister Ruth, and she wished you a very happy birthday, but I didn't say she'd be coming.' He realised he was playing as much to their audience as Reenie, not wishing them to judge him as guilty as he so often felt himself to be. 'How about we go to see her on her birthday, coming up soon, would you like that?'

'If she can't come to see me, why should I?' She raised a trembling finger at him. 'She's no better than me. And she's three years younger, you know,' she told Sally-Anne. Then all the aggression went out of her voice. 'But I would like to see our Ruth. I would like to go home. Will you take me, love? I can't make him, but perhaps you can make him take me home.'

Kerry knelt down in the spot recently vacated by Bella before Peter had a chance to try to spare Sally-Anne any embarrassment. 'Shall we talk about that another day, Reenie?' the carer suggested. 'Will you help me look after all our visitors for now, make sure everyone's got their piece of cake and cup of tea? You always look after your guests.'

It was true. She could no longer bustle about serving, but Reenie suddenly became attentive to Pauline and Connie, as once upon a time in Carlton Close. 'I won't get up, you know where everything is, the kettle's boiled and this little girl will help you to the cake, or one of these chocolates my Petie bought me. He's not a bad boy, really. Just like his dad, a wandering eye, that's all.'

As soon as they cleared the double-door exit, the girl took his arm. 'So your mum knows all about your wandering eye, Petie. What made it wander to me?'

'She would tell you to stop fishing.'

'What do you mean?'

'For compliments. You're beautiful, Sally-Anne, and you know it.' He was careful not to turn to face her as they walked, linked, towards his car, knowing any sign of seriousness would be likely to frighten her off. 'You were great with Mum, I want to thank you for that. Can we talk about you coming with us to East Anglia for the day, visit her sister like you can tell she wants to? I'd pay you full shift rate, cos I'd expect you to help me look after her. It may be her last chance.'

'Don't be so morbid, Pete.' But she squeezed his arm. 'It's a lovely afternoon and I've got to admit I'm glad to be out in the fresh air again. If you promise not to nag me, I might let you treat me to a pint of cider before you drop me off home. If that's not too much trouble?'

'No trouble at all, best idea I've heard all day. How about The Oak on the canal?'

Not wishing to risk losing her to an ill-advised word, he was silent on the short drive to the pub, quiet at that time of the afternoon and with only one narrowboat alongside – he had not been there since before the pandemic, when his memory was of much more traffic. He settled her at an outside table where they could talk without fear of being overheard, suiting equally her desire to smoke. She was already well into a Lambert & Butler when he returned from the bar with their two pints. She had met his suggestion of a half for her with derision and a careful specification of the bottled cider she wanted, with ice please.

'I hope you don't find it upsetting being around Reenie. She's not your responsibility. And I keep forgetting, it's not that long ago since you lost your dad.'

'That's spooky. Are you telepathic or something? I was just thinking about him, Reenie confusing you with *your* dad and all that. Thinking about when he told me I was adopted. So it wouldn't be blood on blood.'

'You're adopted? I never knew that.'

'Well, I wasn't for long. I wasn't at all, actually. It was a story he told me.'

Peter had not heard her speak of Andrew, not been close enough to her at the time of his death to offer other than conventional condolences. Something in her tone made him want to change the subject, something else made him feel she wanted to talk, in a way they had not yet done. He made one stab at restoring a lighter tone. 'What, when you were a kid if you'd been naughty or something? Pretending to disown you, like?'

'I wasn't a kid anymore. No, I was a kid, I *was*, but it wasn't a game. I was a teenager, a young teen when he started saying we weren't the same as a normal father and daughter, the love we felt for each other. Didn't have to be, anyway.'

'Please God, you're not talking about… not Andy?' He tentatively reached out across the table, but she ignored his hands, drawing one leg back to straddle her bench, looking away towards the pub.

'Not good old Andy, oh no, not my daddy. It was all my fault, I was just a stupid kid. Wild child they used to say, back then. He said he would always protect me whatever happened, always look after me. And I did go wild, boy crazy that was another thing I heard about myself. Crazy anyway, with men too not just boys, you must know that part. I survived, lived to have one lovely little girl, my Maddie, but I let another die so this will be the second I've killed off. Don't cry for me, Argentina. This is not my first rodeo. Give me your credit card,' she ordered. 'I need to go to the loo and I'll get us another round on the way back. You look as if you could use a whisky.'

'You got that right. I'll get the drinks. You just go to the toilet.'

She hurried off. He was not far behind, more frightened than anything else that she would run away. He got her a double vodka Red Bull, for the first time without disapproval, and himself a double Jameson's, heavily iced to prevent himself tossing it off immediately and immediately ordering another.

He was on the point of asking the barman if he could go into the ladies to check on – what should he call her? – when Sally-Anne emerged, pale but not crying. She picked up her drink and led him back to their table. She did not object when this time he sat beside her. It was probably more comfortable for them both not to be facing each other, he thought.

'Sally-Anne, that must have been a terrible experience and if you want to say anything else about it, ever, I'll be more than happy – fuck, that's not the word, I'll be more than ready to listen. I had no clue you might already have been in this situation, but you must understand the outcome doesn't have to be the same. You poor kid, I can't say how sorry I am, not just for the past but for the baby you're carrying now. I should have been a lot more careful, a lot more respectful of you.'

She turned to look at him now. 'This is not about you, Pete. I'd have no complaints if every man I've known was as respectful as you. No, I'm the one that should have been careful. It's hard to fall in love – I only did that once, with Maddie's father. Still, I should have known how easy it is for me to fall pregnant and taken more care.'

'Don't blame yourself, don't turn it all inwards. I've done plenty of that and it doesn't help. Cards on the table, I don't know if I should say I love you. Maybe I'm just an old sleazebal_ taking advantage of your youth and beauty, and the wonderful, totally unexpected chance you gave me to get close to it. It would be crazy for us to marry. That doesn't stop me making you the offer as seriously as I've said anything in my life. I'll divorce Margaret if you say the word. God forgive me, I'll do it without enough regret, and make you my wife as soon as legally possible.'

'Don't be ridi—'

'No, hush please, just a minute, I'll soon be done. If that one doesn't suit – and I can see it might not, I'm nobody's dream lover – here's another proposal. I'll put my name on the baby's – on your child's – birth certificate if you like, and if you prefer not I'll still make myself financially responsible for him or her.'

'Yeah, all you have to do is outlive George and Harry, then you can pass on the tontine money my dad so kindly left you all to fall out over. It's not going to happen, Pete. Your fertility tests were what, thirty years ago? I'm not sure how to put it delicately, so I'll be blunt. What about if your old jizz can still produce a kid, like one with two heads or something. I won't risk bringing more damaged goods into the world.'

'There are tests for that sort of thing.'

'Right, and then you wouldn't mind an abortion? Then it would be what, a termination, a mercy killing, a medical intervention. And there's no tests for the damage in my head,' she added.

'You mustn't think of yourself in that horrible way, not as "damaged goods". Don't forget the daughter you're bringing up already, and doing a great job from everything I see and hear. And don't forget the baby may not be mine, with my funky old spunk.' As he had hoped, this drew a smile from her. 'None of what I say is conditional on that. I'm being selfish enough as it is, to want to be with you. Will you at least promise to think about what I've said? Both proposals stand.'

'Well, thank you for them. You're a lovely guy, Pete, but you need to get it out of your head that we can ever be together as a long-term couple. That would be too weird for me, more than I can get my head round. I want someone I can grow old with, I still have that sort of dream sometimes, not the nightmare of my father – someone of my father's generation,' she quickly amended. 'It's not right. Don't push me on it. I'm going to be Billie

Blunt again, don't hang your head.' She raised it, cupping his chin in her hand. 'I'm done with promising men things, Pete. Except I will help you out with Reenie as much as I can. I'll go with you and her to East Anglia in a couple of weeks if you like.'

'I hear you about me. Thanks for talking straight. But the baby, in the meantime you won't…?'

'Don't take it as any kind of encouragement or commitment, but I don't need to do anything about the baby before then.'

And that was as much as she would say.

PART FOUR

TRIUMPH AND TRAGEDY 2020

Le Petit Pierrot

'If they say a second marriage is the triumph of hope over experience, what is a third?' Jane asked. 'Or is it his fourth, fifth, which?'

On the eve of George's wedding, Harry had invited her out to dinner at Market Welham's only French(ish) restaurant, flowers in advance for the terrible state he expected to be getting into after the ceremony the next day. Uneasily aware that his own next marriage, which he was now convinced could only be to Jane, would be his third, he framed his reply carefully.

'I'd say a third marriage is one between hope and experience, with every prospect of a happy ending. This may be George's fourth, but one was over before they brushed the confetti off their clothes. In his case I'd say it's a last fuck-you throw of the dice, or throwing in the towel if you prefer, almost a gesture of despair.'

'My heart bleeds for him. How flattering for the bride. When she could have done so much better with you.'

That had to hang for a minute as *Le Petit Pierrot* waiter brought their first courses. Harry had been joking him when he asked if they served foie gras but the kid's snotty reaction had not pleased him. Buttering the toast for his anodyne opener, he tried to reassure his partner, hoping she was only ragging him for form's sake.

'I don't pretend to be any kind of catch, Jane. Every day I tell myself how lucky I am to be with you.' That raised a faint smile as well as her eyebrows. 'I left Jackie behind a long time ago, and I wish you would.'

'Has your friend left as many broken hearts behind as you?'

'I meant I forgot about her, stopped caring for her if you prefer, not that I was the one who did the dumping. Look love, if this is about George, let's talk about George. You've got a down on him, and he's my best mate. I've never heard him speak badly about you, but you must have your reasons. Is it something to do with him and Sally-Anne?'

'What about him and Sally-Anne? What's he said about her? You men, always bragging to each other about your conquests, that horrible term I heard Dean and her bandying about once, body count.'

'Don't link me to Dean. If I knew what happened between George and your daughter, I wouldn't be asking. Me and him have both probably got a lot we shouldn't be proud of in our past relationships – a few regrets, all that bullshit. As Jack Nick said to Helen Hunt, you're helping me to be a better man. Whatever mistakes George may have made, he always kept his relationships with women strictly between themselves. I never once heard him brag, and I never heard a word from him about Sally-Anne.' He felt it best not to mention the brutal language George had used of Jane's daughter not so long ago, when trying to warn Pete off her.

'Omertà, or is it Prizzi's honour, I wouldn't be surprised if you old little Englishmen think of it as something Hollywood like that; keeping your own business between yourselves, women to be fucked or married and ideally one or more for each function.'

She took a decent shot at her large Chardonnay. 'I never had reason to believe Andrew was unfaithful to me, he was more of a homebody, but I wouldn't put anything past any of you. All I heard of what went on between George and Sally-Anne was from Drew.'

'You don't have to say anything else if it's upsetting for you.'

'Damn right it's upsetting for me. The thought of him casually going off to get married tomorrow, while Sally-Anne is still stuck in the same self-destructive cycle, it gets to me. And to the sister of his ex, when was it she died, a week ago already?'

'He's got his own self-destructive cycle going. The quacks have already told him to stop drinking or else cirrhosis will take him before too long.'

'Sorry, but haven't they given him the answer then? Look, let's get it over with and see if we can enjoy the rest of our meal – go on, help me out with this whitebait, I can see you've been eyeing it up.' She pushed her almost untouched plate to the centre of the table before continuing. 'Sally-Anne had her problems as a teenager, and maybe I should feel guilty about her upbringing in some way, but he was old enough to be her father, she was just barely sixteen. Sixteen, else I would have had him prosecuted, let me tell you. I probably could have anyway if it had been today, but it wouldn't have lessened the shame for our daughter.'

'So it was a proper affair?'

'Come off it. Doesn't an affair somehow suggest adults to you? It was one lost weekend, she didn't come home from Friday to Sunday while we thought she was staying with a friend, that's what she'd told us. We might never have known about him at all if he hadn't told her dad about it.'

'He did feel guilty, then?'

'Who knows? He wasn't coming round to ask for our daughter's hand in marriage, that's for sure. Maybe he didn't come round, maybe they met somewhere else, naturally I wasn't involved in whatever those two *mates* discussed. All I heard was from Andrew. I tore into him – if you think I'm hard on you at times, Harry, you ain't seen nothing yet – when I thought he was trying to justify George in some way at the expense of our child. He tried to make me admit she had been getting wild, was most likely already sexually experienced, looked older than her age, provocative did he say, could have passed for eighteen or more.'

Harry struggled to envisage the woman who had so confidently offered herself for inspection in his flat at the golf club a few months ago as an innocent teenager, until he remembered his own daughter at that age.

'I wasn't having it that Sally-Anne was practically to blame, making the running with someone so much older. She had been difficult, that was true, but you don't expect puberty for teenagers to be plain sailing – for them or their parents. Sometimes I think the only real talent men have is making girls feel guilty for saying no. There's always been that pressure. Maybe I was looking for danger in the wrong places. In our day, a dab of lippie was enough to get served in pubs long before official drinking age. To be honest, for her I was almost more worried about drugs than about sex.'

'And I suppose you wouldn't want to be ugly but being as beautiful as you and Sally-Anne only attracts more male attention.'

Harry was trying to be supportive, show a half-intelligent interest in an area he realised he had woefully neglected (yet been blissfully lucky with) during the upbringing of children in his own household. She swatted away his cracker-barrel philosophy and corny compliment. 'I'd like it not to be all about beautiful or ugly. Anyway, Saint George hadn't realised how old or who she was, or else he would never have got involved. He swore that, apparently, but I got the impression the age wouldn't have mattered to him as much as the name. You lot always liked to think of yourselves as family. For Christ's sake, my husband put you all in his will.'

'We did ask, Jane. Asked if you minded.'

'I didn't mind at *you*, any of you, it was Drew's sense of guilt.'

'Guilt about what?'

'I don't know the ins and outs, but didn't you other three get made redundant at the same time? Andrew was almost at full retirement age but played his part in the rightsizing – he was annoyed they called it that, I remember, said job-cutting was the proper term. He got a hefty bonus for his contribution to bringing the numbers down, plus a last-minute pay rise to bump his pension up. I don't blame him for that, but he was never the same in what turned out to be our last years, especially after Sally-Anne left home and school together, both as soon as she possibly could. And it was too late to get to the bottom of his shame or whatever it was, because he went and fucking died.'

Her voice had been both accelerating and increasing in volume, until she was letting the whole restaurant know that someone had fucking died. 'Jane, how about we step outside for a minute? We needn't come back if you don't want.'

'Embarrassing you, am I? Or embarrassed for your friend. I'm embarrassed for myself now. You're right. Let me go to the loo, or should I say *toilette*. Clear up the rest of the horse doovers yourself or get them cleared away, and we'll be all civilised again.'

As Jane moved away, Harry called amiably across to the next table, where a woman had been glancing back over her shoulder every time Jane's voice rose a notch. 'You want to change places with your missus, mate, so she can get a better gander? Or we can go outside, and I'll give you the whole story. Fill you in.'

The woman turned a sharp face and major décolletage to face him. 'You'd be the one to get filled in if you want to mess with my Ronnie. I thought the pensioners' early-bird special was only good in here till half past six.'

'Is everything OK, sir?' It was Ronnie a senior waiter addressed, the one who had shown them to their table before leaving the fetching and carrying to the kid.

'I'm sorry.' Harry stood and laid the napkin from his lap across the remains of his and Jane's starters. 'We'd been enjoying our anniversary dinner so much until now, maybe a little too much for other diners who only come here to avoid being seen together in public. Cancel our mains will you, and do put on my tab a drink for this charming couple. I'm still happy to have our little chat outside if you like' – he paused on his way past the shaven-headed boyfriend – 'just say the word.'

'Nah, you're fine, matey.' Ronnie looked him in the eye with evident amusement. 'I'll take a pint of Stella before you tootle off.'

'You enjoy your evening,' Harry wished the couple sincerely. The bitch had come back with a good answer, and he realised the younger man had given him a pass.

Jane was glad to leave *Le Petit Pierrot*, offered to call it a night but Harry had a better idea. 'I should have known not to hope for our Parisian ambiance in Market Welham. Over there you expect the serving staff to look down on you, the other customers can't understand what you're on about and couldn't care less. King Henry's Taverns are a safer bet for the likes of us.'

The Man at Arms crowd was bigger and loud enough at their own tables not to be concerned at what was happening on others. Jane was subdued through their main course steaks – with chips, forget the frites – but the dine-after-nine freebie bottle of wine made her more talkative as they shared a sticky toffee pudding.

'I didn't mean to go off on one earlier, Harry. It was a lovely gesture to take me to the Pierrot, I hope you didn't have to pay for our mains there as well. Let's not bother with it again, save the French for Paris as you said. I wasn't being fair on you, or on your mate. George might not have been the father, she would never say, never name anyone.'

'Whoa, hold up, you mean Maddie…'

'No, good Lord no, she was born years later, what are you thinking? Sally-Anne was *much* younger when she fell that first time. I was going to say suddenly fell, and I know the conception only takes a second, but it was too long before I became aware. And that hurt, that she was talking to her father about it before me. He wanted to go with her to the clinic, but I wasn't having that.'

'All right not Maddie but this first… baby, was that George's then?'

'I don't know, I told you. I never heard that. Andrew wouldn't say, I still don't know how he came to find out before me, he clammed right up on it. Sally-Anne never said anything to me either. Several times I thought she was wanting to confide something, but she could never quite bring it out. It broke my heart when she asked me if she was adopted.'

'*Adopted*? Sally-Anne?'

'Yes, it was a crazy idea. That's what I said. She wouldn't tell me what put it in her head. Something about she felt she wasn't good enough to be our child, so different from her dad and me she could hardly believe she was really ours. And there were no brothers and sisters, was there anything I wanted to tell her? I ended up having to get out her Baby's First Album – in which she'd never shown the slightest interest – certificate, lock of hair, handprint, photos of her first days with me, weight at birth, length, the whole nine yards.'

Big baby, Harry did not risk saying. 'Darling, I can understand more now why you were getting so worked up. Might she have been – were you? – thinking about adoption for her own bab?' They were sitting side by side on a leather banquette, backs to the wall, so he could put his hand on her knee and give it a squeeze.

'We should have, more than we did. I remember Andrew was dead set against it. He thought it best to get it over and done with almost before anyone knew rather than have her go through the whole pregnancy. Give herself a new start.'

'And she agreed?'

'She was as much against the idea of giving birth as he was, as I recall. But maybe she was influenced by him, always a daddy's girl. It was a hard time, maybe none of us were thinking clearly. If she knew who the father was, maybe that had something to do with it. It was her choice, I'd like to think that, but I wish now I'd argued stronger against something so… terminal.'

'I'm sure you did your best, Jane. And she's got Maddie, couldn't be a sweeter kid. I don't doubt Sally-Anne still has her moments' – again, that particular moment in his flat – 'sometimes makes the wrong choices like that toerag Dean, or Derek for that matter, but has she got a self-destructive streak like George?'

'I don't know whether George is self-destructive or selfish. I hardly got a chance to know his son either. Look, I didn't want to lay all this on you tonight, Harry. You were the one who asked. I feel disloyal talking so much about Sally-Anne with anyone but her father. She's a grown woman now and she is a great mother. Maybe a better one than me. So can we leave it now?'

'More than happy to, I didn't expect that to take over our evening. I was more hoping some frogs' legs might help me hop all the way to your place.'

'If you think I can be bought by a fancy dinner, you're very much mistaken, Old Henry. On the other hand, since you've sprung for two… and we're not getting married in the morning. Do you suppose George and that woman will be respecting tradition and not sleeping together tonight?'

'I've no idea but hold the thought. About us getting married, that is. I'm glad I didn't have a ring with me tonight with that rubbernecking bi… couple on the next table, but it's in my mind. And you're in my heart. Can we start living together, Jane? Please?'

The Stag

Jackie and Sally-Anne met George and Harry at the doors of the registry office. It was a curious little huddle of hugs and kisses, Harry thought, warmed by a double brandy he and George had just taken at the Carpenters' Arms after some trouble deciding what drink might be enough out of their common round to mark the day. The groom had slept with both bride and best woman, the best man had slept with the bride but nobly declined to do so with his prospective stepdaughter.

The deed was soon enough done, the couple following the registrar's instructions without accepting her invitation to add any 'special words' of their own. The darker deed had already been done, Jackie announced – perhaps she and Sally-Anne had also enjoyed a livener – when Harry said he would do his best to look after George during their stag party. 'Wouldn't want him to fail to come up to the mark on his wedding night.'

'No need to bother about that, Harry. We did it this morning. So we can both get as shitfaced as we like now.'

'I told you it was an arse-about-face kind of wedding,' George uttered almost his first words of the day apart from those echoing the registrar.

Although the bride and groom had opted not to use their own soon-to-be jointly licensed premises for any kind of celebration – mindful that it had recently held the wake for her sister and his partner – the four of them did go from the registry office to the White Horse before parting. Jackie was happy to take up Sally-Anne's recommendation to check that their head barman for the day was ready to receive the punters from the dot of noon. Mason was a nice enough lad, a willing enough worker, but not high on initiative and it would be the first time he had been left in sole charge.

Arnie Collier, the only man who had spent more hours in the pub than George over the last ten years, was already perched on his bar stool, *Mirror* open at the racing pages in front of him with his customary Guinness that Jackie noted approvingly Mason had served with the proper ratio of head to body. Harry was equally pleased that the lad brought out on cue the bottle of champagne in a bucket of ice – Sally-Anne's idea, which he had been happy to fund.

'Here you go, Tesco's finest, no speeches or anything but it wouldn't be right to start our parties without one drink together.' Sally-Anne busied herself pouring for them, still standing at the bar.

'I knew it wasn't from our cellar.' Jackie giggled. 'We shall have to do some Pimm's later, Sal, being as I'm now officially Mrs Pym. I won't offer you a glass, Mason.' She was suddenly all business again. 'No drinking for you until either George or me gets back in tonight. We're the only people you can't chuck out however badly we behave, but if you see any sign of trouble brewing call my husband here – he'd better be close around town to sort it out while we're in the big city. Lock up at twelve as usual, and we'll sort you out a wedding drink tomorrow if we find the place still standing.'

George had not wasted his time offering Arthur a glass of champagne, but poured him a generous tot of Bushmills accepted with a brief nod of thanks. If he realised a wedding had taken place, Arnie was not letting on and George wasn't dressed up for one. He did, however, break the habit of a lifetime in joining the other three of the party in a champagne toast.

If there was any embarrassment at their past relationship, it was on Harry's side rather than Jackie's, though it was easy enough not to speak to each other outside a general conversation. He was careful after last night's talk to look for any spark between George and Sally-Anne (surely Jackie had no idea there might once have been) but saw nothing. She asked him for a quick word before they parted, George antsy about his promise to be in the Rifleman's and in the chair by twelve thirty.

'Harry, will you be seeing Pete today?'

'Any minute now, as it goes. Why?'

'I'm worried about him.'

'You're not the only one. And your mum's worried about you.' He decided if he was going to be part of this family it was time to start putting his shoulder to the wheel. 'Listen, I hope you and Pete are only friends, not part of each other's problems. He's always been soft with women. This is strictly between us. His wife Margaret was a nurse when they met, he'd slashed his wrists after some bird dumped him, daft fucker. And now he's got Reenie going round the twist to cope with, she always helped keep him grounded. I think he'd not long been living away from home when he got into…' He made a throat- rather than the historic wrist-cutting motion. 'She would have told him not to be an idiot. He's like an innocent around women, that's what I'm trying to say, liable to make a twat of himself.'

'I don't know what Mum's been saying about me, but whatever it was I wish she'd kept it strictly between me and her. You're a man of the world, Harry, you were smart enough to know not to touch me. If your friend was more "innocent", he's got no business being at his age. That was some first date story between him and Margaret, but I can't be responsible for him behaving like a kid. He thinks there's a chance of something serious between us.'

'Whatever gave him that idea?' Maybe he should have supported George in warning Pete off, seriously. Except they never spoke seriously to each other. 'I wouldn't touch her with yours' was about the limit of mates' advice to each other, often trotted out before the man did touch her with his own. 'I can warn him off you and let him cry his heart out on my shoulder – not today mind, not on a stag do for fuck's sake – but you need to promise you won't be sending him any mixed messages. Make it clear he's got no chance.'

'I don't know how much clearer I can be on that. Thing is, I do feel sorry for him with Reenie, sorry for her too. She was a woman I could admire. So I've sort of offered to help him out with her, one day next week.'

'That's a lifetime project, the poor old gal won't be getting any better. And maybe nor will he if you're always hanging around there.'

George clapped Harry on the shoulder on his way by. 'No rush, I'll see you at the Rifleman's when you're ready. Cheers for the champagne and for standing for us today, thanks, Sally-Anne.'

'You're welcome, George. And you go on, Harry, enjoy your stag do. What have you got lined up, stripograns? Or are you really going for it, dommies *and* crib. I'll bet you're back in here before us tonight.'

'I'm counting on you to tell your mum we were, whatever happens. We'll finish off our chat later. You take care.' Harry followed his mate out the door.

There was less traffic among the Tuesday-Thursday gang in weddings than funerals. George had not been selective about his invitations, nor specific about the sequence of events. Jimmy Bradley was increasingly leading the committee as other members grew tired, infirm or shy of being out in a pandemic. George had asked him to make the announcement on his behalf a week earlier, with a reminder the day before.

'George is taking the plunge again, some people are gluttons for punishment,' said Jimmy, with only two failed long-term relationships behind him. 'We all know he's his own man, so rather than stag weekend or night, it's a stag day next Friday at the Rifleman's. No fancy dress, no food – we all know his motto, eatin's cheatin' – and he'll be putting a tray of Jameson's on the bar for a half twelve kick-off.'

Pete was standing guard over the tray – the guvnor had done George a deal on two bottles, the second in reserve for the moment – when his fellow tontiners walked in not a minute late.

All happy drinking sessions are the same, all unhappy ones have their own dynamic. It was jolly enough for the first few hours as the golfers came and went. George had stationed himself in his favoured position at any bar, corner with back to the wall, standing or rather leaning for hours not a problem. He shook hands with a score of men. Jimmy was the first, setting up a kitty with a generous kick-start as he explained from the gang's multi-million lottery winner, Mark Jones. Swanning around in Spain most of the time, Mark still showed up occasionally at MWGC and had Jimmy keep him up to date with the gang's weekly results and news ('What a sad bastard,' Franny Rowland had remarked on hearing that). He had transferred a sub, amount judged nicely between being a good friend and showing off too much his new-found wealth.

Despite the healthy float, Jimmy did his best to make sure no one dodged their obligation to return George's opener, not even Arthur Harrison. Percy Parsons, the former president going round in a buggy these days and taking a seat at the bar, came in with Jack Roberts. Graham Cook, Chit Paudel, Brian Hammond, tontine consigliere Nick Gregory in his lunch hour, all put in appearances. Jimmy and Barry Knighton were still friends, still cool, for all that Barry's daughter and the younger man were no longer a couple. Franny Rowland, Carl Bracknell and Billy Jackson came in after their usual Friday three-ball. The Rifleman's was in any case part of Billy's daily round.

Leaving room for each incomer to offer salaams and congratulations to George, Harry and Pete were by unspoken agreement pacing themselves in pints of bitter for what they expected to be a long day.

'Have you been to see Reenie this morning?' Harry asked. 'Kerry tells me she's settling in at Melwood.'

'I go to see her every day. It's not good. I'm thinking of taking her out, tell you the truth.'

'I thought it was supposed to be one of the better ones. Or is she getting better herself?'

'Are you kidding?' He gave something between a snort and a laugh. Harry wondered if Pete was already feeling the effects of the alcohol, despite their relatively sedate pace.

'Will you bring her home, then? Wouldn't that be even tougher, on you and Margaret.'

'She wouldn't let that happen if Reenie was fit as a fiddle, like she always used to boast she was. Margaret has to self-isolate. She tells me we'll soon be in another lockdown anyway, and she should know with her NHS background. I can't let Mum go through that.'

'None of us will have an option. If we do, let's hope they're not as cruel to the old folks as they were last time.' Without caring to enquire why Margaret would be a special risk case, Harry agreed a lockdown was more than likely; one more reason on top of Ellen's bullshit ultimatum, on top of his feelings for Jane, to make him move more quickly towards a live-in arrangement with his girlfriend, something more permanent than a bubble born only to burst.

'I won't let them be. I won't let her suffer.'

Harry was surprised at the intensity of his friend's assertion. 'Maybe I should have asked at the start how you are, not how your mum is.'

'I'm all fucked up, tell you the truth, Harry. How did Sally-Anne look this morning? Did you notice anything about her?'

'She was fine far as I could tell. You're not letting her get under your skin, are you? I hope she's not the one making you feel fucked up. She's not worth it, mate, you've got to give up any ideas you might have about her.'

'If only it were that easy. You might be a bit kinder to her if you're going to be a proper stepdad. You don't know her if you think she's not worth it. You can't.'

'All right, keep your wig on. Let's talk more later, when it's quieter. I'm going over to try and rescue George, Hammo's been bending his ear for ten minutes now. He'll only stand so much before telling him to shut up or piss off.'

By one thirty, both bottles of Jameson's had been dispatched, and by three enough pints to satisfy the landlord his discount on the spirits had served its purpose of priming the pumps. Consciously or unconsciously echoing stag days of their youth, George suggested it was time for a change of venue. Billy Jackson, Franny Rowland and Jimmy joined him, Harry and Pete in a route including the Prince, Queen's, Crown and Half Moon, where Billy camped and Franny decamped. The other four decided to go for a couple of frames of snooker at the Poke, on the high street above what had once been Burton's.

Like them all, the hall had seen better days, no longer enough throughput to justify keeping beers on draught, only one of the eight tables lit when they walked in. Playing doubles, though none of them was a major talent it was soon clear that whoever drew Pete as partner would lose. Jimmy made some spectacular pots but was more interested in selecting tunes from the jukebox than which red to go for. He became more fidgety yet after taking a phone call, before admitting to the others that he would have to leave them.

'I'm not ducking out or nothing, and I'm not taking a snack break. I'd forgotten I had something on with my boy, James. I told him I'd see him tomorrow, but he says it's tonight or don't bother.'

'Yeah, we'll believe you, thousands wouldn't,' Harry said. 'You can prove it when you bring him back with you.'

'He'd more likely want to join the hen party, camp as a row of tents, but I do my best with him. Old Baz, his grandad, was having a pop at me this aft.'

'You go on, family first, kids are the most important thing in the world.'

'Says the only one of us who hasn't got any. You've never had a reality check, Goodie.' The abbreviation of Pete's surname rather than use of his given one was not affectionate. An early sign of drunkenness in George was a tendency to talk. When he started to do so, it was not always pleasant stuff he came out with, though there was no great force behind his jab.

Pete did not contest the point. 'I think I *will* take a snack break, just for a Micky D, some ballast. I shan't be long, will you two still be here?'

'Someone's got to finish the fucking frame, and we've still got minutes on the lights.' George had fluked in a red and was now lining up an ambitious pink.

'Yeah, go on, Pete. I'll call you if we do move on somewhere, not too many places left to go.'

'And me, Harry, call me as well please.'

'I don't know who made me fucking social secretary, but yeah, all right.' Jimmy had an odd attachment to the three of them, almost like a kid tagging along. No wonder his own kid had problems, if that was what the father-in-law had been getting on his case about. You could sometimes disengage from the ex without her family getting the memo to leave you alone.

Jimmy and Pete left the Poke together. When George closed out the frame, rather than rerack and start another, Harry suggested they sit down.

George was becoming argumentative for the sake of it. 'I reckon we should be getting out of here if we're not going to play. Only bottled beers or canned shit nowadays. Christ, what's the world coming to?' They had opted for ciders on being given that grim news. It was a while since any of them had been in the joint, which had suffered like many others from pandemic lockdown as well as a demographic decline in popularity of the sport of afternoon boozers. 'Unless you want a game of crib? Before Goodie gets back, he's a liability to play anything with, got his head up his arse.'

'Let's see if either of 'em come back. My bet is Jimmy no and Pete yes. Can you ease up on him, George, else it's going to be a long night?'

'Go easy on him? Who's being hard? I haven't said a dicky bird to anyone. A stag's nothing without a bit of aggro.'

Harry was finding it hard to focus on his own line of argument, but felt he had to persevere. 'Mate, he may be sensitive about not having kids. Like maybe it wasn't a matter of choice for him and Margaret.'

'What did I say? I didn't say it made him less of a man or anything did I? I didn't say he was a fucking eunuch. Then he might have had cause to complain. If he had the balls.'

'Come on, George, he's our mate, remember. He's going through the mill with Reenie, and I think he's in deeper with Sally-Anne than's good for him.'

'In deep with her, nuts deep most likely. She's never going to change, that one. Bad news from the start. Dam…'

'George, don't forget I'm going out with her mother now. She's like family to me.'

'Yeah, well you know what I think about that as well. I made my position clear on going out with a mate's wife. Perfectly clear.'

'A mate's widow as it goes, a wife maybe I agree but I don't need lecturing from you. What about a mate's daughter?'

George had been slouched back against the wall, but now he sat up straight. He took up his pint and studied it, half empty. 'Are you trying to wind me up, Harry? Do you want to go outside?'

'If that's…'

'For a smoke, you dipshit, that's all I'm going out for anyway. You keep on nagging at that same old bone, let's suck the marrow out of it then throw it in the bin. I tell you what, get me one of them cigars you favour from behind the bar, a man shouldn't be stuck on roll-ups all through his wedding day. Your round I think, an' all. See you in the smoking lounge, I'm going for a slash first.'

'I asked already, he's got no cigars.' Although giving them up was one of the ways Harry was helping Jane to help make him a better man, he had persuaded himself gradually (each time the groom had to step out, though in the Rifleman's he had not lacked company from other TT members) that it was not fair to make George smoke alone on his stag do.

'Go and get some from the minimart downstairs then. Jesus, I remember this place when the smoke was like heavy cloud cover, nearly blocking out the table lights. And get us a pack of cards while you're at it, them fuckers sell everything.'

After the windowless gloom of the Poke, Harry felt like he had as a kid going to the pictures for a matinee, surprised to find it still light when he came out afterwards. Puffing slightly back up the stairs, he made his way to what George had ironically referred to as the smoking lounge. It was past the bogs, gents to the left a two-man urinal and single cubicle. In case of urgent need, men could normally take the door opposite, as vanishingly few ladies visited the old snooker hall. George was still occupying the men's shitter, judging by a dreadful fit of coughing and what sounded like a violent vomit clearly audible through the high, open toilet window onto what was no more than a small square platform above the metal fire escape.

Any more than three or four smokers outside, and some would have to sit or stand on the stairs.

A tiny three-legged round table was the only furniture, up against the corner of the railings. Harry put the two new bottles of cider on it, hoping he would not have to drink them both, beside the tinny ashtray half full of butts, including two or three from George's own roll-ups.

Their brief separation or his boke had restored something of George's good humour. 'Filthy stuff, cider, only for kids, but clears the palate.' He picked up one of the bottles. By way of cleaning his teeth, he took a short pull, swilled the liquid around a moment then arced it – a controlled expulsion, a spit rather than a puke – over the railings, without troubling to look if anyone should be passing in the back alley below them. 'Where's these smokes, then?'

'The look on your face, Harry' – accepting the Henri Wintermans slim panatella – 'when you thought I was offering you outside. Come on, we're mates, you can say things to me I'd let nobody else in the world get away with. Just don't abuse the privilege. I'll say no more.'

Harry thought as his friend lit up the cigar he meant this literally and that he would have to begin a tiresome list of questions again. He wondered if he had the energy. After his first spout of smoke though – it looked as if the stupid bastard was dragging it down into his lungs like a cigarette, not just targeting the mouth area for cancer as was accepted best practice – George continued.

'You know there's that spell of weddings and second weddings and kids' christenings and confirmations and suchlike when you're not just mates out together, you come to know each other's families a bit. Sometimes the women get on, which can be a mixed blessing. Then, till the kids start getting married theirselves, unless they piss off and do it abroad or don't want anyone but their mates along, there's a gap when you don't see so much of them. I reckon it must have been in that gap young Sally-Anne grew up. Grew up enough to fool me, anyway.'

'You couldn't tell she was a teenager?'

'Nothing wrong with teenagers, mate. At least that was how I was thinking then. I'd not long left Melanie, living in that shitty little flat I still call home but before my luck turned with Em. Looking back, I was having a last stab, pretending to be young still. Turned out the bird that split me and Mel up preferred me when I was attached, so I was on the loose, getting into more bother than usual. Doing the doors at Giovanni's didn't help, everybody likes to think they can take on a bouncer. So I was being a proper cunt,' George granted, 'but I won't have anybody *thinking* – and you of all people should know better – that I was into little girls. She's poison – I heard you earlier, I'm being kind calling her that – but she was a woman, no doubt about it. Fuck me, Angela was only sixteen when we got wed, and Louise already on the way.'

How well Harry remembered the prettiest girl in the year below them at school, who had chosen George from the pick of her own class and their own. She came to repent her choice, but they were together for over ten years, with another daughter Alex and son Paul following Louise.

'It was Sally-Anne made the running, if you must know. I'd sorted some little shit who was bothering her, turfed him out, and I could see her looking at me after that. Thought she was grateful at first, not *that* grateful though. Wasn't till next morning, when she teased me for not recognising her, I found out she was Andy's daughter. She knew me all along, just didn't let on. Maybe she had a thing for older men. If I'd had any idea, I would have run a mile. It would have been almost like incest, worse than banging a mate's wife probably, I'm with you on that.'

'You sent her straight home then?'

Neither of them heard someone behind them entering the toilet.

'Well it *wasn't* incest with Sally-Anne, was it? I told myself that. Even if it had been, it was too late. Don't forget I was still pissed. Still horny too if you want all the gory details. I'd done some coke. I realised it couldn't go on, but I did stay with her for the rest of the weekend, didn't treat her like a slag. And she enjoyed it, she ever says she didn't she'll be lying. Christ, I took her to dinner at that poxy French place as I remember, one and only time I've been in there.'

Neither of them heard Pete leaving the toilet. He made it downstairs to the street before vomiting, full hands-on-knees bringing everything up, whisky beer cider burger bun, finishing with bile. Still looking at the bespattered pavement, he heard a woman whose voice reminded him of Reenie's passing behind him: 'You ought to be ashamed of yourself, man. There's kids around here. What sort of example is that to set them?'

His eyes were streaming. A *Big Issue* saleswoman came up with more solicitude than 'Reenie' had shown, or hoping to stop him further polluting her patch. 'Are you all right, sir?'

'Yeah, I'm fine thank you. I'm fine, don't worry. Here you go.'

He pressed a twenty-pound note onto her with further thanks for the magazine. He got round the corner out of her sight before ripping a page from it to spit into and wipe his mouth as best he could. Weren't you supposed to feel sorry for them, not the other way round? He felt sorry enough for himself. His half-formed plans for a way out crystallised. He ordered an Uber.

'There, satisfied now? Speak up, because I'm not going to talk about this ever again.'

George had 'fronted up' to Andy during the week after his adventure with Sally-Anne ('felt I had to do the right thing by him'), first phoning to say they needed to have a serious talk about her. 'I give him the option of home advantage if he wanted it, but said he might prefer to meet somewhere else, away from his women. He come straight out to see me, round at my place. He was good as gold about it. I was ready to let him take a free swing at me if he wanted, told him so, but I suppose that was never his style. He didn't seem surprised, more relieved if that makes sense. I don't know what the fuck he was expecting me to tell him. He said she'd been a lot of trouble lately. She was his daughter, but he could see how a man might be tempted by her. Some malarkey about all he could do was try and keep loving her, look after her till she came through it, hoped it was just a phase or something. I'm trying to give you the whole story so you'll shut up about the bastard once and for all, but I can't remember exactly what he said. We're going back a few years. He played the white man, I did think that.'

'And he must have told Jane about it?'

'You tell me.' Having stubbed out his cigar, George clearly wanted to move on, both from the topic and the Poke. 'I'd never had much to do with her, but I think they were a solid unit, doubt he kept anything from her. She's never been exactly overjoyed to see me anywhere since, you may have noticed. I can't say I blame her for that.'

'So that was the end of it. No fall-out?'

'No, I just told you, he was good as gold. Mates should never fall out over a bird, and we didn't.'

'Not that. I mean, did you use protection?'

'You what? Jesus wept, Harry, now I'm getting worried about you. Are you more interested in the mother or the daughter? I'd of made a video for you if I'd known you wanted to see it going in, bet she woulda been up for it an' all.

Seeing from Harry's unsmiling face a reply was still expected, George went on in an exaggerated tone of weary patience. 'I always say I'm allergic to rubber, thought you knew that trick yourself. I might make the effort if they were worth it, if they insisted and put one on me nicely, but it's got to be for them to ask. I don't remember Sally-Anne making a fuss about it, so I assume she was taking care of herself. I know she's got her daughter, but she came years later, and there was never anything between us, not after that once. Well, them few times. I hope her own girl don't give her as many problems as she did poor Andy and his missus.'

'Come on, let's get out of here. You were right, I can't take any more of this cider.'

They passed through the town-centre Bell and Bull, both into their karaoke evenings though not yet at the stage when groups of kids would spill between them performing their party pieces to each other. While neither man was drunk enough (or ever had been) to consider taking the mic, they were both flagging now. Harry had called their other two friends, to learn that Jimmy was committed to his stepson and to go straight to voicemail on Pete's phone.

'Where the fuck are you, mate? The three musketeers are a man down, all for one, remember. It's bad enough pissing off to put something down your throat, even if it is only your fingers. Or are you giving it large with Jimmy and his boy in some gay club? We're still at it, me and George, one for all balls to the wall, just leaving The Bell. Unless we find you in The Bull doing "YMCA" we'll be starting the serious part of the day's drinking without you. Give me a call when you're ready to come back to the stag, you tart. I shan't be ringing you again.' He stuffed the mobile back into his pocket.

'Looks like my faith in Pete was wrong, George, you win the bet. Twatooks might have answered his phone though. I thought he kept it on all the time, case Reenie pops it.'

George was unsympathetic. 'What's the point of putting her in a home if you still gotta be on call twenty-four seven? Probably can't hear it if he is in one of these disco pubs, wouldn't think one cunt fancying hisself as Elvis could make such a racket. That's the wonder of you, is it bollocks.

Fucking lightweight, Goodie. Knew he'd duck out. There's not many I can count on to stay with me like you do, Harry boy.'

Resolved to stick with the single groom for as long as he was wanted and could remain conscious, Harry was glad to know the former still applied but increasingly felt the urge to close his eyes. He was almost relieved when George himself suggested they complete their pilgrimage where it had begun, a long shift earlier.

Harry remembered re-entering the Horse, but not leaving it. The next day he knew only they had sat facing each other with cards then dominoes in their hands – Sally-Anne's prediction had not been so very far out, though he recalled no saucy sexagenarians – not who had won, usually the most important marker of an evening for them both.

'Look at 'em sitting there like two pieces of furniture. They can hardly lift their pints. When did they come back, Mason?'

'Not late. You're not that late yourself, boss, thought you were off clubbing in Brum?'

'We got as far as Cov, but more for shopping than supping. Then when we got back here with a few of the girls, this one had me on a tight rein.' Jackie threw an affectionate arm around Sally-Anne. 'I always thought she liked cocktails as well as cock, but it was mocktails all the way for her in Prezzo's. She bullied me into eating some pasta with her, would you believe.'

Sally-Anne was careful in disengaging herself from Jackie's arm to place it securely on the bar counter, in case her friend had been leaning on her for physical as well as moral support. 'Had to spoonfeed you it, practically. My mission today, the one I chose to accept, was to keep you company and out of bad company. I knew I wouldn't be able to keep you sober, give up on that long ago. As for the spag bol, look where the liquid diet got your husband and his best man. Never mind lifting their pints, I doubt they could find their way into a bag of crisps now.'

'My husband. I've never been married before, you know, and that's the best I can do.'

Fearing a maudlin turn to tears from Jackie and tiring of being sober all day among drunks, Sally-Anne tried to keep it light. 'Well the other bookend, bellend I should say, is next door to being my dad nowadays. Things could always be worse. I bet he thinks they are, with the prospect of me for a stepdaughter!'

'You're like a proper daughter to me, babes, never had one of them neither. But hey, no regrets, no regrets. Mwah, zhunna regretta ree-enn… If my lump thinks I'm carrying him up the hill to Bedfordshire he's got another think coming. Start as you mean to go on. Made sure I had a sample before I bought though, he's not bad in that department.'

Lurching between drunken song and lucidity, Jackie must have caught Sally-Anne looking over her shoulder at the barman. 'Don't worry about Mason getting embarrassed, he's not as big a ninny as he looks. You head off now, Mase, come round when you like tomorrow and we'll sort you out.'

'I'd better go and sort Harry out.' Sally-Anne moved towards the two slumped men, the only remaining customers. 'I doubt if Mum will want to see him tonight but I can get him back to his little hidey-hole at the golf club.'

'Little shithole more like, I'll order an Uber for you both, on me. Cos you are the wind beneath my wings…' Even the undemanding Bell or Bull crowds would have booed her off the mic. 'No, you've been a great wingman, wingwoman I should say, Wonderwoman, thanks babe. Soz if I cramped your own style drinking. I can look after myself when it comes to boozing, I thought you knew that.'

'No bother, Jackie. Between you and me and the two amigos over there – looks like Pete had the sense to bail on them – one of us has to be the responsible adult.'

The Road Home

Peter Goodwin did not have his phone on silent. He was selective over the next week about which calls he answered. He let most, including those from Sally-Anne – the ones that would have lit his heart as much as his screen only days before – go unanswered, and never dialled into his voicemail. He had a lot to do before taking Reenie out on Friday.

Although he had initially offered to pick up Sally-Anne for their trip to Manea in the Isle of Ely, she had said she would prefer to meet him at Melwood House. Nine o'clock sharp they had agreed, so he did not expect her any time before nine thirty if she showed at all. Pleased to learn Kerry would be on shift that morning, he had asked her if she could have Reenie up, dressed and ready to go by eight thirty please. When he arrived at quarter past, so she was, sitting in the common room, coat on, handbag (empty but for tissues) clutched to her chest.

'I was about to go. I don't have to depend on you, I've got my bus pass.' Her tone was defiant, her eyes watery.

'That's good, but being as I am here I might as well give you a lift.'

'She's been a bit… lively this morning, Peter. Didn't have a very good night. They told me she was up and down wanting to get started, frightened she might miss the bus. I made sure she was showered, she's had her meds, wouldn't eat any breakfast, just a coffee, she's probably excited.'

'Thanks, you're an angel. Right then, Mum, let's get going if you're in a hurry. Say bye bye to Kerry, and thank you.'

'I don't need you to learn me manners, boy. Other way round.'

'Quite right. Take my arm then, madame, s'il vous plaît.'

'Now you're just showing off. You can pack that up right away.' Her smile was worth his mock gallantry.

'We can put Mum in the wheelchair to take her to the car if you like. I've got it here ready so you can use it at the other end.'

Pete no longer found it strange to hear Kerry and other staff refer to Reenie as if she were their mum as well as his. He was happy to share her around. 'I don't know… All right then, thanks.'

Kerry was surprised he wheeled her to the Hyundai's front seat. 'I thought Sally-Anne would have bagsied shotgun. Do you want me to go onto the road and fetch her in? I'm guessing she's out there, having a smoke?'

'No thanks, I've got it. Fetching her from home. Mum can't hear anything sitting in the back, and I want to be able to talk to her as we go.'

'Fair enough. Don't be upset if she nods off, like I say she didn't get much rest last night.'

'That'll be fine, too. Thanks for everything. You've got Reenie done up lovely.'

Kerry looked doubtfully at his sweatshirt, tracksuit bottoms and trainers. 'I hope I'm not being nosy, Pete, but I thought you said it was your aunt's birthday party. Are you going dressed like that?'

'Nobody cares what I dress like. It doesn't matter.' Seeing her taken aback by his tone, he tried to compose himself. 'You're absolutely right, Kerry. Sorry if I snapped. I've got a change of clothes in the boot.'

'Lord, glad I asked now cos I'd clean forgotten the bag for Reenie with a drink, couple of snacks and change of clothes of her own… extra pants, you know.' She lowered her voice, although the old lady, eyes fixed on the windscreen in front of her, did not appear to be listening to them. Pete would need to switch the wipers on when they left, it was beginning to rain hard. The roads would be getting slippy, but that did not worry him. 'I'm glad you said Sally-Anne would help you with that. I would have changed my shifts and come with you if she couldn't. We're all so fond of Reenie, love her stories. Sounds like she was quite a girl in her time.'

'Quite a girl. She was that.' He managed a smile, thinking behind it her time was gone now and wondering if he had ever been 'quite a boy'. 'Thanks for everything, you know…' He held his arms out palms up and for a moment she thought he was going to move towards her for a hug. She was either mistaken or he thought better of it, turning and moving quickly to put the car between them. 'One more favour if you don't mind?'

Opening the driver's door, he ducked briefly inside then hurried back to her with a thick brown A4 envelope. 'Can you give this to Harry next time you see him, please? It's only some pensions bumf from our old company I printed out, been meaning to give it him for a while but keep leaving it in the car. Sorry to impose on you, hope you don't mind.'

'Well OK but I might not…'

'No rush, doesn't matter if you don't see him for a day or two, still be sooner than I will. It should all be clear, you can tell him he doesn't need to wade through the whole thing, everything's all right basically. Everything's fine.'

'OK, if you're sure it's not urgent.'

'No worries. You take care. And thanks again.'

She went to wish Reenie a safe journey one more time, but preferred not to disturb her as the old lady's eyes were closed, her mouth slightly open.

Kerry had enough respect for official papers not to throw them on the floor of her locker to join gym kit, towel and accumulated rubbish. There was a partition shelf at the top for small items, above her shorthouse eyeline, where she poked up the bulky envelope, briefly resentful. For all Peter had on his plate, let him try putting in a few shifts at Melwood if he thought she had nothing better to do than be his messenger girl.

Returning to the breakfast service, in which some of their residents always needed assistance or encouragement, Kerry was surprised not twenty minutes later to see Sally-Anne waving at her before coming into the common room.

'Thought I'd surprise him being on time, early in fact, still not ten to nine, you're my witness. Don't tell me I've beaten Pete here. Where's Reenie?'

Putting a spoonful of porridge into Emily's mouth, which would explore it for a couple of minutes before she swallowed or spat it out, Kerry guessed there must have been some miscommunication. 'He's been and gone, took his mum and said they'd pick you up on the way. You'd better call him and sort it out.'

Sally-Anne, phone already in hand, suspected at once it was useless. Their arrangement had been clear. 'OK, thanks Kel, excuse me a second. I'll get out of your hair and call him from outside, can never get a decent signal in here.'

'Righto, he's probably at yours by now. Good luck and have a nice day with them.' When the other woman did not reappear, Kerry assumed she had managed to pick up with Pete. She knew she would not hear of their trip for a couple of days after going off shift, since she was taking her two-day break, for once coinciding with a weekend.

Though tech-savvy compared to many of his peers, Pete had never bothered to connect his mobile to the car so that he could take calls hands-free while driving. He had it on silent in the space for drinks, keys and the like between him and Reenie, where he saw a call from Sally-Anne coming through. He had no more intention of taking it than he had for the last week of taking her with them. They were finished now and he felt a certain liberation at being out on the road. He hoped he was offering her a similar clear road to freedom.

Reenie woke with a start and a soft cry as they were passing the Peterborough turn-off on the A14. 'Where are you taking me now? Off to another loony bin?'

'No, Mum, we're going home. We're on our way.'

'That's what you tell me. Can you turn that row down a bit, I can hardly hear myself think.'

'You'll miss PopMaster, remember how we always used to listen to it? Ken Bruce.'

He wondered whether he had really expected the quiz to bring something back to her, or to bring her back to him. She had taken as keen an interest in the music he listened to as in everything he ever did. He turned the volume down, without much regret, to where he could barely hear it so she could surely not, for all that Kerry had managed to fit her with one hearing aid, the one on his side as it happened.

Reenie suddenly became agitated, rummaging in her lap and pawing feebly at the glove compartment.

'What's the matter, Mum? Do you need the toilet?' Please don't let her start trying to undress herself.

'Where is it? Did I give it to you? I hope you haven't left it behind?'

'Left what behind?'

'My sustificate.'

'What certificate's that, Mum?'

'You know, the one I got from the Queen, from Lizzie. When I turned a hundred.'

'You won't… oh, I'm with you now, the certificate and the lovely card she sent you, signed by her and everything. Yeah I've got it, don't worry. We'll be able to show it off to Aunt Ruth if that's what you're thinking. How long ago was it now?'

'You should know, you would make me have that big party at your football club. Ruth was always the jealous one, but she'll never catch me up. Are we going to see her today then? Will our mum be there too?'

He steeled himself against the note of entreaty in her voice. 'I don't know, Mum, let's hope so. Let's see when we get there.'

'Once we've got home and had a cup of tea, we'll see, fair enough? My own home, Willow Drive, Wisbech Road, Manea. That *is* where we're going, isn't it?'

'That's right, Mum. We can see how we feel once we get there.'

'Do they know we're coming? If they do, we can't very well *not* go and see them, can we?'

'No, they don't know.' That much was true. 'I didn't want to tell them in case you had one of your poorly days and we couldn't make it.'

'I expect you're more interested in seeing Sally anyway. I wish you'd stop mooning after her.'

'I'll do my best, Mum. Sally-Anne couldn't come today, like she said she would, but she did tell me to give you her best.'

'Give her *my* best an' all. But I'm not talking about that little girl. You know very well who I'm talking about.'

Of course he did.

'She was a lovely girl, had her in our house like she was family from the first.' Reenie changed from reminiscence to scolding as she wagged a finger at him. 'And don't think me and your dad couldn't hear you creeping to the spare bedroom in the night. It didn't matter as long as you weren't using the place like a hotel, that's what Georgie said. We all thought you'd get married, have a do in church, then the Legion and everything. Her mum, Olive, she was lovely too.'

'I don't expect we'll see her today, Mum.'

'You'll be lucky! She was older than me.'

Sally had been his first love as well as his first sexual partner. If not quite childhood sweethearts, he had thought they would spend their whole adult lives together. When she came to think otherwise, he couldn't see much purpose to the rest of his. So the wheel turns; this time there would be no nurse prepared to go beyond her duty of professional care.

'Sally, she would have given me grandbabbies. She had a whole houseful of 'em for Olive, and that Margaret was too mean to let you have a single one. One would have been enough, Petie.'

'I know, Mum, but maybe it's not too late. Maybe Sally-Anne can give us one.'

She looked sharply at him. She was fully there behind her bright eyes. 'Now you're just being daft. I *knew* that was what you were up to behind my back. Just don't go killing yourself again over a girl, that's all I'll say. I won't be around forever to keep an eye on you, and your mother won't rush to save you this time.'

'No, I don't suppose Margaret will. Better off without me, I should think.'

Reenie did not disagree. As if she had said her piece, she relapsed into silence. She started taking an increased interest in the pancake-flat landscape soon after they hit the A141 towards March.

'Why have you brought us this way? You know I don't like it. We always used to go through Peterborough. I hate these narrow roads along the rivers and waterways, and you will go too fast. I don't know how many times I have to tell you, Pauline Clarke's mum and dad come off straight into the sixteen foot when she was a girl, Mr and Mrs Trundle, the times we used to have. They wouldn't let her see them before the burial once they'd pulled 'em out, only thing she got back was her mum's handbag.'

'You tell me every time, Mum, no trip would be complete without that story. I've got it off by heart. Not such a bad way to go. No seatbelts in them days, most likely gone before they hit the water, no suffering, a nice clean death. They died while they were still alive if you look at it one way.'

She was staring at him intently. He chose to see understanding in her eyes. If not, there was no fear. 'You're safe with me, Mum, you know that. If you feel worried, look, you can help me steer. Put your hand onto the wheel, come on it's time you learned to drive, now you've got your sustificate and everything.'

He reached out a hand to take hers, unsnapping both their seatbelts on its way. Did he need an excuse, a piece of business, to hold his mum's hand as he had always planned he would when the time came? He placed it on the steering wheel, felt her fingers curl around that as he rested his own left hand lightly on her right. Reenie *was* trying to steer, exerting pressure on the wheel, trying to push it towards him, away from the river on their left.

He had noticed a feature on the grass verge he did not remember from his youth: painted poles about the height of a man every twenty yards along. No effective barrier, they perhaps lit up in the dark like cats' eyes to guide drivers. Too late for the Trundles. He turned his face towards her. 'I love you, Mum, that's why we came this way.'

He forced the steering wheel to the left with his right hand, left hand down he remembered from his earliest driving lessons. He kept his eyes on his mum, would not have left her for the world, the first face dear to him the last he saw as he sped them off the road.

Within ten days, on Halloween, Prime Minister Boris Johnson declared a second lockdown to prevent a 'medical and moral disaster' for the NHS.

PART FIVE

CLOSING THE RING 2021–2025

Valentine Bouffe

Ever-reliable Prime Minister Johnson kept his Halloween pledge that Christmas 2020 would be 'different, very different'. So was Valentine's Day 2021, when England was in its third lockdown.

The waitress brought the two ladies a glass of Prosecco each. 'Compliments du chef, mesdames.' She bobbed before returning to the kitchen. She was soon back (it was not far) with their salmon and prawn cocktail starters, before sitting down to join them. She giggled when the chef himself brought her own prawn cocktail with a glass of Diet Coke.

'Très bien, très bien,' he said, returning with almost equal speed if nothing like Maddie's gamine grace. He sat down with his pimped-up scotch egg and pint of Doom Bar. 'Bienvenue à la maison de Harry. My home eez your home.'

'Merci beaucoup, monsieur. We had a lovely time last year at your… er, cousin Maître Albert's place by the Seine. I'm sure this will be just as good. With excellent service too from the young lady. I hope you let your staff keep all their tips.'

'Mais fer sure.' If he could not keep up the language, Harry could camp up a French accent – not for nothing had he letched over the suzzied serving wenches through all those eighties episodes of *'Allo 'Allo!* 'And I'm sure we will all be satisfied with the work of our sous-chefs Messieurs Marks et Spencer.'

He had not himself been as familiar with the work of those gentlemen before moving in with Jane over four months earlier, just early enough to say it was not the second lockdown that had driven them into the decision. The horrendous queue for the M & S Valentine's Dine In deals had provided food he could put hot on the table, without troubling the three females now sharing it with him. Apart from her sterling work as garçonne (was it?), Maddie had come up with the menu idea and design, the ornate offering of **BOUFFE DE LA SAINT VALENTIN 2021** chez **ATELIER MAÎTRE HARRY**.

BoJo's comments the previous June about coming slowly and cautiously out of hibernation might have been more seasonally appropriate in a February, but Harry could not say he had been unhappy during this latest period of enforced seclusion. Christmas had been a muted affair, hardly a time for celebration when there was so much separation and bereavement in the air, not least among their own families. Harry would not compare it to Jane's loss of her husband or George's of his long-term partner, but the death of Pete and Reenie on their way to East Anglia had hit him hard. Harder than the separation from his own wife Ellen, certainly. The fact he could soon convince himself that had been the right thing to do for both of them did not spare him feelings of guilt about his record as a husband. He missed Kerry too, and – last and least but far from nothing – Judy. He still caught himself wondering how he would be received if he went round and offered to take her out for a walk, still had hopes she would be released into his full-time care. Old dogs could not be forgotten any more than old habits; some had to be fought for as others had to be fought.

'And then there were two,' George had opened their first Rifleman's conversation after Pete's death, which they talked about only briefly. Harry did not like his friend maintaining it was a double suicide, whether at Reenie's request or her son's instigation and execution. While that thought had occurred to him too, he did not want to make his mind up on it. He could not decide if intent made things somehow better or worse than dumb bad luck. When he came to give his condolences to Pete's widow, how little time he felt had passed since he was doing the same to Jane.

Sally-Anne had seemed more affected than Pete's best mates, though she insisted it was 'not my place' to attend his funeral. She had taken to her bed, not the only person to do so in periods of lockdown but unlike most emerging from it evidently and heavily pregnant. Harry supposed Jane must have known long before he did. He asked no questions and was offered no information. While he wanted to play a full part in his new family, he was grateful to have been spared the knowledge as long as he had, let alone involvement in any discussions there might have been between mother and daughter on keeping the baby rather than taking the same path as in Sally-Anne's teenage years. He was content to watch her grow, quietly at home rather than out and about town, until now in her eighth month the bulge was setting her significantly back from their Valentine supper table. He had ordered three of the sharing meals to give them more options on desserts – a Cheesecake aux Noisettes had his name on it – rather than to feed five, but was glad to see the expectant mum looking fit and well, eating regularly if not for two, drinking less than for her former one and not smoking for anybody.

With a proper French disdain for vegetarian options, they had split evenly for main courses between steak frites and what were called love parcels, pulled beef and truffle with truffle mash. He had forewarned Sally-Anne that he would appreciate time alone with Jane downstairs once their feast was done. She suggested to Maddie that they take themselves off to TV in her big bed (she showed no signs of missing anyone else to share it with) to eat their profiteroles and watch a movie together. Did the younger generation never call them films anymore?

'And now, for our own pièce de resistance, what can I offer madame, an amusing little tarte au citron s'il vous plaît?' he asked Jane, absurdly pleased with the hug Maddie had given him before disappearing.

'So kind, monsieur, and please do call me Jane. I am not a how-you-say brothel keeper.'

He laughed. 'Yeah, it was getting a strain to keep putting on the frog, but you can't beat their food.'

'It was a great idea to do this, Harry, thank you so much. I couldn't help thinking how different this year would be. Let's hope that next we'll be able to visit your cousin in Paris again.'

'That would be great. I feel a family tradition coming on. And it's lovely to be part of a family that's growing, in the middle of so much loss.'

'We're not out of the woods with the pandemic yet.' Jane touched the wooden table before changing the subject. 'I almost feel pregnant myself after that delicious dinner, stuffed anyway, can we leave dessert till later… like tomorrow. Let's eat cakes for breakfast in bed, do something proper decadent and French.'

'I like your thinking. Coffee, though? Or how about a fine Napoleon brandy?'

'On condition that I make the drinks. I feel guilty to have sat here while you sweated five minutes trying to switch on the microwave. And would you mind too much if I had a whisky rather than a brandy?'

'Not at all. I'll take a whisky too. You know, just how you normally make it for me, big and stiff. Can you manage that?'

'Oh, I think so. Now you've shown you're capable in the kitchen, I'll be expecting to see a bit more of you there.'

'What's that old joke, heaven is a Frenchman in the kitchen, hell is an Englishman? Be careful what you wish for.'

'Maybe I'll have to look further afield then. Wasn't it supposed to be Italian lovers in heaven?'

'Don't even think of that. I got it, angel in the kitchen, lady in the living room... well, off you go and get the drinks, I'll tell you the punchline later.'

Comfortably full – Jane was right, the cheesecake could wait – in front of the open fire with its guard down, he felt so too were most reserves or barriers between them. Their few months to date of living together, mainly in full lockdown or with complicated restrictions on movement, were an intense beginning to their own family way. Both worked hard at not falling out, at giving each other space as far as pandemic living conditions allowed. Sharing a bed like a married rather than a courting couple was a pleasure he had not realised how much he missed, while they were still fresh enough together to take delight and release in each other's bodies. Harry did not wish to jinx things by dwelling on the thought that he had never been happier, but it would keep popping into his mind.

He was glad she had chosen whisky. Although buying the Napoleon had felt apt for his soirée, on offering it he was reminded that the last time he drank brandy was on George's stag day, the last time they had seen Pete. They had not said goodbye that evening, he'd just buggered off for a McDonald's and never come back. Harry did not beat himself up over any abuse he might have dished out in the voicemail he vaguely remembered leaving Pete, that was only banter between mates. He did, however, regret not having made time to find out how disturbed he was about his mother, Sally-Anne, whatever – if it was enough to have taken deliberate action on that last drive rather than suffered a tragic accident, perhaps distracted from the road by antics from poor Reenie. He might then have gained some insight into why Pete had chosen to name him in his will, a 'significant beneficiary' as the solicitors had put it. Not a straightforward one though, not a few quid to organise an annual piss-up in his memory. Harry had not mentioned anything about it to George, in fact had hardly spoken to him during 2021. They had never been great ones for talking over the phone.

'Thank you, love. Come and sit here beside me.' He had put the small snacks table handy to hold the drinks between them in front of the settee. 'Maybe we can use some of the money from Pete to fund holidays abroad, not necessarily just France. Right now, I can't think of a better use for it.'

He sensed her annoyance before she spoke. 'Do you have to bring that up tonight? You and your damned inheritances. I wish I was so loved by my friends that they always put me in their wills. I told you already you don't need to spend it on me or us, we're fine.'

'Believe me, I was more surprised than anyone. So I was with Andy, but that was shared between his mates – in a cock-eyed kind of way, if you don't mind me saying so. He never said a word about it in advance, and nor did Pete. I'm not desperate for his money, and nobody wants the tontine cash with the conditions attached to that payout. I suppose they'll have to do probate and everything, it's just bugging me what he said about the legacy, according to the lawyer. I've puzzled over it so much I know it word for word. That I should use it 'in the way you will know is best, if not immediately then in the fullness of time'. He always did have a tendency to flowery language did Pete, told us once he had dreams of being a writer then we ripped the piss out of him so much he never mentioned it again. Come on, mate, just leave me your golf clubs. I'd know what they were for, if not how best to use them.'

'I feel like I've heard the phrase more than you. I wish you'd stop fretting about it. Whenever the money comes through, do what you like with it. You mustn't let people control you from the grave. If Drew had told me anything about his tontine idea, I'd have told him he was off his rocker. It was beyond… I don't know, macabre, is that the word? If you're that worried about it, give it to Margaret. You were all good enough to make me the same offer with Drew's weird bequest, do the same for her.'

'I did think of it. I heard from Ellen she got house, pension and everything else from him, including a hefty life insurance payout, so she won't go to war about any other legacies. And I can't help thinking, if he wanted her to have it, why leave it to me in the first place?'

One of the things they had learned in living together was to be careful around each other in mentioning their former spouses. 'Why don't you just be grateful that a friend would think about you and stop stressing? Do like that poor man said in his last words, whatever feels right to you. You might be better off thinking about your own will than his if you're serious about divorcing Ellen. You know once you do that, all previous ones become invalid. Same in cases of death. I've got to get round to my own.'

'I haven't got a previous one to make invalid, so that's not an issue. But you're right, I should be thinking about it. And while we're at it, leave me out of any changes to your own will. Like you say, I'm popular enough as it is.' He could not resist one last plea for guidance or instruction. 'So you really don't think I should do something for the bab on its way? Don't think that might have been what Pete had in mind? He thought a lot of Sally-Anne.'

'I've told you before, Harry.' She had, and he knew he would be well advised to drop the whole subject if it was not to undo all his good work in the kitchen. 'Anything like that you must talk to Sally-Anne, not me. All I'll say is, never mind a sniff of the barmaid's apron, it's a hell of a tip to leave one. And I'm glad you've already checked his wife or widow is well provided for. I'll say one last thing. Don't you *think* about teaching Margaret golf.'

He seized eagerly on her lightening of the tone. He saw he had been wrong to bring money up at all. It was only the memory of brandy that had sent him riding off on that hobby horse. He had not asked Sally-Anne to give them the room because he did not want her to hear of his legacy. Keep it simple, stupid. 'I love you,' he said, taking her hands in his and giving her a kiss that tasted of whisky on both sides.

'Um, that was very nice. I'm beginning to feel I could do with an early night myself. And never mind the movie.'

'I'm with you on that. What was that main course you had?'

'Harry, are you pissed, or what? Here's me getting all romantic and all you can do is go off on tangents. Thinking about your stomach, now? You kill me. Like a mini beef wellington wasn't it, with mash?'

'God I'd never make a stand-up, trying to find these links for a speech ain't easy. You were meant to remember it was a love parcel… So then I could say…' He was relieved to find the stiff little box exactly where he had placed it before dinner, down the side of the settee behind his pawing left hand.

He clumsily rolled himself onto the carpet, now gripping the box behind his back, almost knocking over the table with their drinks on it. It was in the way, but he was already on his knees, conscious that he was beginning to look ridiculous. 'So then I was going to say, "I have another little love parcel it would make me very happy if you'll accept," but it sounds too cheesy now. Not your fault. Please, Jane, please accept my Valentine gift.'

The saleswoman had wrapped up the box for him, a neater job than he could have managed (and the least she could do, he had thought, after she sweet-talked him well above his initial budget). Jane took and held it for a moment, then almost tore away its bow. She did not hesitate either in attacking the box.

'Harry, it's lovely. Is it what I think it is?'

'Jane, I want to marry you. That's why I'm on my knees. I want to do it properly this time. Will you marry me, please, darling?'

'Isn't there the little matter of you being still married to someone else? Are you allowed to propose in that position, and I don't mean on your knees? Will you be able to get up again?'

He persisted. 'I've said the words, Jane, because it was important for me to do it and for you to hear them from me. That's my commitment. But when you ask about the ring, that is exactly what *you* think it is. Make it whatever you want, but don't make me take it back. There's no strings to you accepting it. For me, it is an engagement ring. If you choose to wear it, put it on whichever finger you want, call it whatever you like.'

'Would you like to put it on my finger? *You* can choose which one.'

She placed the ring, the stone gleaming up from its box, back on the table and extended her hands to him, palms down. He had not expected to progress quite as quickly to this stage. 'It may not fit exactly, she said at the shop they can adjust it either way.'

'Getting cold feet already?' She looked at him steadily. 'Haven't you noticed anything?'

God, was he supposed to comment now on her nail polish? Then he realised what she meant. All her fingers were bare.

'I didn't want to be forward, but I thought it was time, to show my own commitment to you. Not to minimise the years I wore his ring, but I needed to take off the one Andrew gave me – half a pound of butter and still quite a struggle, let me tell you.'

He went straight to third finger left hand, where the diamond engagement ring fitted smooth and snug.

Maundy Thursday

Jimmy Bradley had never heard the term Maundy Thursday for the day before Good Friday until he joined the TTers with Uncle Will. By definition it always falls on a matchday, but it was not marked by them until 2021.

Boris's third and what would prove final COVID-19 lockdown ended on Wednesday, 31 March 2021, setting the gang up nicely to celebrate the next day, which happened to be that year's Maundy Thursday. It was also the day Sally-Anne gave birth to a daughter, Peta, but she never blamed the father for being out on the golf course.

Jimmy had become established in the committee, usually reading out the scores and distributing the prize money collected on the day. He refused point blank to take charge of the gang's funds on any other basis, admitting to Percy Parsons that cash passed too freely through his hands at times; he would not risk that happening when it was not his.

If he had a problem at times with impulse control, Jimmy's brief speech on Maundy Thursday 2021 was one of his happier spurs of the moment. He had no list. There was no churchy giving of thanks for having passed through the pandemic ordeal. Not everyone had, and nobody could say it was over yet. The gang had not lost anyone to death from COVID-19, but some members had not played even during the periods when they could in 2020 and looked unlikely ever to return. One of these was Cecil Ransom, oldest of them all to whom Percy sometimes referred as 'father of the chapel'. That was another phrase lost on Jimmy, who did not have Cecil in mind when, after doling out the winnings, he asked for a couple more minutes from the day's exceptional turnout.

'I'm way behind the years of TT membership that so many of you have, and I can only talk about those I remember. I'd still like, now we've got the band back together, to mention former players who've taken the fairway to heaven. Help me out with any I may miss, please. My first is the one who introduced me to this group, taught me I hope how to be part of it: my uncle, Will Gallichan.'

Jimmy paused a moment, then went on with more confidence, more names and the growing attention of the gang. None of them interrupted, itself a rarity. He had no thought of making it an annual thing, but the TT gang are great ones for traditions of all kinds. It's settled now, every Maundy Thursday.

In 2021 the most recently departed Jimmy mentioned was Peter Goodwin. George Pym's brief 'Well spoken, lad' afterwards meant a lot to him. The third tontiner Harry Unsworth was not with them but providing fretful logistical support around the birth of Peta to Sally-Anne, Jane and Madison.

It was not until 2022 that Sally-Anne and Jimmy started going out properly, albeit cautiously. They already had history when she woke him up at Emmeline's in town one Saturday night before they turfed him onto the street, the club about to close. 'Why are you such a fuck-up, Jimmy?' she asked him.

'I'm a pisshead drunk with a gambling problem. Why are you such a fuck-up, Sally-Anne?' He was too far gone to realise how close he came to a punch in the face. Instead, she laughed. 'Er, let's see, sex addict, two kids with no dad in sight, still working behind a bar more than anywhere else, will that do?'

'You had me at sex addict.'

There was a good turnout on Maundy Thursday 2025, a warm day with more of May than March to it, 17 April late within the range of Easter dates nobody knows how they fix. Jimmy did not mind being in the last four-ball drawn, of seven. With the security of ninety minutes blocked out for the group (another legacy of COVID, before which there was no booking of start times, so they all had to crowd the tee box whatever the weather to discourage interlopers), the committee made the draw inside the clubhouse, using gambling chips with names on them rather than marked golf balls. Today Jimmy would have more time for a coffee before going out, less for beer after coming in. The fact that Sally-Anne was on one of her now rare shifts meant it was no bad thing to be sober(ish) and help her shut up shop afterwards, less tempted to go into town than he might otherwise have been. Mason was on duty for three hours until she arrived at two, when he might come to the buying side of the bar to indulge the taste for strong lagers that got him fired from the Horse.

Mark Jones could have afforded to commute daily from his Costa whatever to play with his friends, landed his helicopter on the thirteenth fairway. Not that any of them were jealous of his lottery millions. Not much. Nearer in age to each other than to most of the TT gang, Mark and Jimmy had always got on well, remained in regular touch by email and WhatsApp. Today they were in opposition, Mark partnering Baz Knighton and Jimmy teamed with Harry.

Jimmy had never actually married Baz's daughter Barbara. They were already separated by the time he and Sally-Anne started getting serious. He remained grateful to both Knightons for taking a punt on him in their different ways. Barbara had ultimately been disappointed, no denying that, but Barry recognised the good shift Jimmy put in at his company. With Sally-Anne he was now on one of the upswings in a roller-coaster professional career – the highs and lows not always coinciding with those of his parallel boozing and gambling gigs – making a good living working from home as an independent software engineer, a proficiency of surprisingly little help in his abiding search for an infallible roulette sequence. He still helped Barry out – in his own time and on his own dime, as the Americans say – with his company's books and systems, without regret that the business would now never be his. His regrets for Barbara, although he had never abused her mentally or physically, he could only show by staying in touch with James. Coming to terms with Maddie as a stepdaughter made him painfully aware how short of the mark he had fallen with the boy. His attempts to make things better were sometimes clumsy. 'Look, mate, I honestly don't mind you being gay, and I know it's none of my business. But do you have to be quite so *gay* about it.' James proved as ready to laugh at him as Sally-Anne and Maddie were, and readier to call him out on his bullshit. Their relationship was a work in progress, but progress was made.

Harry, undergoing his own process of re-education in the Wood women's household, was not shy of passing on lessons learned. He became instantly suspicious of his younger drinking buddy when he took up with Sally-Anne. Jimmy did not make the open-top bus in 2023, but by the time it came to Harry and Jane's February 2024 trip to Paris (another quick-setting celebratory tradition) Sally-Anne made it clear that if he wasn't welcome – paying his own way, naturally – while Madison was free as ever to go with them, she and Peta would not be. Harry was over a barrel and knew it. He doted on the baby nearly as much as on Maddie.

Club pro Cliff Lambert has added Maundy Thursday to the last round before Christmas as one when he'll be outside his shop as the TT gang make the turn, offering tots of port, brandy or a combo of the two – another thing beyond Jimmy's ken until he joined the group. Today he had already passed the memorial shrub for Uncle Will halfway down the sixth fairway, at which he always blew him a kiss he would never have accepted in life. Harry's turn would come on fourteen. For the moment they all raised their glasses to the flagpole, at full mast so no one dead this week. Three holes down, Baz and Jimmy were in critical condition but not quite there yet.

Jimmy found Harry almost as protective of Sally-Anne as her real dad (whom he had hardly known) might have been, and did not blame him for that. At the time of George's wedding he'd been hanging out a lot with them both, one of his top-of-the-cycle drinking jags, too pissed to notice whether Pete Goodwin was suffering and if so how much. That stag day, the last time any of them saw him, was one when Jimmy behaved himself in pooping the party to see James. He did not recall ever having a conversation with Pete apart from his mates, and when they left the Poke together that afternoon there was no reason to start one in the street. Afterwards he knew better than to take a stance on what was clearly an unresolved issue between the others. George was convinced that Pete had staged an accident to cover up a suicide – murder-suicide, if you wanted to be melodramatic about it. Harry never directly contradicted that view, but did not like hearing it expressed.

George had always been difficult to contradict. Marriage did little to mellow him. Whatever ambitions he and Jackie had for the Horse were not helped by second then third lockdowns almost before they had their feet under the tenants' table. Sally-Anne said, once she could return to work there, it was as if they were keeping the place open more for their own benefit than that of the punters.

The two remaining tontiners kept up their Friday drinking sessions for a while beyond the death of Pete, if not at the Rifleman's in restricted periods (when Jimmy sometimes made a third) then on George's own licensed premises. Neither of them was scrupulous about the letter of lockdown law. Still, they were not much together for a while after everyone came blinking into the post-pandemic light.

The family dynamics, with Jackie and Jane hardly bosom pals, were complicated further by what appeared to be some reconciliation between George and his son Derek, once again back on the Market Welham scene and living in the pub with his dad and his latest stepmum. Some thought Mason hard done by in losing his job at the Horse, sacked by the ruthless Jackie after worsening his drinking habit during long afternoon sessions when he and her husband had the place almost to themselves. He learned to play crib, before Derek took his place behind the bar. Perhaps nobody could persuade George to cut back on his drinking; neither his son nor this wife was a likely candidate so much as to try.

Jimmy already knew there was something between Derek and Sally-Anne during first lockdown and into the Eat Out to Help Out spell when Boris allowed the whole country to go crazy. Although they did not much discuss that period when they got together over a year later, he understood why she wouldn't stay working at the Horse once her sometime boyfriend reappeared. Jimmy chose not to go there – in solidarity with her, not from any fear of the shithead, he told himself – which limited his contact with George to MWGC among the TT gang.

It became a race, at the pace of a kiddies' egg-and-spoon, between liver and lights to switch off first once George was diagnosed with lung cancer in late 2023. Harry was the one who told Jimmy, asked why their mate had not signed up for the Christmas hamper. 'He's been having all the tests, see if there's anything to be done. There is, but only to give him a few extra months. He's decided he "don't want any of that chemo shit", says he can put poison enough in his body without the quacks' help.'

From then on, Harry did make a point of more regular contact, visiting him at least twice a week as the tumour grew and George shrank. A mixture of diffidence and a wish not to see the tall man reduced prevented Jimmy from doing so. Sally-Anne, encouraged by Kerry, the longer-tenured stepdaughter of Harry with whom she had grown matey, was taking a new path as a care assistant, helping people with confirmed medical needs rather than listening to the problems of befuddled barflies. She had not yet replaced Kerry at Melwood House to cover her maternity leave.

'I don't want to know any more about the mechanics of it than I imagine you do about James's love life, Jimmy, but you can see from the size of her, such a tiny thing she is normally, Kerry's definitely having the baby herself, none of this surrogate crap. I'm happy for her and Sav if that's what they want, what else can I say?'

That was a rare light-hearted comment from Harry. Though he had a stable home base with Jane, of which Jimmy was coming increasingly to feel part, Sally-Anne told him they had agreed not to get married in a rush, felt it better to be 'absolutely sure'. He knew Harry had been something of a run-around, without casting any stones. Those days seemed to be behind him. There was little temptation to booze on his visits to George, who had lost not only the ability to take his drink but the appetite for it. Jimmy's personal theory, kept to himself, was that Harry was not pushing harder for his own wedding because it would have been too cruel on his mate; impossible not to ask him to stand as best man, but any thought of a stag do a terrible reminder of how far he had fallen. George did keep up the smoking, still rolling his own and somehow contriving to get enough past the staff to burn holes in his bedsheets at Melwood House, where Kerry might have had a hand in helping him to get admitted. With the turnover in that field, Sally-Anne had every prospect of keeping a job there if she wanted one as and when her friend returned to work.

Baz needed to hit his driver nowadays to have a hope of reaching most of the par three greens, but he was usually straight and steady with that. He left one stiff on the eleventh hole, winning it with his shot over Mark. Jimmy chipped in flukily on twelve, putting them now only one behind. Queer's lead, he remembered Uncle Will would call that in less enlightened times.

Thirteen was halved but fourteen as a par five was one that favoured Mark, who could hit the ball twenty or thirty yards further than the other three. The only one with any hope of reaching the green in the regulation three strokes, he would probably have to win it for his team, as it was lately a double-bogey hole for Harry.

Sure enough, Mark flew his third shot comfortably over the creek to within ten feet of the flag. 'Lot of money went into that swing,' Baz remarked without rancour. 'Good hit.' His and Jimmy's balls had been further forward than Mark's, but from three shots. Harry dumped his fourth into the water at a point where it still marked an internal out of bounds. He made no pretence of trying to spot and fish his ball out, crossing the earlier bridge than the one at the green.

'Would it be right to go with him, pay me own respects like?' Mark asked Jimmy.

'No, leave him alone. You know today's a special one. I asked him if he wants to say a few words later and he wasn't sure. Good lad for offering though but.'

Jimmy knew what the plaque said beside the tree whose roots he had helped liberally to wet at its christening in January as the Tontine Acer. No nonsense about friends reunited, no comforting couplet, just three names with years of birth and death: Andrew Wood, Peter Goodwin and George Pym. George had left them in November 2024. There was space for a fourth name, that of Harry Unsworth who stood in front of them, his sun-faded flat brown cap in hands. A Christmas present from Ellen when Judy was still a pup, he had worn it all these years despite the chew marks on the stiff brim his wife said had ruined it. They were still wrangling over custody, Sav and Kerry unexpectedly keen to keep the dog, when Judy sickened over the winter. His last walk with her was to the vet, where they told him no amount of money could make it better. Petting the rough and torn edges of the cap between finger and thumb before replacing it on his head, Harry did not ask who had won the hole when he rejoined the others as they were leaving the green.

Paris 2025

While expecting Harry to be down at the loss of his oldest mate, Jimmy did not realise his feelings were more complicated, related also to Sally-Anne and Peta, until they went to Paris three months after George's death. Harry and Jane would go to the same restaurant every year to celebrate Valentine's, not religiously on the day itself as the break had to coincide with Maddie's half-term. Jimmy and Sally-Anne would take care of the kids that night, usually a quiet one at the hotel which would certainly be the case for the older couple when it was their turn to babysit. Splitting male and female one evening had also worked well, to allow the men the pick of a televised Champions League match.

Part of the fun for Maddie was a sparrow-fart train to London to catch Eurostar for Paris by lunchtime. The rooms were not ready, so they left the luggage in reception to have a leisurely meal. Sally-Anne and Jimmy decided to announce their big decision, hoping it would get things off to a good start, cheer Harry out of his slump in mood. More importantly, it would give them time to bed things down with Maddie in an environment where they could both give her undivided attention if she needed it. Peta, already almost four and due to start school in the summer, often needed that attention, but they did not expect a great deal of interest from her.

Paris is worse than Market Welham for eateries with soft-play areas for kids – where are their Premier Inns with Brewers Fayre? – but Jane and Maddie had scouted one up online. Sally-Anne gave Jimmy the nod after they had ordered desserts, beers for Harry and him and wine for the women already topped up.

'Maddie, you can leave the table for a few minutes while we're waiting for the sweets, if you don't mind keeping an eye on Little Miss Itchy-Britches here. We'll call you back when they come.'

Jimmy thought Jane's reaction was too prompt for their news to have been a total surprise. She put a hand on one of Harry's as she replied. 'That's great. It may give this one a jolt, how about a double wedding? Have you fixed your date yet?'

'Not before speaking to you two. This summer, we're thinking.'

'We need your consent. To look after the kids while we go on our honeymoon, I mean.' Sally-Anne had made Jimmy speak for them both but joined in now with a laugh – she was a wine or two up on her new reduced average. 'That might put the mockers on a joint do, but I think I can speak for my future husband in saying that you crazy young fools have our blessing.'

'And what about the kids? Do they know?' Harry was not smiling, not getting carried away like the two women.

'We're going to sit them down tonight while you pair are out canoodling over your lovehearts dinner. Peta already knows me as her dad, so we don't see any problem there, and Sally-Anne thinks Maddie will grow to accept me. I hope I don't need to say I'll do my very best to be a worthy stepdad to her.'

'Yeah, well, you and me both. I don't want to piss on anybody's strawberries, but I hope you've thought long and hard about the commitment, Jimmy. I know how hard it can be, and what a balls-up I've made of it myself at times.'

'You've done all right so far by me, Harry.' The placatory register was something else Sally-Anne had been working on. 'And you obviously did well by Kerry too, enough for her to call you Dad, like you've heard Maddie already trying out with Jimmy.'

'Yeah, I'm sorry, I shouldn't let my own mistakes weigh you down. I've been a proper gloomybollocks since… you know, congratulations to you both. Is this the time to order champagne or what?'

'Let's save it for our last night if you don't mind, if we haven't maxed out the cards by then. I'm sure you'll be doing yourselves well tonight, so you can raise a glass for us then if you have a mind to.'

'We'll do just that. And thank you, Harry' – Jane squeezed his arm – 'for admitting to exactly what you have been lately, with us. Fair play, you've kept up a brighter front for the kids, they haven't seen a right old Grandad Grump. Not to minimise the grief we've all gone through these last few months and years, but we're in Paris now, in springtime. Sally-Anne and Jimmy have got us off to a cracking start, let's build on that, look forward not back. There's none of us free of mistakes or regrets, I'm sure.'

'Amen to that, Mum.' Sally-Anne thrust her glass towards Jane almost aggressively. Harry picked his up too.

'To the future,' Jimmy said.

Harry had to take a ribbing from Jane the next day when they visited Notre Dame, about it taking him longer to get her up the aisle of St Andrew's than it had the notoriously indolent French to rebuild a whole cathedral. If his single days were numbered, he was more exercised by the other upcoming marriage than his own. When Sally-Anne and Jimmy returned from their quiet dinner – a single bottle of wine between them, how their old younger selves would have mocked (Jimmy's, ever cunning and extremely tenacious of life, was still slyly asking how long he thought it would last) – he was sitting at a corner seat in the hotel bar with an eyeline to the entrance.

'Footie go to extra time, mate?' Wouldn't you like to have watched it yourself, old younger Jimmy whispered.

'No, United pissed it. Never a doubt. They may still show the goals if you want to take a pew at the bar and watch the round-up. Sally-Anne, I've got something I'd like to talk to you about if you're not too tired. You look more sober than me and your mum were last night. She says I've got to do it, get it off my chest, else I'll drive her crazy.'

'So whatever it is, you've already talked to her about it?' Sally-Anne was suddenly on guard.

'Some. It's complicated.' Harry ran a hand over his number two cut, resting it on the back of his neck before looking up at her again. 'To be honest, I'm glad she has to stay with the kids while I'm down here.'

Although there was no reproach in his tone, Jimmy offered to go up and relieve Jane so that she could join the other two in a nightcap, saying he could watch the telly just as well in the room.

'No need for that, mate. We'll only be a minute or two. She doesn't know everything that I do, and quite frankly I don't think she wants to.'

'Yeah, that sounds about right.' The bitterness in Sally-Anne's tone surprised both men. 'Well OK, but I'm not going to make Jimmy sit at the bar while you bend my ear in the corner. Whatever you have to say, I want him to be with us.'

'If you're sure?'

'I am. Come on, stop pussyfooting around, we're all adults, veterans of a few heart-to-hearts you might say. I doubt anything you want to tell me will surprise us much.'

'I'm glad to hear that because I feel like I'm caught up in a whole web of half secrets, not knowing what to say to who or who knows what.'

'We're not flies to be scared of webs, Harry. They only grow if you let them. Let's sweep it all away one time. Tell us what's on your mind.' Harry looked more unsure of himself than Jimmy had ever seen him. Sally-Anne went on more gently. 'If it's about George, you needn't worry…'

'It's not so much about George. I felt I could only talk to him about some of the things in… history. Didn't want to lay parts of it on him in his last days, for all I never met a man with less regrets about his life. And his death landed the tontine money on me, more a curse than a blessing – we'd all felt that somehow from the beginning.'

'I hope you weren't planning to offer Sally-Anne cash behind my back, Harry.' Since she'd insisted on him being there, Jimmy was not going to sit like a dummy. 'I can look after her. Maybe I wasn't always a good bet, but please don't insult me.'

'We look after each other, babe.' Sally-Anne corrected him gently. 'He's right, Harry. But we will take a drink off you, wherever the dosh comes from. Can you give us three Grey Goose on the rocks, please?' she asked the barman as naturally as if he had been English. 'When in France, might as well drink the local firewater and if everyone's flush why not go for the premium stuff? Make 'em big ones. We're going to take a seat over by the window if you don't mind bringing them to us.'

'Of course, madame.' He looked miserable, perhaps at the thought of having to bestir himself as the waitress covering table service had already clocked off.

Harry was not much happier than the barman, clearly impatient for him to be away rather than fussing about pouring the drinks – he had a heavy hand, no messing about with jiggers or optics, which would normally have drawn more approval than the muttered 'Merci' as he withdrew.

'Haven't been able to get a word out of him all night, but he understood you fine, Sally-Anne,' Harry said, taking a slug of vodka, not bothering with the ice she had waved the waiter away to serve with her own bartending skill (not that there was much call for iced drinks in the Horse or MWGC). 'I don't want the tontine money. I only realised how much I didn't want it when I found out why Pete left me some as well. I think it would be fairer – no offence, Jimmy, this is no reflection at all on you – I think that money, Pete's, should definitely go to you, you and your baby girl.'

'But Pete's been dead, God rest him, what, over four years, isn't it? Took their time about reading the will, didn't they? And why should I have more claim to money from him than from my own father? You're not making any sense, Harry.'

'It wasn't the will as such. It was me that didn't understand it. I didn't have all the information.'

'Nope, still not with you. I know you've had death on your mind, losing George and all. Did you have a séance and speak to Pete on the other side?'

Jimmy was relieved to see Harry smile before answering her question with another. 'You know when Kerry went on maternity leave?'

It was Sally-Anne's turn to show impatience. 'Maybe I should have asked sooner, have you been getting stewed in front of the football all night? Mum says you do go off at some weird angles. She may be used to it but we're not. What's Kerry got to do with it? Or wait, no, perfect, give her the fucking tontine money, whatever Pete left too if you like. For her bab, she's a sweetheart and never mind our own modern family here in Paris, she's been like a sister to me.'

'I've had a couple, that's all. Trust me, I needed 'em if I was going to bring this up. When Kerry went on maternity leave, Sav… that's her partner' – he looked at Jimmy, who knew it already – 'cleared out her locker at Melwood and found something addressed to me in it. Kerry was mortified, couldn't have been more apologetic for forgetting or mislaying it, something Pete gave her on the last… just before he died. She said he hadn't made a big deal of it, and she was run off her feet at the home.'

'So this was before George died, cos I'd already taken over from Kerry – tight bastards never give me a locker – when he came in for his last fortnight, bless him. What was it, then? Christ, don't tell me it was a new secret will: "I hereby solemnly revoke all previous and bequeath" stuff like in them old Sunday teatime telly serials, Charles Dickens, men with baggy trousers and sideboards.'

Sally-Anne's bluntness again raised a smile from Harry. 'That takes me back, at least you got them in colour, we were watching the same stuff in black-and-white. All the loose ends get tied up, everyone happy except the villain who's gone up in a puff of smoke by then. It wasn't quite that, but it did help me understand a lot of things.'

Jimmy was baffled, not to say bored. 'I'm glad for you, Harry, but I haven't got a scooby what's going on. It was always *Bullseye* for us on Sunday afternoons. Unless your legacy includes another round tonight, I'm happy to leave you to tell it all to Sal, she can let me know in the morning what I could have won.'

'Let's hear him out.' Sally-Anne summoned the barman and his Grey Goose, though the ice had hardly melted in the bucket he had left them. 'What was it, Harry? You'd better tell us now, after all this build-up.'

'There were two things. A letter to me, then a whole screed headed "Melwood House". That was some dark shit, I'll tell you. I couldn't get through it.'

'You're talking about where I work, Harry. I hope you're not going to come out with horror stories like you hear about some homes cos I can tell you…'

'No, love, don't get on your high horse, it was nothing like that, no ill-treatment of Reenie or anyone else. It was more the way he wrote about his day-to-day visits to her, some of it he was trying to make sound funny for all you could tell it wasn't, not at all. If you think I've been down in the dumps lately it was nothing compared to him. He said in it he was only writing to help him cope, but it didn't work. He still ended up in the river.'

'So you think now it was deliberate?'

'I wish I could still kid myself it wasn't. "If you see me again before reading this, I must have failed to have a fatal accident on the road to Manea." That was one of the bits in his letter to me.'

'But why give it all to you? Was he trying to lay a guilt trip on you, somehow?' It had been a long day and Jimmy was disposed to give up on their conversation altogether, finish his vodka and head off to bed, with or without Sally-Anne.

'No, it wasn't that. He said I didn't have to read all his stuff on Melwood – there were other things mixed in there too, about other relationships.' He paused for a moment, looking at Sally-Anne. If he was expecting her to speak, she disappointed him. 'He didn't want to leave it about for anyone else to find. Mainly Margaret, I suppose. He said I should destroy the letter once I'd noted down the important bit, in case anyone ever came to query his cause of death. Something about suicide invalidating life insurance, I don't know, he must have looked into it all.'

Sally-Anne was following him more closely than Jimmy. 'The important bit? And what was that?'

'You know what, I think he'd cracked by the end, balance of his mind disturbed or whatever the phrase is. If he *had* enclosed another will, his letter and diary might have been enough to invalidate it. DNA tests. You want me to go on?'

That question was again directed at Sally-Anne, with the same intensity as his earlier look. She was equal to it. 'Go on.'

'There was a lot of explanation about these services that help you trace your family tree and stuff like that online, track down long-lost relatives. Don't they have telly programmes about it? Similar to COVID tests, swab in the gob and job's a good 'un, send it off somewhere and there's your DNA on file as long as you pay 'em to keep it there.'

Bored was definitely the word for Jimmy now, and still confused dot com. 'If he's on the point of topping himself, why would he be chasing long-lost family?'

Harry did not take his eyes off Sally-Anne, who told him to go on while giving Jimmy a quick smile.

'Where I come in is, he's put all this information into my care. Not that I'd know a DNA if one smacked me in the face, but he give me a code and said he'd sorted it with Gene Jinnees – sound like shysters, right, but knowing Pete he would have checked that out too – for me to have full access to his information and the same rights to share it as he had himself.'

'And you started wondering why our little girl is called Peta? Is that it, Harry?'

'Not only that, Sally-Anne, he said he'd had a few chats with you about... well, about her future, from before she was born.'

'Look, Harry, you can look at me now.' Jimmy was tired of being made a spectator, neck swivelling from one to the other. He had never liked tennis. 'Let's get this sorted once and for all. If Sally-Anne threw Pete a mercy fuck back in that crazy summer, it doesn't matter. I'm Peta's dad.'

'I understand, mate. Credit to you for thinking that way. All I'm saying is, the money Pete left me should go to her if it turns out that… you know, the biological dad.'

'I'm the biological dad, the birth father, the baby-daddy. You don't have to tell me about DNA tests.'

'All right, Jimbo, calm down. I'm going to call for the bill' – Sally-Anne made the universal scribbling gesture to the barman – 'that's enough Grey Goose for one night. Enough wild goose chases too, like you've been on, Harry. You only had to ask the living, not wait for messages from the dead. Will you let me talk now, both of you? I do happen to like the name Peta for a girl, *and* it was a nod to your mate, a little tribute. I felt close to him, and more than sad when he died. I felt guilty. My head was all over the place coming out of first lockdown, out of the relationship with that scumbag Derek. You could say my body was all over the place as well, I won't deny it. Pete wasn't a mercy fuck any more than you were, Jimmy. If anything, I was the one pleading for something the only way I know how.'

She turned back to Harry.

'There was one night when me and this one…' she continued. 'You don't need the gory details, we've admitted to each other our own memories of it aren't the clearest. It didn't even amount to a fling but… it was one night. I didn't give it a thought, about fathers, not while I was denying the possibility of a child. I wish I had the chance to tell Pete he made me think about that. I can't say for sure if I would have gone through with… well, once Pete was gone, although he didn't say or write me a final word, I took a message from his death. There was too much of it around. Then me and this fuck-up' – she tipped her head briefly leftwards at Jimmy – 'hooked-up properly a year later, and the rest is… not history, the rest is our future. It was something Mum said when Peta was about eighteen months old, something about the shape of her mouth that made me start thinking, looking at her more closely than ever.'

'I've gotta be honest, Harry,' said the fuck-up fiancé, 'all babies look the same to me and I wouldn't have dared hope. I never tried to get a fix on the dates, just told myself the timing couldn't be right. I was scared. I knew I couldn't love her more if she was my flesh and blood than I already did. What I couldn't tell was, if I had a name for the father might I love her less. Sally-Anne had to bully me, the tests were a piece of piss, no question of anything that might hurt Peta. And there it was, the winning ticket, ninety-nine point I don't know how many nines. So I won't need to adopt her, like I want to Maddie.' (Jimmy still had a way to go in convincing Sally-Anne of that one.) 'Only a matter of registering and changing her surname before she starts school. It may be going out of fashion, but we both think it will be nice to give her a different-gender same-name married couple for parents.'

Harry had obeyed Sally-Anne's injunction and kept quiet. The couple did not know if he had taken it all in; he looked dazed, drunk, both. When he spotted the surly waiter fifty euros after signing the drinks to his room, they knew it was in a happy way. He hugged them in turn, clumsily hard, and they saw him safely upstairs.

Roll of Honour

'Order, ladies, please, the very best of order.'

With a good field of twenty-eight players, there were four prizes, which Jimmy announced as usual in reverse order. 'In fourth place today, with thirty-eight points, are Graham Cook and Franny Rowland.' Franny went up (cursing quietly to himself) to get the return of their stakes, a quid each.

'In third place, with forty, Barry Knighton and… his partner. Two pounds each.' To good-humoured jeers Jimmy moved coins a foot across the table to Baz and trousered a single two-pounder for the girls' Christmas fund.

Brian Hammond and the insurance guru who had spoken to the whole gang about tontines, Nick Gregory, were second with forty-two Stableford points for £3.50 each. As Jimmy announced his name, he wondered if Nick had ever been engaged by Pete Goodwin about reasons for life insurance payouts to be turned down.

'And today's winners, with forty-three points for a fiver each, are…' The TTers would have no truck with their emcee spinning it out like the two Geordies on telly. 'Harry Unsworth and Mark Jones.'

Bet your back's aching after carrying him round, Mark.
Money always goes to money.
Don't let it change your life, kid.
Talk about Costa del Crime, that's robbery all right.

Mark was embarrassed to be in the spotlight, but they had won it fairly, if not quite as comfortably as they had beaten Baz and Jimmy. Dormie after the fifteenth, they had wrapped it up on sixteen. Harry, who had sent the gang's gazillionaire up for their shared tenner, took no pleasure in the win. Perhaps he was nervous about the prospect of speaking in memory of George, if that was what he intended to do. Jimmy had given him the option, telling him if not he would say a few words himself, while hinting that wouldn't be the same.

The subs collected on any given Tuesday or Thursday were usually not entirely distributed in prize money. A modest float was kept to subsidise the summer awayday and Christmas hamper. The committee had agreed it as a legitimate use of this fund to put a bottle of whisky behind the bar each Maundy Thursday, but today Harry had insisted on paying himself for two bottles of Jameson's. 'Let everybody drink their fill. I wouldn't want George thinking I got cheap on him.' He had similarly paid for the Acer tree and the whole trip to Paris, the latter despite Jane's protests. It was the opposite of the money from the two legacies burning a hole in his pocket. He did not want to touch a penny of it for himself. Sally-Anne had resisted another generous offer until Jane warned her it was making him almost distraught; then she agreed he could give Maddie and Peta substantial holdings in premium bonds, with her as the nominated parent to look after them on the girls' behalf until they turned sixteen.

Jimmy was happy to distance himself from the funds, especially the tontine money after reading Pete's agonised outpourings under the title of Melwood House, but ranging over so much else. Although Harry must have either kept or destroyed the letter to him, he had been as reluctant to hang on to the much heavier material recovered from Kerry's locker as he was the cash. He had asked Jimmy to put it through a shredder. The fact he gave it to him at all (why could he not have ripped it up or burned it, old school?), without saying anything about whether he should look at it first, made Jimmy think he wanted him to, was seeking a way to share its burden. Whether this was fanciful or not, he got through the whole lengthy document, as Harry had said he could not.

He had been warned; it was a hard read. Jimmy did not want to believe what Pete seemed to infer about Sally-Anne's father, of whom he had never heard anyone speak badly. Certainly not Sally-Anne (unless her general silence about him signified something), nor her mother. He had never understood the saying from the Bible about letting the dead bury the dead, but guessed Harry was going by another old saw with Jane, letting sleeping dogs lie. Not exactly sorry to have the additional information,

Jimmy resolved never to discuss it with Sally-Anne unless she came to him. She emphatically did not want to touch the wodge of papers from Pete. He shredded it.

Never mind Harry, it was always a trial for Jimmy to get up and speak to the gang, hands not much steadier than when he first joined and could hardly place the ball on its tee peg for the off. He was learning in AA meetings to associate periods of such performance anxiety with alcohol as a contributory rather than mitigating factor. GA for the gambling helped him not to follow up the small win of a successful five-minute informal speech to friends with two hours of losing their sympathy becoming increasingly voluble and finally obnoxious. It was a process. When Sally-Anne complained that he might as well carry on with the vices since the work he put in against them took up just as much of his time, Jimmy said that was why he would not let her see anyone else about her sex addiction.

Some years there are new additions to the roll, some not, but it will never get any shorter. Having asked everyone to take themselves a glass of the whiskey from the bar – only a tiny percentage of the gang would toast in tea or a soft drink – Jimmy took out his piece of paper. The numbers on it since his first effort in 2021 were swollen not only by post-pandemic deaths but by men who had been and gone before his own memory, yet within that of older members. He made his usual apologies for any omissions and mistakes in the order of passing, but none for taking his uncle out of that order and giving his name first. That was an article of faith for Jimmy, a way to help him get through the rest of the list without faltering. Sally-Anne's presence behind the bar, her own glass at the ready – they would wait until wed before thinking about a baby brother for the girls – did not hurt in that either.

He read: 'Will Gallichan; Adrian Smith; Robert Laws; Liam Prior; James Gorst, Charlie Thornley; Bob Yorke; Alan Wallis; Mick Brooks; Pete Marshall; George Ramsden; John McShane; Andrew Wood; Dickie Meakins; Barry Rowlett; Peter Goodwin; Iain Atkinson; Alan Bateman; and George Pym.'

As agreed, he looked to Harry for a signal. He gave the briefest nod, face set while Jimmy spoke again. 'I do know George lived his last months with great bravery, fighting to the last, but it is more fitting for someone else to speak, his best mate through a lifetime.' Everyone knew who he meant.

Harry remained in his seat beside Mark, though his settling of himself in it made it look for a moment as if he would stand. 'It's a lot easier for me to speak without George here, because he wouldn't have held with it. He would have told me to shut the fuck up, for Christ's sake. Pardon my language, Sally-Anne, but I'm only being true to what my old mate would have said.

'George was a man's man, a phrase you don't hear so often nowadays and if you do you might think it means something different from what we did when we were growing up. It meant to us being a man you count on as a mate, a drinking mate very often, a playmate whether at cards, dommies, darts, pool, snooker, football. Football until you get too old and have to start chasing smaller balls around the countryside. It meant one you would chase women with, share your wins and losses of them, sometimes compete with for them.'

He looked over again at Sally-Anne. 'I apologised to Sally-Anne a minute ago, but a bit of bad language is the least of it. Being a man's man didn't mean you would treat women well. You might do, but usually only as long as it suited your own needs, your own manliness. Whether you had a lot or a few of them, you would usually end up hurting them, sometimes beyond repair or reparations. I was thinking of all this when I spent a couple of minutes with George, Pete and Andy out there on the fourteenth under their tree.

'Under *our* tree I should say, because I belong with them as if my name was already written on the plaque. I'm no better, and I won't brag about being any worse than my mates. I was happy, proud to call them that in life, George above all, and I'm not going to dob them in for anything, anything at all, now they're gone. We won't see their like again, that's a common enough phrase, but maybe we were all too much of our time and that time has passed. So, as well as the traditional toast, to absent friends, I'll ask you all to stand with me' – he suited action to the word – 'and join in a special one for George… to a man's man, a great mate, who knew what it was to be loved by women. May we all be so lucky, and work harder to deserve that love.'

Fuck me, talk about coming not to praise but to bury him.
With mates like Harry, who needs enemies.
He wouldn't have dared say it if George was still here.
There's a lot of people dying now that's never died before.

Jimmy said enough, went through all his illness without a scrap of medication.

I hear Harry earned a pretty penny when he pegged out, should be more grateful.

Makes you think though, maybe our day is done.

Nah, the TT gang's survived forty years already, good for a century.

Most of us have always been good to our wives.

Yeah, he should only speak for himself and his so-called mates.

I might treat my missus better if she still looked like Sally-Anne.

Harry and Jimmy kept their clubs in lockers at the course, so they could take the Uber home with Sally-Anne in a bit. There were only the three of them in the bar now. Most people were sensible about drink-driving, so there wasn't much point in keeping the bar open beyond teatime.

'Hardly worth taking this with us, but it's plastic glasses now I've got the dishwasher running.'

Sally-Anne brought out the last couple of inches of Jameson's, separated three cups from the coffee machine and poured them the last knockings.

'Harry, I want to toast you for that little speech, never mind it went down like a lead balloon with most of the old-timers here. I only hope you can stick to it, make Mum happy. Let's do that double wedding thing after all, to hell with it. We'll take the kids with us on honeymoon. I hope you heard the bit about looking after women, Jimmy, even if you didn't know what the hell he was rambling on about in the past.'

Jimmy knew.

THE END

www.ingramcontent.com/pod-product-compliance
Ingram Content Group UK Ltd.
Pitfield, Milton Keynes, MK11 3LW, UK
UKHW011300060925
462636UK00001B/64